"Richly layered scenes, intriguing characters, and a compelling story all skillfully woven together to create a delightful debut novel that I devoured from beginning to end. Well done, Kit! What's next?"

Melody Carlson, *Romantic Times* Career Achievement Award winner and bestselling author

"Kit has a winsome way of using words to paint heart-touching images in *The Color of Home*. I paused as I was reading and lingered over her lush descriptions and clever development of the relationship between Audrey and Cade. A lovely story!"

Robin Jones Gunn, bestselling author of over one hundred books, including *Tea with Elephants*

"Not only is Kit Tosello's *The Color of Home* overflowing with evocative sensory details and a strong sense of place, it is also an inspiring story of finding healing and a place to belong. I could not put this stunning debut down."

Amanda Cox, Christy Award–winning author

"From page one, Kit Tosello's vividly told tale of rediscovery places the reader in the midst of a Pacific Northwest town and its endearing people. By the last page, both will feel like home. This is a must-read for fans of small-town contemporary stories centered on intergenerational connections."

Sara Brunsvold, Christy Award–winning author of *The Extraordinary Deaths of Mrs. Kip*

The Color of Home

The Color of Home

Kit Tosello

Revell
a division of Baker Publishing Group
Grand Rapids, Michigan

© 2024 by Kit Tosello

Published by Revell
a division of Baker Publishing Group
Grand Rapids, Michigan
RevellBooks.com

Printed in the United States of America

Library of Congress Cataloging-in-Publication Data
Names: Tosello, Kit, 1961– author.
Title: The color of home / Kit Tosello.
Description: Grand Rapids, Michigan : Revell, a division of Baker Publishing Group, 2024.
Identifiers: LCCN 2024005992 | ISBN 9780800772697 (paperback) | ISBN 9780800746452 (casebound) | ISBN 9781493447251 (ebook)
Subjects: LCGFT: Christian fiction. | Romance fiction. | Novels.
Classification: LCC PS3620.O78 C65 2024 | DDC 813/.6—dc23/eng/20240212
LC record available at https://lccn.loc.gov/2024005992

Scripture used in this book, whether quoted or paraphrased by the characters, is from the following:

The Holy Bible, English Standard Version® (ESV®). Copyright © 2001 by Crossway, a publishing ministry of Good News Publishers. Used by permission. All rights reserved. ESV Text Edition: 2016

The Message. Copyright © 1993, 2002, 2018 by Eugene H. Peterson. Used by permission of NavPress. All rights reserved. Represented by Tyndale House Publishers.

The Holy Bible, New International Version®, NIV®. Copyright © 1973, 1978, 1984, 2011 by Biblica, Inc.® Used by permission of Zondervan. All rights reserved worldwide. www.zondervan.com. The "NIV" and "New International Version" are trademarks registered in the United States Patent and Trademark Office by Biblica, Inc.®

The *Holy Bible*, New Living Translation. Copyright © 1996, 2004, 2015 by Tyndale House Foundation. Used by permission of Tyndale House Publishers, Carol Stream, Illinois 60188. All rights reserved.

Emojis are from the open-source library OpenMoji (https://openmoji.org/) under the Creative Commons license CC BY-SA 4.0 (https://creativecommons.org/licenses/by-sa/4.0/legalcode).

Cover design by Mumtaz Mustafa

Published in association with Books & Such Literary Management, www.books andsuch.com.

Baker Publishing Group publications use paper produced from sustainable forestry practices and postconsumer waste whenever possible.

24 25 26 27 28 29 30   7 6 5 4 3 2 1

Of one thing I am perfectly sure:
God's story never ends with "ashes."
Elisabeth Elliot

I've made LORD GOD my home.
Psalm 73:28 *The Message*

For Dad,
whose voice still guides me

And for Auntie Midgie,
whose real name was Marguerite,
like the daisy

One

MENLO PARK, CALIFORNIA

Audrey

I should have dialed back the melatonin in favor of chamomile tea years ago. Because this time when I dreamed about Dad there were no flames. Still, from what I can tell about the target demographic of sleep-aid advertisements, women my age aren't supposed to wrestle so hard with their pillows at night. Should I worry? See a doctor?

In my dream, the day was dry as wheat and bright as gold. There we were, just the two of us, caught in a tender moment in a tidy patch of green lawn next to a white clapboard cottage. It was late September in Central Oregon's high desert. I know this because the wild fields of rabbitbrush that lay beyond the fence had transfigured from summer's drab olive to school-bus yellow.

I know this too because I lived it, that moment in that place. At the time, I'd never seen a true autumn, hadn't realized that a thing could be one way today and a different way the next. What does a California girl know of seasons? I had no idea, for example, that by some surreptitious ordering of the universe, on some random day that no human can foretell, a family of geese will take to the air and honk their goodbyes.

Or that we have no say in such matters.

I was just a waif of a girl, maybe nine years old, crouching beneath that honey-colored sky, cradling a root ball. Bits of soil slipping through my skinny fingers. When my father planned a horticultural birthday caper for the dear woman who raised him, he'd offered me a starring role—even though it meant missing school. Everything in me tingled with such an anointing. I possessed my dad's favor. He desired my companionship!

We'd arrived under the day's waning heat and set to work at the southwest corner of the tiny home where Dad grew up. In the end, this side of the house would be trimmed in Shasta daisies— genus *Leucanthemum*, Dad explained—like a pristine white cake with yellow-and-white flowers piped around the base. Daisies for my great-aunt Daisy.

Dad turned to receive the plant from my small hands into his large, gloved ones, but a sudden uproar in the scrubby golden field next door interrupted the motion, commanding our attention. With loud honks and a ruckus of wing flapping, a skein of Canada geese went airborne. It seemed to me quite the hasty decision.

Dad stopped working to watch, rested a dirt-caked boot on the step of his shovel as the birds clambered into a loose V. Already they'd cleared the blue roof of the historic farmhouse across the road, the main lodgings of the Sugar Pine Inn. Formation tightening, wings pumping, they angled toward the far tree line.

"Are they a family?" I asked.

Dad did that narrowing thing with his eyes that made long creases appear above his high, summer-bronzed cheekbones. My cheekbones. The same look he wore while calculating a landscaping bid. He offered a slow nod to the sky. "I suppose they are, Audrey. I suppose they are."

The geese had all but disappeared into the clouds, which now glowed like warm buttermilk as the sun slipped behind the mountains. The seedling still rested in my hands, suspended mid-journey. "So how do they know when it's time to leave?"

Dad removed his Oakland A's baseball cap, wiped the sweat from his brow with the back of his wrist, and scratched his mussy blond head. "I don't really know, hon," he said, replacing the cap. "They just do, I guess."

Maybe that's why the moment's indelibly scored into my memory—on account of Dad's not knowing. There were mysteries to which my father didn't hold the answers. Which, to me, meant no one did. And he seemed somehow okay with that.

Something I'll never be.

We watched the family of geese fade into soft, unending light. Measured and purposeful. Spread out in such a way that they couldn't lose sight of one another.

So no one got left behind.

———————

"Grande sugar-free hazelnut latte. Half-decaf. Light foam. Extra hot." Enunciating each detail on my scribbled list, I will the green-aproned hipster to make my order the highest calling of his day. If only I possessed Jedi mind tricks. "Oh, sorry," I add, heat rising to my cheeks, "and half a stevia stirred in. Here—need this?" I offer up the neon-orange square of paper stuck to my fingertip, which is trembling noticeably.

The barista's thin handlebar mustache stretches wide over a pandering smile. Does it really matter if he mistakenly pegs me as one of those self-important, high-maintenance women—the kind I swore never to become? Okay, yes, it bothers me. A lot. I stuff a five I can't afford to part with into the tip jar.

"Sorry. It's not for me," I say, leaning in. "I'll have a small light roast. Please." *I'm just a simple girl, you see.*

"So, a tall brewed coffee."

"No, a small—oh, I mean yes." To detract from the accursed face flush, I laugh and toss my long and unruly auburn curls. How am I the only person with breath and a pulse in the Bay Area who doesn't speak Starbucks lingo?

On the other hand, I speak fluent Dairy Queen, which ought to count for something.

"The smallest tall you've got." I add a wink. "Actually, um, let's make that a decaf."

When I give the barista my name, he scratches it on the cup in black Sharpie, leaving the *e* out of Audrey. His eyes, two dark espresso beans, twinkle with politeness. But I read something else—condescension, perhaps. I'm being paranoid again, of course. I've probably just caught an unsettling glimpse of myself reflected there.

I can't recall ever, even as a teenager with funky hormones, being so easily rattled. But lately I've been forced to wonder . . . what good is magna cum laude if you're easily intimidated by a barista?

I'm sardined in the pickup area next to a woman with a flawless updo who smells like the Nordstrom perfume counter. The bold mustard shade of her Kate Spade satchel calls to mind the Midas-touched shrubs of my dream. Even as espresso machines hiss and the morning rush shows no sign of slowing, I hold on to a measure of solace from that slow and simple afternoon spent with my dad, the one I relived last night.

Just like that, better aromas flood my senses—remembered ones. Juniper. Sun-warmed peat. Lake air. As if it's already tomorrow, and I'm already five hundred and fifty miles removed from here.

I expect the usual tinge of sadness in the mix, but this time it doesn't come. Instead, I'm oddly comforted, and this feels like a betrayal.

After all, I've worked for years to unknow every recollection of our family's annual summertime visits to Aunt Daisy and Uncle Dean. Of a country road and a picturesque inn. Of trail dust caught in my throat and velvet horsehair between my fingers. Of a carefree child in a land of wide-open front doors and welcoming arms.

Because it was also the place that stole my oxygen.

So I've moved on. Am I winning at life? Crushing it?

Ask me later today.

My purse vibrates, and I startle. Mom's soft features fill my phone screen, but I hurriedly click the decline button. Why not just send a text, Mom? Working women haven't got time for impromptu phone calls. I fidget with a napkin. Twist it into a corkscrew. Use it to buff out a tiny dull spot on one of my blush patent-leather slingbacks.

I'm headed in the right direction, I think. At least I've got a roof over my head in one of the world's most expensive housing markets. Never mind that it's the least desirable room in a sixty-year-old bungalow with four black smudges out front where shutters used to hang, or that it smells suspiciously of mold. Or that I room with three younger women, none of whom know how to refill the ice cube trays or would notice if I went missing until rent came due.

But here's what I hold on to. I work for Pilar DeSoto, the trendiest interior designer in Silicon Valley. Already I can drive through the rolling Los Altos hills and point to dozens of grand, sun-drenched estates made grander thanks to my contributions. Not that I have anyone in my life to show them off to. But still. I have to believe it would make my father proud.

I square my shoulders and stretch to my full height. All five-foot-three of it.

Of course, Dad would also want me to have Harriet's engine looked at. Harriet's my eight-year-old Kia, and lately she doesn't seem to espouse the same conviction my dad held about the evils of credit card debt. But I've got a plan. Assuming today's client meeting goes well, I'm considered the obvious choice to replace Pilar's top design assistant and inherit her coveted salary. A salary that recently went up for grabs when she made an abrupt exit—under hushed circumstances.

At least, Joshua and Keiko are convinced the position is mine to lose. I never have any idea what Pilar's thinking.

Thus, my last-second Starbucks detour. I wouldn't normally bend my budget for overpriced coffee when a box of tea bags will last me two weeks. Well-timed kissing up is a professional skill, right? Remind me to add it to my LinkedIn profile. And if this coffee bribe leaves a good taste in Pilar's mouth before I abandon her for a couple weeks, well . . .

Better to save the cornball puns for Uncle Dean. I'm not in Oregon yet.

At the sound of her name, Chignon Lady hikes her purse strap higher on her shoulder and retrieves her drink. While she departs with an air of purpose, I flick through a Pantone color deck in my mind, landing on . . . hmm, let's see . . . *Saffron.*

It's self-soothing, this game of mine, assigning just the right color name to this or that. In fact, for her Kate Spade, I'll go with Mimosa instead. Final answer. Pantone's Color of the Year for 2010. No, that's not right. That year was all about turquoise—which, back when I was studying interior design at Sacramento State, struck me as uninspired. I'm more open-minded these days, after seven years in this game.

I emerge from the café's warmth into a web of silvery dew and the drone of commuter traffic on California Avenue. The chilly May mist invigorates, and the nutty aroma of Pilar's over-fussy latte confection smells like my salvation. And just like that, I'm transported from this cookie-cutter Menlo Park strip-mall parking lot, populated by a virtual clone army of Teslas, to the warmth of Daisy's kitchen. I can taste every decadent note in her signature dessert, a sugared hazelnut torte. Dad's fave. My mouth waters.

Was I really once that wide-eyed child with copper curls, up on my toes sprinkling coarse sugar on the marionberry scones that made my great-aunt a small-town celebrity? Scones destined for guests of the Sugar Pine Inn. An image appears of the quaint resort, a semi-elegant B&B-meets-dude-ranch sort of affair, and I wince. After more than a decade of practice, I know how to slam on my emotional brakes before my heart hits that spike strip and re-punctures.

But for the first time in as long, I tease my mind open, consider the potential upsides of revisiting my old summer stomping grounds—tomorrow, in fact. Charity Falls, Oregon, where even in June the air smells like Christmas trees. It's not exactly a pleasure trip, which seems fitting. Daisy's in a vulnerable place, and I'm the one she reached out to. We always did share a special connection. Do we still?

I'm surprised how much the answer suddenly matters to me.

So. My bags are packed—big-girl panties and all the rest. Tomorrow I'll leave behind the trappings I've come to depend on and get behind the wheel of a car I'm pretty sure I can't. But I won't park my emotions there just now. This sense of dread I awoke to is due to more than the dream or my impending road trip. First I've got to knock the Boatman meeting out of the park. No worries there, though. I'm prepared.

I'm probably overprepared.

Someone lays on their horn, and my shoulders flinch. In the nearby intersection, a Lexus driver thrusts his arm out the window and gestures wildly at another car. Jittery, I set the two coffees on Harriet's roof. Droplets of dew freckle her recently waxed finish. I shuffle through my purse for the keys, but they're not in the usual pocket.

My fingers rummage around the silky lining while I simultaneously peer through the front window. On the passenger seat, there's the stack of mail I haven't had a chance to go through, including that curious padded yellow envelope from Aunt Daisy. But no keys. And they're not easy to miss, what with the bright, rainbow-colored plastic lanyard my eight-year-old niece crafted for me. Terror clenches my chest. I soothe it with self-assurances. *No worries. All is still well. You simply set them down inside.*

Legs cinched tight inside my pencil skirt, I quickstep back to the café in my accursed heels, hold the door for the woman exiting, and offer a smile that's embarrassingly insincere.

Inside, forest-green walls sway and the coffee-shop din drifts around me with an odd, faraway cadence. *Just breathe.* Sure enough, my keys rest peacefully beside the napkin dispenser. But as I turn to leave, something catches my eye. Someone has left the latest edition of *San Francisco Style* magazine flung casually on a sofa. I angle my head for a better look. There's no mistaking the woman staring back at me from the glossy cover.

Skin, flawless. Hair, inky black and precision cut. Eyeliner, flicked up at the corners. Signature red-rimmed glasses. The bold headline reads, "Designer on the Rise."

Pilar.

Well then. This should ensure a celebratory mood at the office today. Good thing, because this might be the first time I'm late to work in, well, ever. At least I won't show up empty-handed.

But wait . . . was that . . . was that a hint of movement on the roof of my car? I'm a ways off, so maybe I'm imagining things. *Oh no, no, no, no.*

I pick up my pace.

Too late. The two coffees are taking a roller-coaster ride down my front windshield.

A plunge. A midair flip. A crash. Eighteen bucks' worth of brown liquid and foam gushes heavenward, rains down on Harriet's white hood, and then dribbles down the fender. The two paper cups hop to the pavement and tumble in random directions like drunks leaving a bar.

Welp. One more reason I'll never be a fan of Karl the Fog, as the soggy marine layer that often creeps this far inland is affectionately known to some. Or Starbucks. Nor, it seems, have I done anything to help secure my own destiny as a designer on the rise.

Two

CHARITY FALLS, OREGON

Daisy

Audrey arrives tomorrow.

Luckily I remembered where I stored the lavender potpourri she sent me some time ago, heaped some in a cut-glass dish, and gave it a home on the hearth. It's a bit on the overpowering side, to be honest. But something had to be done. I keep pacing the rooms of this drafty old place, imagining how Audrey will regard it after so many years. I swear this here knotty-pine paneling darkens more every decade, and it's closing around me like a fist.

I must have been around Audrey's age when I drove that Meals on Wheels route to shut-ins—old folks in old houses that smelled like old books and cat dander and dementia. Is that me now?

Was it wrong to ask her to come?

I'm horrified that I've dragged her away from her life. If she'd wanted to come, she'd have come a lot sooner. But what choice did I have? Even with her help, how on God's green earth will I uproot from this place?

Out front, the Oregon grape hedges have gone rogue, and I swear those aspen shoots that poke up through the front-step cracks are mocking me. It's like they know I can't in good conscience use that awful, toxic weed killer that Dean used to spray. They know I'm helpless.

I should've at least planted some color in the window boxes. It's practically summer. Why does everything have to be so ding-dang hard these days? Once upon a time, this was a welcoming place. Once upon a time, I could run out and buy a half flat of marigolds at the drop of a hat.

At least the birds don't judge or miss a visit. And there goes Myrtle Rose, eyeing a starling from her cushion on the window seat and twitching. Such is my world now, and God knows I try to be grateful. It's just me and a wheezing refrigerator and the occasional snores of the old man in the bedroom. A man who disappears from me a little more every day, like a bar of soap.

That's him stirring now, clearing his throat. Oh, I've a few minutes yet. If he doesn't knock over his water glass again. *Deep breath*.

I'd like to believe seventy-six isn't so old. Lord, I remember Granny Margaret chasing hens and baking her cement cake and even shoeing horses well past my age. True, Granny Margaret wasn't harried, trying to help her husband hold on to his peace and his mind. And I bet she never lay awake worrying she might be losing her own. That wasn't her cross. But for crying out loud, the least I can do is plant a few posies.

Lately I catch myself staring out the window for heaven only knows how long—at the mountains, or the sprinklers, or some random plastic grocery bag rising and falling on a gust of wind. I'd like to think I've been contemplating deep, important things. But no. Just staring, point-blank.

Judy's daughter waltzed through here yesterday with her fancy window cloths and her tote full of organic cleaning potions that she makes herself with some kind of oils. When Judy calls today to ask how it went, as she surely will, I'll say that her girl did a fine job. She did in fact set things to right. I just wish I could figure out where she put my egg slicer. And I must admit, the guest room, which of course will always be Danny's room to me, smells fresher. Lemongrass, she said. I don't hate it. Still, after she left, I re-wiped the kitchen surfaces with Pine-Sol. Now *that's* what clean smells like.

There's Dean's low murmuring now, and the sounds of him fumbling for his glasses on the nightstand. I have to confess it somewhere: Hearing him awaken makes my stomach quaver. And not in the way it did all those years, day after day, when his Ford crunched over the gravel, alerting me he was home from work. How many times did he come in and land a sloppy, wet kiss on my cheek while reaching around to sneak an oatmeal chocolate chip cookie off the cooling rack? Countless. I miss that dance.

My jolly early riser now sleeps away what he used to call the meat of the day. Which is probably better for both of us. But something inside me is breaking. And something is hardening.

God help me, I don't want to be crusty.

I picture Audrey here, coursing with purpose and promise and beauty, and I can't help but think what an artifact I've become. This isn't only about Dean. I hardly recognize myself anymore.

Lord, for quite some time, you've been my chief companion. You'd think by now I'd be some kind of holy. But, okay. I'll keep dragging my cross down the Via Dolorosa if that's what you ask. So make me brave today. And could you maybe just send me a sign or something? I believe you're there, of course. But sometimes, well, you know. Forgive my unbelief.

Oh, and traveling mercies for Audrey while you're at it.

Three

Audrey

Arriving at DeSoto without a peace offering in a paper cup, I can only pray Pilar's in one of her more gracious moods. Come to think of it, how long has it been since I actually formed a prayer? She may have approved my time-off request weeks ago on the team's digital calendar, but I'd sure feel a whole lot more comfortable if she'd acknowledge it directly to me.

Forced to parallel park along a side street, I'm burning minutes I don't have to spare. The visor mirror reveals wiry auburn-and-gold strands of hair projecting maniacally, the frizz I've come to expect from doing life on this humid peninsula. And somehow I've smudged my mascara. I look like a deranged red hen. "Lovely," I mumble, digging for undereye concealer.

Inside, I'm greeted by the gentle piano strains of Pilar's new-agey Spotify channel and the aroma of sandalwood. I spot her immediately, leaning against the East-meets-West bamboo island I helped design and laughing—borderline flirtatiously, in my opinion—with a silver-haired gentleman in a slate-gray tailored suit. His booming voice rolls toward me like a thundercloud. This must be Bill Boatman, one half of the couple with whom I'm to meet. If so, *ugh*. He's early.

I shoot a good-morning to Joshua, Pilar's executive assistant extraordinaire. He looks at me questioningly. No doubt wondering why I have nothing to show for the detailed drink order he provided. I shrug. He nods his dark, pomaded head toward the conference table where he has set out my AutoCAD and hand-drawn renderings, along with a folder containing the Boatman bid. I mouth a silent thank-you.

Let's hope Mrs. Boatman is here somewhere.

Pilar and her guest turn to watch me clickety-clack across the hardwood just as I narrowly miss walking face-first into a large palm frond. At times like this, why can't I simply flip a switch and shut down this odd, off-balance feeling, this ever-increasing self-consciousness? Now is no time to be a spaz, or worse, overcome by one of the panic attacks that have plagued me of late. About those I've wondered, why me, why now, at twenty-eight, six payments away from sole possession of a Kia, with a womanly gait and practically never a pimple? My mother believes hormones are the culprit, complicated by stress. She's been pestering me for a while now to take some time off.

Well, Mom, the time off is coming tomorrow, but it doesn't exactly promise a spa getaway.

From a distance, Mr. Boatman resembles Jay Leno. Closer now, he smells like thousand-dollar bills dipped in Ermenegildo Zegna's Roman Wood cologne. Unfortunately, I know this scent, having recently dated a guy with a yacht for six months too long.

"Audrey . . ." Pilar purrs my name, drawing it out like it has a long cheetah's tail. She scans me from head to heels, and her lips part. Something hasn't pleased her. "How was Priscilla, dear? I was just telling Bill here about her urgent call this morning. You were so good to drop off the swatches. Bill, this is Audrey Needham. I don't believe you've met."

It takes a few hurried mental calisthenics, but I catch her track. *Ah, Priscilla. Wife of a certain household-name tech guru.* An errand I ran last week. So we're telling half-truths now, are we? "Priscilla's fabulous," I say. That much is probably true. "Wonderful to meet you. Will, uh, Marlene be joining—"

The front door flies open. Marlene Boatman sweeps in, appearing less composed than I'm used to seeing her. Still classy, though, in her usual neon polo and golf shorts. Gold bangles tinkle from her wrist, and she's clasping the hand of a toddler boy with nut-brown curls. His giant bug-eyes rove the studio like he's just entered Legoland.

There it is now, my confidence returning. After several previous consultations about their remodel, Marlene and I have an easy rapport. And kids—well, kids are in my wheelhouse. This one has heart-melting dimples.

While leading the Boatmans to the conference table, I detour along the way to swoop up a chain of Formica color chips and a stack of quartz countertop samples to entertain the grandchild, whose name, I've learned, is Billy. I set them on the floor next to the conference table, and the child happily plops down onto his rear.

Within minutes, any resemblance between the ensuing meeting with the Boatmans and the way I'd seen it going down in my head has dissolved. In short, Mr. Boatman's appraisal of my interior renderings of his stucco Silicon Valley castle-to-be falls just shy of contempt. This, despite the fact that it's exactly what Marlene and I have discussed in detail for the past three weeks—a sweeping Italian farmhouse-style kitchen—light and bright but with rustic, old-world elements and layers of texture.

Unlike her husband, Marlene leans in, spellbound, as I present each feature of the room at the heart of their remodel. A commercial-sized Viking range tucked into a wall of weathered stone that soars to the apex of their massive, thick-beamed ceiling. Cream-colored cabinetry with a sepia wash. Three copper sinks.

Twin islands with a rich, chestnut stain and hefty, ornate turned legs. Oversized Umbrian limestone pavers.

And the coup de grâce, a hand-forged, iron-and-wood chandelier, six feet in diameter, which I designed in collaboration with an award-winning artisan blacksmith from Montana and sketched in meticulous detail. Its price tag is enormous too, but fair. Besides, it's arguably the focal point of the kitchen and great room combined.

Bill Boatman clears his throat and narrows his eyes. "And exactly what is *this*?" He gestures to what is clearly meant to depict a decorative ceramic rooster atop one of the islands, a hand-drawn detail I included merely for a spot of color and whimsy. Every kitchen needs a chicken, I like to say. This time I refrain.

"Honey, that's nothing. It's just a chicken," Marlene says.

But Mr. Boatman's displeasure increases like a gathering storm, until it's effectively sucked every molecule of the Zen atmosphere Pilar prizes out of the studio. He condescends, nitpicks, and vetoes. Why would he pay good money to make something new look old? Where are the renderings of his wine cellar? Is his wife out of her blooming mind? His eyes dart between the two of us as if we're in some sort of cahoots. Is it too early in the day to offer a client a nip of chardonnay?

From her glass office across the showroom, Pilar shoots me concerned looks. On the other hand, I get the feeling Joshua is trying to send me good vibes. As if sensing the tension, little Billy sidles up next to his grandmother. He wraps a chubby hand around her calf. "Horsey," he says, pointing toward a shelf above my desk.

"Miss Needham is working, Billy. Please don't interrupt." Marlene's voice sounds thin.

"It's okay." I offer up the object that caught his eye, a cast-resin figure of a girl galloping on a bay horse, her long red hair flying behind her. At his grandmother's nod of approval, Billy looks shyly at me through lashes I'd kill for and carries the figurine to his spot on the floor. I'm only a little worried. I do love that figurine, a gift from Aunt Daisy on my seventeenth birthday, something I recognized at once was laced with deeper meaning. *Remember all the good years and who you were in Oregon*, it spoke. For sure, there'd been many happy summers—fifteen to be exact—and she wanted me to hold on to those memories. Not just to the painful reasons I've never wanted to return.

"Oh, for heaven's sake." Mr. Boatman makes a show of pressing his hefty forearm onto the table, peeling back the cuff of his sleeve, and checking his Rolex. Sweet Marlene's stricken look tugs at my heart. I feel her joy de-escalate as if it were my own. Still, she retains some poise and gushes with gratitude about all my "hard work." But I see tears pressing, and I can't help thinking, *Please don't acquiesce, Marlene.*

What I wouldn't give right now to kick off my cruel shoes and join Billy on the floor. Mercifully, the couple agrees to discuss the design and bid at home, signaling an end to the meeting. We all consult our e-calendars and strike on a date to reconvene several weeks from now, taking into account the Boatmans' trip to the Amalfi Coast. Pilar emerges to spritz the clients with compliments on their way out. Marlene's hair color, so flattering. Their grandson, a cherub.

After scoring a coy smile from Billy as he's whisked out the door, I waste no time liberating my toes from their patent-leather prison. Dropping to my knees, I'm eager to clean up the scattered reminders of a meeting-gone-sideways.

Pilar's legs, in knee-high, black stiletto boots, appear before me like jail bars. I crane my neck to look up at her. "Have you ever considered, Audrey," she says, "that clients like the Boatmans are here, first and foremost, for an exceptional designer? Preferably one who is agreeable? And *not* for a babysitter?"

Much as I'd love to stand eye to eye with Pilar, she towers over me. The "agreeable" part is what really grates, considering how often she's advised me to exude confidence during presentations. I feel blindsided. So I break eye contact long enough to set down the makeshift toys I'm cradling. "Thank you for covering for me this morning." I hate how timorous my voice sounds. "I—"

"I covered for *me*, Audrey. Everything you do reflects on DeSoto."

"I understand." Where is this coming from? I'd heard Pilar hand out some spine-tingling reprimands, but never to me. What's happening here? Could it have something to do with my first-ever scheduled time off?

"Your role is to make the client feel they're the most important person in the universe. William Boatman happens to be CFO of the largest biopharmaceutical company in the country. He deserves our deference. Instead you fawned over the little boy."

I'm pretty sure I disagree with her. Vehemently. "I, um . . . I'm not sure how much you heard, but he was super condescending, both to his wife and to me." I'm surprised by my steady voice, which belies that whooshing sound in my head.

Pilar shrugs. "Audrey. Now I realize this may offend your delicate sensibilities, but it wouldn't be our business if he kept a den of concubines or dumped his company's hazardous waste in the Pacific. If he can afford beautiful spaces, he deserves our regard the moment he walks through that door. This is what we do, Audrey. We sell beautiful spaces where our clients are king. A man like Bill Boatman isn't going to change his mind because his wife asks him to. He must believe it's in his own interest. Do you see what I'm saying?"

My mind is like a roulette ball spinning, and I can't get it to land on an appropriate response. Hopefully, the question is rhetorical.

Pilar lifts one of my sketches from the conference table. "I see your passion here. Your work . . . exquisite as usual." She returns it to the table. Folds her arms tight. Angles her head, as if assessing the whole lot of it. Or computing the total sum of my value to her. "Your sense of color and balance—these are skills I had hoped to utilize. But . . ." Now she looks at me pointedly through crimson cat-eye glasses. "There's more to this job than pretty pictures."

Had hoped? I perceive a threat in her use of past tense. I know for certain my hand sketching gives us a competitive edge. Most design firms rely entirely on SketchUp software. She has to be bluffing. We're short-staffed. She *needs* me. Doesn't she?

"Thank you, Pilar. I'm sure I still have a lot to learn. And I hope to contribute here for a long time." My words hang in the air like shiny bubbles, floating and vulnerable, and perhaps not a thousand percent sincere. That last part takes me by surprise. *Is* this really what I want?

Pilar inhales deep, then continues on an exaggerated exhale. "Well. For now, *my* first order of business is to see if, by some miracle, this project can be salvaged." She angles toward her office. "Speaking of which," she says over her shoulder, "Joshua, you'll need to call Brad and tell him I can't make Simone's recital. And get me a dinner reservation for three at Arabella—by the fireplace."

Outside her office door, Pilar pivots. "It appears I'll be spending my evening on damage control."

Circumstances seem to demand I work through lunch hour as a demonstration of loyalty—and besides, I've got a drawer full of instant cups of soup. But I've also got an appointment scheduled. If I hang my nail girl out to dry again, she'll have no choice but to charge me. And tomorrow's locked down.

My desk calendar has no power to produce a solution. In tomorrow's box, under "Saturday," is one word, inflexible as a mountain range. *Oregon*. In fact, if I hope to arrive at Daisy and Dean's at any sort of decent hour, I'll have to leave at sunrise. Especially now that I've finally got around to listening to Mom's voicemail.

The prospect of an Oregon visit lurks in half shadow. But after today it also beckons like an escape hatch. What would Tawny say?

I can easily imagine my best friend advising that a little self-care is in order right now. I'll keep the appointment.

When I return, Joshua isn't his usual chatty self. I set down what's left of an Oreo Blizzard on my desk before approaching Pilar's office. Somehow I've got to shatter this fragile silence surrounding my impending absence. But a gut punch stops me cold.

Pilar has my Boatman folders open on her desk. The sketches lay fanned out, and the CAD file sits open on her computer screen. Sweet vanilla cream curdles on my tongue.

"Something I can do to help?" I manage to say, despite the strangled feeling in my throat.

She doesn't look up. "That won't be necessary, Audrey. Thank you."

I've been excused. But something still has to be bridged. We can't keep dancing around the fact that I'm leaving for two weeks. "Alright," I say, smiling with my voice, since she won't look at me. "Well, please don't hesitate to call me while I'm out of town. If any questions come up"—*for instance, about the ideas Marlene has been communicating* to me *for weeks*—"or if there's any way I can help with . . . anythi—"

Her desk phone buzzes, followed by Joshua's voice over the intercom. "That's Keiko on line one returning your call." Pilar takes the call, and I make myself vanish as gracefully as possible.

Does she think she can woo Keiko back early from maternity leave? Is she reassigning my project to her? My stomach churns. Questions niggle, and Joshua may hold the answers. In fact, I sense a secret or two burning within him. But he values his position too much to risk spilling the tea with me.

On the bright side, Pilar makes an early exit. There are no awkward goodbyes, because there are no goodbyes at all. By five thirty, I'm alone in the office and my to-do list is done. Rain pelts the windows. When did the sky burst open? I riffle through each of my active project folders, making sure everything's tidy and alphabetical in case my coworkers need to refer to something while I'm away.

What have I been thinking? Two weeks may as well be forever. Could the timing be any worse? As much as I want to help Daisy, I can't afford to risk losing my job. But to bail on my great-aunt? She's the closest thing to a grandmother I've ever known. My eyes float to the padded envelope she sent, still unopened. The slant of her handwriting, although not as smooth and flowing as it once was, is as familiar as my reflection. No way could I stomach disappointing her.

All I need is a compromise. I slip a manila folder containing the specs for my newest assignment, an interior update of a prominent attorney's office, into my briefcase. Surely there will be hours to fill when I'm not helping Daisy. I'll find a coffee shop with Wi-Fi. After today, further ingratiating myself to Pilar feels yucky, but at least I might recover a sense of control.

Launching into my standard end-of-the-week routine, I clear my spam folder. Slide my laptop into my attaché. Dust my cherrywood desk and shelves. I pause to study the galloping-horse figurine. With one hand, the rider grips the reins. With the other, she secures a cowboy hat to her head. Her expression communicates determination, and something else. Something unbridled. I reposition it slightly.

As I return the microfiber cloth to the top drawer, I swear my tin of Prismacolor pencils whispers to me. How strange it might feel to be without them for so long. Slipping them into my briefcase feels strangely empowering.

Finally it's time to investigate Daisy's mysterious package, which I've been saving like a carrot for this moment. I tear off the tab. When I turn the envelope upside down, out slips an audiobook on CD, and I have to chuckle. How old-school. I'll bet it never occurred to my seventy-something-year-old, classic-literature-loving great-aunt that automobiles with built-in CD players are fast going the way of the chaise and four. Good thing my Kia's an older model.

Still, it's *Mansfield Park*! Which means my Jane Austen collection is now complete—the collection Daisy began contributing to when I was a teenager. She remembered.

I unfold the note.

> *"It's such a happiness when good people get together—and they always do." Pleasant travels, sweetheart. I appreciate you.*

At the line from another Austen novel—*Emma?*—my cheeks lift into my first full-on smile of the day.

Several moments tick by while I turn the gift over in my hands and simply enjoy the soft patter of raindrops. For the first time today, peace arrives, and with it, clarity. I open my briefcase, remove the new-project folder, and place it on my desk for another day.

Oh, Daisy. I'm there for you.

It looks like I could be waiting for a break in the rain indefinitely, and suddenly I want out like never before. I make a run for my car, into the gathering darkness. Then I slow. Turns out, I don't actually mind the cool, bracing drops on my head and cheeks as I walk up the now-empty avenue. Streetlamps glow through the mist with gold, diffused light. Runoff from the cloudburst courses into a drainage grate and burbles underground. The air smells purified. A city is baptized.

I lift my face. *Oh, Lord.* Let the aroma of my day run in rivulets and be washed away . . . sandalwood mingled with the stench of failure.

Four

The following morning, I depart under the gray light of predawn. Merging onto the 101 is a breeze this time of day, so what's got my body wound as tight as a bowstring? *Name the tension.* It's a maxim I heard recently on a therapist's podcast. Actually, Dr. Everything's Going to Be Okay, I'd rather not.

Alright, fine, I'll do it. For starters, I've worked hard to get where I am, and now I'm . . . what? Leaving things to fate? Also, the price of gas is gross. Only a fool would embark on this journey with so little financial reserves. And on top of it, I've committed to two stops before my drive begins in earnest. What if there's a traffic delay? I told Daisy I'd arrive before dinner, and I couldn't stand for her to think I'm not a woman of my word. This whole leaving-things-to-fate thing isn't me, and I don't see how it ever could be. I'm not that girl, I guess—the one in the horse figurine. Not any longer.

I cue up the *Mansfield Park* audiobook and practice box breathing. Hey, if it works for Navy SEALs . . . Pretty soon I'm so spellbound by the British narrator's snappy telling, the two-hour drive northwest to my old hometown of Davis flies by.

As always, Crepeville hums with wakefulness, and the air is thick with the aroma of bacon and naughty carbs. Tawny and Ava are curled over their cell phones at a window table. "Still smells like heaven," I say, approaching. "And old times." We share hugs all around and I remark on Ava's rounding tummy.

Gorgeous, elegant Ava positively glows. "Another boy!" she gushes.

As always, being in the same room as Tawny has a grounding effect on me. Pretty sure my blood pressure dropped the moment I saw her. "Sit. Relax," she says, turning to me. "I went ahead and ordered you the Athens Scramble. Hope you don't mind. They're so busy, and I know you can't stay long."

"Perfect."

"Really? Oh, good." Tawny visibly relaxes. "I was worried your tastes might've changed now that you're killing it in the big city."

"C'mon. Get real. This is me."

"I know." Her brown eyes are soft. "You'd never go all bougie on us."

Seeing that the girls have already got their drinks, I start to rise from my seat. "I'll just go order a—"

"Earl grey?" As if on cue, a blond waitress materializes delivering a steaming mug of tea. Of course Tawny nailed this too. Why should I be surprised? I offer her a wan smile that I can only hope communicates half my affection. I haven't felt this seen since, well, since the last time she and I hung out. It's been months, and the blame falls squarely on my shoulders. I'm sure I could stand to spend a little less time measuring my progress and a little more time engaging with my people. *Be present, Audrey.*

Ava is two parts Penélope Cruz and one part Goldie Hawn. Her stunning eyes are never not drawn into an inquisitive expression, like a newborn. It's the oddest but also the cutest thing. She wakes up that way and I'm pretty sure she falls in bed the same. Now Ava peers at me over the top of her mocha. "*So . . .* Tawny tells me you're not dating the yacht-club guy anymore. What's the story there?" Leave it to her to go straight for this topic.

I'm loath to spend our little bit of time together on ancient history. But while Kyle and I haven't spoken in several months, I haven't caught up with Ava in even longer. Hopefully she'll accept a thumbnail version. "How 'bout I just tell you how it ended?"

Tawny shoots me a wink and excuses herself to go visit the ladies' room. For her, this is old news. She and I have maintained an active text thread ever since cell phones became a thing.

"Well, let's see. We spent a Saturday afternoon walking around the Arts Guild—surprisingly his idea. This, by the way, was a Valentine's Day plan he'd had to postpone. Which was great with me because, you know, we weren't in a relationship."

"Yes, I know. Just *dating friends*." Ava gestures, placing air quotes around my term.

"Anyway, he knew I'd always wanted to go. We had lunch in the Blue Garden and wandered the art shops. The hydrangeas weren't in bloom yet, so that was kind of a bummer. But still, it was nice. Then he suggested we hit Kepler's Books. Again, I was surprised."

"Yeah, that's totally your jam."

"We took in an author reading. But, I don't know, Ava. It was all just so ironic."

"What? What was ironic?"

I slowly swirl the tea bag by its string, unlocking more of its heavenly bergamot scent, and remembering. "For me the whole day fell flat. I could tell he was just doing all this to please me." As I speak, I'm intentionally prodding my heart, testing the tender middle, the way I learned from Daisy to check the center of a snickerdoodle for doneness. Nothing. There's no goo, no give. I may as well be talking about someone else's love life.

"And that's . . . bad?" Ava appears far more injured than I remember feeling. "Am I missing something? That sounds sweet."

"I mean, he was trying. Kyle's not a bad guy, mind you. He's thoughtful. He's got charisma—"

"By the boatload?" Tawny's back, just in time to interject. Ava and I groan.

"But you know me," I say. "Better to be alone than with some-one who doesn't share my interests." I don't mention my suspicion that Kyle didn't entirely share my values either. Or my faith, such as it is.

Ava stares at me blankly, then blinks. "You mean like your in-terest in design?"

I look to Tawny for help. Sure enough, where Ava falters, Tawny comes through. "Nature, poetry . . . don't forget, Audrey's still our hippie in high heels," she says. "And then of course there's that special place she holds in her heart for cringeworthy dad jokes." She dabs a napkin at her lips, which are turned up in a smirk.

A new sense of gratitude sweeps through me, for having kept my heart detached and therefore unscathed. Suddenly I relish the prospect of tossing a few more shovelfuls of soil over the deceased non-relationship. "Exactly. And it hit me—what am I thinking, dating a guy who only ever wears Sperrys without socks? The only thing he reads is the West Marine catalog. I mean, I love the ocean. Just not so, you know, up close and personal. Give me the mountains any day. They don't undulate."

When Tawny and I clink mugs, her princess-cut solitaire flashes. Secretly, I'm not convinced her fiancé knows what a diamond *he* has in Tawny. Ava blows out a breath, then lifts her mocha and joins our toast. "Fine," she says. "Good riddance to Kyle."

Later I'm poking at the last bits of spinach and feta on my plate when Ava thrusts her phone screen toward me. "Audrey, have you seen this app—Clurk? Never mind. You already have it, don't you? I knew it! Ugh. Jared's got me on this major budgeting thing—it sends me a text when I get anywhere close to our monthly limit on stuff. I'm already in the red zone on dining out—and I've still got two weeks to go. I'm doomed!" She laughs, in her Ava way—which is to say, loud and rapid-fire and often experienced by patrons two tables away. "Oh"—Ava rubs her belly—"baby kicks! I think he's taking my side."

Ava's not wrong. I do like that app. And I love Ava. Ava is a hoot. Tawny and I inherited her as a roommate at Sacramento State, and she stuck. It's just that the entirety of the life wisdom she's eager to offer begins and ends with finding an eligible McDreamy clone with a Dr. Derek income. I find it endlessly entertaining that she doesn't see the irony in having married a CPA.

Today, though, I'm coveting some overdue, deep-talk-with-Tawny time. She's my person, my go-to for meaningful emotional expeditions. It doesn't hurt that she's pursuing her master's in counseling. She and I go all the way back to seventh grade, and even then she had a settled soul.

"Gah! I need to get going," I say, stealing a glance at my Fitbit. I unzip the lipstick compartment of my purse.

Tawny manages to look both disappointed and supportive.

Ava pouts. "You *will* be back to help me with Liam's room, though." A statement, not a question. With a baby brother en route, Liam's graduating from the nursery to his own big-boy room. "You promised."

Standing to collect my sweater, I smile. "I can't wait to help." Now that I think about it, maybe Daisy won't need me for the full two weeks. Maybe I'll get the deed done and come back early.

"Wait, wait. You can't leave yet." Ava reaches beneath the table and produces a Victoria's Secret bag. Tawny waggles her eyebrows.

"What's this about?" It's nowhere near my birthday.

Ava waves her hand dismissively. "Oh, don't let the bag throw you. It's just a little something I thought you might want for your trip. To be honest, I'm regifting, okay? Don't judge. I never even took the tags off. You keep it. In fact, I insist." Again she adds one of her short blast-laughs.

Beneath a layer of tissue paper, my fingertips land on something soft. Flannel. "Oh, you're too cute," I say, lifting out a forest-green plaid shirt. But then I lay a hand on my heart. Perhaps I'm not embarking on this journey alone after all.

"Not my style," Ava says. "Or yours, for that matter. But at least you'll fit in. In Oregon." She pronounces it Or-ee-*gone*, and with disdain. "I hear it rains there all the time. Ew."

For a brief second, I'm tempted to defend the place I once adored. To say, "No, that's a common misunderstanding. My dad grew up on the *other* side of the Cascade Range, not the rainy side. It's all forest and stream and high desert and sunshine. *And it's beautiful*." But I don't.

"Just promise me, whatever you do, girlfriend, don't buy the ugly shoes. Remember my cousin who moved to Tahoe? Now she's got that whole, you know, pinesy-woodsy thing going on. If you come back wearing those ugly river-walking shoes, we simply can't be friends."

Our collective laughter's like an echo from long ago, pealing with an adolescent brand of hope. Like a song you know every word to but which no longer rings completely true no matter how loud you sing. The kind of song that once had me believing that all that stardust shimmering across the night sky was put there just so I could rearrange it to my liking. Or that God would do it for me if I simply prayed enough and toed the line.

I'm suspicious of this particular kind of song. And I wonder if it has led me afield. Maybe even galaxies away from where I belong.

But this morning, I'll take it. Laughter feels luxurious, like a soul massage. And before I've even left the parking lot, Tawny texts.

> Let me know when you get there so I don't worry.

I really have been blessed with two mothers.

～～～

My actual mother, the one from whose womb I of course sprang three weeks early, wheedled me into a brief pit stop at the old family house after breakfast with the girls. Not that she was there. Nor will anyone I know ever live there again.

Despite the added detour, I'm making good time now and haven't even given the deserted house on Sunset Terrace much thought, thanks to the whims and woes of the Bertram siblings of *Mansfield Park*. In fact, when I stopped at a gas station just past the California-Or-uh-*guhn* border, I accidentally thanked the attendant in a Regency accent I didn't know I was capable of. I just wish I'd thought to check the oil level back there. I'm not too crazy about the position of the temperature gauge while Harriet and I have still got some climbing to do.

Here, though, this narrow ribbon of highway hugs the contours of a vast sapphire lake. Clouds drift across a cornflower-blue umbrella of sky. I, too, feel suspended and gauzy. Adrift, somewhere between what was and what will be. Could I ever hold things so loosely that I might ride on God's exhale? Allow him to direct my course wherever he decrees? Unlikely.

Yet somehow my mother has learned to do this, to let go. Even to embrace new challenges. I picture her learning to reach out in practical, relational ways to Indigenous people on reservations throughout the Southwest. How lit up she and her new husband, Jeffrey, are about enhancing the lives and culture of Native Americans.

Mom's okay. I don't need to carry a burden for her any longer. Still, I should have offered to stage the house for her. What's the matter with me? *You're too self-focused, Audrey. That's your problem.*

Earlier, when I arrived at my childhood home, I sat staring through swaying windshield wipers at the bright-crimson real estate sign out front, working up the courage to use my house key for the final time. Inside, the vacant house yawned. Rain mumbled against the windows, and our same old refrigerator sighed from the kitchen like a ghost. I barefooted it across a newly carpeted living room, past naked walls and empty bookshelves, catching sterile whiffs of fresh paint and citrusy floor polish. In the backyard, rain pelted the soft-pink cabbage roses and Dad's blossoming citrus grove.

Shouldn't there have been some lingering aroma of our humanity, a sacred thrum forever resounding from the four lives lived there? Of fish-taco Tuesdays and fend-for-yourself Fridays. Of Sunday soup days, when we had always been encouraged to invite a friend—or better still, a stranger.

Of Troy and me bickering over the inanest things. Dad, restoring order with one sharp look. Mom, calmly reciting a verse from Ephesians: "Let everything you say be good and helpful, so that your words will be an encouragement to those who hear them."

Then, overnight, a match was lit to all of it. And nothing could ever be the same. A few weeks later, Troy left for college, Mom laid her apron to rest, and every day became fend-for-yourself day.

Sniffling down a sob, I pop open my glovebox and scrounge for a Kleenex. Or napkins. Anything. What's wrong with me lately? Why do I feel jelly-legged, like I've just stepped off Kyle's sailboat? It doesn't help that Harriet and I are navigating a strong cross breeze.

I prefer to think of Mom on her better days—stoic, marching chin-up in survival mode, reacclimating to full-time work as a middle school teacher. I've worked to forget the nights she refilled her wine glass several times, raved like a madwoman when Cricket the geriatric Corgi peed indoors, or broke down in sobs over a bag of spinach gone spoiled. If she even came out of her room.

I guess we each coped in our own ways.

Anyhow, I now carry in my possession the item she asked me to fetch from her and my dad's old bedroom, and it is lovely. Her vintage hard-shell suitcase. A thing of huge intrigue for me as a child, the way it was always stashed on the highest shelf of her closet. Pale-blue casing. Chestnut-brown leather corners. Cotton topstitching. Weathered latches. I love that romantic old piece, and now it's accompanying me to Oregon. And then home again.

When I try to visualize home, uncertainty billows through my insides. Now more than ever, home is gossamer. Colorless. Perhaps even a fable.

A surge of renewed gratefulness warms me that Mom eventually emerged from what she calls her dark night of the soul. And that when my portion of Dad's life insurance ran out and I became one of those revolving-door adult children, she always welcomed me home to regroup, to save up for another college term. I think of those as the friend years—Mom coming out from the shadows, finding her new groove, inviting me into her life, interested in mine.

Until, that is, a couple years ago when she met Jeffrey at some kind of ministry conference and stopped relying on our friendship. At first, the idea of Mom remarrying was a big fat *ew*. Celebrating last Christmas with Jeffrey's extended family, all of them strangers to me, made me feel the stabbing pain of Dad's absence more than ever.

My throat constricts and I swallow back a wad of emotion. Through trembling lips, I struggle for just one smooth breath. *Not now.* I channel all my anguish into an old, familiar fury and smack the steering wheel hard, three times. *No, no, no!*

When did I stop listening to my book? With shaking fingers, I'm about to hit the back arrow when I notice a dark SUV riding my bumper. How long has he been hovering like that? *Idiot.* Or for that matter, the rest of the cars stacked up behind me? Oh, dang. I'm the idiot, and I need to get it together. But I can't imagine traveling much faster on this gusty, winding stretch. Fine. I'll speed up a bit and pray there's a passing lane ahead.

I press play on the CD deck. Roll my knotted shoulders forward twice. Then backward twice. It'll be over soon. In a few hours, I'll arrive in Charity Falls.

Well, isn't this ducky. Now the knotting has relocated to my stomach.

Okay, so helping Daisy is inconvenient. And potentially excruciating. Plus, I've taken a huge professional risk. But is love that isn't willing to be inconvenienced even love at all?

Five

By the time the Charity Falls city limits sign comes into view, my eyes burn. For the last half hour, the lowering sun has been glaring at me through a smear of bug guts. I'm relieved to flick on my blinker and exit the sleepy two-lane highway before it bisects downtown Charity Falls.

And just like that, I'm on it—the old country road to Daisy and Dean's place. How strange. Everything feels at once familiar and also like a scene from someone else's life. How could it not, after thirteen years? Years in which I've shape-shifted from a gawky teen into my late twenties. I've only ever traveled this route from the back seat of my parents' car.

Same town. Same road. Different Audrey.

I roll past City Hall, a historic-looking Greystone with an elaborate wrought-iron timepiece crowning the clock tower. Not exactly as Gothic as the one in *Harry Potter*, but it's the one that informed my imagination when I read that series in my youth. Next comes a new-looking residential area with meandering rows of modern Craftsman homes, humble in square footage but dripping with charm.

And then I'm in open country.

At my first broad view of the Three Sisters mountains, snow-streaked and glowing, I gasp. I'd forgotten how the late-day light paints them orange and luminous. And how close they are. Part of the Cascade Range, the three peaks are nicknamed Faith, Hope, and Charity. Noble and friendly names for mountains that are somehow, well, noble and friendly. I couldn't begin to tell you which is which anymore, though. Before them waves an amber field of wild grasses, perfectly backlit.

I'm tempted to stop and snap a quick image to share on my socials. This landscape deserves to be shared.

Still, my stomach is clenched in anticipation of what I'm about to come upon—in less than half a mile. No way to visit my family without passing the Sugar Pine Inn. A carousel spins in my mind, in rapid clips like a TikTok reel. Faces I once knew. People I've never met. How many thousands of guests must have chalked up memories of their own at the inn since I last visited? Since . . . I swallow hard. Since everything changed.

I imagine couples exchanging vows in the gazebo. Children splashing in the pool, their voices echoing to the tips of the pines. Smiling families returning on horseback from a leisurely trail ride. Aromas accompany that last image, of sun-warmed hay and saddle leather and horsehide, ever wafting across the road and descending over Daisy and Dean's place.

On one such afternoon—around two thirty, to be exact—there was another smell. Smoke. My mind falls open to that dog-eared place. But no. I won't finish the thought.

I don't suppose any of those giddy faces in my carousel have a clue about what happened that hot August day.

From a ways off I spot the behemoth tree that inspired the inn's name. No turning back now. Next, the blue roof of the two-story farmhouse comes into view. But just as quickly, familiarity melts into confusion.

It's not simply that the ranch fencing is missing boards and thirsts for paint, although this in itself is unusual. But the half circle of cabins, ever sweet and tidy, are boarded up and drowning in a sea of weeds. I can't compute this. What happened to the lush meadow of orange and blue wildflowers? The pond?

An old, rusty-red pickup languishes where the gazebo used to be. Heaps of dead branches where picnic tables once rested.

I roll by at a crawl. Pine cones and debris litter a swimming pool that doesn't appear to have seen water for a decade. And the farm-house itself—now there's a hot mess. Someone has boarded up the lower-story windows and sunroom. Gingerbread trim dangles loose. The once welcoming porch has lost sections of spindled railing, like an elderly woman with tooth gaps.

Worse, the place seems all cried out as if resigned to its fate.

I hadn't allowed myself to imagine this moment, this reunion. But if I had, never in a million years would it have gone like this. What exactly happened here? I drift to a stop on the shoulder. "Hey, Siri," I say, my voice sounding strange to my ears. "Search Sugar Pine Inn, Charity Falls." Hopefully, my great-aunt and uncle aren't watching out their windows. I could easily pitch a pine cone from here to their driveway almost directly across from the inn.

Swiping through search results on my phone, I land on a local newspaper headline: "End of era for Sugar Pine Inn?" It's dated eight years ago, when the property was evidently put up for sale. The owners, June and Todd Milligan, Daisy's longtime employ-ers, had retired. Which all makes sense. That's when Daisy retired as well. But someone must've purchased it by now. Why haven't they kept it up?

It's no wonder my hands tremble, being so close to the inn and all. I'm just not sure why I'm so hot and bothered about its demise. I wrote this place off when I was fifteen. Why should I care? In fact, I don't. I don't have to care. I refuse to let it wield any power over me.

I chuck my phone into my bag. *Soldier on, girl. This is not your fight.* I don't need another thing to grieve. Stuff happens.

RIP, Sugar Pine.

One thing's for sure. I will not speak of this with Daisy or Dean. We're all doing the best we can to live in the here and now. Yesterday's gone. I'm zipping my lips—and my heart.

Besides, suddenly I can't wait to see my great-aunt and uncle.

Six

Daisy

If Audrey's put off by my appearance, she's a brilliant actress. "You look *uh*-mazing," she coos, then drops her duffel on the porch and bends to wrap me in a full hug. Her voice surprises me, so earthy and sweet. Womanly. My heart puddles like warm tapioca. Can she not tell I'm barely being held together with string, like an overdone pot roast?

"Oh, fiddle. Same old saddlebags," I say, patting the widest part of my hips.

You'd never guess my niece and I share the same pear-shaped body type. But at five-foot-nothing and shrinking, I'm like a short, squat Bartlett standing next to a graceful d'Anjou. Audrey's still such a petite thing, but to my tired eyes she's lithe and glamorous. Has she really been wearing that flowy spring skirt and those white kitten heels for six hundred miles?

But shame on me. I should know better than to stub out a compliment like the butt of a cigarette. What kind of example is that for a young lady?

Within moments of being back in Audrey's orb, I perceive that we somehow still share more than our similarity to fruit, or lack thereof. Intangible things. Things I suddenly yearn to rediscover together, if she'll have it.

"Gosh, it's been too long," Audrey says. But then she drops her bright, teal-eyed gaze. Her lovely lids flutter. Are her eyes wet? "I'm sorry, Aunt Daisy. I'm really sorry it's been so long. I don't know wh—"

"Hey." I hold my palm upright, firm as a stop sign. "Let's not give it another thought. Too much catching up to do. Come right on in. I've got Danny's room made up for you."

Too late, I recognize my blunder. At the mention of Danny, Audrey flinches like I've poked her with an electric cattle prod. But the careless words are already out, and now, if I'm not mistaken, the atmosphere carries a subtle charge. To distract, I start gabbing like a fool as we cross the living room's hardwood floor. I can't help myself. I just keep prattling on about all the ways she should make herself at home.

Audrey wears a smile, but we both know what's being left unsaid.

Danny's bedroom glows peach with the golden hour's first blush. "Here, set your things on the window seat. Plenty of room in the closet if you'd like to hang things up. You look so ding-dang pretty! I just love that soft shade of blue on you with your coloring. Is it comfortable?"

"What, this?" Audrey fans the front of her wrap skirt. "Super comfy. See? Stretch fabric. No wrinkles."

I'm breathing a sigh of relief, thinking we've moved past the awkwardness, when Audrey turns to me suddenly. "Is there a car wash in town?" Her eyes dart around the bedroom, everywhere but on me. "I drove through this huge cloud of weird, kamikaze bugs a ways back. Like one of those plagues in the Bible. I should probably wash them off before they're stuck forever. Would you mind?"

I knew it. I've said the wrong thing. Or maybe she's nervous, knowing Dean's due back any moment. One of his Rotary buddies took him out for a drive and possibly for a short hike along the river. Heck, I'm nervous too—what if Dean falls? His gait is so unsteady these days. In fact, shouldn't they be home by now? So maybe I've projected my own anxiety onto Audrey.

And then I see it. Or perhaps a certain Someone Upstairs reveals it to me. Despite her Grace Kelly facade and the confidence with which she carries herself, there's something fragile about Audrey. Timid. Birdlike, even. What she's gained over the last thirteen years in poise and intellect, she's lost in self-assurance.

She hasn't been too busy to visit. She's been too afraid.

Audrey

I don't know what exactly I expected. But at first Uncle Dean doesn't appear to have roamed as far down the murky trail of Alzheimer's as I'd feared. He knows me! At least he insists he does, becomes all curmudgeonly when Daisy throws him an assist.

"Dean, honey, look! Look who's here," Daisy says, as she ushers Dean and his white-haired friend toward the kitchen table, where I'm about to pass out from gastronomic euphoria. Until the old dudes arrived, Daisy had been sitting across from me, delightedly watching me consume her baked ziti casserole, each bite bursting with melted mozzarella and good olive oil and some kind of magical marinara.

But now Daisy's eyebrows are raised and she's fast-nodding at her husband, like one of those dashboard bobbleheads or a preschool teacher. Odd. She was never high-strung. "It's Audrey. You know . . . *Danny's girl.*"

"Of course I do," he says, leaning away from her, looking offended. I'm struck by the new gravel in his voice. And its weaker volume. But still it's glazed with that syrupy twang from his childhood roots somewhere in the South—Oklahoma, I think. If I had to liken my Uncle Dean to a donut, he'd be a maple bar for sure. His bald spot's still endearingly shiny, and I'm pretty sure I detect an echo of his old playfulness.

He turns to me. "By golly, it's Danny's girl. Well, whatdaya know? How 'bout that." When I hug him, he feels unsteady.

And observing him alongside his bright-eyed buddy, I can't deny the changes in him. Changes for which I'm totally unprepared. Once a solid evergreen, Dean's now more of a withering vine. He's lost height. He's shed weight. In square footage, he's lost a whole person. Most of all, he's lost pieces of himself. Gone is his hearty presence, the way he invigorated a room just by being in it. Instead I see hesitance. Uncertainty. Maybe even fear.

Of course, he's probably at his worst right now, tired from the day's exertion. A sharp stitch pierces my heart, a feeling I've never associated with my wisecracking uncle. Empathy. I don't need to be all anxious around him. I just need to care. And I do. Oh, God help me, I do care.

"I went ahead and fed her," Daisy's telling him. "Poor thing's been driving all day. Isn't she a vision?"

The admiration in her eyes is excruciating.

Daisy keeps up her constant stream of guiding words. "Come, sit down now, Dean. Over here. No, not there. Here. This chair, honey. Rob, won't you stay and join us for dinner?"

I observe. I watch the way Dean shuffles to his seat at the head of the table. How he's oblivious to the fact that his friend is saying his goodbyes. Like he can only focus on one thing at a time, and right now his mind is occupied with operating the salad tongs. I watch the way my petite aunt bustles around this shadow of the man who for the last half century has been her person, tending to him with a kind of devotion rarely seen, even if it is tinged with exasperation—because I can see that it is.

Yeah. I care more than I had any idea.

Shoot. This wasn't the plan.

Seven

I awake to warm, diffused light that insists on being reckoned with. And silence. No, not silence exactly. There's music reeling in my head, incompatibly upbeat for the break of dawn in disorienting circumstances. Tuning in, I'm confronted with one of Mom's seventies anthems. Really? What have I done to deserve Fleetwood Mac between my ears first thing in the morning, belting, "Don't stop thinking about tomorrow"? Electric guitar solo and all. *Yesterday's gone*—yeah, I know. You can go now.

Really. Please. Be gone.

Rewinding to last night, the last thing I remember was this deep marshmallow of a mattress swallowing me whole the moment I climbed in. I try to recall any dreams, but nope. Just a solid night's sleep in—and this is a weird thought—in what's probably the same bed my parents slept in when we visited each summer. Back then, Troy and I always crashed on the living room floor in sleeping bags. Mornings brought the *shlip-shlip-shlip* of Aunt Daisy's slippers across the kitchen linoleum and the intoxicating smell of bacon.

I sit up and sniff the air. No bacon today.

Are my memories even real, or did I fabricate them with wishes and watercolors? This faded floral quilt. The cotton, so soft. How long has it been in the family? What stories could it tell that I've never thought to ask?

Enough of this. I slip my toes into the dense, forest-green area rug and make my way to the window. What I need right now is some sunlight and a to-do list. But when I open the blinds, I'm met with an angled view of the inn. It's as if the ghost of a jilted Victorian bride is peering at me from behind that row of weepy, overgrown cedar trees. The place gives new meaning to the term *distressed*. Well, this is unfortunate. Another assault I hadn't counted on so early in the day.

After lowering the blinds, I turn to face my duffel. This kind of workday calls for hard-boiled willpower and yoga pants.

The Victoria's Secret "Pink" toiletry bag containing my toothbrush and the like sits atop a mid-century dresser, surrounded by three silver-framed photos. Dad's high school graduation portrait. He and Mom, younger than I am today, grinning wide while cutting a tiered wedding cake. And one of all four of us, in which preadolescent Troy has his hair slicked freakily to the side and I'm missing my front teeth. There's an odd dissonance between my glossy pink bag and these photos. I can't really name it.

I've never thought much about this being Dad's childhood bedroom. Could this old thing have been his dresser? The top drawer grumbles when I slide it out. Empty. Nothing to see here but a vacuum of stale-smelling nothingness. And perhaps, if I'm lucky, an invisibility cloak.

Yesterday's gone. That's obvi.

———

A tangible hush hangs over the living room. Pine paneling infused with furniture polish and memories. A fire crackling in the hearth. This part of the house feels sacred, like a chapel in the woods.

"Look at you, up with the sunrise and every bit as lovely," Daisy says quietly, slipping off her readers. Curled up among the folds of her trademark zippered velour robe with an open book in her lap, she looks adorably elvish. Like Tinker Bell, with that pixie-cut white-blond hair. She gestures to her chair's twin on the opposite side of the fireplace. "Come. Sit."

I'm disarmed. I've walked straight into the most enticing invitation I've had in I don't know how long, and I'm powerless to resist. So what if Daisy's fourteen-year-old short-haired calico rescue kitty is giving me the stink eye from her bay window cushion? The poor, sweet old thing. Now I understand why Daisy hasn't shared photos of Myrtle Rose in a long time. There comes a time when a cat is . . . how can I put this delicately? When a cat is no longer photogenic. I pet the orange patch behind her ear, hoping she'll warm up to me.

"Whatcha reading?" I ask Daisy.

"Would you like some coffee? I'll go get you a—"

"Oh, please don't get up. I'm fine. Really."

She looks at me penetratingly, holding my gaze as if to weigh my words. The smile that follows is so genuine and loving, and communicates so much, that my chest squeezes and I'm afraid I might cry.

She holds up the cover of her book. "It's . . ." She clears emotion from her throat. "It's a biography. Ever heard of Hannah More?"

Oh, thank God. We're sticking to book talk. I shake my head.

"And how do you like *Mansfield Park*?" Daisy asks.

Reflexively, my gaze flies to the golden-oak bookcases that flank the brick fireplace and wing out all the way to the corner in either direction. "Loving it, of course. Oh! You must have it in print. Maybe I'll keep reading while I'm here." I'm up now, roving the shelves for Daisy's collection of Jane Austen titles and not finding them where I remembered. Her assortment of owls are still scattered about, though, perched here and there among the books.

Some are ceramic, others of carved wood or colored glass. Wise and whimsical touches, like the woman of the house.

"I've thinned out my books. Had to. So much has to go. Look there," she says, pointing.

I locate a complete set, all similarly dressed in fading dust jackets. My great-aunt has easily reduced her library by more than half. I stiff-arm sadness and turn *Mansfield Park* over in my hands. And then, as if by habit, I also slide *Pride and Prejudice* off the shelf. I know this one so well, I may want to just snack on it without commitment.

"I can't thank you enough," I say. "It made the trip go by so fast. I wasn't driving a Kia up I-5, I was bouncing through the countryside in an open carriage."

Daisy's eyes shine. And suddenly there she is—the younger, more carefree auntie I remember. "Yes! A *barouche*!"

I nod at the book she's holding. "So, who was she, Hannah More?"

"Unsung hero of the eighteenth century. Remarkable woman, a writer. Helped abolish slavery in England, along with William Wilberforce."

"Oh. Wow." I used to be more inclined toward that type of book. True stories of fearless world-changers. Corrie ten Boom. Harriet Tubman. Condoleezza Rice. No doubt Aunt Daisy remembers my whole Pocahontas phase. But lately I'll choose escapism over inspirational every time. Unless you count the ebook I keep attempting, *5 Rules for Life*, which bills itself as the remedy for "women who can't seem to get it all done." Fittingly, I can't seem to find time for that one.

Without thinking, I tuck my feet under me, then reconsider. Should I settle in or offer to make breakfast? Visit awhile or get our day rolling? What happens when Dean gets up?

Daisy's feathering the pages of her book, wearing an expression of longing. "Can you imagine effecting that kind of change?"

What? Say it ain't so. Daisy's life may not be flashy, but if it hasn't contained divine purpose, no one's has. She can't really be questioning her own contribution. Can she?

A muffled voice travels the hall, and Daisy's eyelids flicker. And in that brief sliver of time, I perceive the truth. She's more on edge and less stoic than she portrays. "I'll just go check on him," she says. "He's always been one to talk in his sleep. Says the darndest things."

When Daisy returns, she moves her book from the seat of her chair to the side table, exchanging it for her coffee mug.

"So, how can I help today?" I ask. "I'm here to help."

Daisy begins reciting her list of projects. Then she breaks off and puffs a sigh. Her pixie shoulders slump. "Oh, Audrey. There's so much to tackle. To be honest, it's all so overwhelming. Anything would be helpful. And truly, having you here is already giving me a lift. What do you feel like doing?"

I'm speechless. She may as well have asked me to translate the preamble to the Constitution into Farsi. I turn this strange concept over in my mind like I'm sampling a new, exotic tea blend. What do I, Audrey Needham, feel like doing? What do I *feel* like doing? Sort dishware? Haul junk? Pack owls? Go back to bed? What have feelings got to do with anything? Must. Take. Charge.

"You know what? Never mind. It's Sunday. We'll start tomorrow. Now tell me, what do you think of our Fanny Price?" Daisy wraps her hands around her yellow mug and leans in, wide-eyed, awaiting my review like a kid watching a parent open their handmade present on Christmas morning.

So we're back to book talk. And a day of rest. Alright, I'll take it. But just one day.

"Hmm. I'm still not sure," I say. "She's no Elizabeth Bennet."

"No, she's never sharp. Nor a meddler like Emma, however well-intentioned."

"I know, right? I want her to meddle!" I lift Daisy's ancient copy of *Mansfield Park* to my nose and inhale. The pages smell like a warm vanilla cookie. "Fanny's got such amazing insight, but she keeps her opinions to herself. I think that makes her kind of a weak female protagonist, don't you? So I'm not sure yet if I'm a fan of her."

Daisy turns to watch the low fire dancing in the hearth, as if it holds all the answers. How does she do it? You won't catch me staring at a fire. Sometimes even candles make me edgy. I brush the thought away.

"Or does that make her strong?" she says, finally.

"What do you mean?" Warm tingles run through me. I've missed this. Momentarily, I can't remember any of the reasons I've kept my distance for so long.

"Well, like you, I admire Fanny's discernment—"

"Yes, she reads people so well," I say.

"She's no feminist."

I love that Daisy filters things like a millennial. "Not even."

"But she has discretion. There's power in that. She knows her mind, but she also knows how to hold her tongue."

"Maybe to a fault," I say. "I don't know if I could've held back from slamming Miss Watson, letting Edmund know her true character. And, *come on, Fanny*, let him know you're in love with him! But what did you just say? Do you think . . . do you really think it's possible to know your own mind? Pretty sure I know mine less every day."

Daisy chuckles. "Good question." She hums thoughtfully and returns her gaze to the fire.

Minutes pass, and we remain like this, suspended in a comfortable silence. Another thing I haven't experienced in forever. A cozy cup of tea or coffee is beginning to sound just right for the moment at hand, but I'm unwilling to shatter this fragile ambiance.

At last Daisy clears her throat. "Maybe she's just being true to herself. You know, it could be that she doesn't pass judgment because she sees herself as needy too. In need of grace."

"Then I'd say she's too good to be true."

Daisy smiles and cocks her head playfully. "I might be tempted to agree. If I'd never met anyone like her."

"What? Aunt Daisy, why are you looking at me that way?" She can't think I'm anything like this particular fictional heroine. An orphan, surrounded by privileged people behaving badly.

Daisy raises her eyebrows and pins me with a look. "Honey. When you were a just a little bitty thing, you were already calling out injustices. You remember! You could sniff out a lack of integrity like a bloodhound. Remember—" At this, Daisy throws her head back in a laugh. "Remember your campaign to get the city to change the lighting allowed at night?"

I feign defensiveness. "Hey now. Migratory birds travel at night. Light pollution throws off their GPS." And causes a million other problems, not the least of which is making it impossible to stargaze. A memory surfaces of the party my fifth-grade teacher threw when the city council voted to institute a dark-skies ordinance, restricting the kinds of commercial and residential lighting used in our town. Warmth spreads through me. It's still a proud moment, now that I think of it, in what seems like another lifetime.

"I'm sorry . . ." Daisy shakes her head, grinning. "I'm not smiling because it's funny. You were just so, so . . . *audacious*. Didn't the local TV news come out to your school and interview you? As I recall, your parents said it touched a lot of folks. Bet it inspired some to take more of an interest in civic matters. Especially kids!"

I guess that *was* pretty alright. "Yeah. Mom loves to tell those stories too. But see, you just said it, I wasn't very good at keeping my ideas to myself."

"Well, I guess there's a time and a place. And I'll bet it's gotten you into trouble a few times."

Had it? Not lately. When was the last time I stood up for a cause? These days I've become someone who caves, even when I disagree. Snippets of my last conversations with Pilar flash through my mind, and my skin runs hot. Should I have spoken up to her? Which reminds me, I never checked my phone today. Normally I scroll through email first thing. How strange that it never even occurred to me. My stomach tightens at the thought that a simple missive from Pilar wields the power to pierce the invisible barrier between where I sit today and my real life.

I'm a girl in a bubble, and right now I'm very okay with that. "I'll take it under advisement," I tell Daisy.

"And, like Fanny, I'm sure you must feel . . ." Daisy's eyes soften and I sense she's treading carefully.

Oh no.

"Perhaps, at times in your life, you've felt . . . displaced?"

Now there's a word I've never thought to apply to myself. I picture some child out of a Dickens novel, a ragamuffin. A street urchin with coal smudges on her cheeks, holding out a worn hat, begging, "Tuppence, kind sir?" Of course, my story has never been like that. I had both parents until I was nearly sixteen. My problems have been of the first-world kind, so by contrast I had it pretty good. Why then is my throat tightening as if Daisy just prodded something tender? I feel like an ant under a spyglass in the hot sun, seized by the impulse to squirm away.

"Interesting," I manage to say, twisting the ends of my hair. "I'll give that some thought too." I rise a little too hurriedly, working to keep my voice light. "But first, I'll take you up on that coffee." I set the two books in a neat pile on the worn, discolored circle in the middle of my tufted armchair, then bend to plant a kiss atop Daisy's head. Against my lips, the bone of her forehead feels surprisingly close to the surface. Her skin may be thinner now, but it carries the same familiar scent. Oil of Olay, I remember now. As a little girl I used to like to mooch a dab, rub it into my cheeks. Feeling sneaky. Sneaky and grown-up and soft.

She pats my hand and winks at me. "Fine, have it your way, sweetie. But here's something you can't dispute." I head to the kitchen, her voice trailing after me. "Like Fanny, you have an aunt who finds your presence extremely comforting!"

Eight

My Monday visit to The Box Office is by far the first of its kind. Never before have I experienced an office-supply store slash mailing center slash knitting shop. But the place is a well-stocked wonder, and I emerge onto Birch Avenue having accomplished my morning mission. I've found everything needed for Saturday's yard sale—price stickers, poster board, and a black Sharpie as fat as my wrist. Oh, and one unpremeditated purchase. A sketchbook.

I mean, you never know.

So this is late May in Charity Falls. I've only ever visited in the peak of summer, plus that one weekend in early fall when Dad and I surprised Aunt Daisy for her birthday. A barely-there breeze carries the musky scent of juniper. Okay, it's pollen, and my eyes itch. But it's a distinctive smell, reminding me I'm not in Kansas anymore. Or in my case, I'm nowhere near Meta, Google, or Apple headquarters. Driving a Tesla Model X here would turn heads for sure.

Instead, I'm in Subaru Land. All-wheel-drive vehicles topped with cargo boxes crawl like turtles everywhere through town. Some sport brightly colored kayaks. This street, one jump over from the main drag where the cross-state highway cuts through town—also at twenty miles an hour—is like all the rest at the town's core, which is to say, adorable. Lined with mature conifers and old-fashioned streetlamps. Fronted by quaint, touristy shops with Western facades.

I shield my eyes from the sun. Across the street and down a block, a building I'm pretty sure used to house a candy store back in the day is now something called Sweet Reads. Intriguing. I stuff my purchases in the car, then jaywalk like I see others doing. Oh my. On closer inspection, I see a second sign that reads "Used Books & Tea." Um. Books? *And* tea?

That's my kind of welcome.

Annnnd I'm about to enter when my phone rings. "Hi, Mom. Hey, I'm just—"

"Hi, sweetie, did I catch you at a bad time? I just had a quick minute. Thought I'd check in."

I move out of the way so a couple can enter the shop. "No, of course not," I say, casting a longing look through the window of Sweet Reads. I can tell it's my vibe.

"How's everyone? I haven't heard anything since you first arrived."

"Mind if I call you back in a bit, when I'm not standing in the middle of the street?" At my teeny exaggeration, I wince. *Liar.*

"Of course! Of course! No worries. I really just called about the suitcase."

My mind's as blank as the pages of my new sketchbook.

"The blue suitcase," she adds.

"Oh, yes. I got it." Pretty sure I already told her this.

"I mean, what did you think?"

What kind of question is this when I've painted the picture of me standing in the middle of a thoroughfare? "It's beautiful. I love it, Mom. I thought I already mentioned that. Thank you so m—"

"Did you open it?"

Open it? "Actually, I assumed it was empty." I swear that thing was light as a feather. "Look, I promise I will. I'll open it and call you back later, okay?"

"Okay. Oh, but no, that probably won't work. We're teaching two more classes on the reservation today. And with the time difference . . . let's plan for tomorrow."

Leave it to Mom to one-up me in busyness lately. Except that her kind of busy carries a different quality. It's like her work energizes her, while mine leaves me brittle, like a rubber band that's all stretched out and shriveled. Still, who do I think I am, rushing my self-sacrificing, humanitarian mother off the phone? Selfish me.

I try to act poised as I enter Sweet Reads and not like a girl with a heart-eyed emoji where my face is supposed to be. But the smell! Warming spices of ginger and cinnamon mingle with the sweet, woody aroma of old, disintegrating books. And do I detect bergamot? Come to mama.

Minutes later, I'm seated at a bistro table in the front window, savoring the best London Fog of my life, made by a guy with a slight British accent, while my eyeballs gorge on my surroundings. Every detail speaks to my soul. Overstuffed floor-to-ceiling bookshelves. Deep armchairs. A cozy little reading nook with toss pillows, one of which is embroidered with the C. S. Lewis quote, "You can never get a cup of tea large enough or a book long enough to suit me." Above the pastry case—and so far I've been victorious in resisting the croissants—hangs a rustic apothecary shelf filled with glass jars of tea.

An adjacent room offers a touch of Downton Abbey—a vintage, rolled-arm sofa of crimson velvet with books scattered messily at one end. There's even an orange tabby lounging on the third step of a narrow wooden staircase that leads to—oh glory—more books.

All of it just begs to be captured in my new sketchbook. I hurry to my car to retrieve it like an enchanted zombie. Like I imagine I'll feel when I'm about to be kissed for the first time by the *right* man. Even my face tingles.

Perhaps an hour slides by, but who can say? Right now my only anchor points in the entire space-time continuum are the rainbow of colored pencils littering my table and my second mug of tea. I'm in the flow, feeling the old magic.

At some point, a blast of rich, deep laughter erupts nearby, breaking the spell. Over at the register, the clerk or whatever his title is—book barista? tea-rista?—is joking with a tall, sandy-haired customer. They act like old, unhurried friends, and I watch them for a minute. This place is like the anti-Starbucks.

Tall guy, the one with his back to me, wears a faded sage long-sleeve with some kind of tree logo across his broad shoulders. Huh. The wear on his jeans looks to be the result of actual real-life wear rather than a design element. For some reason, this strikes me as refreshing. Not to mention that they fit him, well, for lack of an actual men's fashion term I'd find trending anywhere online, *naturally*. Instinct tells me he doesn't care whether he's trending or not.

Very nice.

I probably shouldn't notice such things. On the other hand, artists must be keen observers of the world around them, am I right? I'm playing artist today, so I'll chalk this episode up to a job hazard.

Green-shirt guy turns his shoulder suddenly. I look away. Adopt a deeply pensive, furrowed-brow expression. Rap my pencil on my chin as if pondering my next masterpiece. Which is all very silly. What are the chances he happened to notice me over here at all, let alone had a clue that I was admiring his, uh, jeans?

Just as I settle back into my work, adding a bit of detail, a shadow falls over my table, followed by a voice. "Very nice." For a nanosecond I startle, then freeze. Apparently, it's a thing—the startle-freeze response. That voice. Deep, as rich as my ginger chai latte, and a little too similar to the one I just heard joking with the tea-and-book-clerk guy.

Very nice? The next nanosecond feels oddly more akin to the length of time spent in after-work traffic on the 101. Finally, I dare to turn. But apparently green-shirt guy wasn't trying to elicit a response. Just sprinkling the air with good vibes on his way out. A bell rings as the door closes behind him.

Oh snap, what just happened? *"Very nice"*? Does the clean mountain air give Oregon guys powers of telepathy? Had I thought it out loud?

A coincidence, that's all it was. And I'm going to shake it off . . . right . . . *now*.

But curiosity tugs. Casually I twist my shoulders to one side then the other like I'm doing seated Pilates, so tea-rista dude doesn't suspect that I am, in fact, stealing a quick peep out the window at his buddy. *Digging keys out of his front pants pocket.* I lock my fingers behind my head for the next twist. *Getting behind the wheel of an old pickup. Interesting.* And one more rotation. *Backing into the street.* He's driving one of those classic two-tone Ford pickups from a bygone era in a powdery seafoam-ish color. Bright sun glints off the polished chrome trim and nearly blinds me. Aqua Sky, that's it. Pantone's 2003 color of the year.

Well. How weird was *that*?

My phone chimes and I jerk. Gosh, I'm jumpy. Probably just a notification from Clurk that I've overrun my personal luxuries budget. Should I check, or keep drawing? I waffle, mildly disoriented. Check? Or draw? I resign to digging for my phone. That whole episode with Mr. Very Nice has chased the magic off anyway. Session over.

I stare at a text from Pilar, feeling the last bits of helium in my joy bubble deflate.

Please respond to my email.

No. I don't wanna. As a matter of fact, I resent the intrusion, Pilar. Still, I begin gathering my things. Whatever it is, it'll have to wait until I get back to Daisy and Dean's.

In spite of the heat of guilt prickling my cheeks and the clench-ing in my stomach, or maybe because of it, I don't head directly for the exit. Instead I follow my feet and end up in front of an inspired display of loose-leaf tea packages.

"Just this bag of Earl Grey?" the clerk says with a kind smile and that pleasant British lilt. I'm guessing by his silvering temples and the way he carries himself that he's the owner.

"Yep. That'll do it. Great place you have here. Oh, actually, I had better get a, um . . ." I reach into a bin filled with stainless-steel basket infusers for sale. "One of these." Somehow I doubt my coffee-addicted great-auntie has any kind of tea setup.

But now the gentleman has his head cocked, straining to get a peek at my sketch pad. "Would you, uh, mind if I take a gander?" he asks.

I shrug. "Sure."

"These are phenomenal," he says, flipping through my sketch pad. "Would you . . . *wow* . . . you wouldn't by any chance be open to selling these, would you?"

"Oh . . . I hadn't really thought about it." That's putting it mildly. I've never sold a drawing in my life. "I mean, they're sort of unfinished. Just rough practice sketches."

"No, these are really canny. Absolutely charming. I'd love to share them on social media. Maybe even frame this one." He's running his eyes over the one with the red sofa and the cat. I like that one too.

He introduces himself as Ian Witherspoon, bookseller, tea blender, cat dad.

"I don't know that they're frameable, but—"

Ian offers to pay me in store credit. "I'm sorry," he says, "I really have no idea about these things. Wouldn't have an inkling how much to offer. Would . . . I don't know . . . would a one-hundred-dollar gift card be fair? They're probably worth a great deal more. One fifty?"

I chat with my inner pragmatist. It's a short conversation that goes like this: *Don't be proud. This is a win-win.* Besides, he's an unusually pleasant sort of man. "Okay, sure. That would be great."

Outside, I tilt my gaze and take in the deep-green ponderosas, heavy with young pine cones, and the sheer-blue skies beyond. My sense of wonder is being reawakened, and it feels like a prescription I didn't know I needed. Reflexively, I exhale a thank-you, send it fluttering on the breeze. Perhaps two weeks of this will be just the thing after all.

Now that I think about it, as a whole, my first excursion into town has been . . . *very* nice.

If only I could shake this strange pit of dread in my stomach.

Nine

Daisy

No matter how many ways I've tried to tell Judy I would never in my lifetime make the switch to one of those K-Cup coffee dealios, she's gone and bought me one. The woman's a peach, of course, and I know she figured it would somehow lighten my load. But truth be told, I've never minded making the coffee, and I haven't been without a Mr. Coffee machine since 1977, so I'da certainly never got around to figuring the darn thing out if she hadn't included a training session. Well, the deed is done. And now my old, dependable coffee maker is just one more in a mountain of things I hope to fob off on someone else at the yard sale.

"I was just beginning to wonder where you'd gotten to," I say, when Audrey sweeps in through the kitchen door. And me, still sitting here on the floor and without a plan for lunch. She leans across the pots and pans littered around me to give me a sideways hug and a peck on the hair. Poor thing probably got a nose full of hairspray.

"I have a crush," she announces.

I raise my eyebrows. "That didn't take long," I say, drawing Audrey's warm, throaty laughter.

Her eyes dance. "I'm in love with Sweet Reads. You know, that little bookshop on the corner of Birch. Oh, and I brought us something. Earl Grey."

I'm impressed with the dramatic flair with which she produces a bag of tea along with some kind of shiny contraption that looks like an upside-down top hat. But no doubt my blank expression gives me away. It's not that I've never heard of it. One of my old girlfriends used to be fanatical about that kind of tea. I've just never tasted any evidence that me and tea are, in general, a match made in heaven. "Uh. Woo-hoo?" No point disguising my lack of enthusiasm.

Audrey plants her fists on her hips. "Oh, come on. What could be better than you and me and a cuppa?"

Now there's an easy question. Not much. Not much could be better. Although I'm not convinced tea adds anything to the equation. "For you, my dear, I'll give it a try."

Audrey's eyes take in the mountain range of items surrounding me. "Can I help you here? This looks . . . you look like the patron saint of kitchen gadgets."

She's right. Why on earth have I collected three flour sifters? What retired woman needs more than one angel food cake pan? For that matter, do I even need *one*? "No, thanks. I'm afraid I'm the only one who can decide what's worth keeping."

Audrey fishes out one of my favorite doohickeys from the pile I created when I dumped a drawer upside down on the counter. "What's this even for?"

"For opening pop cans without breaking a nail."

"Ohhh, for soda."

"Huh? You mean pop."

"In California, we call it soda."

"Well, that's just silly."

"So, what else can I do? Need me to bring some more wood in?"

"No, honey. Thank you, but that there is the last of it." I gesture toward the fireplace, to the half-dozen juniper logs left in the rack by the recliner where Dean is napping. "We've pretty well made it through the season, anyway. Mornings aren't so cold anymore. I'm ready to be done with it until . . ." *Until November,* I almost say. *I'm ready to be done with it until November.* But we won't be here in November. Our small apartment in Whispering Pines—the memory-care place that bills itself as "the perfect option for older adults who need a little extra care but want to maintain a fun and social lifestyle"—won't have a fireplace.

I try to conjure up a sense of relief at my future life of ease. After all, I'll never have to hassle with it again—the physical effort, not to mention the mess. But the truth is, I like my warming fires in the morning. I like it when the house smells sweet and smoky all the way back to our bedroom. I even like the way the wood stacked on the porch out front says, "Come on in and get comfy."

You're being a sentimental ninny, Daisy. Everyone has to face these things. We just don't realize they're so close at hand until they're on our doorstep, knocking. It's simply our turn.

Already, last fall, when our cord of firewood arrived, I had to sneak behind Dean's back and ask the church secretary if they could send over a couple young guys to do the stacking. Dean insisted on helping—the doctors say it's important he feels useful. But Lord, was I a blubbering mess, watching them work together, assembly-line style. Dean loved it. And I learned, or at least I'm *beginning* to learn, how deeply touching it is to be on the receiving end of a helping hand.

We've had our last firewood delivery. Last Christmas in this house. For me, there'll be no more quiet Januarys watching the snow flock the blue spruce out front. No more Aprils witnessing the sudden birth of spring-green leaves on our aspens out back. To everything, there's a season. A time for everything under heaven. No one's ever been successful in changing this precept.

Every new chapter means the demise of another. Which means

that when we move, our present will become our past. History, broken off in chunks that won't ever again feel quite real.

Thing is, this life we've known . . . these aren't pieces I want to let go.

Audrey's experimenting with the pop-top opener on a can of sparkling water. I hear a pop and a fizz, and she grins at me, victorious. I wink, then turn away so she doesn't detect the tears prickling behind my eyes.

Drawing a breath, I steel myself. Just like that paltry stack of firewood, my days here with Dean are dwindling. Nothing to be done for it except answer that ominous knock on the door. And do it with all the grace and dignity I can muster.

I stretch my right leg out painfully. "Audrey? I may need you to help me get up from here."

Audrey

Retreating to the bedroom, I exchange my light sweater for a simple tailored blouse and add lipstick. I need to feel the part before opening Pilar's email. Which is funny. Why do I feel like I'm putting on a costume? At least I'll look the part from the waist up if whatever's going on at the office requires a Zoom call.

At the small corner desk, I fire up my iPad, and a series of notifications descend from the top of the screen. I quickly turn away, resisting the urge to read those truncated messages, and distract myself until every app has loaded and I know I'm good to go. It would help if my aunt and uncle's Wi-Fi wasn't as spotty as Julia Roberts's brown dress in *Pretty Woman*. I'll make do.

I wipe my sweaty palms on my thighs, and my fingers run over something firm in the pocket of my leggings. My lips curl into a smile. A pleasant remembrance warms me from the inside out as I fish out the Sweet Reads gift card. I tap my phone awake, and within seconds I've become Sweet Reads' newest Instagram follower.

Maybe I've sunk into procrastination because now I'm gliding my thumb over the words engraved on a small stone paperweight. "Let us not grow weary of doing good, for in due season we will reap, if we do not give up." A fitting Scripture for Dad's room, what with the horticultural metaphor and his unswervingly servant-hearted disposition. Which brings to mind that autumn-hued memory of him and me. The one that actually, now that I think of it, took place right . . . I move to the window. Right out *there*.

Again I picture it. Dad resting his foot on the shovel, adjusting his A's cap, grinning contentedly at me. Like there wasn't anywhere he'd rather be in that moment or any higher cause than planting bedding flowers, *with me*, for Aunt Daisy.

Only now, those flower beds are a disaster. The daisies we planted have been strangled out by weeds and swallowed up by a disorderly hedge. Bet they never even bloom.

When I cast a gaze around Dad's old room, a familiar hollowness fills my chest. Sometimes grief feels like a bottomless black hole in the middle of a road that I . . . *Must. Steer. Around.*

Deep breath. I clench and unclench my hands. Back to work.

Turns out, I've only got three work-related emails. One's from Pilar, with the subject line "PLEASE READ" in all caps. *Geez, Pilar. Take a chill pill.* There's one from Joshua, and one from a client named Sasha. Sasha is a successful thirty-something women-trepreneur who's constantly checking on the status of her sexy, twelve-thousand-dollar furniture suite. This doesn't ruffle me. She will have received my out-of-office auto-reply, so she knows I'm unavailable. Sasha will get her arctic-white Dresden sectional with matching pouf and Carrara marble coffee table soon enough.

The only other email of any concern is a Google reminder that my rent's due. I make a mental note to Venmo that later, even though there's a good chance it won't leave enough in savings to address whatever's going on with my car. I don't dare drive Harriet home with that overheating thing it's doing. Mental note number two: Ask Daisy where I should go to get the engine looked at.

My aunt is one of those rare people who never learned to drive. Which has always mystified me. And yet I've never thought to ask why. Although, she does look awfully cute on her yellow bike. What was that corny old song Uncle Dean used to sing to her? Oh, yeah.

> Daisy, Daisy, give me your answer, do.
> I'm half-crazy, all for the love of you.
> It won't be a stylish marriage, I can't afford a carriage.
> But you'll look sweet upon the seat of a bicycle built for
>   two.

And then she would swat him with a kitchen towel. Ha!

What am I thinking? Elvish women pushing eighty don't ride bikes, do they? How does my aunt get around town? I picture Tom Hanks stuck on a deserted island, so lonely he's making conversation with a volleyball. Does Daisy ever even get off this island? How thoughtless I've been not to ask.

Anyway, Dean must have a relationship with a good local mechanic. Tomorrow I'll book an appointment and pray it's something minor.

Not until I've batch-deleted a gob of promotional emails, with the exception of my new coupons from Target and Barnes & Noble, do I finally obey the inner voice that's been jeering at me. *Slacker! Wimp!*

Okay, fine. I'll open Pilar's message.

Audrey,

A personal matter has come up that requires I take a leave of absence. While I'm out of pocket, DeSoto will not be moving forward with any new projects, only wrapping up jobs already in motion. As soon as possible, I need you to communicate to Joshua the precise status of all client relations, any expectations they may have outside of the paper trail—purchase orders, etc.—that he already has access to. Please allow him to be the one to communicate with your clients, as he knows the script.

Between Joshua and Keiko, we've got things fairly well covered. You'll be paid through the end of the month, including any outstanding commissions. Beyond that, I can't make any promises. But it would help to know your level of interest and commitment as I consider how things will be structured in the future.

I've stopped breathing. *What in the . . . ?* I circle back to re-read the words, but now they swim around on the screen. My fingers fly to my temples and press. By the third read-through, my heart's about to thud out of my chest and I can't make heads or tails of what any of this means. Especially now that something dark and ominous has slithered around me, and it's squeezing. An anaconda. A giant, murderous anaconda. So this is how it all ends for me.

Is this a joke? Shame heats my face. Somehow this is my fault. I've failed. Hand shaking, I click to open Joshua's email. His is brief and corroborates Pilar's. He's right to the point. Uncharacteristically impersonal.

Audrey—

Please give me a call asap so we can get all of this figured out.

Okay . . . okay . . . It's going to be okay . . . The voice inside sounds meek and unconvincing. Still, I give her props for trying.

Yes, I certainly will be calling you, Joshua. But first there's the matter of this boa wrapped around my lungs.

Ten

The next morning, dawn lights a fire in the sky. With hot reds and oranges reflected off its dormer windows, the abandoned Sugar Pine Inn appears aflame from within. This swirling, molten-lava sunrise is like nothing I've ever seen. But not unlike the roiling thoughts that ambushed me the moment I awoke.

How do I respond to Pilar's dismissal? Is it a trumped-up story to get rid of me? Payback for leaving?

Where Daisy and Dean's gravel driveway meets the road, I inhale and fast-walk right, in the opposite direction of the inn. What am I even doing here? This place isn't real. I shouldn't allow myself to be sidetracked in some enchanted Pacific Northwestern Shangri-la while my actual life decomposes six hundred miles south. With each pounding of my Nikes on asphalt, I borrow power to declare my current inner truth.

I'm about to be gut honest, God. What are you even thinking? At the moment, I'm pretty sure I could do a better job than you. Are you even listening?

I turn a corner. Ratchet up the pace. Break into a run. I want nothing but to connect with my physical self. To find where I begin—the real me. The one Dad called insightful. If I can just recover my powers of reasoning, maybe then I could put things back in order from the ground up.

Away now from cars and houses and electronic devices, my inner disquiet feels out of place. I imagine calmly delivering the news to Daisy that I need to return home, but I can't find a way to spin it. Could it possibly be that, for better or worse, here is where I'm needed more? How is it a life can hop the tracks and look nothing like the day before? I can't operate without a crystal-clear course any more than a moving train can negotiate an open field.

I run past a sprawling ranch where a half-dozen freckled long-horns graze. In the shade of a pine tree, a heifer nurses her brown calf. Now and then she swishes her tail lazily. Next, the pavement rolls past a soggy green marsh, where thin-legged birds stand stock-still. I sense I could learn a thing or two from them. Ahead, the road rises sharply—my mission, should I choose to accept it. Three garishly large homes cling to the lush hillside. It appears even Charity Falls has attracted some elite citizens who love their stucco.

I set my sights on the crest of the ridiculous incline. Breathe deep. Gun it.

Hamstrings burn. Chest aches. *Push. Keep pushing.*

At the top of the rise, I curl at the waist. Drop my hands to my knees. Steadying myself, I gulp for air. My heart hammers. At last I look up and out, and awe descends. I'm staring at a measure-less, dizzying view in all directions. I count at least seven shining mountain peaks. Red skies have softened to rose. I seem to have emerged in a cathedral without walls.

Okay, technically I'm always in one. It's just harder to recognize when I'm down in the weeds. By far this beats any human-made, twenty-thousand-square-foot cathedral dangling off a mountain-side.

Inside, my landscape may be unstable. But where my breath-ing's erratic, these mountains stand rock-sure. How is it that my life has changed so much yet all this has not? For a moment this doesn't sit right with me. All this time, over all these years while I've stayed away, forest and meadow exhaling a silent hymn. And they'll be raising a hallelujah long after I leave this place.

Given the vertical pitch of the road, when I collapse onto the pavement I haven't got far to fall. Maybe if I ground myself here, gaze long enough at the mountains, some of their strength will rub off on me.

I'd forgotten.

I'd forgotten it was possible to ditch the noise in my head. To feel God's presence in my pores. His heart whispering to mine. For years now, my spiritual life has looked like fixing my stare on the corner of my ceiling, sending up rote prayers or the occasional panicked plea for intervention. At times I've sensed my thoughts actually made it beyond the drywall, that I was heard. When dark dreams unsettle me, I find a measure of peace reciting Psalm 23 like a lifeline, words Dad taught me line by line as a child.

"I have all that I need. . . . I will not be afraid, for you are close beside me."

But from where I sit now, the tender breeze feels like an embrace. This pine-scented sanctuary evokes church. And today's sermon, the one playing on the air, speaks to my limited understanding of God. Judging him through the lens of my experiences will never change who he is. Accepting this? Now there's the struggle.

At long last I stand and brush road dirt from my palms. Descending the hill, I'm determined not to pummel myself anymore, at least not until I connect with Joshua. This situation with DeSoto Design isn't my doing. It can't be. Since when would Pilar hesitate to let me know I'd messed up? No. Something serious has happened. Illness? A lawsuit? But right on the heels of her shining moment in *San Francisco Style*? So odd. It isn't like Pilar to retreat from a fight.

Nor should I.

Still, as I turn into Daisy's long driveway, slowing my pace and deepening my breaths, there's something I have to acknowledge. An idea that flickered to life back there in that mic-drop moment on the hillcrest. Something nonsensical, really. A faint pinpoint of light. A kind of weird knowing.

Something new is in the wind. It's uninvited. It's unnerving. But also, just maybe, if I'm willing to accept it, it's blowing my way right on schedule.

In practical terms, nothing has changed since yesterday.

Dreams still dashed? Check.

Boa constrictor of despair still in place? Check.

Vacuous nothingness where I need a plan B? Triple check.

Still, I can't deny this unexpected modicum of inner peace. I'm not doomed. I'm only detoured.

I fish out my yoga mat from the trunk of my car and wonder, *Could I ever have what it takes to fall forward?*

Or am I being summoned to a fight?

My eyes snag on that curious blue suitcase. May as well carry that inside too.

～～～

Daisy

The oatmeal is about thick enough and releasing a fragrant cloud of steam when the kitchen door flies open. I startle, flinging oatmeal from my wooden spoon. "For crying out loud." I lay a hand on my chest. "You just about gave me a heart attack, Audrey. I didn't even know you were up."

In all seriousness, my poor ticker is unaccustomed to surprises.

Audrey's eyes are bright and her fair cheeks carnation pink, alive with the glow of exercise. Could this be the same girl who, just last night, seemed to be carrying the weight of the world?

"I'm so sorry, Daisy." After wrapping me in a side-hug, she holds up a roll of yoga mats and arches her eyebrows. "Hey, I just happen to have an extra . . ." She uses a beguiling tone, as if she were offering me a plate of chocolate éclairs rather than a half-inch-thick berth for torture. "Pilates?" she says.

"Believe it or not, Miss Stretchy Pants, I have my own mat. There's a strength-and-balance class in town I like to . . . well, I used to attend."

Audrey's gaze lingers on me. She flips on the electric kettle. When she unfurls her bag of tea, the scent of citrus billows out. I do believe bergamot is growing on me, at least in concept.

"I've been wanting to ask," she says, "are you able to get out at all? I mean, are you able to do anything, you know, fun? Ever? Would it help if . . . would you be comfortable with me staying with Dean so you can get out?"

"Oh, bless your heart, honey." Loath to appear too pitiful, I explain how Judy picks Dean and me up for church sometimes—although not so much nowadays since he's a real slug to get going in the mornings. "Judy and I enjoy doing our grocery shopping together," I say also, as if that settles the matter. *Unless, of course, Dean is in a mood and refuses to go to the drop-off memory-care place.* In that event, Judy does my shopping for me. But I don't say this.

Maybe it's time to break down and have Audrey give me a lesson in online shopping on my cell phone. But that feels like conceding defeat. It's a slippery slope to isolation.

I fetch two bowls from the cupboard. "And, of course," I say, adding a lilt to my voice that sounds false to my own ears, "I can always take a spin around the block on my bike. At least, I will when the weather warms up a tad more. I've gotten pretty persnickety about the temperature." Also, there are only so many windows of opportunity when I'm comfortable leaving Dean alone. But I don't say that either.

Audrey nods thoughtfully.

I drop a spoonful of raisins into my oatmeal. "Well, I do have a friend who's always nagging me, or I should say *inviting* me, to go to a caregivers' support group. And I suppose one day I'll go. But with so few hours Dean's okay apart, and so much to be done here at the house . . ." Good Lord, this topic makes me run at the mouth. I'm doing my best not to sound wistful, but I'm wearing down.

"Besides, if I had my druthers," I finally confess, "I'd prefer to help out with the prison-letter ministry ladies, once I . . . well, as soon as I get back into some kind of routine." *In other words, when hell freezes over.* If wishes were horses, beggars would ride, Granny Margaret would say. I don't voice this aloud either, but I see no sign of returning to any sort of familiar routine in the near future. If ever.

No sense raking up thoughts better left to mulch.

Before I know it, I'm on a mat parallel to Audrey's, and she's got me stretching like the Little Mermaid under the curious gaze of Myrtle Rose. I've even changed into my butter-yellow-camouflage-print leggings, which Audrey says are a "good look" for me. I'm not sure what it is—the exercise, the leggings, or possibly the vow I've made to Audrey that I will join the prison-ministry ladies next week—but something's got me feeling footloose and fancy-free. I'd forgotten the sensation.

In fact, we're on our fourth pelvic tilt and I'm beginning to lose control of my giggle box. Oh my word! When was the last time I heard myself giggle?

To top things off, Dean comes schlepping into the room with his hair about as disheveled as I've ever seen it—note to self, get that man a haircut—and he's dressed himself as if for a day at the office. Except that his best dress shirt is buttoned all wrong and only half tucked in, and he's cinched his belt around a pair of too-big slacks that haven't fit him right since George W. was president.

I can't help myself. The bewildered look on Dean's face! He's watching us exercise with such amusement. What else can I do but burst out laughing? "Oh, Lord!" I manage to say, collapsing on my mat. Letting the laughter have its way with me.

~

Audrey

When Dean rounds the corner looking adorably pathetic, Aunt Daisy completely loses it, descending into hysterics. I have to admit, his expression at finding his wife of over fifty years stretching her hips toward the ceiling and giggling like a middle schooler is too good.

I can't keep it together either. I'm a goner! Just like that, I've joined her in the land of snort-laughs and hysteria. But it's okay because Dean's snickering as well. In fact, he's even got that gleam in his eye I haven't seen in a long, long time. And when he points a shaking knotted finger to where the cat lies paws-up on the coffee table, I sense things are only going downhill from here.

"You know . . ." he says, stumbling over his words, then clearing his throat. "You know why that cat is so relaxed?"

Oh boy. Color me a sucker, but for old times' sake I'm going to step right into this one. "No," I manage to say between laughs. "Why, Uncle Dean? Why is the cat so relaxed?"

"Well, don't you know?" He pauses and winks at me. His hair's sticking up as if a donkey licked him from behind. "It's because she got out of the rat race."

That's it, I'm done for. I can't even. And this unraveling feels like a long time coming. Like all I've been carrying, things I didn't know had been pinched up inside me, decompresses all at once. It's like when UPS delivered my memory-foam mattress, and I freed it from its too-tight shipping box. I'm literally coming apart. I can hardly breathe.

Something like champagne bubbles through my veins. An unlikely vintage of aged heartache with back notes of joy. And then . . . I'm free. Free to see it—the fleetingness of this brief but holy moment. And the fact that I'm here for it.

I *get* to be here for it. If only for today.

For an instant, I'm just stupid-thankful for these people. And for the wonderful, awful absurdity of this . . . whatever this is. A line from a favorite poem whispers an answer. *This is my one wild and precious life.*

"Oh, mama, I needed that," I say breathlessly.

As always, though, caution rides shotgun with joy. I know better than to drop my guard and leave it down. It's one thing to be reminded I'm not alone, like what happened on my morning run. Like what just happened here.

But hope . . . well, hope is dangerous. To hope is to play with fire.

~

As soon as I'm out of the shower, I lift the suitcase onto the bed. Gosh, it's divine. I re-tuck the bath towel around me, then sit and run my hands over the leather details. One thing I vow not to do is stash this beauty away in a closet like Mom did, never letting it see the light of day. In fact, this girl's going to be on a thrift-store hunt for another case, maybe even two, in graduating sizes. They'd be lovely stacked against a wall. Set a plant on top—at the moment I'm picturing a blue star fern in a rattan vessel—and *voilà*, I'll have a vignette. And bonus—storage!

Alright, Mamacita, what could be so precious? I've never been made aware of any family heirlooms. The two metal thumb latches are stiff and require a bit of effort. Each eventually releases with a gentle pop. I'm not sure what I expected to find inside, but this is not it.

The powdery blue interior is empty. Vacuous. Did Mom have a senior moment? Is an empty suitcase some kind of metaphor? Is she trying to impart something deep and inspiring here? But then I peek inside the stretchy satin pocket, where a dozen or more papers of various sizes peek back at me. Huh.

Also, who knew Mom kept so much of my old artwork? Locks of wet, wavy hair fall forward as I curl over the papers, quickly riffling through a time capsule of my earliest, most rudimentary art. They seem to be organized chronologically, from juvenile finger painting to explorations of other media—watercolor, chalk, pencil.

This is sweet, don't get me wrong, but rather a letdown. Here's the obligatory stick-figure portrait of my family, which could appropriately be titled "Four Smiling Triangles." Maybe we're all wearing dresses. I should be amused, so I paste on a smile. But that makes the disconnect even more plain. This is an ode to what once was, and my heart's not having it.

From the bottom of the stack, I remove a sketch of Tawny I did for a college fine arts class, an attempt at photorealism. *Ouch*. How embarrassing. I remember thinking I'd done so well, but from where I sit ten years later, I can easily see all the things I got wrong. My face heats.

With zero urge to revisit any of the in-between pages, I return the stack to the pocket, decidedly unimpressed.

And you call yourself an artist?

Eleven

I'm pretty sure the gawky, curly-haired kid behind the paint counter at Homer's Hardware is attempting to flirt with me.

"New in town?" he asks, leaning across the counter. The guy's about six-foot-three, thin as prosciutto, with thick, wire-rimmed glasses that seem to contradict his head-to-toe cowboy vibe. Like if Napoleon Dynamite dressed for a rodeo.

"Just visiting," I say. *Not here to make friends, dude.*

His jaw drops in mock stupefaction. "Do you always buy paint when you're *just visiting*? What happened? Damage your hotel room?"

Only one of us thinks he's funny, and it's not me. I'm sure my attempt at a smile lacks something in the execution. "Just doing some work for my aunt and uncle."

Some work that will only be a drop in the bucket. The entire exterior of Daisy and Dean's house could use a makeover before they sell. Maybe I'm not the one to do all the things, but I can at least give the picket fence a fresh coat of white. And yet, what am I doing painting fences and prepping fifty-year-old junk for a yard sale when I should be updating my portfolio? Or finding some way to demonstrate to Pilar—how had she put it?—a level of commitment.

82

Ugh. I would take a choppy sail around the San Francisco Bay with Kyle and a barf bag over this emotional yo-yoing. *Lord, I didn't mean that*. Still, I've been haunted all day by my phone conversation with Joshua.

"Listen," he'd said, lowering his voice to a hush despite Pilar's absence, "it has something to do with her marriage. I have no idea exactly. She's all over the place. Yesterday she flew in and started barking orders. Now she's gone dark, isn't even responding to my calls. I'm just treading water here. I need this job, but . . . I don't know, Audrey. I'm not sure how long I can hang with this. And Keiko's . . . well, you know Keiko. Zero boundaries. She doesn't know how to say no to Pilar, even if it wrecks her home life."

"Do you need me?" I asked. "Should I come back? I can. I can come ba—"

"Girl, no." Joshua had been adamant. "You do your thing. I'm proud of you. Besides, you're so brilliant, you can write your own ticket."

Write my own ticket? A flattering concept. But I don't deal well in unknowns. Never have. My problem is, I operate best in the linear, and right now the lay of the land is anything but. I say, tell me what I should do to be successful and I will slay. Give me linear or give me debt!

There was that drafting internship my professor lined up for me before I even completed my degree. After only three days I was promised a full-time job upon graduation. Which was where I rubbed shoulders with Sacramento architectural designer Peter Flatow, who invited me on board. Everything so nice and linear. Eventually, Peter introduced me to Pilar—which, he told me not so long ago, he always regretted. Said he'd hated to lose me but that I was always destined for "bigger things."

Does it then follow that some people are destined for the smaller things? Is that the endgame for me—keep going until I find something *biggest*?

Napoleon the Buckaroo pats the top of a gallon can of standard ultra-white exterior. "This is the one you want?"

"Yep. Acrylic latex, right?"

He inserts my can into the shaker and flips it on. The machine convulses loudly. Now there's a familiar old sound. "So, what's your project?" he asks.

I stall, sensing he's bursting to drop some knowledge. I'd prefer not to reveal my own. Having worked in the paint section of Home Depot during college, I could run this department with my eyes closed. Neither do I care to dumb down. Luckily, I catch a break.

"I'll be right back," he says, jogging away in long strides down the main aisle in response to a page over the loudspeaker. Evidently his real name is Silas and he's "needed in electrical."

Mentally I travel back to Joshua's words. Even if he's right, even if I were in a position to write my own ticket, how would I decide? What do you do when you could do anything?

Ka-thud, ka-thud, ka-thud.

The paint shaker keeps knocking out a rhythm, a tune that was once the background score for a girl I used to know. Yes, Daisy, a girl *displaced*. Shaken. Shaken hard. A young woman desperate for wisdom and direction, willing to listen to anyone who cared enough to guide her. Those voices had affirmed her, helped her plot a course, but one that had ultimately terminated in a cliff. Now what?

Just do the next right thing.

The words settle across my mind. Spoken by a voice in my head, yet somehow also not. A gracious truth bomb, a banner over me, an imperative. But from where had it originated? The Spirit of God? Eh. I'm dubious. Although, okay, I'm willing to allow for the possibility. More likely it's something I once heard Mom say. Or an inspirational meme I've seen online.

Regardless, the words are like honey on my lips. Guess I'll just have to let them drip there until I understand their meaning.

What *is* the next right thing? How will I know? The only thing I'm certain of right now is that there's a fence waiting to be painted. Alrighty then. To that end, I unfurl my shopping list and go in search of a sanding block.

Absently, I watch a young, chestnut-haired girl enter and make a beeline for the giant red gumball machine. The thing's as tall as me, with an enormous globe on top filled with gumballs in a rainbow of colors. It's got a see-through middle section where you can watch your gumball spiral down the chute. The girl—she's maybe eight or ten years old—plunks a coin in and stands watching her prize descend. Most of her hair has escaped her ponytail and her round, olive-skinned belly protrudes over too-small orange bike shorts.

Compassion stabs. I can easily imagine kids on the playground teasing her.

Suddenly her golden gumball stops halfway down the track. She spins toward the front checkout counter as if seeking help. No one's there. I walk the few steps to stand next to her. "Uh-oh," I say with a smile. "Hmm." After peering around as if to make sure no one's looking, as if the girl and I share a secret mission, I give the machine a quick hip bump. The gumball resumes its journey. I score a quick grin from the girl, and then she crouches to retrieve it.

"Hey, nice catch," I say, then wink.

Her smile is huge, but there's timidness in her whispered thank-you. And those mocha eyes, beneath Selena Gomez lashes, contain a look I've seen before. She has the appearance of a child in want of . . . something. Whatever it is, it makes me sad, and I really don't have room for sadness. I scan the area for a parent. "Bye!" she says, heading for the exit. Outside, she turns and waves at me shyly and pops the kickstand on her bike.

"You are good to go," Silas says once I've gathered the remaining items on my list and circled back to the paint counter. He sets a wooden stir stick on top of my can but leaves his hand resting there. I move to grab the handle. "But not until you promise to cut down on all those wild parties in your hotel room."

This kid's getting on my nerves. "I'll sure try," I say.

Evidently my response is worthy of a fist bump.

"I'm only messin' with ya!" he says, a little too loudly. Like, is this the social norm in Charity Falls, or is it just this guy?

At last, I'm released to jump into the checkout line. But, like a foghorn, Silas's sudden loud, jocular voice jars my nerves. "Hey, we don't serve your kind here!"

Fortunately, a kindly voice behind me in line answers, "Oh, hey, Silas. Alright, then. Fine. Guess I'll just have to drive to Lowe's." Then a chuckle.

Phew. Silas hadn't been addressing me. I feel a stab of compassion for the awkward paint clerk. We all need friends. He's simply trying too hard.

"I'm only joshin' with ya," Silas continues. "What're you up to, Cade?"

"Just giving my dad a hand with some things."

Gotta give the guy behind me points for patience. Not to mention his choice of soap, some subtle combination of basil and mint. Also, I feel like I've heard that voice, that easy, smoky laugh, somewhere before. Not likely.

"Huh," Silas says. "Kinda funny that I've never met your dad."

Okay, so maybe I'm not so special after all. Maybe this kid sticks his nose into everyone's business.

I'm about to give in to the temptation to turn and sneak a peek at the great-smelling human behind me when I reach the front of the line. Daisy instructed me to give the clerk her name, so I do, adding that I'm her great-niece. Who knew there were still homey places in this crazy world that let you say, "Put it on the account"?

You'd have thought I said, "Stick 'em up," the way the matronly bottle-blond cashier freezes in place upon hearing my name. Her hand flies to her mouth. "Oh my. Oh. My. Stars." And then with a kind of hushed reverence, she says, "You're Danny's girl." She scrutinizes my facial features. "Good Lord, yes. Yes, I see it. Oh my. Welcome! Welcome, Audrey. I'm Jan."

"You . . . knew my father?" My voice is tremulous. The idea of meeting someone who knew Dad is beyond astonishing.

"Shoot, yeah! We were classmates. Oh, dear, I'm so, so sorry for . . ."

I nod quickly so she doesn't have to finish. "Thank you."

Jan's shaking her head as if remembering the accident. Which, of course, forces me to. "Mm-mm. Your father was just about the nicest man. The world lost a good one." She tucks a copy of the receipt into my bag and hands it to me with genuine tenderness. "Nice to meet you, Audrey. You give my best to Daisy and Dean now."

I feel her eyes on me as I leave.

I'm in a bit of a daze over the "Shoot, yeah, I knew your dad" thing. But then something familiar snaps me to attention. A relic on four wheels, painted aqua-sky blue and parked right in front of Homer's. Dots connect. *Aha.* So, the guy behind me is the tall, sandy-haired dude from Sweet Reads. If I heard right, his name is Cade. I suppose he got an earful about me as well.

Guess the clichés about small towns are true—where everybody knows your name and all that. I have to concede, I'm charmed. Who wouldn't want to live in a world where people are generally kind and friendly?

And yet.

And yet I'm tormented by a pair of dark, yearning, young eyes looking up at me from beneath raven lashes. Eyes that testify to the existence of something undeniably *un*friendly. No doubt, beyond Charity Falls' quaint facade lies a world of need. I open Harriet's rear door. *Sheesh.* In addition to offloading this ten-pound can of paint, now I need to find a way to offload a heavy heart.

I could sure use a distraction. And that's when I notice the sign across the street.

Twelve

How much design work could there be in such a small town? This is the question that's been dogging me for the past two days, ever since I noticed the small storefront across the street from Homer's Hardware. High Desert Home & Design. Enough business that they might throw me a freelance project while I'm here in town?

Like it or not, I've got to adjust to the idea that my length of stay in Charity Falls has become far more open-ended than my bank balance. Let's just say my nest egg is missing both the yolk and the white.

At the moment, I'm a *displaced* design professional—there's that annoying adjective again—in need of gainful employment. Temporary employment, of course. Let's hope very temporary.

Although I've just passed a small wooden sign in the front window inviting me to "experience rustic elegance," instead, upon entering High Desert Home & Design, I'm experiencing raging claustrophobia. The whiffs of nutmeg and pine are cozy, but the small space unfolds as more of an overstuffed Western boutique than a design studio. All pretty things, if only they weren't so heavily layered. Every nook is crammed with chunky furniture, leather pillows, and tchotchkes for sale, with red price tags that—*gasp*—are as bold and visible as Hobby Lobby's.

I have to smile, though. There's no shortage of chickens. Still, this place wouldn't exactly be conducive to creativity. In decorator terms, it's what I'd call noisy. I'd hate to imagine what Pilar would call it.

Nevertheless, what the showroom lacks in feng shui it makes up for in tasteful wall art. Images of the magnificent Cascade Mountains in every season. The turquoise waters of the nearby Metolius River, world-renowned to fly-fishers, are well represented. And then there are weathered barns and other ranch-life settings.

I'm particularly drawn to a large stretched-canvas print of a bay mare and her foal nuzzling. Just their faces. I move closer. Tousled strands of straw-colored hair frame the mother's expressive gaze. It's crisply rendered, using intensely saturated colors. Somehow the artist struck a magical combination of realism and dreamy transcendence. A real statement piece. *Love.*

"Hi there. Can I help you?"

The woman who greets me wears jeans, short suede booties, and infrared lipstick. Suddenly the belt of my skirt feels stifling. My heels, ridiculous. I've even touched up my manicure, removing every trace of white paint from my nail beds. Well, almost. When I get into a project, I'm all in.

"This is lovely," I say.

"Oh, yes, one of my favorites. Local artist. Those eyes, right? You can view the original painting over at the art center."

I nod. "Captivating." Together we admire the piece for a moment before I introduce myself. When the woman shakes my hand, her platinum ponytail swishes and she casts a furtive, head-to-toe appraisal of me. Ruby is her name, and although her smile never wanes, if I'm not mistaken her response cools the moment I begin listing my credentials.

"Is there something we can do for you?" she says.

"I'm in town for . . . for a time. I wonder if perhaps you could use any help. I work independently." I mean, in truth, I've never worked independently before, but I don't see why I couldn't.

"You say you're from . . . ?"

"California. The Bay Area."

"Ah," she says.

"Or perhaps someone to man the sales floor part-time?" *Someone to dust your gewgaws while you worry about the clients?* My offer, and the concept of taking a step back from design work, comes as a surprise to my own ears. "I've worked in customer service as well." *Although it mostly involved either pizzas or paint.*

"Well," she says, glancing toward the back of the studio where an older woman sits focused on her computer monitor, "I'm sorry, but my mom and I handle pretty much everything here. We don't have any current plans for adding staff."

She doesn't look sorry. The word *petulant* drops into my head for the first time in my life, and it seems more fitting. There must be a classic novel to thank for such a timely adjective. Maybe *Little Women.* Anyway, clearly Ruby wouldn't consider me a fit even if she did have an opening. Still, tight smile intact, she produces her business card and invites me to email a résumé.

"You know," she adds as I turn to leave, "a lot of businesses in town need extra help for summer. On account of the tourists."

My instinct is to politely brush off the suggestion. But then again . . . *hmm.* If indeed this whole "stuck in Charity Falls" ordeal is an opportunity to rethink my future, maybe it couldn't hurt to take a brief time-out from the design community. It's a fresh thought, anyway.

"Come to think of it, I'm pretty sure Homer's hiring." Ruby gestures across the road just as a certain tall, gangly paint clerk steps out onto the sidewalk in front of the hardware store. Purple plaid shirt tucked into Wranglers. Ginormous rodeo belt buckle glinting in the sunlight.

Probably not my top choice of work environments. But then

again, I do know paint. I'm just suddenly super confused. I feel like I've crossed into an alternate universe. How can this possibly be my real life?

For a while I recline in my car, listening to my singer-songwriter playlist. Anything Ray LaMontagne-esque will do. Somehow, I've got to gather my senses. Bring order to insanity. No, more like I need to recover my pride, which took a gigantic hit back there with red-lipped Ruby.

I close my eyes. A slide guitar and the lyrics to "Gravity" perfectly match my melancholy frame of mind. Something inside me awakens, and when I recognize what it is, my chest feels broken open. It's a stunner. *Shame*. Who knew John Mayer could preach to my soul?

Somewhere along the line, I've bought into the story that I belong to a venerated social group. I mean, we're the tech giants. *The* innovators. Aren't Bay Area people an oracle for all mankind—and me among them? We've even got the 49ers! But rather than being impressed, Ruby seemed put off.

So, props to her. She detected a superiority complex in me. And she was spot-on. *Ouch*.

Now here I sit in my nondescript car in a town no one's ever heard of, thinking maybe I'm not all that, after all. And I'm staring at the Help Wanted sign in the window of Homer's Hardware. *Hello, I'd like to upgrade from Bay Area designer to the rich and famous to hardware-store cashier*, said no one ever.

"Keep me where the light is," I sing along softly. Again, louder. "Keep me where the light is." This time my voice breaks with emotion. How silly.

Maybe it's not so silly because a single tear rolls down my cheek. There's no denying this sense of lostness, of wandering in a deep forest without a compass. That's it. That's what it is—I've never felt so disoriented. Do I stay or do I go? Should I fight for a sense of normalcy or flow with whatever comes my way?

This time when I close my eyes, I'm enveloped in a kind of warm tenderness. My questions are not falling on deaf ears. The God who met me on that hill is also here in the car. Waiting for me to reach out.

Lord, you know how I am. I'd like to think I've got this. But the truth is, I'm stumbling in darkness down here. I don't got this. So please—

My lips quiver. Something heavy lays on my chest. The weight of what I'm being asked to surrender. What I'm *ready* to surrender.

Please guide me. I need you.

Clarity arrives in the form of an acute need to hear Tawny's voice. I legit could use her input right now. My thumbs fly, composing a detailed text, and within minutes she FaceTimes me.

"Where are you?" I say. All I can see are cream-colored ceiling tiles in the background.

Tawny speaks in a hushed voice. "Library. Studying for finals." She pans her phone to give me a quick 360 and introduces me to the girl working across the table from her. "So. You want to know what I think?"

"Hit me," I say.

"Sure? Because you won't like it."

"A hundred percent."

"I think, Audrey, that sometimes we can reason our way through our circumstances. You're really good at that. But other times, well, we just have to live our way through. Like what happened to me when I found my birth parents. I was frozen for a while, not knowing how deeply I should get involved with them."

"I remember."

"And then, I took the step in front of me."

I nod slowly, letting her words sink in. *Like doing the next right thing.* "You're not wrong," I say. "I don't like it. But . . ." I let out a long exhale. "I hear you. Thanks, Yoda."

"Ha. And hey, Audrey?"

"Still here. Still contemplating."

"I have your back. I'll be praying. Also, if you need an Oreo Blizzard, don't overthink it. Go for the big one."

I stick out my tongue at her like we're back in middle school.

"But then again, what do I know?" she adds, shrugging. "I'm just an almost-thirty-year-old, sleep-deprived caffeine junkie with no marital prospects."

"Wait, what?" I say. "The marital part."

She waggles a bare hand. No ring. "Engagement's off."

Stoicism aside, there's no mistaking the emotional catch at the end of her words, and my heart sinks. "Oh, Tawny."

"Let's connect when I can talk more, okay?" she says. "Gotta go."

And just like that, two facts crystallize. It's not all about me. And things could always be worse.

Thirteen

Charity Falls may not be the land of innovation but, hallelujah and amen, they do have DQ. And now that I know I'll soon be pulling a paycheck—I start next week at Homer's—I cruise the town with a surprising sense of ownership. And an unctuous sugar-and-dairy concoction that feels like something in between a celebration and a consolation prize.

My worst fear didn't materialize after all. And I can name it now. After I talked to Tawny, I entered Homer's, anxious that if I hadn't fit in with the local designers, the hardware folk might just laugh me right out of town.

But that Jan's a real mama bear. Before I could even fill out the application, she'd ushered me to where Homer himself stood making notes on a clipboard. She passed me off to him like I was some sort of local royalty, all the while drizzling warm and buttery words over me.

Homer Rudloe walks with a hunch, but he walks fast. He led me down the main aisle toward the back office, repeatedly popping his polished bald head up like a hairless parakeet. Checking each aisle, acknowledging a blue-vested worker here and a customer there, while I quickstepped along behind him.

In a scrawny little office with lackluster wood paneling, I spent the first moments of the interview trying to wrangle a rolling metal stool underneath me. In fairness, Homer had warned me right away. "Careful now," he'd said, a subtle gleam in his eye. "It'll get away from you." Once safely astride, I slid my knees together and tucked my ankles to one side in a way that would do my mama proud.

Across the desk, Homer peered over his glasses with tender eyes and gave his head a scratch. "Well, I'll be hanged. You're Danny's daughter. Golly, I am awful sorry about your father. That was a sad, sad day in Charity Falls. A sad time for all of us. You know, he went to school with my Jimmy."

I hadn't known that, of course. But then, I was beginning to think there were probably a lot of things about my dad I didn't know. "It means a lot to know he's remembered," I said, again trying to reconcile that my father had walked these very streets as a young boy. And that he was still known here.

"Oh, I guarantee you, plenty of folks 'round here remember. He was a good boy. And a good man if there ever was one."

"Thank you." I tried to swallow away the clutching in my throat. Somehow I'd never considered that Dad's accident might have affected others outside our family. *My dad is not a myth here.* Even as this dawning warmed me, it came with an unsettling stickiness. My standard operating procedure was no good here. In Charity Falls, I wasn't allowed to play distant spectator. In some way, I was bound to this place.

"And how's our Daisy? Can't say I've seen her around much, ever since Dean . . ." He let his words drift, and they settled into the space between us.

"She's alright. I mean, considering. She doesn't get out much."

Homer frowned. Furrowed his brow. "Must be awful tough."

"Yes. That's why I'm here. Hopefully I can take some of the load off."

"Good to hear. Very good indeed." Homer nodded absently, still frowning. He'd retreated into a melancholy place, that was clear enough. Appeared to have traveled back to a sad chapter of the past and stalled his mental tractor there.

"Your father, he was a fine landscaper," he said finally.

Just the prompt I needed to get things back on track. Remembering the garden center I'd noticed on my way in, I informed Mr. Rudloe about my experience working with Dad each summer.

Between that and my time at Home Depot, there's a thin chance I was offered the job on my own merit. More likely it had to do with the family connection.

Homer ran a hand over a jaw stubbled with gray, then looked at me pointedly. "Can you give me two months?"

"I took the step in front of me," Tawny had said. But two months? This was a long step. A giant and absurd stretch. "I can," I said with more certainty than I felt. "Thank you, Mr. Rudloe."

"Call me Homer. Ever'body does. And speaking of everybody, I'd like you to try to get to know my customers. Can I count on you for that? They've come to expect a big hullo when they walk through our doors. So treat 'em like they's your neighbors. Which, in a manner of speaking, they are."

"Of course."

He rose to open the door. "We'll look forward to seeing you on Monday then. Oh, and my, uh, grandson, Silas, will show you the ropes. Don't let him give you no trouble." He punctuated that last part with a wink.

I'm pickin' up what you're puttin' down, Homer Rudloe. I'll need to bring my sense of humor.

Outside, quaking aspens lined the sidewalk, their glossy green leaves dancing on an undetectable breeze. A milky swirl of sky and clouds looked to have been painted with watercolors. Charity Falls certainly had its charms. And a growing pull on me that was hard to deny. *Your dad . . . good man . . . plenty of folks 'round here still remember . . .*

A piece of my story is embodied in this place, even if I've allowed it to fade into a dream. *Resistance is futile.* I release a soft hum of a laugh, knowing Dad would appreciate the Star Trek reference. In fact, it's probably what he would say to me right now if he could. *Maybe he did.*

At the very least, I feel him smiling as I pass the countless yards of picket fencing that still need to be painted and turn into Daisy's driveway.

Inhaling deep, I move courage like air into my lungs, into all the parts of me where I remember courage once residing. And as I scrape out the last bits of Oreo goodness with my pink plastic spoon, it occurs to me that Tawny was right again. I should know better than to order the smallest size.

Closing the front door behind me, I still haven't landed on a strategy for breaking the news to Daisy. I'll have to explain that, while my stay in Charity Falls has been extended, it nevertheless is still destined to come to an end. My life, my real life, could never be here. I'll be clear about that.

Uncle Dean is fully dressed and sitting upright on the couch like a guest in his own home. His cane rests across his knees.

"Hi, Uncle Dean. It's just me, Audrey," I announce, as I always do, so he isn't forced to scour his mind for an explanation about this woman who keeps appearing in his home.

My uncle steadies his cane and makes an effort to get up. "Oh! Are we leaving now?"

From the kitchen, Daisy's voice is all honey and cream. "No, dear. Lunch is just about ready. We're about to sit down to lunch, sweetheart."

Dean relaxes and sends me a charming smile. "Can you join us?"

"I would love to."

"Audrey's our houseguest, Dean," Daisy reminds. "I told her she could stay as long as she likes. Isn't that nice?"

I follow my aunt's voice into the kitchen. "So, Daisy . . . by any chance did Homer Rudloe ever have a thing for you?"

"What?" She stops arranging sandwiches on a platter and scowls. "What's all this silly talk?"

"When Homer found out I was your niece, he practically begged me to come work at his store." *Well, that, and he took pity on me because of my past. Maybe I'm laying it on a little too thick.*

Daisy looks baffled.

"I had no choice but to tell him yes."

Her mouth falls open. "You took a job? Sweetie, why would you . . . you didn't need to do that."

"Actually, I did. And you're looking at Homer's Hardware's newest, *temporary*, *seasonal* cashier. It kind of just . . . happened."

Daisy gently brushes a loose strand of hair off my face. "But you're our guest here."

"Well, it's done now. Besides, it's your fault. You got me the job. I can tell Homer thinks you put the shine in the sun. Turns out it's not your credentials that matter, it's who you know."

"Oh, pishposh. I should think you could land a job anywhere in this town. Homer 'n Dean served in Rotary together for years. Come to think of it, he led your dad's Cub Scout troop. He thought—I should say, he *thinks*—very highly of your dad."

"Yeah. He mentioned that." I pop a green grape into my mouth.

She lifts the platter. "Here, I can take that," I say.

Daisy follows me to the kitchen table, chatting incessantly. "Okay, Dean, time to eat. Remember your friend Homer? Homer hired Audrey to work in his store. Isn't that wonderful?"

"Oh!" He watches Daisy closely, taking his lead from her like a puppy. If she's pleased, he's pleased. How unlike the Uncle Dean of my childhood, always trying to get her goat, keep her off-balance. The Dean I remember would have thought this the ideal time to pop off a joke. It would've been, *By golly, Audrey, you better measure up or ol' Homer'll bring the hammer down!*

Or, *Hope you sell a lot of saws, so he doesn't have to cut the workforce in half!*

When I offer Dean my arm and accompany him to the kitchen, he laughs softly and pats me on the shoulder, like I just ran the game-winning touchdown. "Well, whatdaya know. How about that. You're quite the girl!"

Fourteen

Dead vines slither up the brick chimney of the former Sugar Pine Inn. To the right of the farmhouse's boarded-up front door, a peeling sign still bids Welcome. Another to the left commands Keep Out—in fire-red letters.

But is it really trespassing if your family's blood is in the soil?

It's a brisk Saturday morning and the wild, dry, curry-toned grasses shimmer with a hint of dew. Twigs snap beneath my steps. A robin startles. I zip my hoodie and follow him around the side of the inn as far as the old wooden playhouse. How small and sad it looks, still trimmed in bric-a-brac to match the main house but half swallowed up by weeds. Once upon another time the mural painted on its side, of a boy and girl frolicking with a golden retriever, was bright and colorful. Now it's dull as dirt. Her yellow dress has ebbed to beige. His red shirt, to Pepto-Bismol pink.

A flicker of movement catches my eye, and I stiffen. Something alive . . . or *someone?* . . . is maybe ten feet away, around the left side of the old tool shed. I'm being watched—I can feel it. Figures. Serves me right for breaking the law for the first time in . . . ever. With my luck lately, it's a serial killer wearing track shoes.

I may be carrying a hammer, but I'm poised to run. "Hello? Is someone there?" I say. Leaning out, I get my answer. And freeze.

Obsidian eyes are transfixed on mine. A black nose, exhaling steam. Great furry ears. Thick, velvet-coated antler starts—what look to be the makings of an immense rack. *Oh, thank God.* I release my pent-up breath.

"It's okay, buddy," I hear myself say in a voice so calm I can't believe it's coming from the same woman whose heart is sprinting like a quarter horse. Apparently if I'm ever called upon to talk a jumper off a ledge, I possess the right voice modulation. I drop back a step. "See, I'm chill."

Another ten or more big-eared deer rest in the grass wearing freaked-out expressions. That's a lot of ginormous eyes trained on me. At least twenty-two if my math skills serve me right. "Oh, look at your whole gang there," I coo. "Very nice." At least *someone* is enjoying this place. On the other hand, some of these are likely mama does with newborns concealed somewhere nearby in the tall bunchgrass. I'm too close for their comfort *and* mine.

Slowly I back away. "No worries, folks. I'm leaving. Y'all have a lovely day."

Just as well. What had I been thinking, tramping on someone else's land? *Someone who clearly doesn't give a rip about it*—that's what I'd been thinking. But you know what they say about curiosity.

And anyway, it's yard sale day, and this poster isn't going to hang itself.

Minutes later, I'm pounding a nail into a telephone pole when an old, sputtering Suburban pulls alongside me. The window glides down. The driver's a leathery woman attached to a glowing cigarette, with two inches of gray roots leading to hair an unnatural shade of orange. She gestures at the poster. "That Daisy's place?"

"Yes, right down this road, just past the Sugar Pi—"

"I know where it is."

"But we're not—" Already she's off, spewing gravel. "Set up yet. Sheesh." Good thing I put up a No Earlies sign at the driveway entrance. I jog back toward the house. Ugh. And my day began with such peace and promise, watching dawn tiptoe over the pines, painting the snow-brushed mountains apricot—

Good grief, there's that woman in Daisy's front yard. Altogether ignoring my No Earlies sign, she flits from table to table, peeping under tarps like an eager coroner. Meanwhile Daisy's busy chatting on the front porch with a tall, white-haired, cowboy-looking gentleman. Guess I'll have to handle this. I paste on a smile and cross the lawn.

That man, though. Why is he so familiar? I glance over too late to catch a peek of anything but his backside as he steps into the house. But I got a good enough look to know that he had to remove his hat and duck his head to enter. Must be a friend of Dean's. Or wait . . . *maybe*—

"How much for the Crock-Pot?" the orange-haired lady says huskily, without so much as a how-do-you-do.

On the porch, my aunt has returned to her project of assigning price stickers to old record albums. "Aunt Daisy, price?" I call.

She removes her readers. "Oh, hello, Agatha. That old thing? You're more than welcome to it."

Thing is, now I recognize that brown Crock-Pot. In fact I know it well, lined at the rim with tiny orange-and-white flowers and permanently stained. Daisy's hunched over the record albums again. Guess I get to handle this too. "Actually, I'm sorry," I tell Agatha quietly, "the Crock-Pot's not for sale."

Where did *that* come from?

When she clutches it to her chest, the glass lid jangles. "But Daisy just said—"

I open my arms to receive it from her. "Sorry. It stays." Both of our heads turn toward the porch, but Daisy must have gone inside.

"Fine, I'll give you five dollars. Lid's chipped. See?"

I'll need to try a different tack. I yank a sheet off a nearby card table. "Did you see this electric skillet? It's pristine."

Agatha ignores me. Instead she rests the Crock-Pot on the table and starts pulling bills out of her fanny pack. "Here's eight . . . nine . . . ten—"

I seize the moment. Lift the Crock-Pot into the safety of my arms. Agatha lunges. Now we've both got our arms around it. Up close, she reeks of cigarettes and cheap perfume.

Agatha tugs. "Fine, twenty! Don't be foolish, dear, I'm sure Daisy can use the money."

I grasp tighter. The tail of the electrical cord cascades to the ground. What's wrong with this woman? I could easily outpower her. "Agatha, this item is not for sale. I'm taking it inside now. Please. Let. Go." Seriously, what's with her?

What's with you?!

"Audrey! For heaven's sake!" At Daisy's voice, Agatha releases her death grip and backs away, smoothing her plaid blouse. What just happened, and how will I ever explain it to my aunt? I huff up the stairs and deposit the appliance near the front door, taking pains to avoid Daisy's gaze. But I feel her staring at me like she just caught me swiping a lollipop from an orphan.

"Audrey?"

Maybe I'll try feigning nonchalance. "Hmm?" But then I meet Daisy's eyes, her incredulous expression, and let out a long sigh. "It's just that . . . I mean, don't you need it?" I sound whiny and childish. Pathetic. "What will you cook your chili in?"

"Sweetie, the inn's closed. The family's grown. Who in the world have I got to cook for anymore?"

I shrug. "I get it. I just . . ." I visualize Daisy's Crock-Pot sitting on Agatha's kitchen counter and bile rises in my throat. Here's my problem—I can see it now: This dispensing with the things of the past is all happening too abruptly. Never mind the fact that everything about this house—heck, the house itself—is going away. Why does this bother me more every day?

An idea forms. "Maybe you could show me how you make it," I say. "I could keep the recipe going."

Like an electric drill, Agatha's gravelly voice punctures this moment I'm having with my aunt. "Any chance you're ready to share that recipe now, Daisy?" Make that a disc grinder.

Daisy chuckles dryly, breaking the tension. "Maybe . . ." She shoots me a side glance. "Maybe not quite yet, Agatha. Sorry 'bout that."

The woman lifts a shoulder, then resumes inspecting a deviled-egg platter.

"That woman has been trying to get her hands on my chili recipe for years," my aunt whispers. "It's not a magic pot, you know. But . . ." She waggles her eyebrows. "I may have a secret ingredient or two."

Later I'm reorganizing the table of free items when a man wearing overalls and shaped like Wario makes a beeline across the lawn, apparently aimed at me. It's like his legs can't keep up with his paunch. I have the distinct feeling this guy's not shopping for a pink vanity stool or a gallon Ziploc full of never-opened bottles of nail polish. Maybe I can interest him in a trout-shaped lamp.

The man jerks his chin toward the old Sugar Pine. "Young lady, can you please tell me what's going on across the street?" Together our gazes pivot to the blight with a blue roof. "I drive by here all the time, and it's a dirty rotten shame to see the place like that. Why in blazes has it been left to go to pot? No one seems to know."

So I'm not the only one appalled. But I won't do it. I won't let this red-faced ranch dude stoke my outrage. I've so far managed to survive a week in Charity Falls with less than scanty information about the Sugar Pine. It's not my mystery to solve.

Then why are my emotions as taut as fishing line caught on a deep, slimy river rock?

"I wish I did," I say. "But I'm just visiting. The last time I was here, it was still a bed-and-breakfast."

"Right." He strokes his gray stubble. "So you know, then. You know what it was like back when June Milligan had the place.

Me and my wife—God rest her—were regulars for those Tuesday brunches."

I nod. "When that woman with the bird's-nest hair would play piano."

"Exactly!" he says, then slumps. "Ah, well. At least the coyotes get to enjoy it."

"Coyotes?"

"See, there's one hunting over there now."

I train my eyes on the distant bunchgrass. Sure enough, something thin, gray, and doglike roves there. "Oh wow. I've actually never seen one before." That seals it. You won't catch me trespassing there again. My days of criminal mischief are d-o-n-e.

"Well, alrighty then. Thank you," he says, turning to leave. "But I'd sure love to know who's responsible. Shame it's become such an eyesore." The man has no idea how strongly I agree. It isn't like I haven't gently prodded Daisy about this topic, despite my original vow not to.

———〜———

I must be what my dad would've called one sandwich short of a picnic because the next afternoon I again broach the subject of the inn with Daisy. With the yard sale behind us, the two of us are working out back. I've taken to clearing the jumble of last fall's tumbleweeds from where they've collected in the corners of the patio. Carrying them out to the charred crater where Dean used to do his burning is not an easy feat, as large and prickly as they are. Maybe Rotary Rob will be willing to monitor a burn pile. Or a volunteer from the church. That's one job that doesn't have my name on it.

At my mention of the Sugar Pine, my aunt is once again dismissive. "Aren't you at least curious?" I ask, switching from my hands back to the rake.

She doesn't even look up from her task of repotting the six-pack of baby herb plants I purchased for her with my new store discount at Homer's. "As I've said, I'm sure there's a perfectly good explanation." As if that somehow spells things out.

Back off, a voice in my head warns. *Let it go*.

"Is there another pair of gloves I can get for you?" I ask. Although Daisy insisted I wear hers, it isn't like they're helping much. Tumbleweed thorns easily pierce the thin floral fabric, sending shock waves clear up to my shoulders.

With her arm, she brushes a snowy lock of hair off her forehead. "No, thank you. Feels good to get dirt under my fingernails for a change."

I pause my raking. "So you're really not bothered, looking at that eyesore across the street every day?" I shouldn't have said it. But now it's out there. I brace myself, and for a long time Daisy doesn't respond. What insanity possesses me to keep bringing up the place where the man she raised as if he were her own child died so horrifically? I make Adrian Monk look sensitive.

What does it matter anyway? I resume my raking. Into the awkwardness I've now added the scraping sound of metal against crushed rock.

In moments like these, I can too easily believe that hope is a joke, nothing more. Because what feels more real in moments like these—in the air, on my skin, in my bones, and in my heart—is pain.

I feel it acutely in Daisy's silence. When at last her eyes connect with mine, they're darkened with sorrow. "Life moves on, Audrey, without stopping for our permission. We learn to make peace with the things we can't make sense of. I've come to a place of acceptance—at least enough of the time. Only the Lord could do that."

Slowly she brushes the soil from one hand and then the other. "I've had quite a bit of practice, you know," she adds, turning to me. This, tinged with undisguised anguish. She wants me to see it. Needs me to understand.

Daisy squares her petite shoulders. "Someday, though, I believe with all my heart that things will be made right."

Life has been cruel to Daisy. Her afflictions easily outnumber mine. Although she's never spoken of it, I've been told she couldn't have children of her own. And long before my dad's death, she lost her only sister—Sandra, the grandmother I never got to meet. Killed in a rollover accident as a new mom. An impaired driver had been responsible. Ironically, my grandfather, the grieving young husband Sandra left behind, turned to substance abuse. Left the picture and remarried at least twice more.

Yet there'd been a miracle in the middle of the tragedy. Daisy's infant nephew survived the accident unharmed. My father. The reason I have life today.

Now that I think about it, it's no wonder Daisy gave up driving.

Thing is, the closer I get to my aunt's pain, the closer I move toward having to acknowledge my own.

Bending, I wrap my arms gingerly around the next mound of tumbleweeds. The lightweight flannel that was a gift from Ava is no match for these devilish little spikes. A subtle torment, though, in comparison to the topic at hand.

Daisy narrows her eyes, watching me work, then moves to the toolshed and muscles open the sticky old door. She vanishes inside. Moments later she's back, slapping the dust off a pair of thick suede work gloves. "Here. Try these. They'll be too big, but—" Her voice catches. "But they were your father's."

The air smells of dried pine needles and sadness, if sadness had a smell. Wordlessly, she disappears into the house, leaving me here with the immeasurable weight of my father's work gloves resting in my hands.

Leaving me alone. Free to stop fighting the tears. Did she go inside because she needed to shed her own?

Fifteen

"Mind if I give it a try?" I ask Jan as a customer approaches. It just so happens that the day she's expected to train me on the checkout counter is the same day Homer's new cash register system gets installed. Jan's a total sweetheart, adored by the locals. Everyone is her BFF. But tech-savvy she is not.

Add to that a major aversion to change, and by late morning frustration has painted her fleshy cheeks maroon. Three times now, she has let fly a mild profanity followed by a fervent apology. I'm beginning to worry about her blood pressure.

In reality, the new register is simply a glorified iPad.

"Have at it, honey!" Jan says, stepping back. "I'm right here if you need me."

I greet an older man wearing a navy-blue cap decorated with pins and embroidered with the letters VFW. "Thank you for your service," I say. Behind me, a bag crinkles. Jan likes to keep a stash of dark chocolate Dove Promises at the ready. I respect that.

Within the hour, Jan and I have found our footing. She needs my constant help with the register, and I need hers for other protocols. One thing I picked up on quickly is that Homer's in-house credit system exists mainly as a courtesy to local businesses. Only a handful of old-timers like Daisy and Dean still hold such high privilege.

Homer turned me loose in the paint department on my third day. And yet Silas continues to hover like a bubble-eyed drone, towering above me and ever watchful. At least now I'll be able to cover Jan's breaks on the front counter as well. Whenever I'm not needed, I wander the store in my chichi blue vest, getting a feel for the layout. Nothing worse than receiving *that look* from a male customer determined to size you up as mere window dressing. This may be a part-time, temp schtick, but I *shall* conquer.

And hey, I'm putting my employee discount to use as I tidy up Daisy's flower beds. What a difference a little pruning, weeding, and new bark mulch make. Having divided the Shasta daisies Dad and I planted twenty years ago, I'm hopeful they'll make a late-summer comeback. *Which you won't be here to see.* I shrug off a tug of disappointment.

I check my phone again, half dreading *that* call, the one from the mechanic where I find out if old Harriet's going to put me in debtor's prison. But I have to admit, this job has brought me a measure of peace. And at least one new friend.

Her name is Paige. The dark-featured girl with a daily gumball habit has chosen me. Kind of in the same way a shelter puppy with beseeching eyes lays claim to an unsuspecting Petco shopper rather than the other way around. Every afternoon Paige parks her bike, buys a gumball, then lingers at my counter, quietly waiting for me to strike up a conversation.

By now I know what she likes and doesn't like about her teacher, Ms. Barnes. I know she is good at spelling, bad at math, and believes she super-stinks at art. I also know that in her third-grade classroom, Paige's desk is positioned toward the back of the room and she has trouble reading the SMART board. I'm guessing she needs glasses.

Paige spends every recess either swinging on the parallel bars or reading by herself. Her best, and I'm pretty sure her only, friend is a boy named Chase. I know Paige lives only one block away, has an older brother, and a mom who works in a café. I'm still unclear about her father.

What I don't know is why she spends so much time unsupervised. When I was Paige's age, my free time was carefully managed by my parents. Outside of school, I was allowed to be one of four places—at home, at one of my two *approved* friends' houses, or at the community pool under the watchful eye of one of my two approved friends' parents.

"Paige," I say, curiosity getting the better of me today. "You said your brother's at home? What'd you say his name is, Arlo? Does Arlo know where you are right now?"

She's resting her chin on her folded arms, watching me with those chocolate eyes as I reorganize the contents of a drawer. Who keeps seventeen dried-up gel pens anyway?

"Mm-hmm," she says. "He's playing video games. He's always playing video games."

"Is he nice to you? I have a brother. His name's Troy. We didn't always get along when I was your age."

"Yeah, I guess. He gives me a quarter when I'm done with my homework."

"Oh. Well, that's pretty cool." For my next question I want to tread carefully. But I sense I've gained Paige's trust. On the other hand, I'm not entirely sure I want to hear her answer. Something tells me that if I know too much about this girl, my heart's in danger.

I proceed anyway. For some reason I can't help myself. "And your dad? Where is he during the day?"

Paige fiddles with her sleeve. When she answers, she doesn't look at me. "He lives in a castle."

Surely I've misheard. But Paige doesn't blink. I swallow hard. "Oh. Did you just say . . . castle?" Maybe she said the name of a town. Like Newcastle. That must be it.

Paige nods impassively. "Uh-huh. At Strawberry Creek."

Okayy. What exactly am I dealing with here? Before I can figure out where to go next with my line of questioning, a woman approaches with a red shopping basket filled to the brim. I paste on a bright expression of greeting, conscious of Paige slipping off toward the exit. *Darn.*

"Bye, Audrey! See you tomorrow!"

And she's gone, once again leaving me with lingering questions—and this time, with new concerns. Isn't Paige too old for such imaginative talk? Something is definitely amiss with my little friend. But what? Why can't I shake this sense of foreboding?

Sixteen

Daisy

Something unexpected happens when your house gets pared down to the basics. Inspiration moves in. At least, it seems to have struck me. Now that we've cleared away so much riffraff—collectibles that I already don't miss because, as it turns out, they carried very little sentimental value—I like my house better. What an irritating irony. All of a sudden I can envision ways to make these spaces brighter and cheerier. Why didn't I do these things long ago?

Audrey calls it quieting the rooms. She says the more a room is allowed to breathe, the more clearly it will let us know what it needs and what it doesn't. I'm beginning to see what she means.

"What do you think about painting the wood paneling?" I ask. "Would that be worthwhile before we put it on the market?" Even as I say it, I sense the earth beneath me shuddering as my parents do a full turn in their graves. In my family, painting over wood was a sin nearly as unforgivable as stacking something on top of the Bible. But somehow, now that this is no longer going to be my house, all bets are off. I feel daring. Unrepentant, even.

Audrey looks up from where she's sitting crisscross-applesauce on the floor, sorting magazines into piles. "Hmm. That would elevate it for sure. If we painted them white, maybe a warm white, the place could have a real cozy cottage vibe."

"You don't look so sure. You're right, it's a bad idea," I say. "Not to mention it would take a lot of paint. All those dark knots."

"Actually, it's an awesome idea. And honestly, if it was my house I'd probably do it. But . . ." Audrey's voice trails off.

"But what?"

Audrey sighs and gazes around the living room. "It's just that this is the way I've pictured your house forever. It's so cabiny, so rustic. So you."

"Ha! Now look who's the sentimental one."

"I mean, it could be fun. And yes, probably a smart investment for resale. I wonder . . . what if we were to start slowly, maybe paint one of the smaller spaces, like the guest room? Make sure you're comfortable with it."

"No." Who is this reckless woman that's inhabited my body? "In for a penny, in for a pound. Let's just go for it!"

Audrey lays on a thick cowpoke accent. "Well, alrighty then, Miss Daisy. You da boss!" She unpretzels herself, rolls on her side, and does a mermaid stretch. "Oh, hey, about these magazines, can we toss them?"

I cluck my tongue a few times, debating. "The only ones I care about are the *Birds & Blooms*. I canceled my subscription several years ago. But the photos are so lovely, don't you think? Sometimes I enjoy looking through them. I keep thinking they'd be perfect for a craft project. Remember I used to like to decoupage? But who'm I kidding? I'll never get around to it. Go ahead. Give 'em the old heave-ho."

"Okay." Audrey thumbs through the pages of an issue. "But I see what you mean. These are gorgeous images. You could always restart your subscription after you move."

"What a marvelous thought. That's it! I'll resubscribe. It'll give me something to look forward to. Thank you, Audrey. I never would have given myself permission."

Audrey's riffling the corner of a magazine, wearing a faraway look. "Actually, would you mind if I hold on to a few of these? I just got a wild idea."

Seventeen

Audrey

When I open the door to Paige's mother, Nina, on the following Saturday, my fingers are coated with Mod Podge. "Come on in," I say.

"I know I'm early." Nina is a soft-spoken woman I'd place somewhere in her late thirties. When I picked up Paige this morning for our art day, I was immediately struck by her mother's extraordinary features. Her mahogany skin is even deeper than Paige's, but it's overcast with a somber gray. "The café was slow," she says timidly. "Reggie sent me home before my shift ended. But I thought you might like some cinnamon ro—"

"Mom, no!" Paige leans out from the kitchen table. "I'm not done! I'm not ready to go!" Despite her whining, I feel a twinge of pleasure. So Paige *does* like crafts after all. Earlier, when I told her what activity I'd chosen for our first get-together outside the hardware store, she was skeptical. Me too, but for different reasons. For one thing, I don't know much about her story. Should I even be taking this risk, wading into her life?

Also, between the work I'm doing at Homer's and the projects I've agreed to do for Daisy, I have a decently full schedule. Still, somehow I'm finding margin—time and energy for other things. Margin that, for some reason, I've never been able to find around my career at DeSoto.

Daisy scurries to the foyer, arms outstretched. "Hello, I'm Daisy. And what have we here?" Paige's mom pops open the to-go container, releasing a heavenly scent. "Oh my," Daisy croons. "Nothing beats Reggie's cinnamon rolls. And with pecans! For goodness' sake, what a lovely treat. Did you . . . are *you* the one behind his baked goods these days?" Nina offers a bashful smile. "Around here, that makes you royalty! By all means, come join us."

Daisy leads the way into the kitchen, leaving Paige's mother little room to refuse, although I sense hesitation. Whether she's shy, exhausted from her shift at work, or simply afraid to intrude, I couldn't guess. I don't know her well enough. Perhaps it has to do with what I'm pretty confident is her single-mom status. She's certainly got a wounded look about her.

"Here, take my chair," Daisy insists. "I'll just heat these up a touch."

I introduce Nina to Uncle Dean, who has spent the day unusually relaxed, more than content to sit at the table watching the three of us girls cutting and pasting. "And you might know this little Picasso," I say, giving Paige's shoulder a gentle squeeze.

She giggles but keeps working. "Mom, look, I made a vase. But I'm not done. Do I have to go?"

As the coffee maker gurgles, the room sizzles with warmth and chatter and the scent of hospitality. To the colorful array on the table, Daisy adds a sunny yellow platter I haven't seen in over a decade, piled with the icing-drenched rolls. "Isn't my niece so clever?" she gushes to Nina. "She dug these old milk bottles out of the donate pile. First we painted them. And we've been decorating them with birds and flowers and whatnot."

Paige holds her vase up, rotating it to show off the brightly colored birds on all sides. "See, Mom?" she says, laughing. "I made it look like they're kissing. This bright-green one's a swallow. And this one's a kess . . . kess . . ." She looks to me.

"A kestrel falcon," I say.

Dean studies Paige with a sweet, dopey tenderness that squeezes my heart. "How about that." He chuckles faintly. "She did a good job!"

The way Paige's mother perches noncommittally on only half her chair reinforces my guess that she's anxious to get home. Also, she does look tired. "Paige," I say, "yours just needs a topcoat of glue, and I think you're all done."

Eyebrows furrowed, Paige picks up the scissors. "Uh-uh. Look, Audrey. I need to find a flower to put right here."

"Just one more flower, and only if your mom says it's okay. I'm sure she's had a long day."

Her mother nods a go-ahead. I take this as a green light to get to know Nina if she's willing. It's possible she isn't much older than me, but it's hard to say. She wears such a dull patina, like a starling stripped of its natural iridescence.

"Paige tells us she's only got one more week of school?" I say.

"Yes, that's right." I almost miss the uptick in Nina's lips, so brief is the smile that never reaches her eyes. She exhales a barely audible sigh.

"I think she's planning to give her vase to her teacher on the last day. I know Paige is *very* disappointed that school's almost over." I give Paige a soft bop on the nose.

"No, I am not sad! Not. At. All! Mom, can I hang out with Audrey when you're at work instead of Arlo? Can I, can I? Please?" Does Nina not have a plan for childcare during the summer months? Is that some of the weight she carries?

"Paige, honey," her mother says, shifting in her chair, "it's not polite to put Audrey on the spot."

"Well, I don't know," I say in a mock serious tone. "I might have to put her to work. I happen to be in need of someone who likes painting fences, so . . ." With yards of pickets left to go, I truly wouldn't mind any help I can get.

Paige rockets her right hand up in the air. "Me, me, me! Pick me!" This version of Paige, the animated one who spent the day in our company, bears little resemblance to the sullen girl who skulks around Homer's. Unlike her mom, Paige's spirit isn't completely broken . . . yet. And I, for one, am more eager every minute to watch it soar.

DeSoto may not need me right now. But I know a little girl with an uncertain family situation who might. And, God help me, it's starting to feel like the next right thing.

Eighteen

"Mm, mm, mm. To die for." Jan pops the last bite of a buttery marionberry mini-scone in her mouth and writhes with pleasure. "Better stop at two, though. Wouldn't want to bump myself out of ketosis." She brushes a crumb from the corner of her mouth.

I happen to know it's Jan's fourth scone. And also that her dieting efforts are legendary around these parts.

The hardware store's breakroom isn't in fact a room so much as a narrow alcove outside Homer's office. It boasts a water cooler, a dinky microwave, a mini fridge, and a coffee maker that predates Moses with a carafe that'll be stained coal-black till the Second Coming. There isn't enough baking soda in the world to remedy this. Believe me, I've tried. Today, though, I've added a ray of golden sunshine to the cheerless space—Daisy's yellow platter of delights.

Come to think of it, if I calculate correctly, Daisy has baked four times in the past two weeks. The realization brings a sense of warmth and fullness to my chest. Enough to melt another square millimeter of glacial ice from my heart. Why does this make me so uncomfortable? If I've learned anything in the month I've been here, it's that two conflicting emotions can and will cleave to one another like awkward dance partners. In this case, gratitude for the resurgence of life I see in Daisy, intimately entwined with my growing sense of naked vulnerability. I can't seem to have one without the other, and it's got me feeling punchy.

Maybe another scone will provide a momentary fix.

No. What I could really use is some fresh air and a nice cup of tea. So when Silas spies me in the slender alcove and moves my way, I feign like I'm just leaving. "Make sure you try one of the scones," I say as we pass. "They won't last long." With Silas, I feel the need to strike a balance with my tone—part droid, part entertainment director—so my overtures of friendship are never misconstrued. I sense he's been working up to asking me out, and if he thinks he's gonna corner me right here and now, he's got another thing coming. I'd love to save us both the embarrassment.

Silas's shoulders slump. "Oh. Thought I'd find you still on your break."

"Yep, just heading out to run an errand." Maybe I need to invent a boyfriend, someone waiting for me back in California. *Ugh*, no, that would be a black lie. No gray tones about it.

Outside, the sun's rays hitch a ride on my shoulder as I make my way to the corner, then left along Birch Avenue. Sweet Reads is calling my name.

I succumb to the smell of cinnamon in the air and order an iced chai. While I wait, I peruse the poetry section. A Mary Oliver collection tempts, and I thumb through, looking to treat myself to one poem. Something to match my mood. *Hmm*.

"Excuse me. You're Audrey, right?"

That voice. Turning, I find myself looking up into the eyes of Tall Aqua-Truck Guy. Addressing me by my first name? I'm at a loss, off-balance. Although there was that one sort-of encounter in line at Homer's. Maybe he caught my name just as I'd caught his. Cody, I think. Or was it Cade?

I square my shoulders. "Yes, I'm Audrey."

He rubs the back of his neck. "I've, uh, seen you around. With Paige."

"Oh." Okay, not what I expected. When and where could he have seen us? Although it *is* a small town, and Paige and I have been a number of places together over the past couple weeks. The library, for one. Signing up Paige for their summer reading program was a no-brainer. And then there was the day I borrowed Daisy's bike and we rode together to the park so her mom could make a little extra cash cleaning vacation rentals. Devoured a huge picnic lunch and practiced cartwheels on the grass. In the opposite order, of course.

He thrusts his hand out. "Sorry, I should've introduced myself. I'm Cade." We shake, then his hand slips into his pocket. Which for some reason I find adorable. "Look, it's just that . . ." Whatever this guy wants to say, it's obviously excruciating for him. Oh my gosh, is he interested in me? We've never even met. I should probably shut him down right away. Which is a shame, because his eyes are an extraordinary shade of blue.

"It's like this," he says. "Paige has been through a lot."

I nod knowingly, even though I'm still missing most of the puzzle pieces. Far as I can tell, Paige's father may be nothing more than a product of her imagination. And her mother, Nina, hasn't been in any hurry to entrust me with the details.

"She needs . . . I mean, is it true you're just *visiting* Charity Falls? Sorry, it's a small town. People talk."

"Yeah, no kidding." I have no idea where he's going with this, but suddenly my hackles are up. "I'm here through summer. Well, July anyway." My tone is defensive, and I'm not sure why. Maybe because I've just verbalized the entirety of what I know about my life. It's not much, but it's all I've got, and I'm not sure why this person should be privy to it.

Cade's nose flares slightly. "Does Paige know that?" An intensity charges the air between us. *Whoa.* "Look, I'm sure you mean well, but she doesn't need someone who's here today and gone tomorrow, you know." He moves a hand to a hip. "Do you really think that's fair to her? She's—"

"Excuse me? You don't even know me. I happen to care about Paige. A lot. I'm sorry, but who are you to—" I need to flee this assault before the venom rising in my chest spews. This is probably one of those locals who has a thing against people from California. "You know what, never mind."

I've taken three steps toward the counter to retrieve my tea before I realize I'm still holding the poetry book. *Sheesh*. In order to return it to its rightful place I'll have to brush past Mr. Tall and Uptight, traverse the tension-laden spot where he still stands. "Excuse me," I mumble as I pass. His gaze meets mine, and he looks . . . what? Contrite? I strengthen my voice and tint my words saucy. "Wonderful to meet you, Cade. Have an *awesome* day."

So much for small-town friendliness. What a disappointment. At least my friendly drink is ready and waiting.

Daisy

The home phone trills, breaking my concentration. I'm certain I can make at least a six-letter word out of these Scrabble tiles. "I'll get it," I say quickly to Dean. The last time he answered the landline, he unwittingly upgraded our monthly public broadcasting donation to the premium amount. Granted, we thoroughly enjoyed their delightful thank-you gift, a gorgeous basket of Oregon-grown edibles—pears, hazelnuts, a bottle of Willamette Valley wine. But there's no point in letting him struggle through a phone conversation when he's utterly at sixes and sevens.

"Alexa, pause the music," I say with a growing confidence in my authority over the little white box. Willie Nelson stops singing "You Were Always on My Mind" mid-refrain and I shake my head, incredulous. *Hallelujah!* This new system Audrey set up is a godsend. I still remember the days when, if you wanted to request a song, you had to phone the radio station and wait on hold for an eternity. Usually, by the time my song finally came on, my mother had paged me downstairs for dinner.

Caller ID displays a local number, so I pick up. "Hello, Needham residence."

"Hello, Mrs. Needham. This is Margaret Skidmore from Whispering Pines."

My heart rate shoots up to triple speed. While Margaret informs me with warm enthusiasm that our time spent on the assisted living facility's waiting list has finally come to an end, I absently draw circles in the thin layer of dust on the hutch. Come late August, she says, we'll have our choice of two apartments. August. The August that's less than two months away. *Oh dear.*

"Let me just get a pen," I say, then walk in circles like a dog preparing to do his business on the lawn. *You ninny, you were just using one at the table to keep score.* I take scanty notes, nodding as if Margaret Skidmore from Whispering Pines can see me through the phone. But all the while I'm watching Dean monkey with his letter tiles. My husband is *happy.* At least, for the time being, he's peaceful. In fact, ever since that last adjustment in his meds, his symptoms have more or less plateaued. What if none of this talk of selling has been necessary? What if I've moved too fast?

Dean gazes my way, raises his eyebrows as if to ask, "What's next, dear?" I blow him an air kiss as Margaret prattles on. Her words fade into the background, like the muffled-trumpet voice of Charlie Brown's teacher. Time seems to enter a deep freeze. In fact, I could swear I've left my body and I'm watching this whole scene happen to someone else. How very, very odd.

"Mrs. Needham? Daisy? Are you there?"

I clear a frog from my throat. "Yes, yes, I'm here."

"Does that work for you? Friday?"

"Friday?" I'm watching Dean spell a word with his tiles. *C-A-R.*

"For the tour."

"Oh, yes, right, the tour. I'm sorry, what time did you say?"

Her voice is pleasant, unhurried. "Any time before noon."

I make a note of this, forcing my brain to engage. "And we'll need to decide then, about which apartment. Is that right?"

"It would be helpful. But you'll have a little time to think on it."

"Alright. Friday will be fine." Maybe Audrey can get the day off. Or no. Judy. Judy will insist on taking us. She's been dying to size up the place. "We'll make it work."

I don't need to panic. This isn't carved in stone. After all, I don't recall putting my signature on anything yet. If necessary, when I get there I can tell Margaret we're backing out. I'll also call off my realtor friend, Ellen. I'd asked her to act as our agent, but she'll understand that we've changed our minds. No harm done.

I click off the handset and rejoin Dean at the table. My limbs tingle and my head feels like it's filled with meringue. I force a smile. He's sliding another letter onto the board, adding it to the end of his word. *See? He's doing so well.*

I release a small gasp.

C-A-R-E.

Ever so softly, I slip a hand over the top of Dean's and lace my fingers through his. He squeezes gently, and I lean my head on his shoulder. *Oh, Lord. Are you telling me we're okay here? We can carry on, keep things just as they are?*

It's all too much. What if I make the wrong decision?

With my thumb I stroke Dean's gold wedding band. It's looser these days. But ever solid. Love worn. Incorruptible. "Alexa, start the music," I say.

Dean wraps his arm around me. And with that sweet, raspy voice I've loved for so long, he croons over me. "You were always on my mind . . ."

With everything I have, I cling. Cling to my husband. Cling to a truth. This ring isn't the only thing we possess that's been forged to last.

Nineteen

Audrey

Standing tall and white just outside town limits, Charity Falls Community Church has always exuded a timeless, steadfast presence. But until today, I've never had a reason to stop. Even so, I recognize for the first time that this simple wooden structure has forever served, however subconsciously, as a kind of cornerstone for me.

The Needham family has worshiped here for decades. Dad was baptized here. This is where Daisy and Dean have prayed and been prayed over, not only through each of their unfathomable big-L losses but also, I'm guessing, through plenty of small-L losses I know nothing about.

I park Harriet out front, trying to recall the last time I stepped foot in *any* church. There was my brief involvement in that on-campus ministry in college. Didn't take long before I got turned off, though. Too much hypocrisy. Looking back at it now, it wasn't like everyone was insincere. But I couldn't exactly sing with abandon, knowing so many disgusting details about the worship leader's love life. Especially once he started private messaging me. Maybe

I made too hasty an exit, but I couldn't risk losing what meager faith I still possessed.

I'm still afraid if I clutch it too tight, it will slip away like beach sand.

Daisy called it right. I've never had much tolerance for breaches of integrity.

After college, I moved cities—from Sacramento to the Bay Area. I suppose in the back of my mind I've always intended to find some kind of faith community, a safe place, if there is such a thing, where I might one day come to understand . . . no, that isn't it. I don't carry any naive notions that I'll ever understand God's ways. But I do have a growing suspicion I'll never find the peace I crave until I at least come to terms with him.

With its simple portico, arched doorway, and windows so gently Gothic, the main chapel embodies early-American Protestant architecture. A well-maintained clapboard exterior and not one single square inch of pretension. In fact, the reader board I drove past at the entrance made me grin. "Adam & Eve, the first people to not read the Apple terms and conditions."

Approaching on foot, I can't ignore that the whole scene demands to be photographed . . . or painted. Drawn with chalk on a sidewalk. Anything. Crisp winter-white steeple against cerulean skies. Dark-forested mountains offering depth of field. I pivot to retrieve my phone from the car and compose a few shots from different angles. Too bad I don't have my art supplies. But none of this is why I've come. Today I'm driving Miss Daisy.

Inside, the air smells like the pages of an old hymnal, and the receptionist's desk sits unoccupied. My gut tells me that if I pursue the source of lighthearted chatter coming from down a hall, I'll find Daisy in the midst of it.

Sure enough, my diminutive auntie is seated at a large, round table strewn with papers, surrounded by three other senior ladies. "Audrey! Come say hello!" Actually, on closer inspection, the papers are a jumble of envelopes and letters. "Audrey, this is Luanne and Margie. You know Judy. Margie and I just met today, and you'll never guess where she lives!"

She's right, I haven't a clue. I don't even know the names of the neighborhoods around here. So I just smile. "Whispering Pines!" she exclaims. I haven't seen her so deliriously cheerful in forever. Sunlight streams through a window, illuminating flecks of green in her eyes. A light that had gone dim seems to be making a reappearance. "You know, the retirement village that we are, uh, well . . ."

"Oh, sure. What a fun coincidence," I say.

"Ladies, this is my great-niece, Audrey." You'd think my aunt was on a stage, introducing the starring act.

Into her pregnant pause, Daisy's friends begin bombarding me with compliments and we've-heard-so-many-good-things-about-yous. My cheeks warm and I wish I knew how to deflect such unwarranted praise. But I see how this works. My aunt, I realize, set me up.

I'm on to you, Daisy girl.

After all, Judy's sitting right here, and our house is on her way home. Daisy didn't need me to give her a ride. She's been dying to introduce me to her tribe! Which is sweet, except that I don't deserve even a crumb of this attention. A snake-like voice inside my head accuses me of playing at this. I mean, I'm a girl who abandoned her Oregon family for over a decade, indifferent to how it might hurt them. And soon I'll abandon them again.

Maybe it's being on the inside of a church looking out that has me acutely aware of my transgressions. Come to think of it, I'm not sure I've ever used the word *transgressions* until this moment.

But still, it's cute to see Daisy among friends. To know I'm not all she has in the world. Although I am her only family. Well, she has my brother, Troy, too, but he and his family seem permanently tethered to South Carolina. So there's that.

"I'm just finishing up here, sweetie. Help yourself to the snack table over there. You must try Margie's brown-butter cake."

Ack. Set up again.

I'm loading a square of moist, cinnamony cake onto a paper plate when a gentleman enters the room. He's as tidy and friendly as a mid-century reading chair, with wavy salt-and-pepper hair and a dress shirt tucked into gray jeans. "Ladies!" he says good-naturedly, angling toward their table. "Just thought I'd check up on you. How's everyone?" He rests his arms on the back of Judy's chair with an air of casual familiarity.

"Oh, Pastor David," the woman named Luanne says heartily, "you're not fooling any of us. We know you've got a nose for baked goods." The women titter.

"Not even going to deny it. I'm afraid it's my only superpower." Grinning, he heads to the snack table. "Mmm, what have we got today?" I hand him a paper plate and introduce myself. Before departing with a mounding slice of cake, Pastor David christens the ladies with encouragement. "Keep up the good work. You're making a real difference!"

Judy leans out, spying on his movement until he's beyond hearing distance. Then she turns to me conspiratorially. "It's a shame he's too old for you, Audrey. He's quite a catch."

"He's a widower," Daisy whispers, drawing a low hum of empathy from the circle of women.

Luanne isn't so cautious with her volume. "Yes, and it's a shame he's too young for me!" The women explode into laughter.

"So, what exactly do you ladies do here?" I ask, peering over their shoulders. "How does this prison ministry work?"

"I'll show you." Daisy leads me toward another table, this one stacked with books. "Several years ago, we took over this ministry from a local couple. They still finance it, thank the good Lord. In a nutshell, they provide all these resources, and we send them out to inmates who request them."

Part of the long table is stacked with Bibles. And there seem to be half a dozen other titles. I spot a book on prayer and another on forgiveness. Some are in Spanish. I pick up a book with a woman on the cover whose sunny smile reminds me a little of my second-grade teacher. "What's this one?"

"Oh, that is powerful. It's the true story of a woman who encountered the saving love and grace of Jesus on death row. During the years she waited for her sentence to be carried out, she led a remarkable ministry to other incarcerated women. Such a picture of redemption. Absolutely miraculous. This is her." Daisy taps the book's cover.

I can't imagine the joyful, glowing woman on the cover hurting a fly. So I have a hard time reconciling that she's a . . . what, a murderer? "What happened? Was her sentence commuted?"

Daisy presses her lips together in a fragile smile, and I'm not sure I want to hear the answer. "You'll just have to read it. Here, keep this copy. And then, over here are the packages we're about to mail out. See, the prison chaplains provide our list of spiritual resources to the inmates. If an inmate writes us a letter requesting any of these materials, or all, we send them. Simple as that. Oh, and we always include a personal note of encouragement. That's what takes the most time. Here, I'll show you."

Back at the letter table, each of the women tells me about the written response they're working on. "These are the kinds of letters we *receive*," Judy says, handing me three pages covered with row after row of neatly angled penmanship. "We can hardly send a cursory note when they've just poured out their life story to us."

I peruse the first few paragraphs and immediately get sucked in. The inmate opens by describing a loving grandfather who took him to church as a young boy. Then he shares about his broken family. A parent with an addiction. A foster home. No, many foster homes. This man is surprisingly articulate. Not at all what I expected.

"Do they have to tell their stories in order to receive the books?" I ask.

"Oh no, it's not necessary," Judy says. "But many of them do. These men and women are typically at the end of their ropes, grasping for hope . . . and a listening ear. They're often quite candid. And they've got plenty of time on their hands. Thus the tissues. We went through quite a few today." She gestures at the Kleenex box in their midst.

I'm a little rattled. Emotion wells in my chest now that I understand what these piles of letters represent. So much humanity. So much brokenness. But also, desperate attempts to put their lives right. *Reaching out for God.* Each of the envelopes lists the inmate's assigned number, and below it, the name and address of the prison. "Are they all in Oregon?"

"Yes," Daisy says. "We have relationships with chaplains in nine of Oregon's fourteen state-run prisons. It's already more than we can keep up with."

As we chat, I run my eyes across the table strewn with mail, touched by the sensitivity and magnitude of this ministry. But then something stops me cold. I lean closer.

"Excuse me, Judy. Do you mind if I . . . ?" I reach over Judy's shoulder to retrieve an envelope that's peeking out from beneath another. A prickly sensation creeps over me.

Staring at the return address bleeding across the top left corner, I scramble to connect the dots pinging around in my mind. There are other envelopes, too, with the same inky stamp.

Strawberry Creek Correctional Facility.

The hair on my arms stands on end.

"He lives in a castle. At Strawberry Creek."

Wasn't that what Paige said? What can this mean? More specifically, what can this mean for a certain young girl with a daily gumball habit and no sign of a father?

Oh, Paige.

Twenty

Before reporting for my shift at Homer's the next day, I pay a visit to the local thrift store. It's time. Time to break down and submit to Charity Falls' fashion rules. They're quite simple, really. For everyday wear, it's a T-shirt and leggings with a hoodie on the side. Business casual? Ratchet up the dial barely half a notch. Upgrade the T-shirt to a blouse. Add jeans and sandals. And there you have it.

When in Rome, right?

An elderly woman rings up my purchases on an ancient cash register while a second bags my new treasures. She works slowly and meticulously. Her long, lined fingers sport an impeccable electric-pink manicure as she wraps white tissue around the pair of secondhand earrings I selected. "These are quite lovely," she says. They really are, and obviously handmade. Silver-wire tear-drop hoops, each with a single floating glass bead the color of a glacial lake.

And they only set me back four dollars.

Pretty sure I'm getting better service here in this place that smells like mothballs than I would at some chichi boutique. "That'll be twenty-seven dollars," the cashier says. I gaze incredulously at the two brown-paper bags brimming with clothes, including two surprisingly cute pairs of jeans. Much as I hate to question this geriatric volunteer, there's no way her total is right. "Are you, um, sure you got the jeans and everything?"

She adjusts her glasses and studies the receipt. "Let's see here. I count eight items. Pants are half-price today."

"Oh. Then I guess it's right. Wow, that's fantastic."

Returning to my car, I switch out my earrings for the new ones and admire them in the visor mirror. They're exquisite, perfect for casual or dressy. And yet . . .

Oh, who am I kidding? I suppose I was hoping to anesthetize my despair. But even an unusually successful shopping event hasn't worked to quell the nausea that now surges again as I remember my grim discovery. Strawberry Creek is the name of a prison.

Strawberry Creek is a *prison*! And a pair of new earrings will never fix the implications.

Could Paige's father be in jail? What a horrifying thought. Is he some kind of hardened criminal? The poor child—no wonder she's in la-la land. *"My dad lives in a castle . . ."*

Last night I googled the correctional facility, which turns out to be less than a hundred miles northeast of here. Images appeared and my breath caught. With its tall, concrete guard tower, at once I could imagine how a child might view it as castle-like. Is that what Paige meant?

I'm preoccupied with this line of thinking as I start the engine. Harriet purrs, and I draw meager comfort from the fact that at least my car is now healthy. Even if I'm wrecked.

Paige's poor brother, Arlo! What a trial for a preteen boy. No wonder Paige's mom is so tight-lipped. Heck, no wonder Cade interrogated me. Somehow, he must be aware of the family's situation. After all, this is an extremely small town. Maybe *everyone* knows Paige's story except for the girl who galloped in on a horse called stupid, thinking she could right the world.

For all I know Cade is a father, and his kids attend the same school as Paige. For that matter, he could be her teacher. Or her school counselor!

My gut convulses, remembering his rebuke. *"She doesn't need someone who's here today and gone tomorrow."*

Cade was right. I'm *way* out of my depth.

Reflexively, I turn right toward Sweet Reads, instead of left to Homer's. As I wait in line to order a cup of chamomile, my gaze is drawn to the poetry shelves, the scene of our confrontation several days ago. I was so flippant. Worse, I was haughty. A fool.

Not to mention, what have I been thinking, befriending a girl with a wound in the same shape as mine?

~~~

My chamomile tea has long gone cold, and I'm barely treading water. All morning, the paint department at Homer's has hummed nonstop with weekend warriors. At the moment, I've got a gallon of dove-gray interior latex thumping in the shaker for a pregnant lady painting a nursery, and a bearded guy waiting for my assistance with his stain choice.

Not the ideal moment for Cade to show up at my counter. And he doesn't look like he's here for paint. In fact, he wears a loaded expression I haven't got the bandwidth to read.

The moment our eyes meet, a bolt of anxiety surges from out of nowhere. My face goes hot and my pulse races. Really, a panic attack? *Now?* Oh, please, no. Thought I left those behind in California. *Fine. Bring it. Whatever.*

Cade tucks a hand in his front jeans pocket. "I, uh . . . you look . . ."

I look what, nervous? Awkward? Like my head's about to explode?

"Busy," he finishes. "I was just hoping to get a chance to, well, to apologize. But—"

I'm spinning out. The air in here is smothering. *Don't be a dork!* I shake my head vigorously and raise a hand. "Nope. I . . . you don't need to . . ." is all I can get out. My eyes dart to the bearded man with the stain question. Thankfully, he's occupied with reading a brochure.

A question descends from the ether, and I find my voice. "How did you know where to find me?"

"I mentor Arlo Marinovich," Cade says.

"Ohhh. Got it." I'm not sure what he means by mentoring, but it sounds pretty official. Which explains a lot. Gosh, it's hot in here. My neck prickles.

The pregnant DIY woman reappears, and I check the timer. "Just about done," I tell her. She nods and backs away but remains well within earshot of my conversation with Cade. Bearded guy hovers closer to my counter now, eyebrows raised as if to say, *Are you really gonna let that guy—fine specimen of a man though he is—cut in front of me?*

I can't breathe right. Too. Many. Eyes. Beads of perspiration spring from my forehead. I can tell I'm wearing a deer-in-headlights expression, but I can't seem to turn it off. So bright in here.

Escape! But to where? I remind myself to inhale through my nose and that the human body cannot sustain this kind of evil abduction by my nervous system forever. It *will* pass.

Better. I'll get through this.

"I'm sorry," Cade says, "it's obviously a bad time. You're totally busy. I can come back later." In contrast with that hummingbird playing the piccolo in my head, his tone is an oboe played adagio. Has he deduced I'm working to fend off a total meltdown? He turns to leave.

Mercifully, the shaker stops thudding. "Actually, Cade, could you . . . would you mind hanging on?" I manage to sound surprisingly coherent. "I mean, if you have a few minutes. I just need to—"

Cade holds up both hands. "No worries. I'll just circle back in a few." His gentle smile is very school counselor–like, to my thinking. He hangs a right and disappears down the main aisle.

Okay, I got this. I just need to take one thing at a time.

When Cade reappears ten minutes later, I'm swigging hard on my water bottle. It's been torturous and I'm jittery, but I think the episode has passed.

"Can we step outside?" I say. "I'm a little overheated."

Cade leads the way. With fresh air in reach, my confidence makes a reappearance. I might even be ready to act like a normal human being. "Hey Jan," I call to the front counter, "I'll just be . . ." I point outside and try to disregard the fact that she's glancing back and forth between me and Cade and grinning like a weirdo. And what's the meaning attached to that over-the-top wink, as if she's got a false eyelash stuck in her eye? Goofball.

On a cast-iron bench in the garden center, Cade and I turn to face one another. The half smile he offers activates a dimple in his cheek, which is surprisingly disarming. I also can't help noticing that his eyes are charmingly asymmetrical, and in them I detect unusual depth. Sincerity. Just right for a school counselor. Color? This one's easy. Crater Lake Blue. A color I just made up.

I study my hands, then inhale. "I'll go first, if you don't mind. I need to apologize. I shouldn't have responded so defensively the other day."

His eyebrows lift. "Understandable. I did kind of ambush you. And for that I'm really sorry. It wasn't planned. I just happened to notice you there and . . . well, I should have found a better approach."

"Maybe we could start fresh?"

"I'd like that," he says. His shoulders relax and he crosses his long legs at the ankles. He wears leather flip-flops, and his feet are tan. I stare too long at them.

"You mentioned that you mentor Arlo," I say. "What exactly does that mean? I've met him several times. He's quiet, but he seems like a pretty good kid. Considering . . ." I can't finish my thought when so far all I have is speculation about his family's situation.

"Yeah, it hasn't been easy for him. When I moved here a couple years ago, I . . ." Cade's voice trails off. He appears to abandon that thought and restart. "Well. I started looking for a way to get involved. I work in Portland—it's a three-days-on, six-days-off sort of thing. So when I'm here, I'm here with time on my hands."

"What do you do in Portland?"

"I'm an emergency medical pilot." Okay, so, not a counselor.

"Like in a helicopter?" *As in, the kind in which my dad spent his final moments?* I work to shove the image aside.

"Yep. Of course, there's more to life than my job . . ." He says this without pretension, as if he'd been late to the party on this discovery, and he assumes I'm not. "So when I heard about this program through the sheriff's office where they match a mentor with a child who has an incarcerated parent—well, I'd been dealing with some personal stuff, and it just really connected with me."

This hits like a punch to the gut. There it is, my suspicions confirmed. The envelope. The inky return-address stamp. *Strawberry Creek Correctional Facility*. Thank God I've been somewhat prepared for this. Which, I've got to say, is a pretty odd alignment of circumstances. Divine, even.

I have to clear emotion from my throat before speaking. "Sounds like a great program."

"It really is. It's all fairly structured. First you have to take a class, to get a better idea of the challenges these kids face. And they ask for a one-year commitment, that you'll spend a few hours every week with the child. The program's built on the idea that these kids need . . ." Cade hesitates, then adds, "consistency."

"I see." Well, this sure stings. Consistency is the one thing I can't offer Paige, and this guy knows it. No wonder he was concerned. "How did you get matched with Arlo?"

"His mom, Nina, applied for the program. It doesn't cost anything for the parent or guardian. You, uh, might be surprised how many kids are in this situation, even in a small town like this."

"Oh. That's super sad. I don't . . . I don't actually know any of the details. I mean, about why their father's in jail or for how long. I don't mean to pry. Maybe you're not at liberty to say."

Cade takes a deep breath, then slowly releases it. "Yeah, so Vic—that's their dad—was a recovering alcoholic. *Is* a recovering alcoholic. Apparently he'd gotten sober years ago, like before he got married and started a family. But for some reason—this was four or five years ago—he fell off the wagon. Within twenty-four hours he was behind bars. Left a bar drunk, got behind the wheel, crossed the freeway divide, and caused a head-on. Just like that, a woman was killed."

My body falls slack. Such needless tragedy. Everything turning on a dime. Lives hopping the tracks. "I can't even . . ."

"Yeah. It's pretty awful. Manslaughter. I'm not sure where things stand right now with his sentence, but he won't be out any day soon. You know, I'm pretty sure Nina applied for a mentor for Paige too. I think she's been on a waiting list for a long time."

"Oh. She hasn't mentioned that. Look, Cade, I think I understand why you questioned me like that."

"I believe you mean *interrogated*."

I let out a soft laugh. "Okay, yeah. Maybe a *little* harsh." I pinch a half inch of air between my fingers. "Honestly, Cade, I just fell into this friendship with Paige. I don't have any formal training. And you were right, I'm not in a position to make the same kind of commitment as you have. I admire what you're doing, don't get me wrong. Part of me wishes I could take on something like that with Paige." And in this moment, I realize how deeply I mean it. "But I . . ."

I gesture toward the entrance to Homer's. "This here is just a temp gig. My home, my life, my future, is in the Bay Area. Right now I'm a little . . ." Exactly how much should I reveal? "Let's just say I have some things to figure out."

Cade bobs his head slowly and a corner of his mouth tips up almost imperceptibly. It's a subtle change. Even at rest, his face wears a look of mild amusement, in a Ryan Gosling sort of way. Something that had been hard to pick up on while he was upbraiding me in Sweet Reads. "I get it," he says, his voice husky. "I have definitely been there."

Something tells me he has.

"But I'd never do anything to hurt Paige," I say. Who'm I trying to convince, me or him? "Somehow, meeting her felt . . ." I lift a shoulder. "It's hard to explain. It felt meant to be. Maybe I can't be a long-term mentor, but I hope to at least have a chance to boost her confidence, maybe awaken her creative side. You know, she's surprisingly deep and soulful."

He studies me for a length of time before finally blinking. *Intense.* "You seem like just the right person to do that."

"Oh? How do you mean?"

"You're an artist." He says this matter-of-factly, as if he knows something about me I'm not even sure I know about myself. My bewilderment must be easy to read. "I saw your drawings on Instagram," he explains. "On Sweet Reads? My buddy Ian tagged you in them."

"Oh, gotcha. I didn't realize that." Come to think of it, I haven't been on social media for a while.

"They're very good. I mean, I'm no expert, but *I* like them. You really captured the place."

"It's a great place."

"Agreed." Cade raps his fingers on the back of the bench and appears to consider me once again. "Seems like there's more to you than mixing paint."

Seems like there's more to you than I realized too.

"Anyway, I am sorry 'bout the other day." He sits up straight, so I do too.

"Me too. Apparently the poetry section brings out the worst in people. Who knew? Might want to tell your buddy he should post warning signs." I feel fresh wind in my rickety sails. Ready to go another round in the paint section.

Cade breaks into a full-on smile. "In that case, we should probably steer clear of the history section. World War II, Saddam Hussein, and all that." I laugh, maybe a little too hard. But at this point, laughter feels medicinal.

He stands, stretching to his full height, and offers a hand up. His touch is warm. A breeze tousles a lock of his hair. "Well, Audrey from the Bay Area. Guess I'd better let you get back to work."

Twenty-One

Daisy

"Well, Camille, care to chime in?" I hold the pewter-framed photo of my bosom friend under the bedroom lamp and again admire her classic beauty. Shining blond, goddess-like waves. Kind, knowing eyes. If only I could talk to her about this afternoon's tour of Whispering Pines.

"What should I do?" Ever the encourager, Camille would have known exactly the words I need to hear.

We must've been about twenty when this picture was taken. Just before she went off and made her mark. And what a glittering mark she made. Seems like some people are just destined for public adoration. Only a rare few know how to handle it, Camille being one. Lighting up the stage and screen, offering enjoyment to millions. Meanwhile, I stayed. Through those first anguishing years of marriage. The miscarriages. The money woes.

I can admit it now—at times, I'd been envious of my sparkly friend.

"Oh, Camille . . ." How she would've teased me for typing her name into the search bar of my cell phone recently. Googling her, as the kids say, curious to see what came up. Perhaps to make her real again. One thing's for sure, based on my findings: I'm not alone in grieving the loss of Camille Bettencourt.

But I *am* forever alone in my personal experience of her loss. Mourning a celebrity is nothing compared to the mourning of a friend you've only recently regained. I inhale deep, moving air into the place in my chest that aches with sorrow. "We had such great plans, didn't we?" I whisper.

When Camille decided it was time to hang up her acting career, she returned to her hometown, to Charity Falls, alongside her mega-movie-star husband, Nash. Such an unexpected blessing! Never did I dream she would circle back here or that we might have the chance to pick up where we left off decades earlier. To spend our later years getting into all sorts of harmless mischief.

As things turned out, that's all we were given. A chance.

Don't get me wrong, Lord. I'm grateful for it. There was the sailing trip out to Orcas Island off the Washington coast. That winter escape to their lovely vacation home in Palm Desert. And a wealth of sunny walks and book talks and good coffee and ridiculous laughter. A couple years of reconnection. Until . . .

Life changes on a dime, and no one knows this better than me.

I swallow a lump of emotion, grip the frame with both hands, and look straight into my friend's eyes. Knowing I wouldn't trade any of it. Especially the honor of comforting her through surgeries and the ravages of chemo. "Thank you," I say aloud—to whom, I'm not certain. I swipe at the tears I can no longer suppress.

The process of walking alongside a lifelong friend, of having a front-row seat to watch her cancer story unfold, was a lot of things. Bitter. Tender. Infuriating. And also, somehow, faith-affirming. But more than anything, it was an unforeseen privilege. Through Camille's honesty and grace and ridiculously tenacious hope, I gained so much. Not the least of which was the courage to ask for help when it's needed. In fact, I don't know that I would have had the boldness to reach out to Audrey had

I not known that it was just the kind of thing Camille would have advised.

Like it or not—and I don't like it one bit—the Lord brings people into our lives for seasons, not for forever. And the annoying thing about seasons is that they blow in and blow out on time-tables over which we have no say. Only he who is sovereign over the seasons can give us what we need to carry on. Just as, one day soon, I'll be called to carry on without Audrey.

I release a ragged sigh. Then I paste on a smile for my friend, as if I need to reassure her I'm okay. "Darn it, I miss you." *Silly goose. One day in the company of older folks and you're losing it, talking to photographs.* No, really I'm just chatting with a dear friend in the only way possible. Besides, as Dean used to like to say, "We *is* old folks." Yep. Every birthday seems ominous, but once it arrives and I try it on for size, I'd never choose to go back. I have to believe I'll feel the same way about seventy-seven, which isn't too far off.

Wisdom trumps collagen, in my book.

No, getting old is not a curse. But being lonely would be.

And after today, I have to acknowledge that Whispering Pines has more to recommend it than I realized. Both apartments we toured have their merits. The one I keep ruminating over juts out from the corner of the complex at an angle, making it feel less cookie-cutter. In fact, it has a small, sunny dining nook that bays out into the courtyard, with views all the way to Mt. Jefferson. We wouldn't have a stove, only a kitchenette, at least not while Dean is . . .

It's okay. I need to learn to think in these terms. *Not while Dean is with me.*

But, as Audrey has pointed out, air fryers are all the rage. So there's that. I'd have to move fast, though. It's by far the most de-sirable unit in the memory-care section. Later on, who knows. I'll move into a small, fully functional apartment somewhere, I guess.

After today I'm more confident that Dean will adjust. In fact, possibly more quickly than me. Lately, as long as I'm not long out of his sight, he seldom gets agitated. Better to move him now than later, I've been advised. And, oh, to have help with his bathing and whatnot! As Dean's doctor says, he's only going to need more caregiving—never less.

But we only have to worry about *today* today. And remembering the way Dean's eyes lit up when he spotted the pool table, how he hovered over those men playing cards, a tiny seed of hope germinates. He always *has* been more outgoing than me. And what a kick to meet up with Margie and get an unexpected bonus tour of her lovely independent-living unit. She's made her space quite homey, with a navy-and-terra-cotta color scheme. I'll ask her to help me with ours.

Yes, it saddened me to observe some of those dear residents who are further down the dementia road. But it also helped me feel less isolated. Dean and I are on a trying journey, one that will inevitably get even harder. But it's well traveled.

With a corner of my blouse, I dust the small picture frame. "I'll be okay, won't I?" Camille's soft expression hides a strength I know intimately. Strength that bolsters me. "In other news, you'll be happy to know that Nash is doing better. Ha! Maybe you already do. His eyes are still tragic—Lord, he loved you! And overall, he's still drooping from head to toe. But at least he's getting out more. Don't you worry. I'm keeping an eye on him, just like I promised."

I hear a car in the driveway. That'll be Audrey, and she'll have her arms full with the groceries she insisted on picking up on her way home from work. How did I ever manage before Danny's dear angel daughter arrived? And how did she coerce me into spending tomorrow together in the kitchen? Well, if she wants all the so-called secrets to my chili, she'll get 'em alright. Ha.

With a sigh I return Camille's picture to the grouping on my tall dresser, alongside my parents, my sweet baby sister, Sandra, and Danny. "Somehow we're *all* going to be okay," I whisper. "Aren't we, pal?"

———~———

Audrey

Something Cade said today piqued my curiosity. So after work I flop on the guest bed's well-worn quilt straightaway and open my phone. Sure enough, I run into a load of notifications on Instagram. I know it's disproportionate to reality, but this kind of digital pileup makes me feel crazy, like I'm running miles behind in life.

Anyway, my profile has indeed been tagged by Sweet Reads, and not just in one post but a series. Scrolling through comments—things like "Amazing!" and "This is fire!" not to mention countless heart-eyed and starry-eyed emojis—I feel my face warm. Those drawings were *not* my best work! More like warm-up exercises. Looking at them now, I can see things I'd do differently.

Instagrammers are just generous with their likes, that's all.

Let it go. I don't even know any of these people who follow Sweet Reads' account. Except for Cade, of course, and I wouldn't exactly say I know him either. We're what? At best, acquaintances. Once again my thoughts loop back to his lake-blue eyes. That scrutinizing gaze. My vanity wants to believe he was intrigued by me. Yeah, sure, that was it . . . *Ooh, Audrey Needham, mysterious ginger, freckled fly-by-night!* More likely, he was still weighing whether my friendship with Paige is in her best interest.

Even more likely, the man is married. Also, he's an Oregonian. I'm a Californian. Geographics set in cement.

Despite the self-doubts these sketches stir in me, they also bring to mind the freedom—and, yes, the joy—I experienced on my first visit to Sweet Reads, drawing just because. Just because I felt like it. Just because I was inspired. And just because . . . *Say it, Audrey. Just because you* are *an artist.* Why is this so hard to own? Why do I feel the need to justify my natural creative bent? I didn't even choose it. It's one of untold thousands of genes God saw fit to deposit in me by way of my father's DNA. Who am I to dis God's creative choices?

On a whim, I send Tawny a link to the Sweet Reads posts. Partly because I know I can count on her for an "attagirl." And partly because I want to get her super pumped for her upcoming visit to Charity Falls. I have a feeling she'll quite agree on the charm my local tea-and-books niche holds. In fact, suddenly I can't wait to show her all the sights. As if Charity Falls is somehow mine to share.

Moving on to other notifications, I smile at a friend request from Silas. Mm, yeah, I'll just defer that decision to another day. As usual there's a funny meme from Ava, along with a message reminding me about her baby shower. Note to self: shop.

I've also got three private message requests. Yick. Probably trolls. But, no . . . these profiles appear to belong to normal human beings. And—you have got to be kidding me—two are inquiries about where they can purchase my artwork. I let out a loud, scoffing "Ha!" just as Daisy passes my open door carrying a laundry basket. She raises her eyebrows. I gesture to my phone and she smiles.

These people are asking if I have a website or an Etsy. It's seriously insane. I've never once entertained the idea of selling my quote-unquote "art."

The third message is even more of a head-scratcher. A woman opening a new bed-and-breakfast in a nearby town wants to know if I take commissions. Would I be interested in sketching her building for promotional use? Commission work—me? Ohh, and it's such a darling old Victorian. What in the . . . ? All this from a few impromptu sketches? I don't even begin to know how to respond.

Obviously, this one's a no too, right? If so, what's the story with this happy little fairy sprite, the one doing pirouettes inside my abdomen? I mean, I have to admit, the idea sounds fun. No doubt I'll simply accept the compliment and move on. Then again, no need to respond right away.

Besides, *oof*, I'm due to pick up Paige in . . . I check my Fitbit. Ten minutes. And I know just where I want to take her today.

Twenty-Two

As I enter the greige building where Paige is enrolled in a series of day camps, I tap off my earbuds. Paige's leader spots me right away and breaks into a shiny grin. "Hi, Audrey!" Ack, what's her name again? Oh yes, *Miss Brittany*. Perhaps Miss Brittany is super friendly to everyone, but I swear she's been making a point to connect with me. "Paige is outside on the playground," she says. "Back this way."

For so late in the day, the young teacher sure is a chatty and energetic thing. She fusses with her messy bun while leading me down a corridor of color-blocked floor tiles. "Listening to anything good?"

"Huh? Oh, just a novel. And, I'm not sure. It's a little more intense than I'm feeling right now. I probably need to switch to a beach read. But once I start a book, I feel obligated."

Brittany laughs. "Same." She appears to be about my age. Upbeat but down to earth. Under other circumstances, I'd say she has friend potential.

It turns out the city's parks-and-rec department operates under a generous sliding scale. I've caught wind that the lion's share of Paige's tuition has been covered by scholarships. We pass the large, glass-enclosed central room, which today is full of kids wearing loose-fitting gis, practicing karate kicks.

Afternoon light pools around Miss Brittany and me as we pause inside the back door watching a boy scale the play structure. It's a long moment before I spot Paige sitting on a swing. Alone. "You know," Brittany says, "Paige talks about you nonstop. She's a lucky girl to have you in her life." Brittany gives me a meaningful look that tells me Paige's family dynamic is common knowledge here. "It's nice that you can pick her up on the days her mom can't."

"Maybe I'm the lucky one," I say, and it becomes true. A warmth spreads through my chest. Between helping Daisy and Dean, working part-time, and spending more and more time with Paige, my days are never boring. It's nothing flashy, but it feels worthwhile. Which is all well and good for me, except that Paige has no idea it's temporary.

Guilt twists my insides. Cade's apology may have erased the tension between him and me. But it hasn't erased the truth of his original words. Words that still shadow me. *She doesn't need someone who's here today and gone tomorrow . . .*

How do I tell a ten-year-old girl whose life has been anything but secure that everything about my life right now is temporary—including her? I can't keep putting it off.

With a loud clack, Brittany shoulders the heavy-duty door open and kicks a wedge of wood in place to hold it. The smell of sun-baked bark chips wafts inside. She shouts for Paige's attention before turning to me. "Hey, if you're interested, there's a spot open in my book club. First Wednesday night of each month. Disclaimer—we don't exactly take things super seriously. More like, it's an excuse to chat over a glass of wine."

And there it is, an overture of friendship. The first of its kind in a long time. One I'll have to reject. I brush off a twinge of disappointment. Fortunately, before I open my mouth to offer an explanation about my temporary status in Charity Falls, I think better of it. Wouldn't want to spill the news to Paige's teacher before I've told her directly. Instead, I brighten my expression. "Wow, thanks," I say. "I'll keep it in mind."

———〰———

Charity Falls Community Art Center occupies prime real estate near the center of town. That fact, along with its handsome brick-red Western facade, seems to speak volumes about how this thumb-sized town prioritizes the arts. In fact, there's even a small theater next door in what appears to be a historic church building.

I park along the street. "Have you been here before?" I ask Paige.

"Yeah, one time. On a field trip. I saw a guy making a mug. He gave all of us a little piece of clay to take home. What are we doing here?"

"Oh, a potter! That's pretty cool. Did you make something out of your clay?"

Paige huffs. "I made a horse, but it didn't look like a horse. Arlo said it looked like a hippo."

Together we walk a meandering pebbled path where bees hover around fragrant, fully blooming lavender and golden coreopsis. "So then, you like horses?"

"I don't know if I like them. I've never ridden one. Well, with my class, we went to the pumpkin patch this one time. I got to ride in a cart thing, and it had two white horses pulling it. That's all. But Arlo has."

"Arlo rides horses?"

"Yeah, sometimes. With Cade. He has a huge ranch, I guess. Can we get ice cream later?"

I hold the knotty-pine entrance door open for Paige. Why has it never occurred to me that she might be a rich source of info about Arlo's charmingly dimpled, do-gooding mentor? Not that I plan to exploit it. Nor, for that matter, am I all that interested. Just curious, that's all. For some reason, he's a bit of an enigma. "So Cade has a huge ranch?"

"Mm-hmm. Ginormous." She rolls her eyes dramatically. "Or maybe it's his dad's. Yeah, his dad has a ranch." Interesting. So Cade's a horse guy.

Inside the art center, a colorful lobby welcomes us. Paintings line the walls. Most of them appear to be of the same meadow, but from different angles. A flyer announces an upcoming plein air workshop. "Oh, look, Paige. These are all plein air paintings—"

"What are we gonna do here?" She slumps her shoulders for effect.

"I thought we'd explore. You're my exploring buddy, right? Let's see what all's here."

"I know what's here. It's a bunch of pictures and stuff, and a guy who makes mugs."

A listing on the wall reveals that quite a number of local artists have galleries or working studios on each floor, including a ceramicist who must be the one Paige visited. I scan for the one name I'm interested to find. Yep, there it is. *Cara Murray*. Second floor. "Let's start upstairs."

In a small corner room on level two, I turn in a slow circle, gawking. Canvas after canvas is rendered in the same bold, color-saturated, textural style. "Gah! Look, Paige! Aren't these incredible?" Most are of horses, although several feature dogs—the same black border collie, obviously painted with affection. I'm guessing it belongs to the artist. Also, to my amusement, there's a portrait of a white pig against a deep russet background. All bear the same signature style as the giclée print for sale over at High Desert Home & Design. This itty-bitty gallery doesn't do them justice by any means. But still. I'm infatuated.

"Can I help you ladies?" The woman who enters wears her long white hair thick and straight, with blunt-cut bangs. Her tan skin is leathered in a healthy, outdoorsy way.

"Are you the artist?"

Her smile is warm. "I'm Cara Murray." In contrast to her bold paintings, Cara dresses in flowy, neutral layers.

"I'm so—we're so excited to meet you," I say, offering my hand. The artist graciously shakes Paige's hand as well and asks her name. "I'm a new fan," I say. "I ran into one of your prints in town recently. I was told I might find the original on display here, but I don't see it. It's of two horses, just their faces and necks. The mare is amber with a long white blaze. Her mane is light, flaxen really. And I believe her foal is white. Maybe it sold?"

"Oh, that sounds like *Bright Hope*. Out here." Cara guides us back out to the upstairs lobby. And there it hangs. I cock my head and enjoy the flood of emotions it calls forth. "The name fits," I say. "It absolutely glows with hope."

"Thank you. There's a story there. The mare, her name is Henna, came out of a terribly neglectful situation. She's a lucky girl just to be alive. Literally would've starved to death if she hadn't been rescued. A friend of mine took her in and nursed her back to health. Believe me, it was touch and go. At first, we didn't think she'd make it, let alone carry her foal to term. But she did." Cara turns her gaze on the painting. "It's amazing what we can overcome, given the chance. And love, of course."

Feelings well up, and I make the mistake of trying to speak. "The backlight . . ." My voice breaks. I blink back the moisture in my eyes and drape my arm around Paige's shoulder. *Pull yourself together, Audrey.* "How do you describe your style?"

"I like to say it flows between abstract and representational. I'm inspired by nature. Animals especially. My hope is that my work helps draw hearts to nature and to interconnectedness with one another. You'll notice I prefer to keep the background plain. Uncluttered. In our day and age, we have enough trouble avoiding distraction. I try to offer something simple and beautiful, something profound to focus on."

The artist crouches to Paige's level. "Do you like to paint?" A spark lights in Paige's eyes, then fades just as quickly. Cara switches to a sing-song voice. "Because I just happen to be teaching kids' classes this summer!"

"I'm bad at art," Paige says, and inwardly I cringe. Haven't any of my efforts to convince her otherwise gotten through? And yet, I'm beginning to see her tendency toward self-criticism differently. It may be more of a guard-your-heart diversion tactic. And maybe I, of all people, should understand. It's so much easier to spot the mask someone else is wearing than your own.

Once Paige is buckled in the back seat, I hand her the brochure about Cara Murray's art classes for children. "Promise you'll talk to your mom about this?" The brochure mentions a limited number of scholarships for families with financial need. I know from my own past that you have to move fast on those, and it's usually worth a shot.

"You talk to her," Paige says, shoving the brochure back into my hand. I'll take this to mean that she does want to take the class. Also, it represents a vote of confidence. This ten-year-old views me as her advocate, and that's no small honor.

"Okay, I'll talk to her. Now, think you could help me with a kind of tough decision?" I watch Paige's expression in the rearview mirror. She raises an eyebrow. "Should we get ice cream, or would you prefer I take you straight home?"

She really has the sweetest giggle. "Ice cream!"

"Ice cream it is!" I'm feigning enthusiasm. Because afterward, she and I need to have a hard conversation.

So this is it? This is your great plan? Buy her an ice cream. And then break her heart?

152

Twenty-Three

A few days later I wake up agitated from a menacing dream I can't remember and probably wouldn't want to. It's still dark, but my mind thinks it's go time. Solve-all-my-problems-at-once time.

I'm surprised to spy Daisy reclined among the living room shadows. Her eyes are closed. Did she sleep here all night? Before I can sneak back the way I came, she opens her eyes. "Don't let me wake you," I say softly.

"You're not, honey. I'm just enjoying the stillness." She waves me over and reaches to switch on the lamp.

"Oh, don't do that on my account," I say. I'm more than content to curl up in the moss-green chair I've started to think of as my morning chair and wait for daylight.

She smiles. "Elisabeth Elliot believed we should talk to God before we start talking to anyone else. It's not easy to be still. But I find it's worth the effort to try."

"You mean, to pray?"

"Mm-hmm. Well, yes and no." She closes her eyes again and chuckles faintly. "I'm trying to learn to shut up for a change. Listening is so much harder."

Listening? Leaning my head back, I close my lids. How hard can it be? Although . . . this kink in the right side of my neck is distracting. I roll my shoulder twice.

Click, click, click. For the first time, I notice the antique mantel clock's mournful rhythm. Which is fitting. There's been a great deal of mourning in this house.

With the house so hushed, I'm aware of the occasional hum of a passing car. And a soft whooshing overhead. That'll be the air purifier. For sure, I'm relaxed. My pulse is measured. But what exactly am I listening for? Some people claim to have heard the voice of God. Does Daisy?

Could it ever be possible for me? Can I master this?

Fail. You're thinking, which means you're not listening. I curl my body in the opposite direction, but there's that twinge in my neck again. And a rush of uninvited thoughts. Within moments, I've stressed about how I'll entertain Tawny when she comes this weekend—lake or river or both?—and berated myself for once again chickening out on talking to Paige about my leaving. (But what was I to do? She was in such a silly mood! I didn't want to wreck our time together). Furthermore, how can I expect to keep my foot in the door at DeSoto if I keep forgetting to check in with Joshua? And by the way, according to my bank balance, I am in fact three digits away from street-urchin status.

What am I doing just sitting here? These things aren't going to take care of themselves!

Sheesh. *Fine. I surrender. Help.* I know I can't be trusted not to muck up my life without seeking a greater source of wisdom.

Get up, make tea, and save the world, you bum!

This isn't working. At all.

Stay. Now that voice wasn't mine.

He makes me lie down in green pastures.

Okay, then. I'll stay. Not because I have to. Because I'm meant to.

Being, not doing. Trusting, not shoulding. Resting, not reproving.

Easier said than done, of course.

I'm not sure how much time passes before I slowly open my eyes. Against the tender twilight, the mountains stand in silhouette. And although the old farmhouse across the street still languishes among the wild grasses, she wears a surprisingly soft countenance. Like a waking girl in a worn cotton chemise, with tousled hair. Part woman, part child. She may be still, but I see now that she's not without spirit. More like, lying fallow. The slow burn of anger I'm accustomed to feeling when I consider the inn doesn't come. Instead I feel a sense of camaraderie. And compassion. All good hostesses need a break after all.

For sure, though, the inn is an object of neglect. Why does this get to me? Maybe because she's not doing what she was created to do, offer hospitality. And maybe I can relate. Am I, too, an object of neglect? If so, it's no one's fault but my own. Am I doing the things I was created for? *If not, forgive me, Lord. Sometimes I think I catch a glimpse of who you made me to be. It comes to me in waves like the tide and then—whoosh—it's swallowed up again by the insatiable depths.*

When Mom and Jeffrey informed me they were pulling up stakes and moving to Arizona, she explained that she'd discovered the place where her great passion meets the world's deep hunger. Or something similar. I haven't thought about life in those terms in, well, ever. Haven't paused long enough to think about my maker, about how he wired me to function. I've never shared this with anyone, even Tawny, but when my job at DeSoto dissolved, I felt . . . relieved. Like I'd stripped off an outfit that, although fashionable, pinched in all the wrong places.

What would it feel like to be moved by passion rather than fueled by adrenaline and affirmation?

As the sky brightens, everything becomes suffused in sheer white light. A thumb-stroke of peach appears, and just like that the countryside swells with life. Birds materialize out of nowhere by the dozens. Red robins and black-capped juncos hop around the lawn. A northern flicker robed in speckled fur clings effortlessly by a tree hollow. Feeding babies? Stunning.

A woman in running togs and a wide yellow headband runs by. As if it's just another morning, and there aren't tiny miracles occurring all around her.

Stretched out in the bay window, Myrtle Rose watches too. One eyelid's open to half-mast, and her bony tail twitches.

And I sense a rhythm. A sacred song I'm meant to know. A way of being, under the sun.

He refreshes my soul.

Can I learn to be still and know? Can I even learn to be still?

At a soft tapping on my shoulder, I startle. With a tiny smile, Daisy offers her cute little elfin-sized bird binoculars. Like a benediction. What just happened? Have I just stumbled into some rite of initiation?

Should I order a velour robe?

Twenty-Four

"Hey, Audrey. 'Sup?" Silas peers into my piled-high shopping cart. "Looks like you two ladies are up to something major."

"Hey, Silas," I say. "This is my good friend Tawny. Yep. We're painting out a *lot* of knotty pine paneling in my aunt's living room."

"Ah. That explains the stain-blocking primer."

I set two cans of it on the paint counter and lay a Sherwin Williams color card on top. "Would you mind tinting it to this?" I point to the color code.

"Sure thing. Good thinking too. A lot of people don't bother to tint the primer. But you'll get more even color." He turns to Tawny conspiratorially and points his thumb at me. "I gotta keep my eye on this one. She's smarter than she looks." I've grown used to Silas's goofing, but *ugh*. Part of me wishes we'd chucked my employee discount and gone to Home Depot.

Silas pushes his wire-rim glasses higher on his nose. "Alabaster, huh? I've overheard you recommending this shade to customers."

"It's really the perfect neutral. A warm white, but it never pulls yellow. Simple and restful."

"Huh. Good to know. Gonna prime all the knots first?" He's testing me.

157

I grimace. "Yeah, they're really dark." I've been trying to maintain an undaunted attitude, but the true scope of this job is ominous. "It'll be a lot of work. But at least the payoff will be huge."

"V-groove?" Silas enters the formula code and I watch a thin line of color stream into the first gallon of primer. I've got to hand it to him. He's a much better multitasker than me. I wouldn't dare talk to a customer while mixing color.

"Yep."

"Need to rent a sprayer?"

"Honestly, I've never used one, and I don't think I want to practice on my aunt's house."

"Roller or brush?"

"I'm thinking both."

Silas nods and starts the mixer. *Ka-thud. Ka-thud.* "Need brushes?"

"Nope."

"Drop cloth?"

"Oh. Thank you, yes." I turn to Tawny. "Be right back." I head down aisle two, conscious that I've just left my friend, my *person*, alone with Silas. As expected, when I return Tawny's holding her own. Something about her mere physical presence, her vibe, makes the world around her spin a little more harmoniously. She brings out the best in people.

Unlike my vibe, apparently. Silas turns to me, smirking. "So, you brought a crew all the way from California to do your dirty work. Some friend you are." He shakes his head in mock judgment. Then, "Nah, I'm just messin' with ya."

"Hey now!" See? I can be lighthearted too. "We've got some other things planned, right Tawny?" We do hope to cram a lot into her five-day visit. But there's no point sharing our extensive list of possible adventures with Silas. He'd just feel excluded.

"Cool. How can I help?" Uh-oh, now he's being direct. "With

your painting project, I mean. Sounds like a lot. Need some dudes to at least help move stuff out of the way?"

"Oh, I think we're good," I say. "Thanks, though." Why is Tawny spearing me with a look? Okay, in truth, I haven't given a single thought to how we'll move the heavy furnishings. Some of it will need to live in the carport for a few days. But we wouldn't want Silas underfoot. Would we?

"If you say so. Geez. I try to do something nice for a change and she shuts me down." He raises his voice and directs it toward the checkout counter. "You hearing this, Jan?"

Jan grins. Later, while she's ringing up our purchases, Jan checks to make sure Silas is out of earshot. "He's harmless, you know. Believe it or not, he's actually a terrific helper."

Tawny responds before I can. "Well, Audrey's only letting *me* help because I insisted. She's kind of independent like that. Sort of a one-woman show."

Ouch. Harsh.

But here's another thing about my friend. She's quick to apologize. "Sorry," Tawny says, as we load items into the back seat, "I shouldn't have said that back there. And there's nothing wrong with saying no to the guy. That was your call to make."

Trouble is, she was spot-on. "Don't even apologize. You were right. I'm not good at accepting help." And because of this particular character flaw, I've subjected Tawny and Daisy to a heavier workload. This *is* an enormous project, even with the three of us. One we've given ourselves only two days to complete, in order to minimize disruption to Uncle Dean's world. Tomorrow, Rotary Rob will take Dean fishing. And on the following day, we're counting on Dean's willingness to hang out at the adult day-care place.

"You know that I'm still down for this, right?" she says. "You and me, we've always dreamed of tackling a fixer-upper together. Let's think of this as a warm-up. Move over, Joanna Gaines!"

There's never any falseness about Tawny. If she says she's down, she's down. Besides, she's been invested in the progress of Daisy and Dean's place since day one. I texted her the photos of the house as it was when I arrived. Lackluster fence. Overgrown flower beds. Weeds growing up through the driveway. She's a hundred percent into this.

In the passenger seat, Tawny's quiet, staring out the window. "Whoa! Deer alert! There must be—" She points and counts. "There's like ten deer in that field!" I smile. Then she turns to me. "Actually, do you mind if I comment on the Silas thing?"

"Sure."

"I know you're committed to fencing out all unnecessary personal entanglements. But for the record, that checker . . . the one with the big, hair-sprayed bangs . . ."

"Jan?"

"Yeah. Jan is probably right. I think it's safe to assume he's fully aware of your boundaries. Just FYI. As an objective observer."

"Thanks. I receive that." As we pull into the driveway, Harriet's tires crunch across the fresh coat of gravel. When the load was delivered earlier this week, I invited Dean to supervise me while I spread it. Not only did he display surprising enthusiasm, he insisted on helping. The house gleams now, trimmed in neat-as-a-pin flower beds and surrounded by bright-white picket fencing. Daisy's freshly planted flowerpots lend happy spots of color to the porch.

All this progress on the place keeps propagating new motivation within me. Fact is, I've already gone well beyond what Daisy asked me here to do. In fact, most of this window dressing was my idea. We knocked out most of the sorting and packing and donating early on. If my job is already done here, why am I so compelled to keep at it? Case in point—that drab-blue front door. "Call me crazy, Tawny. But I might just repaint the front door too." She cocks her head and scrutinizes it, then nods in agreement. I unbuckle my seatbelt. "Help me think of a color?"

Is it possible I've taken this next-right-thing concept too far?

Twenty-Five

"Still three more miles to the turnoff," Tawny says, monitoring the map on my phone. "And this just in. You have a new text from Joshua." She strips off her sweater. "Woo, it's heating up! Mind if I get the AC going?"

"Here, I'll get it." I switch on the cooling system. "Paige, you doing okay back there?"

"I'm fine!"

"Joshua, huh?" I say, struck by a bracing mixture of surprise and annoyance, way heavier on the annoyance factor. After only five weeks in Charity Falls, I'm puzzled that this feels so much like a dispatch from a former life. I shouldn't have to remind myself that receiving an update from DeSoto is not an interruption. Because it isn't. This—what I'm doing now, sailing up a highway bound for even higher elevations and deeper forests—*this* is an anomaly.

What would be wrong would be for me to continue neglecting my *actual* life indefinitely. It's time I start getting more practical about things. Grateful as I am for the provision my temp job at Homer's has provided, I need real work. The kind that pays the rent.

Still, if I allow it to register, sometimes when I imagine going back to my old environment, to my old bedroom with its tiny window on the world and its musty-smelling closet, my passageways

161

constrict. I suppose this is the natural response for anyone facing the dwindling days of a long vacation. And oddly, my time here has felt unexpectedly vacation-like.

But also like something more. Maybe for thirteen years, I've been needing closure.

Still, I'm on my way to the lake with Tawny and Paige, so a word from my old coworker feels like ice-cold water on this placid summer day. Why do I feel like I just got busted playing hooky? "Can you read it to me?"

"Sure."

Dude, Steffen Beckenbauer just called for you. Asked for your contact info so I gave him your email. Should I give him your cell? Also, WHY is Steffen Beckenbauer calling for you??? Spill!

I think I just had a series of mini strokes. *Steffen Beckenbauer?* My fingers feel shaky on the steering wheel.

Tawny shrugs. "Who the heck is Steffen Beckenbauer?"

"I . . . I . . ."

"Are you okay? Who is this guy?"

For a moment I'm stunned silent. "Uh, he's only the founding partner in Beckenbauer-Vandersteen, one of the most important architectural firms *in the country*. No, make that internationally. I don't get it. Why would he be calling for me?"

"Whoa. Want me to text Joshua back?"

"Absolutely. Tell him to pass along my number." I adopt a breezy tone, which belies the fact that my internal organs have conspired to stage a flash mob in my belly. This feels like a big deal. When we get to the lake, I'll check my email.

But when we park next to Fawn Lake, an area dense with pine and fir, I can't get a decent signal. Not even one bar. Whatever it is will have to wait. Besides, already Paige is out of the car, slinging her bright-orange beach towel over her shoulder and carrying the Styrofoam pool noodle I just bought her at Dollar General.

"C'mon!" she yells. I'm okay. I can be present. This event gets top billing today.

A light wind laps at our tattered quilt as I shake it out and then lower it to the sand. Paige has chosen a spot for our picnic only a few yards from where the lake laps at the shore. Now she bounces with anticipation, smoothing a corner of the quilt. When she drops to her soft brown knees, all that dark mermaid hair spills forward. Her round belly protrudes unapologetically from a large, diamond-shaped cutout on the front of her one-piece. Adorable. Was I really ever that free and unselfconscious? I hardly remember.

This place is a locals' spot, its location a carefully guarded secret. Against a grand backdrop of soaring trees and open skies, the scattering of lake-goers and brightly colored floaties look minuscule and insignificant, like so many rainbow sprinkles. At the water's edge, two boys dig a trough in the silky brown sand with toy shovels. Out in the middle of the green, finger-shaped lake, a downed tree acts as nature's malt shop for the four teen girls draped over it, exchanging secrets. Paige watches them with interest. "Can I go in?"

I stop unpacking the oversized beach tote I borrowed from Daisy and consider the terrain. The reason this lake is so popular with families is because it's so shallow. Many times I was one of the girls on the log. Paige's mom said she's on her way to becoming a strong swimmer. "Sure," I say. "Of course. Just stay where I can see you, okay?"

I shield my eyes from the sun and watch her take a tentative step in. Ankle deep, she squeals, then giggles. "Cold! Come in, Audrey!"

One of the little boys, a towheaded cutie half Paige's size, scolds her. "It's not cold!"

I turn to Tawny, but she's lying in repose in her fern-green bikini with her face to the sun. Guess I'm on my own here. The lake water does feel frigid, but in the best sort of way and only for seconds. The boy's right. I've forgotten how temperate this water is. Just as I've forgotten the weird sensation of sinking your toes into the muddy bottom of a deep-forest lake. I wade in as far as my shins, sizing up the depth for Paige's sake.

"Ew. It's squishy, huh?" she says.

"Be careful, hon. See how it drops off a little right there?" There's a visible ledge ahead, where the shallows drop several feet. We stand together for a comfortable moment, soaking in the day's rising heat. I slide off the scrunchie from my wrist and twist my hair up off my shoulders, high and sloppy. Lake hair, don't care. "Okay, so this is probably far enough. You'll stay in this area, right?" I sweep my arm through the air to indicate a short stretch of beach between two scrubby manzanita bushes. "Like from this bush to that one."

"Yeah. Okay. I can swim, you know."

"I know. Hey, want to help me set out our picnic? I'll race you."

In five or six strides, we're back on our quilt. I uncover a plastic dish of deviled eggs while Paige tears into one filled with little, crustless sandwich quarters. Kid-friendly, because that great-aunt of mine knows her stuff. Paige passes out juice boxes, but not in a way that will ever earn her a waitress job at Kokkari Estiatorio on the Embarcadero back home. She bonks Tawny on the arm with it. "Tawny, get up! Here's your drink! Here's your sandwich!"

"I'm up, I'm up!"

The three of us sit around grinning at one another. "You guys are pretty great company," I say. "You know that?"

Paige grins with her mouth full. She licks mayonnaise off her fingers like we're in some kind of race to see who can finish first. "I'm going in."

Tawny and I recline on our elbows and watch her wade out. "Oh man," Tawny says. "This is just what I needed."

"What, actual sand in your sandwich?"

"Ha. Yeah, that was pretty gritty. No, it's just so restful here."
She reaches for the paperback she brought along.

"Mmm. Agree." A warm breeze caresses my face, and I breathe
deep of all things earthy and verdant. Suddenly Paige is waving
wildly, but not at us. Evidently she knows someone behind us.

Nobody I recognize. At least not at first. Just a family back there
enjoying the pine-shaded picnic area. There's a pretty brunette in
an electric-pink ball cap, who appears to be wearing an infant in a
sling. Sitting next to her is a small blond child barely tall enough to
see over the picnic table. And a man tending the barbecue . . . who
definitely just saluted me with his spatula. I wave back, instantly
aware of the tiny leak that just sprung in my bubble of tranquility.

"Okay, don't look now, Tawny, but the guy I told you about?
He's at three o'clock."

"The mentor guy?"

"Yup. The very same."

Tawny casts a furtive glance over her shoulder. "Huh. So he's a
family man." She sounds disappointed, confirming my suspicions.
Once again she's been fabricating hope for my romantic life where
there is none. Am *I* disappointed? I shouldn't be. I'm sure my sudden lack of peace has more to do with feeling like an amoeba on
a slide under a microscope. Cade is the expert mentor, after all.
And here I am with Paige, right smack in his field of view.

But of course this is silly. I'm not doing anything untoward.
Also, he and I are on solid footing now. Will he think me unfriendly
if I don't go over and say hello? Nah. I'm too relaxed, and the
way we're positioned between them and the lake, I'm guessing
it'll happen organically.

Besides, I haven't had a minute to process the text from Joshua.
Good distraction.

A thought bursts through my lips without preamble. "What if
this is about a job?" By now, news must have leaked that Pilar's
business is on hiatus.

Tawny doesn't bother turning from her reading. "What if what is about a job?"

"The Beckenbauer thing. I just can't imagine why he'd contact me."

"Well, if it is, you'll nail it."

"You're ridiculous. How can you say that? Tawny, his firm has taken the lead on urban renewal projects all along the San Francisco waterfront. Not to mention in New York, Chicago, Stockholm . . . probably, I don't know, Abu Dhabi!"

She angles a look at me and I know I'm in for some snark. "I would just lead with the fact that you put your laundry away on the same day you wash it. That alone separates you from the rest of us mortals."

"Oh ha." I nestle my rear into a more comfy position. "What about you? Have you absolutely decided on Miller Medical?"

After all these years, I'm so used to Tawny's death glare, it's lost its power to shame me. "You know I have."

Repeat after me, Audrey: I won't bring up Tawny's job situation again. I won't bring up Tawny's job situation again. There's nothing more left unsaid anyway. In spite of her freshly minted master's in psychology with a specialization in social personality psychology, she has chosen to stay in Davis and help out in her parents' medical equipment business. With the exception of that college mission trip to Peru—an opportunity I turned down in my haste to snag an internship—the woman has remained in the same town all her life.

Someday, Tawny is sure to be sainted.

Paige, I notice, hasn't shown any interest in swimming or her pool noodle. In fact, I detect a potential earth science nerd in her, the way she plods contentedly through the muddy water, poking a long stick at the lake bottom. "See any fish?" I call.

"No. Just weird stuff. Ew, look, Audrey!" She lifts the stick. Oh, yum. Gooey sludge.

Truth is, I brought a book too. But I keep imagining Cade's eyes boring into my back, and I wouldn't want him to think I'm giving Paige anything less than my full attention. Which makes me envy Tawny over there, with her nose in a historic romance. I really shouldn't disturb her.

I manage to hold out for a beat or two before asking, "Any news from your folks? Will I see your mom at Ava's shower?"

"They're fine. Pretty much the same. And yes, are you kidding? She wouldn't miss it. She's making the cake."

"I haven't seen her in too long." Apart from my family, Tawny's parents, Carl and Janice Miller, are the two adults I've known longest in my life. They're good, hardworking people, and it's one of the greatest unfairnesses in the universe that Carl is dealing with Parkinson's disease. Now that his symptoms have taken a hard turn, Tawny's chosen to step in full-time and help maintain the status quo at the store. They're a tight family. She's the obvious choice. I get it.

But. That doesn't alter the fact that my brilliant friend could accomplish so much if she weren't so uber laid back. She could seriously be the next Brené Brown. Ugh. Facepalm to my *soul*. What am I thinking? She's right where she's meant to be.

"You promise you'll look into that PhD program though?" I say, against my better judgment. *You're doing it again.*

"Already promised."

True, she's still young. If she's not, *I'm* not. Here's something I wouldn't dream of saying aloud. Part of my concern is that, even though things didn't work out with her engagement, next time it *will* be the right guy. She'll get married. Start having little Tawnys and Timmys. And never get around to fulfilling her goals. *Oh, stop it.* Why must I project my unreasonable expectations for myself onto others? The truth is, I covet Tawny's peace. I see the shine of holiness in her humility. Her bikini's pretty cute too.

I, on the other hand, am contemptable. I'm the White Witch

trying to entice my bestie with Turkish delight. Because why would the world need another Brené? Maybe what it needs right this moment is a Tawny Miller, handing out grab bars and toilet risers along with empathy and encouragement to family members adjusting to the changing needs of an aging loved one.

Her phone rests beside my leg. I set to work wiping away the gunk around its edges. "Do you ever even take your phone out of its case?"

"Why should I when I know I'll see you once a year and you'll do it for me?"

A short scream erupts from the shore. Then a splash. *Paige?* Before I can register what's happening, heavy footfalls land next to me. Sand flies up. It's Cade, sprinting to the water as if auditioning for *Baywatch*. Before I can even get to my feet, he's in the lake. Now fully submerged. Now he's a phoenix, rising with Paige lifted over his shoulder.

Her eyes are frantic. "I'm okay! I'm okay!" she keeps yelling.

In an instant, they're on the shore. He deposits her next to me. His eyes are dark, his features twisted. "Are you okay?" he asks Paige, crouching to her level. Lake water weeps from his hair onto our quilt.

"Yeah! I said I'm okay!" Paige looks embarrassed and close to tears. Cade turns his wild eyes on mine. I can't tell exactly what I read there. Recrimination?

"Okay," he says to Paige, breathing hard and nodding robotically. "You're okay." Like he needs to convince himself. And that's it. Turning, he slips back into the shadows, to his forest family.

Tawny wraps Paige in a beach towel. "I was okay," she says again, pleading to be believed. "I just slipped. It scared me, that's all." I fold her in a hug. *Had* she been okay? Not that I don't appreciate Cade's quick reflexes, but I can't help thinking his sudden, dramatic rescue might have been the more upsetting factor. And right now Paige looks a lot more concerned about saving face with the two little boys who watched the whole thing unfold. She pivots herself free from our little hug party.

Tawny and I exchange a look of total confusion. "What was that even all about?" she says.

"I don't know. Guess he read it as an emergency." My attempts at soothing Paige have been more effective than those to console myself. *Had* it been an emergency? *Did* I have everything under control? Cade is an emergency medical pilot. You'd think he'd know an emergency when he saw one.

"Then why is he taking off?"

The site of their cozy family picnic now sits empty. In the distance, two figures head toward the parking lot. Under the weight of the toddler, Cade plods quickly. The woman, presumably his wife, appears to be having a hard time keeping up, between the baby in a sling and the cooler she trails behind her.

Once again, I'm thoroughly disquieted. I've fallen a thousand stories, out of Cade's good graces. And now off he flies, just like that? Leaving me in his jet wash?

Twenty-Six

Daisy

Monday evening, Audrey's filling a pitcher with ice. Our refrigerator's ice dispenser makes the most horrifying racket, a thing I will not miss, so I wait until she finishes before venturing to speak. "Sweetie, I don't mean to be nosy, but you've been hummingbirding around ever since you got back from the lake. Didn't you girls have a good time?" I'm amazed that Dean hasn't picked up on Audrey's frenetic energy. But then, at the moment he's hyperfocused, sorting a box of fishing lures at the kitchen table. Just the kind of task his doctor suggested I supply.

Audrey moves to the sink and turns on the faucet. "I know. I'm sorry, Daisy. It's been a weird day."

"Oh? How so?" Immediately I swipe at the air dismissively. "It's okay, you don't need to tell me, if it's not a good time."

She shuts off the faucet and sighs. "No, I don't mind. That's why I sent Tawny to pick up the burgers. I needed to clear my head. A thing happened at the lake, and *man*, it really shook me." She slumps against the counter. "You wouldn't happen to know a guy named Cade? Drives an old blue truck. I don't know his last name."

"Cade Carter?"

Audrey shrugs. "Maybe. I don't know. He's—"

"Fairly tall? Dark blond hair? Good heart?"

"Um. Yeah, that sounds about right. Although I was going to say tall, moody, and slightly intimidating."

"Oh dear. What happened?"

After hearing Audrey relate the story about how Cade swooped in so dramatically to rescue Paige, I have a pretty good idea what might've been behind it. But it's not my story to tell. Instead, I motion for her to follow me down the hall to my bedroom. Briefly, I smile at the pewter-framed photo before passing it to Audrey. "Do you remember my friend Camille?"

"Of course. I mean, it's hard to forget that you grew up with Camille Bettencourt." Audrey runs her eyes over the photo. "She's so beautiful. I'm glad you got to see her before she passed. I remember you mentioning something about it in a letter."

"That's exactly right, honey. In fact, Camille and Nash moved back here, oh, about six years ago, I guess it was. Yes, that's right. Dean's symptoms weren't yet very apparent. Anyhow, she'd always wanted to retire here in her hometown. Raise horses. And so they did. They built a gorgeous ranch not far from town. Actually, Camille and I were blessed to spend quite a lot of quality time together. Until she got sick, that is. And then, well, I had the privilege to walk through that with her."

Audrey listens keenly. Probably wondering where I'm going with all this. "Honey, Cade is Camille's son. He moved to Charity Falls when his mom got diagnosed."

A furrow pleats Audrey's gracefully arched ginger eyebrows. She looks utterly puzzled. Like I could knock her over with a feather.

Audrey opens her mouth to speak, then closes it. Then opens it. "Oh," she finally says. "So you're telling me his dad is . . ."

"Nash Carter."

"Like *the* Nash Carter?"

"Only one I know of. I don't suppose it's easy growing up in the spotlight with two famous parents. Let's just say, Cade has had quite a lot to deal with." I pat the bed. "Here, let's sit down."

"Oh. Well, yeah. I had no idea he just lost his mom." Audrey rakes her fingers through the top of her hair and leaves them there. "Guess I'd better cut him some slack. It's just that . . . Daisy, I felt so humiliated. In front of Tawny. In front of his family."

"His family?"

"His wife and kids were with him."

"Honey, Cade doesn't have a wife and kids."

"No? Well, maybe it was a girlfriend. Anyway, I was mortified. But thank you. It helps to know he's been going through something."

"Did you know he's a Life Flight pilot?"

"That much I know."

"So he *is* trained to respond in emergency medical situations."

"I've thought about that."

"And, you see, Audrey, there may be, well, *other* circumstances that played a part. I don't know that, of course, and it wouldn't be my place to share it if I did."

"Thank you. That helps. But . . ." Audrey stares at her hands. "Something else happened today . . ."

"Oh?" Clearly, my niece is still carrying considerable weight on those narrow shoulders. While I wait for her to find her way into the conversation, I tuck loose, wavy strands of hair behind her ear. "You got some more color today."

Her face relaxes into a smile, one that nearly reaches her eyes but doesn't quite. "Here's the thing. When I got back, I had an email from an architect. Not just any architect, Daisy. Steffen Beckenbauer. He and his associates have their hand in important projects in all the major cities—I'm talking globally. Mostly high-profile urban renewal projects—like, they've been involved in rehabbing a huge swath of the San Francisco waterfront. Converting old industrial buildings into modern spaces. But they also work with historic residences. I've never even met Steffen, but I've long been aware of his firm. Anyway, among other things, they're working on an update of the Whittier Mansion."

At my lack of recognition, she continues. "It's an old, iconic place in San Francisco, listed on the National Register of Historic Places. You know, in one of those posh San Francisco neighborhoods up on the hill with a view to the Golden Gate Bridge. It's privately owned now, but it has a fascinating history. Anyway, they're assembling a team to come up with a complete interior and exterior color palette change. Which is kind of a big deal. Like, a really big deal. And somehow my name came up. Daisy, this is one of those projects that could open some huge doors for me. I mean, *if* I got in."

"Why wouldn't you get in? Of course you'd get in. I haven't a shred of doubt." Even as I respond, I recognize this as one of those times when a power apart from my own guides my words. Somehow I've stepped outside our conversation, acutely aware that later there'll be emotional consequences from encouraging Audrey in this way. Her enthusiasm is undeniable. And I know my words are true, that they're the right ones for this moment.

I'm also conscious of a voice deep inside, which isn't the right voice, crying, *What about us?* Instead I ask, "What about Homer's?"

"Oh! That's the best part. The site visit isn't scheduled until August. The same week I have to be back for Ava's baby shower. But, first things first. I've been invited to interview over Zoom. They have partners in offices all over the world, so virtual meetings are standard operating procedure. But. I haven't responded yet."

"Why wouldn't you?" I place my hands over Audrey's. "Of course, you must do it."

She nods, slowly at first, then more determinedly. "Yeah. Why wouldn't I? I mean, the timing seems perfect. What are the chances?"

"Tell me about this mansion. What's so strange about it?"

"It's not so much that the house is strange as its occupants over the years. The man who originally built it in the nineteenth century founded Whittier, Fuller & Company, which later became Fuller O'Brien Paints. Anyway, later it was occupied by Nazis, the California Historical Society, and maybe even a ghost or two. It's privately owned now, and—"

The grind of tires on gravel alerts us to a car. That'll be Tawny. Audrey stands. "Aunt Daisy, I have *got* to show you the house. I'll pull it up online after dinner."

Audrey leaves the room and I return Camille's photo to the dresser, setting it reverently atop the white cotton runner embroidered by my mother. For some reason, my soft-hearted niece felt the need to obtain my permission to get excited about this new job opportunity. How is it that, sometimes, what fills one person with joy leaves another bereft?

Mindlessly I remove several spent sunflower petals from the runner. Audrey brought this bouquet home from the farmer's market over a week ago, for me. At night as Dean slumbers fitfully and I lie fully awake, I've loved its cheery reminder that I'm not alone in this. Now, though, the blossoms have begun to shrivel, and a dusting of bright yellow pollen threatens to stain the delicate white fabric.

I consider moving the vase. But what's a little golden flower dust? There are certainly worse things.

I turn to Danny's photo and peer deep into teal-blue eyes that hold the same gentle intensity as Audrey's. *Son, whatever brings your daughter joy and fulfillment, this is what I pray for. I promise I'll never hold her back.*

But it doesn't mean I'm ready to think about her leaving.

Twenty-Seven

Audrey

"Girls, I'm going to have to take a break," Daisy says. "My neck is killing me. Anybody else ready to join me in an iced tea? Or should we go straight to Coke floats?"

Tawny rests her paint brush in the tray and strips off a disposable glove. "Me too. I'm dead. I'll help you, Daisy."

With my arm, I brush a stray curl out of my eyes and step back to view our progress. It's day two. Coat number three is nearly dry, and it already feels like a completely different room. But I can't yet justify a Coke float. Even if it is the Fourth of July. The fun factor went missing after day one, and our meager crew has simply been powering through. Also, it's time to acknowledge the great Sherwin Williams alabaster elephant in the room. If we're going to do this right, it'll definitely take another coat.

"Okay," I say. "I'll join you guys in a second, soon as I'm done with this trim."

Half an hour later, the three of us recline in Adirondack chairs in the shade of the old blue spruce. We're basically paint-speckled lizards basking belly-up in the high desert. When a silver van pulls in, I shield my eyes against the sun. I can't get a make on the guy who gets out of the passenger side. But I recognize the driver, even

175

without his blue Homer's vest. Just as I realize it's Omar from electrical, the van's back door slides open and another familiar form slithers out. Silas.

Tawny and my aunt exchange glances with me, but none of us moves to get up. We're way too chillaxed. And sore. On approach, Silas grins. "By the looks of you fine ladies, I take it we're too late. Already knocked out the painting?"

Daisy lets out a groan that confirms my suspicions. She's more than ready to be done.

"I wish," I say.

"Oh good," he says, "cuz I brought reinforcements. You know Omar, and this is my buddy Andrew. And if you really want to knock it out fast, I brought my sprayer."

I have to say, right now these three guys look as able-bodied as three people ever could.

The timid look both Tawny and Daisy send my way makes me feel like some kind of imperious home improvement dictator. They needn't worry. This time, I won't require any convincing. "Silas," I say, "at this point we would love *any* help you can offer. Thank you. We're pretty fried."

He juts his chin toward my glass. "What are you drinking there?" just as I slurp the last swirls of ice cream and foam through my red-striped straw.

Daisy chuckles. "The same thing you'll be drinking when we are *all done*. Let's go, team!"

The next afternoon, I offload Tawny's two-ton duffel onto the curb in front of the airport. "What did you stuff in this thing, a pine tree?" Maybe it's just my sore arms talking.

Tawny smirks. "Books, duh. It's your fault for introducing me to Sweet Reads. I couldn't exactly pass up all those killer deals, especially with no sales tax.

"Next time we come, I *promise* there'll be more tea time and less painting."

Tawny rolls her shoulders. "Yeah, I am one giant ache. But I figure, every time I move for the next few days I'll think of you."

"And speak a curse over me."

"Never. You know I don't swear. Seriously though, it was worth it. The house looks so charming. I'm just heartbroken for your aunt. Does she really have to sell? Seems like there must be some other way."

"I know, I thought so too. But assisted living isn't cheap. Besides, I think she's ready to be done with the burden of maintaining an old house. That was Dean's thing, and now . . . it's not."

"Well, at least she still gets to live *here*." Tawny stretches her arms toward the horizon with its circle of mountain peaks, and her tone turns wistful. "It's absolutely gorgeous. Someday I'd love to settle in a place like this. Which one is which again?"

"Of the Three Sisters?" I point, north to south. "Faith. Hope. Charity. And yeah. I'm starting to realize that part of my heart will always be here. Part of my story."

"But it sounds like the next chapter could take you some pretty fabulous places."

"*If* I get the Whittier Mansion job. And *if* the firm likes what I do. I mean, Steffen Beckenbauer? I could bomb."

"Audrey, get real. You've never bombed a thing in your life. You're gonna slay."

"We'll see. Either way, it seems like a sign that I'll find work again. And then you and I will just have to somehow break away and come visit Daisy and Dean."

"And Silas, of course."

I laugh. "And Silas."

"Thanks for inviting me," she says, raising her voice over the high-pitched squeal of a jet overhead. "I had such a great time. It really helped get my mind off things. Too short, though."

"I'm just grateful you could get away. I know your folks need you right now. You're a good daughter."

"Yeah, well, don't forget," Tawny says, "you promised you'll let me know what happens with super-intense Ryan Gosling guy."

"Oh, for sure. You'll be first to know when he toilet-papers the house or slashes my tires."

It's never easy to part ways with Tawny. But at least I know I'll see her in just a few weeks, at Ava's shower. And besides, she gives grade-A goodbye hugs.

Twenty-Eight

It's generally accepted that the Trading Post Café boasts down-home friendly service, the best bacon guacamole cheeseburger east of the Cascades, and cinnamon rolls frosted so heavily they make your teeth throb. It's also where I sometimes deposit Paige in the afternoon to wait for her mom to get off work.

On the Saturday following Tawny's visit, Paige hops super quietly onto a well-worn stool at the diner-style counter, then waits for her mom to turn and notice her. Nina's returning what looks like a chocolate silk pie to the pie case, and I'm suddenly acutely aware that I haven't eaten in hours.

"Oh, manahuu, sweetheart!" Nina cries, when she turns to find her daughter's playful expression. "You surprised me!" Paige beams. It's not the first time I've heard her mom toss out what I assume is a tribal language term.

When Nina turns to thank me, her eyes are tender. "I appreciate you," she says. There's been a detectable change in Nina's disposition since we first met. She still looks worn—I mean, of course she does, she's single-parenting two kids and working six days a week. But she seems less discouraged, and I'd really like to believe I had something to do with this.

"My pleasure," I say, and guilt stabs. I have got to tell Paige and Nina about my departure in a few weeks. Still, I take comfort in

179

knowing Paige is on the waiting list for a more permanent mentor through the sheriff's program. Somehow it will all work out. It has to.

Paige leans out to give me a goodbye hug.

"Oh, I almost forgot!" Nina slides her hand into her apron pocket. "Cade Carter asked me to give you this." She produces a slip of paper and my stomach tilts. "His number. He asked for yours, but I didn't think it was my place to give it out." She tips her head in a cheeky way, scrutinizing my response. The implication's clear. She's dripping with curiosity. And I didn't even know Nina had a sassy side.

I narrow my eyes and shake my head as if to say, *Move along, Nina, there's nothing to see here.* I can do sassy too.

But in truth, I'm rather curious myself.

———— ⌇ ————

If Cade's handwriting is any indication, he's a man who puts great care into things. Many of the professional draftsmen I've worked with don't boast such well-ordered penmanship. I've also never stared at a phone number so long in my life. I've been sitting here on my bed, frozen, ever since returning from the café.

Way to lob the ball into the far reaches of my court, Cade.

I'm no coward. If I can interview with Steffen Beckenbauer on Tuesday, I can make a simple phone call. But which is better, text or call? I keep coming back to this: If Cade plans to level more criticism at me, I'd rather not hear it aloud.

Finally I compose a brief text. Now that he has my number, I tell him, he's welcome to connect.

Minutes tick by. No response. For all I know he could be up in a helicopter, saving a life. Which, after all, seems to be his thing. Saving a lonely, troubled, small-town boy. Rescuing a girl from drowning, never mind that the responsible adult was ten feet away and the girl was never in any real danger. I toss the phone onto my pillow and debate joining Daisy and Dean in the kitchen. Judging by the smell of melting cheese and browning sausage, there's frozen pizza in my future. But I no longer have an appetite.

Instead I pick up the phone again. Three conversation dots ripple across my screen. I swallow. Then wait.

> I'd like to try to explain. Would you be willing to meet me? Sweet Reads? Or wherever . . . Tomorrow at 2? If not, I'll understand.

See? That wasn't so painful. Too bad I just wasted the last twenty minutes overthinking which way to communicate. I vow not to overthink my response.

> Sweet Reads works. See you then.

Now what are those traitorous butterflies doing, pumping their wings and fluttering around behind my breastbone? Not my beloved monarchs. They would never. Probably some kind of devilish Oregon species. I did *not* come to Charity Falls to meet unattached men, especially emotionally complicated ones who publicly castigate me on the regular. Even if we do have a favorite bookshop in common. Even if he comes with an embossed-in-golden-foil stamp of approval from my favorite aunt.

On the other hand, it wouldn't be an altogether bad thing to cultivate a, well, neighborhood chum—yeah, that's it—especially when said chum has access to horses. If there's one activity I'd still love to introduce Paige to before I leave, it's riding. File that under things to do *after* I determine why Çade keeps lashing out at me.

Meanwhile, I could accomplish a lot before two o'clock tomorrow. Having updated my resume and identified several Bay Area design companies of interest, I simply need to pull the trigger and reach out to them. What's been stopping me? Also, I've got loads to do to prep for Tuesday: Research the architecture period Whittier Mansion represents. Familiarize myself with Beckenbauer-Vandersteen. Commit to memory the highlight reel of their company's accomplishments. Why is my stomach clenching? Maybe because I'm being vetted by one of the most innovative design firms in the world. *No big deal.*

Oh, but I do love a challenge. So there's that. Raising the bar never failed me in the past. I'm just rusty. Off my game. I roll my shoulders. This beastly tension has always been price of admission to the prosperous life.

An urge to call my mom takes me by surprise. Or maybe my brother, although with the time difference in South Carolina I'm probably too late. No, it's my mom's voice I'd like to hear. It's been a minute.

So I do. Once again, when I ask how things are going with her work on the reservation, she dismisses the triple-degree heat out of hand and instead gushes with a kind of settled satisfaction. And as dust motes dance in a wide beam of golden light spilling from the window, I'm left afterward to ponder a quote she dropped on me, something from Henri Nouwen, one of her favorite writers.

"The main question is not 'How can we hide our wounds?' . . . *but 'How can we put our woundedness in the service of others?'"*

An alarm clock ticks, and I sense golden hour stretching its arms to me like open country. This far north, the sun doesn't set until nearly nine o'clock in July. That's another two hours. I've come to savor these final soft moments of each day, watching the sun lower itself behind the mountains until all that's left is a dark, jagged silhouette against a pale blond canvas.

Is now the time? Yesterday after work, I happened upon a homeless-looking easel at the thrift store. Before I knew it, I'd purchased a basic palette of watercolors. What if I could capture this magical lighting?

Or what if I stink at plein air? I haven't painted outdoors since . . . since . . .

I slide out the blue suitcase from where I stashed it and set it reverently on the bed. With a soft click, the case opens, releasing a scent I didn't notice the first time. The perfume of vintage silk mingled with aged paper and long-dried pigments.

I riffle through my old artwork. Here's one I did when my fourth-grade class studied California's missions. My parents decided to make a family vacation of it, road-tripping south to Mission Santa Inés. We stayed in a cute little Danish town and ate jam-filled pancakes called ebelskivers. I can taste their sweetness on my tongue as I hold the watercolor between my fingers.

I can smell the bright, fresh-cut grass where I sat cross-legged under a cloudless sapphire sky sketching the mission's facade. Running my finger over the arches of the front corridor, I admire— yes, admire—the creamy buff color I chose for the adobe. And the waves of its red-tile roof. Okay, maybe this isn't so bad. In fact, for a kid about Paige's age, it's pretty decent.

Somehow I know what I'll find if I keep searching. And then it's in my hand. An eleven-year-old's depiction of a pristine, blue-roofed farmhouse with a welcoming front porch and patches of sunflowers. The Sugar Pine Inn, back in its glory days. I let the other pages fall away.

I'm surprised by my level of detail. Whoever painted this did it with love and passion and an eye for the kind of cordial beauty that makes the world a joyful place.

I'm that girl.

Yes, now's the time. I grab a protein bar and my blue-and-green flannel overshirt. I'll snag a bottle of water from the fridge and let Daisy know I plan to eat later.

Recrimination murmurs over me. *You're ditching responsibility, Audrey.*

I mute that merciless taskmaster. She lies.

〜

The next morning, two watercolor paintings sit side by side on the small desk. Touched by the tender fingers of early light, they tell two very different stories. One speaks to beauty and hope. Would it be fair to call it naivete? Perhaps. What matters, though, is this: Real art doesn't lie. That artist, the girl with two long amber braids who inhabited my skin eighteen years ago, told the story in her heart. And her painting will never stop telling that true story.

The second painting, the one that finished air-drying last night, is certainly more sophisticated. It depicts the same subject as the first painting, a classic 1930s farmhouse, originally constructed by the town's first mayor, later a tourist destination, and now in near ruins. This story is every bit as honest. Except the artist imbued it with sadness. She could hardly do otherwise.

I may be a novice with watercolors, but right now I'm oddly content with the new painting. Where the juvenile version is simple and bright, with cheery hues that don't stray far from primary colors, my new golden-hour painting features subtle contrasts. I've leaned heavily on tertiary shades. Amber tones, soft yellows, and muted grays testify that melancholy can be beautiful too.

Interesting.

And this is my story to tell. Maybe one day I'll be able to look at these two paintings and reconcile their very different stories. Or maybe I'll always reside here in this tension, unable to escape the pulsing ache of loss but growing in gratefulness for things as they once were.

The words my mother shared seem to have penetrated while I slept, awakening a fresh supposition. God hasn't tasked me with hiding my wounds.

That's it. I've been in hiding. And for years, it's rendered me powerless.

Nothing I do will ever bring my father back. That's an injustice I can't fix. But what of the property's neglect? Having lost so much here, most notably my hope, my childlike faith, haven't I of all people the right to respond to the inn's grievous disregard? There has to be something I, Audrey Needham, can do to remedy it.

What if I could redeem my father's death by hastening the inn's return to life?

The last time I searched for information about the inn's ownership, I came up empty. This is going to require a deeper dive. And I'll make it a carrot, my reward once I'm fully prepared for my interview with Herr Beckenbauer.

Is this what Henri Nouwen meant by putting woundedness in service to others? I'm not sure. But something's taking flight in my chest.

Twenty-Nine

I arrive early and wielding my glorious Sweet Reads gift card lest there be any awkwardness in which Cade feels he must pay for my drink. The owner, Ian, and I are on a first-name basis now. Only one table sits open, a round two-seater by the window, the same table where I parked for hours that first time I visited Sweet Reads not long after arriving in Charity Falls. Where I recovered my joy in making art as a natural response to the world around me. Where, of all people, Cade Carter poked his head over my shoulder and affirmed my efforts.

That was the day I learned to keep art supplies in Harriet's trunk, to always be ready on a whim. Here's another lesson learned: Creativity has a unique way of inviting others into our story. Which is why it feels so vulnerable. So, come what may, I'm determined to share my two paintings of the Sugar Pine with the property owner. Might seeing their juxtaposition and hearing the heartfelt story behind them inspire him or her to action? It's a superlong shot, but it's all I've got. And I haven't felt this brand of excitement in forever.

Maybe it's muscle memory, because sitting here again, inhaling the sweet steam rising from my green tea latte with honey, my hands virtually twitch with desire to hold a pencil. Except that an aqua-sky-blue pickup just pulled in out front.

The moment Cade enters, he shoots me a pained look. After ordering, he settles into the empty chair across from me. "Thanks for meeting me, Audrey. Seems like apologizing to you is my new thing."

I offer a tight-lipped smile. "You've certainly been getting some practice."

Cade scrubs his hand over his face. "Look, I—" He's interrupted by his buddy Ian waving him over to pick up his drink. "Excuse me a second."

"Let me try that again," he says upon returning. "Actually, maybe I should let you go first. You have every right to be upset. C'mon, let me have it."

Maybe it's due to the bracing aroma of chai spices emanating from his mug. Maybe I have the art therapy to thank. Or maybe it has something to do with Fanny Price. But I'm feeling emboldened. I refuse to disguise my hurt. "It's true," I say. "I didn't know what to think. I got this vibe like you were judging me, as if I were incompetent to supervise Paige. Which made me question myself. But here's the thing, Cade. I'm not incompetent. Not one bit."

I exhale. "But hey, I hate it when people rant. Especially when it's me. And actually, I want to say that I'm sorry too. I didn't know about your mom. I'm so very sorry for your loss. I didn't realize that you're . . ." *Don't say the son of a Hollywood A-list couple.* "I only just learned that your mom is my aunt's friend Camille."

A muscle in Cade's jaw twitches. He takes a long breath and stares momentarily out the window. His eyes return to mine. "Thank you." Clearing his throat, he shifts in his chair. "Yeah. It's been hard. But it's no excuse for being a jerk. I overreacted— *big-time*. It had absolutely nothing to do with you. That's what I came here to say."

Okay, maybe I'm not entirely calm and collected after all. I didn't realize how much I needed to hear that. My eyes fill, and I work to hold back the tears. If I blink, they're going to roll. Cade reaches across the table, lays his warm hand over mine. "You did nothing wrong, Audrey."

Oh geez, there are those sincere blue eyes. My bottom lip quivers. "Thank you." I want to say more but the words catch in my throat. I want to say that being responsible for Paige isn't a thing I take lightly. That I've been tormented, replaying the event at the lake over and over, to make sure I hadn't fallen down on such an important job. I want to say that *I love Paige* . . . but the truth of it is more than I can bear. I wipe the corner of my eyes with my finger, then scan the table in search of a napkin. No luck.

Cade's already on it. "Pardon me," he says, addressing an older gentleman at the next table. Cade hovers his hand over the man's napkin stack. "May I?"

"I get it," I say, dabbing at my eyes. "I mean, I know what it's like to lose a parent."

"I'm sure you do." His brow gathers. "Sorry about your dad. He seems to have a lot of friends here."

It makes sense that Cade would know about my dad, would know a piece of my story, his mom being such close friends with Daisy and all. But still, it continues to catch me off guard when Charity Falls locals talk about him with a tone of such familiarity. I let out a soft, sniffly laugh. "Yeah," I say, "more than I realized."

"What was that like for you? Losing your father so young—I mean, if you don't mind talking about it."

For some reason, I don't. But where to start? "Are you by any chance a *Harry Potter* fan?"

He raises a questioning eyebrow. "Sure. I totally fell down that rabbit hole back in the day. You?"

"Big-time."

"Been to the theme park?"

"At Universal Studios? No. So please don't gloat. I once had the chance. But," I sigh, "sadly, work has always taken priority." I take a deep breath. "Anyway, back in high school, my friend worked at a movie theater. The newest one was coming out, and we got to go to the midnight showing before opening day. Must have been *The Deathly Hallows*."

"Part one or two?"

I smile, remembering. Tawny and I were seniors, so it hadn't taken much to obtain special dispensation from our parents to go out so late. "Definitely two. Anyway, we were super pumped. And we were watching, and we were into it. All of a sudden there's this loud crackling noise. The screen goes black. And there's this eerie silence in the theater. A pregnant silence, you know? Like time stopped. Everyone starts looking around in disbelief. One moment, we were all on this fantastical ride together, soaring through the experience. And now here we are, gazing around in the darkness. We're like, *What just happened?*"

Cade nods attentively.

"Slowly reality hits. It's over for us. All around me, mumbles and groans erupt. Finally, a woman walks to the front and says she's sorry, the filmstrip broke. 'Your movie will resume shortly,' she says. And eventually it does. But it's too late. The spell's broken. The magic's gone. Somehow, it had seeped out. It was as if we all lost faith in the story.

"Anyway, my dad's accident was like that, like a filmstrip snapping in two. It was so abrupt, so unexpected, it felt like our lives stopped. Like my story, the story I was anchored to, was over, or maybe it had never been real to begin with. I wanted to ask, *What just happened?* Only there was no explanation. Inevitably, life restarted. But it was never the same, especially at first. It was . . . colorless."

I swallow back a surge of emotion before venturing forward. "My family and I, we just kept on marching, going through the motions." *And maybe I still am.*

Cade leans back, rubs a hand over his jaw. "That sounds . . . horrible."

"Yeah, I kind of went from being embedded *in* my story to watching it unfold like it was happening to someone else. I was like, what's this girl named Audrey going to do next? Oh, she should probably go to college. Does that make any sense?" I sip my latte, struggling to steady my quivering hands.

Cade's intense gaze is hard to read. A slow nod. "Yep. Makes *a lot* of sense."

I smile. "Thanks for listening." And I do feel better. When was the last time I tried to verbalize it?

Cade stares into his chai. "I, uh. I had a similar experience. Except, in my case I brought it on myself. That's one of the reasons I was so glad you agreed to meet me. I've been wanting to explain." He searches my eyes. "Maybe you heard about it?" At my blank expression, he continues. "Never read the tabloids? Celebrity gossip?"

I scoff. "Not really. There are so many better things to read." I make a sweeping gesture toward the rows of bookshelves.

"Well, you can google it, but I'd rather spare you the dramatic TMZ accounts."

"I'm sure I'd prefer your version."

As Cade begins relating the story of how he grew up in Malibu doing more than his share of drinking as a teenager, a memory gets tickled. Years ago, I was vaguely aware of some paparazzi photos splashed over the internet of Nash Carter's wild child, a party boy. Something tragic had happened. Something tabloid-worthy. What was it? I listen, seized by a sense of dread.

"My parents were away, working together on location," he says. "I promised my mom I would have my little bro's back that weekend. Instead I was an idiot. Brought him with me to a beach party. It went late into the night. Eli was fourteen, a strong swimmer. So when I saw him in the water, doing some bodysurfing in the moonlight, I didn't think much of it."

The details are coming back. If only I could stop what's coming next.

Cade drops his eyes, thumbs the handle of his mug absently. "I didn't know someone had offered my brother beer. Maybe something even harder. Truth is, I was pretty wasted myself, so . . . Anyway, there must have been a riptide. I . . ."

He jerks his head away, then seers my heart with a look of undisguised remorse. "Eli drowned, Audrey. On my watch. I didn't even know he needed saving."

Before I can slap a hand over my mouth, a gasp escapes. There it is, a story that must have made it to the mainstream news outlets, maybe even the cover of *People* magazine. Because I do remember now. A fuzzy mental image comes into focus of a grieving Nash Carter and Camille Bettencourt standing graveside, holding hands. I do the math. I must have been fourteen when it happened. The same age as Cade's brother.

I push a heavy breath from my chest. "Geez." What words can I offer that aren't woefully inadequate? There are none. "I can't even imagine what your family must have gone through. What *you* must've gone through. I'm so sorry." Clearly, I can now understand why he flipped out on me at the lake. And it's no trouble to muster the grace to cover it. I lean closer. "How did you cope?"

"I didn't, at first. I ran. Moved to Hawaii. Surfed, partied, tried to bury my shame."

Trying to imagine this earlier version of Cade brings an ache. That guy is not this guy. "But look at the good person you became anyway," I say.

"Well, I don't know. Regardless, I'm who I am today not in spite of my past but because of it. I'd never be able to help save others unless I'd been saved myself. I mean, I have regrets. Serious ones. They'll be with me always." He takes a deep breath. "Thankfully, my counselor helped me see the difference between regret and shame. Regret says, 'I've done wrong,' while shame accuses, 'I *am* wrong.' I'm learning to accept that my identity in God's eyes, accepted and loved and somehow *forgiven*, means that I make mistakes and carry regrets. But I'm never meant to carry shame."

"Are you saying you became a Christian?"

"It's been a journey. It *is* a journey. At first, once I cleaned up my act, I'd say I was more of a moralist. I thought being godly was about what I portrayed on the outside. Being a good boy for a change, you know? Proving myself. Trying to make up for the past. So yeah, I called that Christianity." Cade purses his lips, then shrugs. "Eventually I gave up trying to be a good person and just became a disciple. A learner. Which had to start with the me no one sees. Thought about being a youth pastor—seemed redemptive. Even started seminary. But after a while I felt sure it wasn't a fit. A good plan, just not the right one for me."

"How did you decide? I mean, how did you know the right plan for you?"

For the first time since he arrived, Cade's smile emerges. "I used to like to run up Haleakala. Clear my head. There was this place up there that was, you know, *my* place. Where I'd go to think and pray. And one day I just knew. Had a weird peace about it. Like peeling off a too-tight wet suit. When I quit seminary, I felt relieved. I was already working toward my pilot's license. I stayed in the islands for a while doing heli-trips for tourists, finished college. Moved to the mainland, worked as an EMT in the LA area, eventually got into what I'm doing, flying for Life Flight."

His eyebrows furrow. "When Mom got sick, transferring to Portland was a no-brainer."

"Mmm," I say. I'm still processing. The kind of healing Cade describes, the kind of restoration I see in the man before me, is nothing short of miraculous.

"I know that look," he says. "And I get it. You probably think I hole up in my room watching Kirk Cameron movies."

I chuckle. "No, that's not it. I'm just stunned, I guess. And I'm always interested in how people make decisions, especially big life decisions." I finish the last sip of my tea. "Do you mind me asking, is that why you're involved with the mentor program? Because of what happened to your brother?"

"A hundred percent. I had great parents, but with their work schedules I didn't always feel seen. And when the press started labeling me a bad kid, I believed them. I started to own that identity. So yeah, if I can help even just one kid feel seen, prevent them from acting out in destructive ways like I did . . ." Cade's voice trails off.

He stares out the window before turning to me, his features hardened. "You know what they call these kids with incarcerated parents? *At risk*. They hear that label spoken over them, and they buy into it. I want them to hear that they're at risk for doing something amazing. Because I was once that kid, and that's what I needed to hear."

I sit back. "Wow. I never thought of it that way."

A silence falls over us, tinted gray with a shared grief for Arlo and Paige. But it's a comfortable silence.

Eventually I sense the need for levity. "So, since you've been around . . ." I begin. *Oof.* Hadn't intended it to come out so charged with innuendo.

Cade stops sipping his drink midslurp. His eyebrows shoot up.

"Traveled, I mean," I quickly add. "You're not a lifer here in Central Oregon."

He nods. "I've done some traveling."

I motion with my eyes to a redheaded man just exiting the bookshop. He looks like he does his shopping at a big-and-tall-outdoorsman store for both reasons. "Then maybe you can tell me. Are mullets back, or is that just a Northwest thing?"

Cade chances a look at the guy, then winks in a good-natured way. *Winks!* "That, city girl, is a logger thing. Just one of the many acceptable hairstyle options for men around these parts." His wry smile kindles something warm inside me. *Rein it in, girl. He may be taken.* "Is that a problem for you? Is our sense of fashion too lowbrow? Would you have us all in suits and skinny jeans?"

I grin. Seems Cade, too, wants to demonstrate that we have officially moved out of the shadow of misunderstanding and into the sunlight of friendship.

My attention's caught by some activity outside, where cars in both directions are slowing to a stop to allow a pair of mule deer to amble across the road. "Also, I'm pretty sure I just saw two deer use the pedestrian crossing . . . like people."

He laughs. "Yeah, they do that. I have absolutely no idea why."

"Well . . ." I watch the two deer graze on a patch of grass. "To answer your question, I like Charity Falls just the way it is." *And I'm going to miss it.* "And hey, thanks, Cade. This was nice. I don't get out much."

He takes another napkin and wipes the table, like it's second nature to tidy up after himself. "Sure. Thanks for listening. And again, I'm sorry I got so triggered at the lake. Obviously, I need to work on that. I promise I'm not a complete jerk. And if I've botched my apology in any way, well, I'll never hear the end of it from Ronni. She was super embarrassed."

"Ronni?"

"My sister, Veronica." So, *not* a girlfriend.

"My nephew was pretty upset too," he says.

"Your nephew?"

"My man Griffin. He was with us at the lake. Great kid. He'll no doubt run a small country someday. They're out visiting from Minnesota. Ronni comes as often as she can. Living so far away when Mom got sick, that was hard on her. It's good medicine for Dad, having her here. He got to meet the new baby, Gabe."

"I'm sure it means a lot to him."

"Yep." Cade slathers on a thick Scottish brogue. "Whatever yeh say, blood's important."

I drop my jaw in mock disbelief. "Hagrid!" I say, laughing. This final development skyrockets my level of respect for Cade Carter. His cheeks flush adorably, which isn't lost on me.

It's also not lost on me that earlier he alluded to a secondary purpose for inviting me here today. Dare I ask? Nope. No point. Not when there's nowhere for the two of us to go from here.

Chums it is, and chums it must remain.

Thirty

A week later, red volcanic dust billows around my car and I'm forced to drive at a snail's pace. The last part of Cade's directions has taken me down a seemingly endless red-gravel road. Stubby juniper trees pepper the high-desert landscape, their trunks twisted like they've been slowly writhing for decades. I half expect Clint Eastwood to jump out from behind the sagebrush.

That said, the musical score filling the car doesn't exactly evoke *The Good, the Bad and the Ugly*. I'm amazed at the beatboxy rhythms Arlo is able to coax from my iPad. After Cade bragged on Arlo's musical aptitude, especially his interest in drums, I downloaded the free version of GarageBand.

Meanwhile, his little sister stares out her window, looking none too happy. Now and then she shoots Arlo a death glare. Paige has been excruciatingly vocal about her strong preference to hit the town's splash park rather than try something new today. She doesn't do well with surprises, and visiting the Carters' ranch was a last-minute change in our plans. Cade texted the invitation only last night, returning from Portland after pulling back-to-back three-day shifts.

Days I had filled sanding and priming Daisy and Dean's front door, working at Homer's, kickin' it with Paige, and attempting to move my inn-rescue project forward. While I'm no closer to identifying the property owner, I'm working on a plan B.

When again Paige whines, "It's so hot," I can't disagree. *Lord, let this go well today.* It's fine if horses don't turn out to be her thing. But she won't know until she tries. Either way, I'm confident she'll be in good hands with Cade.

The man is an anomaly. It's not often you get such a strong sense of a person before reaching the bottom of your teacup, even if it's one of the oversized mugs served at Sweet Reads. Apart from his sophisticated penmanship, Cade Carter exhibits other noble qualities. It's a rare guy who possesses strength and kindness in equal measure. Not to mention, he's self-effacing—I mean, the guy is chronically honest. When we chatted at the bookshop a week ago, he veered from grave to goofy in ways that made me tipsy. But at least now I understand his uber-serious side. I really do.

This guy has been to hell and back and somehow managed not to adopt a victim mindset. It's astonishing, really.

If nothing else, meeting a man like Cade has reawakened my romantic optimism. Someday, when the time *and place* are right, there may be a guy for me. Not just any guy. *The* guy. Cade brings new meaning to the measure of a man. Next time, I won't compromise. It's not enough to share like interests. He'll have to be a person I admire. And I would hope to be a woman he admires equally.

And there's the rub.

I've come to realize that dating Kyle last winter was an act of insincerity. If he hadn't been so cool and noncommittal, if he hadn't stayed at arm's length, I'd have kept him there. I didn't want Kyle, I only wanted to feel less alone in the world. So shame on me. Truth is, I'm not sure I can be trusted with someone else's heart.

Besides, a next-level man such as Cade Carter would logically be attracted to, well, a next-level woman. Someone who has their stuff together. Someone more like Tawny. I won't pretend to be someone I'm not.

It's hard enough to focus on the details of my real life without adding a cerulean-eyed do-gooder to my list of distractions. And that's exactly what I must do now—pinpoint the next right step for me professionally. I'll have to trust that my personal life will follow.

With the Beckenbauer-Vandersteen interview behind me, I'm breathing easier. Now I can move on to the quest for a permanent position while I wait to hear if I'm invited to take part on the Whittier Mansion team. Until I see the offer, I won't know exact terms, but it's only contract work for the duration of the project. Several months' income at best. Regardless, adding it to my portfolio would practically guarantee a career with some other exclusive Bay Area design firm. And maybe, someday, a partnership.

A handsome fieldstone entrance comes into view, with a black-iron gate for which Cade texted me the code. "We're here!" I sing enthusiastically, in part to quell my own nerves at the sight of Nash Carter's stately home. No, stately isn't exactly right. Masculine and gracious is more on the mark. With its mix of natural materials—honey-colored stone, heavy wood beams and pillars, and dark-brown siding, the sprawling residence would probably be termed "mountain modern." Of all the expensive homes I've visited, and I've crossed the thresholds of more than my share, I'd call the Carter ranch one of the most tasteful.

Arlo wastes no time. I've barely pulled to a stop in the wide circle driveway bordered by attractive waterwise landscaping before he's hopped out of the car, carelessly tossing the iPad onto the seat behind him. Off in the distance I spy a large equestrian complex topped with four cupolas. Again, gracious despite its size. I'm still taking in the whole scene when the massive front door opens, and out steps Cade. He's wearing a T-shirt the color of his eyes, his customary blue jeans, and light-colored cowboy boots that look as if they've seen plenty of action. For some reason, I can just as easily imagine Cade mucking out a stable as attending the Golden Globes or strolling a beach at sunset.

Better not linger on that last visual.

He raises an arm in greeting. Closer now, his quick smile at seeing me ignites something in my chest, a part of me I had no idea was so willing to catch fire.

A spark of excitement flashes in Paige's huge dark eyes. Maybe she's up for this adventure after all. The interior of the Carter home smells like leather and pine, with a hint of vanilla. Or maybe the scent trails behind Cade—I can't be sure—as he leads us through a broad, welcoming foyer, past a curved leather sectional and a copper-trimmed fireplace set into a massive wall of stone. I like to imagine Camille had a hand in selecting the muted desert color palette and Pendleton wool throw pillows. And she must have loved candles. This was her place of refuge and retirement, Daisy had said, even as her husband remained semi-active in the film industry.

"Show us the way, Arlo," Cade says. "You ladies ready to meet the horses?" Arlo puffs out his chest and marches down a wide hall off a gleaming chef's kitchen, then opens a door that leads to the garage.

"How many do you have?" Paige asks.

"Horses? Three. Actually, only two right now. Our other horse is on loan for the summer. Doing some important ministry work."

I level a look at him. "Your horse is . . . in ministry?"

There's that sly grin again. He really ought to trademark it. "You could say that."

"Actually, you already did," I say.

"Did what?"

"Say that your horse was in ministry." I'm enjoying this entirely too much.

For a moment our eyes tangle playfully. "Right you are," he says. "And I stand by it."

The garage could easily house six cars with room to spare. Still,

this fleet of vehicles is surprisingly modest compared to those be-
longing to many of Silicon Valley's boy and girl wonders, successful in their own right but not exactly household names like Cade's
parents. Revered, but not necessarily beloved. Besides Cade's truck,
I spot a white Escalade and two sedan-shaped vehicles hiding under
black covers. He presses a button and the garage door closest to
us whirs, rising to reveal a flood of sunshine and sweeping vistas
in back of the house.

Arlo scrambles onto the back seat of an ATV that looks like
it's built for fun. Shouldn't he have a helmet? Cade hops in front
and gestures to a second ATV parked next to his. He asks me, "Up
for driving one of these?"

Paige's eyes widen. I've never driven an ATV, but this one looks
tame enough, I guess—utilitarian, really. Roof above, cargo area
behind. I shield my eyes and regard the stables. "It doesn't look
very far."

He laughs at this. "But this is more fun, right?" He turns the
key, and his engine purrs. "Key's in it!" he shouts over his shoulder. Aaand, the boys are off. Arlo turns back with a smug grin
for his sister.

At the slightest touch of the gas pedal, our ATV bolts like
a quarter horse at Pimlico. Instead of being alarmed, though, I
laugh. All previous concern about helmets dissolves on a musky,
midday breeze as I throw my head back and roar. I also slow down,
because Paige is gripping the side bar and looking wide-eyed at
me as if I'm certifiable.

Cruising more leisurely now along the wide path, I feast on
the view. The Carter estate perches along the ledge of a vast dry
canyon, a steep-walled gorge punctuated with rocky outcroppings.
As if God dragged a finger through a great pile of ground nutmeg
and then stuck in some boulders and trees. Far below us, a red-
tailed hawk hovers between canyon walls.

I inhale hot, spiced air and congratulate myself for having been so bossy on the topic of sunscreen. Sans shade trees, my bare neck and shoulders bake. Paige and I exchange grins. The ends of her dark ponytail whip in the wind. Even after I return my eyes to the path ahead I can still feel her eyes studying me.

She shouts over the engine's low whir. "Can you braid my hair like that?"

"Like mine? Sure, I can French braid your hair."

All too soon we reach the commodious stables and I've no choice but to decelerate. I park my new favorite toy next to a white diesel pickup coated in a film of red road dust. The four of us enter the building at the same moment a white-haired gentleman wearing a baseball cap exits. He raises his head and I gasp. Hopefully no one noticed. I hadn't meant to make that face out loud. Guess I've underprepared for crossing paths with Nash Carter this morning.

Don't give off any ditsy starstruck vibes.

"Hey, Pops. You know Arlo," Cade says.

Arlo flips his overgrown hair off his forehead. "Hi, Mr. Carter." Man, this kid's going to be a lady-killer.

Nash gently grips Arlo's narrow shoulder. "Great to see you, buddy. How ya doin'?"

"This is Arlo's sister, Paige," Cade says. When Nash offers his hand, Paige's cheeks color. Instinctively, I lay my arm over her shoulder to embolden her.

Nash then turns to me. "And I gather you're Audrey."

Oh man. Having met my share of famous people, I can tell you the experience is typically anticlimactic. That is, with the possible exception of Michelle Pfeiffer. The woman oozes an otherworldly elegance even in a sloppy bun and no makeup. But for the most part, celebrities are shockingly normal and about as naturally glamorous as the next person.

Nash Carter, on the other hand, is larger than life. Literally. The man is every bit as tall as, if not taller than, his son. His signature thick, salt-and-pepper mustache and eyebrows are completely legit. And now that I'm meeting him, I'll wager a guess that the characters he portrays on-screen are written with no one but Nash in mind. Because every gesture is familiar. The way he rests one hand loosely on a hip and squints playfully when he looks you in the eye, not to mention his trademark slow, gravelly drawl—it all smacks of his on-screen persona.

Exchange his cap for a Stetson, slap on a pair of holsters, dangle a hand-rolled cigarette from his lips, and you've got *A Man Called Desperado* or Jedediah Boone in *This Godforsaken Land*.

Sure, Nash's true age is apparent in the way his shoulders round forward. His celebrated, weathered face doesn't glow quite as bronze as his movie stills would have you believe. But this I find endearing. Academy Awards aside, the man is a recent widow.

Nash's crow's feet deepen, and his eyes hold a softness that disarms me. "I gotta say, you've sure done Daisy a heckuva world of good. Their place looks great. You know . . ." He plays with the edge of his mustache. "I saw you once, at the yard sale. Your aunt pointed you out." *The man on the porch.* "Sure glad you came out on the winning side of that slow-cooker showdown." He chuckles and my face goes hot. Not my most shining moment. "Anyhow, honored to finally make your acquaintance, Audrey."

"Likewise," I say, willing myself not to appear as addled as I feel. "And I'm so sorry for your loss. Sure wish I'd had a chance to meet your wife. She seems like an amazing woman."

An amalgam of appreciation and grief flickers in Nash's eyes. "Quite. You know, Camille would love that you're all here today, 'specially if you make sure to give Fancy some extra attention." He pivots to face the barn. "That's her baby."

"Who's Fancy?" Paige says.

Nash grins. "Fancy Nancie's her name. But mostly, we just call her Fancy. She's the paint. You'll meet her. A real princess, kind of like my Camille. Now y'all stop talking to a silly old man and go. Have a good time."

"Thanks, Pops," Cade says.

"Oh, yeah—and the fridge is all stocked up with ice-cold drinks." Nash pats Cade affectionately on the back before turning to depart. "See ya back at the house, son."

I can't help thinking how lucky Cade's nephews are. I'll bet Nash Carter makes one heckuva grandpa.

Thirty-One

On the Carter ranch, Arlo transforms before my eyes into a competent buckaroo. While I braid Paige's thick locks, he halters a muscular chestnut gelding named Copper all on his own. When Cade suggests he lead the horse outside for grooming, Arlo readily complies.

Paige eyes their retreating figures with a mixture of admiration and discouragement. I'm guessing she figures that if her brother has mastered something, she shouldn't even try. I get it. I've been that girl, growing up in the shadow of a talented sibling. When we were kids, Troy received so much praise for his musicality I quit piano lessons. And I loved the piano.

"Oh, she's gorgeous!" I say when Cade leads Fancy Nancie out of her stall into the breezeway. "Paige, doesn't it look like she got splashed with paint? What do you think, does she look like a brown horse that got splashed with white paint or a white horse splashed with brown?"

Paige toys with the end of her braid and shrugs. I'm a dork, and I need to stop trying too hard.

"Here," Cade says, handing a brush to Paige. He runs her through a few basic horse facts, including the importance of grooming. "Horses are a lot like us," he says. "They don't like surprises—sudden movements or noises. So just chill. Be yourself. She's going to love you."

Paige looks doubtful. Tentatively she touches Fancy's thigh with the brush. I bet if I gave her the option, she'd bolt right this second. "She doesn't like me," she says. "See? She keeps looking at me." Paige backs away, dropping the brush. "I know she doesn't like me."

"Hmm," Cade says, "I have an idea." He releases the knot tethering Fancy Nancie and offers Paige the loose end of the lead rope. "It's okay. Go ahead. Take it. Good. Lead her this way." Outside, Cade opens the gate to a large round pen. "See? She's following you."

"She has to. I have the rope."

"How do you want her to feel about you?" He sounds genuinely curious.

The old, dejected Paige is back. The one I haven't seen in a while. The little girl without a friend in the world who rested her dark head on my counter at Homer's.

I see more clearly these days how my own level of self-assurance is to my dad's credit. When he told me, "You can do anything you put your heart and mind to, Audrey," I believed him. Does Paige's father speak courage to her? I don't suppose it's easy to accept a motivational speech from a man under lock and key.

Finally Paige answers, and with more vehemence than I'd expect. "I want her to be my friend."

"Friendship takes time, Paige. It takes work, right?" At this, Cade casts a side-glance my way. Which sparks a sensation in me that's altogether disproportionate to the concept of friendship. There is only one appropriate response to inconvenient chemistry. Ignore it.

Let. It. Die.

I scale the fence and settle my buns on top of it, curious to see what Cade could possibly have in mind for our frightened little filly named Paige.

"Alright now, Paige," he says. "Go ahead and let go of Fancy.

Good. You're going to communicate with her, let her get to know you. But we'll let her make her own choices."

Good policy. I presume we're still talking about horses.

Cade now holds a lunging crop, and he instructs Paige to stand with him in the middle of the pen. He asks her, "Have you ever trained a horse before?" and I conceal my smile. "No?" he says. "Then you're going to have to let me puppet you. Ready?"

I'm mesmerized by the man's unhurried manner. He's like the child whisperer. "Now, let me be clear," he says, placing the crop in her hand, "this isn't a whip. We never, ever use it to hit a horse. It's just an extension of our arm. We use it to tell the horse what we want her to do. So, see, when you hold it out and step toward Fancy, she'll know you want her to move away. And when you step back, she'll know you want her to come forward. Got it?"

With one arm wrapped around Paige and a hand guiding her wrist, Cade moves Paige toward Fancy, just one step, then maneuvers her arm to slowly raise the crop. Fancy swishes her tail and begins trotting in circles around the pen. "Excellent. See how her eye is fixed on you, and her ear is turned toward you? You have her attention. She's doing what you ask."

Paige doesn't blink. She's a hundred percent focused. As she and Cade slowly pivot in the middle of the pen, Fancy continues circling them. Her mane and tail flutter behind her like black and white ribbons. Her circles tighten and grow closer to the middle. I suppose this makes less work for her. She must be getting tired of this trotting business.

"You're doing great, Paige," Cade says. "Now, answer me this. Do you think a horse would pretend to like someone?"

"I don't know."

"Horses don't know how to lie. They can't pretend. Let's invite her in now." Cade guides Paige to lower the crop. Fancy halts. "Extend your free hand. Now step backward with me."

Fancy lowers her head, contemplating, then makes a slow bee-line for Paige. To my amazement, the child doesn't flinch.

I hold my breath.

"Okay, Paige. Just stay there." Cade removes the crop from Paige's hand and leaves her alone in the middle of the pen with the horse. "You're fine. I'll be right over here."

Fancy dips her muzzle. Paige pets her forehead. Moisture presses behind my eyes, and an inner electrical charge raises the hair on my arms. Using slow movements, I pull out my phone, frame a photo. Paige's fingers explore the thickness of Fancy's mahogany fur. The horse looks relaxed. Remarkably, so does Paige.

Cade's low, well-modulated voice soothes. It's not unlike his father's, I realize. If only I could sync my wild internal metronome to its tempo. "Okay, Paige. Do you trust me?"

Who wouldn't?

"When you're done petting Fancy, I want you to turn around and walk away." Paige's head snaps around. Her eyes plead with confusion. Cade gives her a reassuring smile and a nod. "It'll be okay."

She runs her hand down Fancy's white blaze and strokes her cheek a final time. "Bye, Fancy," she whispers, then turns away.

"You got this, Paige," I say.

Head hanging, she walks toward me, slowly covering the distance of ten or fifteen feet. I don't tell her what I see happening behind her. Instead I tighten my grip on the fence and brace myself for her moment of surprise.

Arlo's watching too, quietly approaching from the opposite side of the pen.

Fancy is following Paige. The same way Myrtle Rose has taken to following me around the house, even into the bathroom. The horse's head is mere inches from Paige's, and Paige has no idea.

At the unexpected dampness of Fancy's nostrils nuzzling the

back of her neck, Paige squeals and spins around. "Fancy! You silly, silly girl! Where'd you come from?"

"Looks like you've made a friend," Cade says.

"I guess." Still, Paige clings to her insecurity like a shield around her heart. Ugh.

"She likes you, Paige. Horses can't lie, right? Still don't believe me? Walk away again."

Paige takes several long steps, then stops. Looks over her shoulder. Again, the sweet paint has followed. A few more steps, and she turns again. Still Fancy shadows her. Paige smiles—a genuine smile that brightens her features and sends a lump to my throat.

Arlo scrambles to the top of the fence. "Hey, nice going, sis!"

I draw a shuddering breath and chance a look at Cade. I'm startled to find that he's watching me. Silently, I mouth two words. *Thank you.*

Thirty-Two

Daisy

When Audrey returns from her shift at Homer's and drapes her handbag over the kitchen chair, I paste on a smile. "Alexa, pause the music," I say. So much for Michael Bublé. So much for the pity party I've been queuing up.

"There's a Subaru in the driveway with a real estate logo," Audrey says. "Is that your friend?"

I put a finger to my lips. "Shh," I say, then draw her attention to the living room, where Dean is absorbed in the TV news. I don't know how he can stand it, really. All those red-faced pundits with ridiculous hair tasked with raising everyone's blood pressure. I doubt he gets anything out of it.

"Yes, that's Ellen. Is she still out there?" I peek around the curtain. "Hmm. We said goodbye ten minutes ago."

Audrey slips off her shoes. "She seemed to be chatting on her Bluetooth. How did it go?"

"It went well, I think." Is it possible it went too well? "I showed her around. Then we mostly talked outside." It had felt odd not to get Dean involved. Who would've ever thought I'd have to do something like this on my own? Who'd have thought I *could*?

Dean, that's who. He's always said I'm capable of more than I realize. And now . . .

Now he looks at me so helplessly, as if I hold the key to great understanding. Like Danny did as a child.

I offer Audrey the yellow cookie plate. "Here. Maybe this can tide you over till dinner."

"You baked!"

I'd forgotten how easily a batch of snickerdoodles comes together. "She said it's a perfect time to sell."

"That's great news. Right?" Audrey pours herself a glass of milk.

"She said the house is ready to show, although I might want to replace that old dinosaur of a refrigerator with a stainless steel one. So all the appliances match. But otherwise, she was very complimentary. Says it has curb appeal. Desirable location. The cozy factor."

A warm rush of appreciation floods me, for Dean's fastidious maintenance of this old place for so many years. That man of mine has been faithful on every level. Danny, too, coming up from California to give us a hand with the bigger projects. And now, his daughter. "Audrey," I say, and my voice catches, "all the things you've accomplished here . . . they've made such a difference. I'm utterly in shock at the listing price she suggested. We have you to thank."

"The things *we've* done, Daisy." She raises a cookie in triumph. "Team Needham."

"Not to mention Tawny and your work pals."

I know Audrey sees past all my rah-rah. We're dancing around an elephant in the kitchen. This is getting too real, too fast.

"How are you feeling about it now?" she asks, unwilling to let me off the hook so easily.

I exhale long and heavy. "Oh, you know. Surrendered, I guess. It's one of those both-and situations I'm learning to accept. I can be brave and scared at the same time. I'm wistful, of course. This house has been good to us. But it's only a house. I figure the Lord who met our needs every day here will meet our needs every day someplace else. My heart will catch up with my head eventually."

I break off half a cookie. "Have a seat, honey. We haven't had a chance to catch up since you took Paige out to the ranch yesterday."

Despite having worked on her feet all day, Audrey comes visibly alive. "Have you seen their horse setup? Oh my."

Good thing I know better than to call attention to the adorable flock of new freckles peppering her nose, the ones that bring to mind little-girl Audrey. Instead I admire her silently. This is hardly the same girl who showed up at our door last month, skittish and pale. This is a woman who has found her sparkle.

"Oh! I've got pictures." She pulls out her phone and scrolls. "Look, here's Paige—her first time on a horse, Daisy. Isn't that sweet?" A burst of warmth fills me. Nothing could've prepared me for seeing the young girl beaming with pride on the back of Camille's horse.

"And then look at her here. After a few minutes she got bored of trotting and took Fancy into a canter!" Audrey's ascending joy even distracts Dean from his television watching. She carries her phone into the living room to show him the photos, and he nods appreciatively.

"If you don't mind me saying it," I say when she returns, "you look . . ." I don't want to say anything she might interpret as manipulative.

She's still scanning the photos and smiling to herself. "I look . . . ?"

"Like you're in your element."

"You know, Daisy, I do feel like I've recovered something here. Something I'd, well, misplaced." Movement outside catches Audrey's attention. "There she goes."

I turn to see Ellen's royal-blue station wagon turning onto the road.

"She probably jumped right online to alert her colleagues that the cutest house in Charity Falls is coming on the market. What did she say about the front door? About painting it red?"

"She thought a little lipstick wouldn't hurt. But you have got to promise me that you'll stop after that. You've already outdone yourself. Spend your last two weeks relaxing. Chilling, as you call it. I mean, when you're not working at Homer's."

"I'll try. But—and I know how you feel about this—I do have one more thing on my list. I've decided to look into what's happening with the inn."

No. "Burn your list. Enjoy yourself."

"I looked up the tax lot in the county records online. I know who owns it."

A jolt passes through me. Here she goes again, meddling where no one should be meddling. "You can do that?" I start pulling random ingredients out of the fridge so she can't read my alarm. "What are you doing? It's my night to make dinner."

"Oh. Oh, yes. Habit."

"You can leave out the chicken. I'm thinking enchiladas. Anyway, yeah, it's all public record. But the thing is, it's listed as a corporation. Elijah-Grace or something like that. Does that mean anything to you?"

I give a nonchalant shrug. "Huh. Well. Certainly sounds as if they prefer to remain private. Some people do."

"Maybe it's not a name. Could be a religious reference. Hey, can I show you something?" Audrey disappears into the guest room and I blow out a long breath.

She returns with two paintings. "You might remember this one," she says. "Obviously I was young when I did it." She hands me my readers and I slip them on.

I press my hand to my chest. This is a child's watercolor painting of the Sugar Pine, back when it was vibrant with color. "I do!

I remember you carried a patio chair out to the middle of the field. Your mother and I kept checking on you. This is charming."

"Here's one I did the other night."

"Oh, Audrey. This is stunning." I carry the painting to the window and study it in the late afternoon light. "You know, even in its current state, the old house has a kind of poignant beauty. You've captured it."

"Like you said, I need to make peace with the place."

"Now this, Audrey, seems like a healthy means of coping. And your depiction is really quite compelling." Now, please, *please*, can't you leave it at that?

"Here's my thought. If I can share these paintings with the property owners, it might be an in. Nonthreatening, you know? Just a girl with a story. And maybe they'd be willing to answer my questions. Are they going to bulldoze the whole thing? Or is there hope for it? I'm also wondering about what's involved in getting it listed in the historic registry. If it's a developer who's sitting on it, that could really put a kink in their plans."

Audrey lathers her hands at the sink. "I know I'm playing the sympathy card. I don't know why, Daisy. But for some reason, I need it to turn out good."

Oh, dear girl. This is obviously about Danny. If only I could explain. Tell her I want to help, but my hands are tied. Instead I say, "I love your heart."

"You're the one who reminded me of my inner crusader." Audrey looks around for a place to wipe her dripping hands.

I offer her a towel. "That you are. I just think, honey, in this case, why not give it some time? Pray about it. I'd hate to see you stir something that's better left alone."

"How could that be better? You said yourself that strangers knock on your door wanting to know what's going on over there. I've been asked too. Seems like the whole town would love to know. And maybe to find some recourse."

"Unless they have a perfectly good reason for keeping a low profile." That's it. I've said too much.

"Seems to me if people are keeping a low profile, it's calculated. Probably some detached out-of-town developer who doesn't give a rip about Charity Falls. And I'm going to find out who."

Oh dear.

Thirty-Three

Audrey

On the last Wednesday in July, Homer's is quiet. Quiet enough that when my cell vibrates inside my purse under the paint counter, I hear it. And since I'm still on pins and needles waiting to hear from Beckenbauer-Vandersteen, not to mention two other firms for whom I polished my resume top to bottom, I scramble to retrieve it before it goes to voicemail.

"This is Audrey Needham."

It is none of those firms. But at least it's not a robocall. In fact, it's a real, flesh-and-blood, pleasant-sounding woman. "Hello, Ms. Needham? My name is Lucy Montgomery. I'm with the *Mountain Messenger*."

"Oh," I say. "Hello." What's this, yet another small-town nicety? The local paper calling in person to offer a subscription?

"We spotted one of your flyers in the grocery store—well, my editor did. And he'd like to know if you'd be interested in—what I mean is, I'd like to interview you. If that wouldn't be a problem." Ms. Montgomery doesn't sound entirely sure of herself. But despite all the flyers I posted around town in hopes of drawing attention to the plight of the inn, this is the only bite I've got. One that might just qualify as a big fish.

"You want to know . . . ?"

"We're interested in knowing more about your efforts to save the old Sugar Pine Inn."

With a heavy thud and then a clatter, my purse slips from my arms to the floor. Who cares if my lipsticks and intimate whatnots are rolling in all directions—this is it, the break I've been hoping for! "In that case," I say while scrambling to retrieve them, "where would you like to meet?"

———————〜———————

At first, when I arrive at Sweet Reads later that afternoon, I don't see anyone who resembles my idea of a reporter. I place my order, then channel my inner Elizabeth Bennet and take another turn about the room. A thirtyish brunette engrossed in a book has potential. At least, she's a more likely match for the voice on the phone than anyone else. "Would your name happen to be Lucy?" I ask.

The woman's pretty face brightens. "Is yours Audrey?"

Her features are delicate, like her handshake. I take a seat beside her on the red-velvet settee.

"Well, this is fun," I say. "I love this place, but I've never sat in this particular spot before. Nor have I ever been interviewed for any kind of publication for that matter." Good grief. I'm way too amped, and overly chatty.

Evidently it's contagious. "Actually," the woman says, tucking a strand that's come loose from her bun behind her ear, "that's perfect. Confession—I'm new at this. So I hope you'll bear with me." She digs out a spiral notebook and pen from her bag. "I mean, I was a journalism major. U of O. Gooo Ducks! I've been working for the paper since I moved here several years ago. Proofreading, editing obits, that sort of thing. And now my editor says it's time for me to get out there and give it a go. Guess we all need a little push sometimes, right?"

Not all of us. Some of us can conjure up a cruel amount of pressure and apply it to ourselves. "Okay then," I say. "Let's give it a go."

The woman flips through page after page of her notebook before finally coming to one that isn't already covered top to bottom in words. So many words.

"Looks like you do a lot of writing."

"Oh." Her cheeks flush. "A little. Nothing important." For an awkward moment, she simply stares at me, smiling.

"So, um, where shall we start?" I say.

"Oh yes. Let's start with the flyer. It's wonderful, by the way. You're quite talented. Can you tell me about it?"

"First," I say, "I wonder, do you know how long your editor— what's his name?"

"Well, it's Samuel Peabody III. But everyone just calls him Sam."

"Gotcha. I'm just curious how long he's been with the *Messenger.*" I don't see any way around it. To share my story effectively, I'll have to include the details of my family's blackest day. If her editor has been in this community for any length of time, he already knows a version of it.

But no one has ever heard my version. What little I know of that day usually comes to me in vivid, sharp-edged fragments. Can I even assemble them in a coherent way?

"I'm not exactly sure," Lucy says. "A long time. Sam isn't what you'd call, um, young. I'm pretty sure he arose from the Central Oregon soil and has Metolius River water running through his veins." I smile. The woman is a writer alright.

Well, in for a penny, in for a pound, as Aunt Daisy likes to say. So I tell her about sunflowers and scones and the piano lady. I describe the gazebo and pond, white weddings and wildflowers. It all tumbles out like scree down a mountainside. How Dad's mom was killed in a car accident and so his aunt and uncle stepped in to raise him as their son. The emotional weight of this settles across my chest as if for the first time.

"So he'd grown up working at the Sugar Pine," I say.

"Working?"

"Aunt Daisy was their cook, and since she lived right across the road, my dad started young. Dishwashing, yard work, mucking out stables. Everything." I tell her that this was where he fell in love with landscaping, which became his career. That he went to college in California, got married, raised his family there. I don't know how much of this the correspondent needs, but I figure she can decide.

"Anyway," I say, "he never stopped coming up here, especially later, as Daisy and Dean got older and needed more help." What I don't mention is how often I resented it. Like the time he missed my blue-ribbon moment at the middle school science fair. It wasn't just *my* project. It had been *our* project.

And like the time he'd never returned.

Which means my story has arrived at the precipice of the awful day.

I clear my throat. *Steady on.* And then I tell Lucy Montgomery about four horses and a two-week-old foal with golden fur. About how most of the inn's outbuildings dated back to the forties, including the barn. Original shake roofs, lumber dry as kindling.

"This barn, with the blue roof?" The reporter produces a copy of my flyer, points to the painting I did at age eleven. "It's lovely."

Tightness claws up my throat. I swallow. "Yes, that's it."

I steel myself. And then I proceed with the story of an oppressively hot summer afternoon. Of the stablewoman departing with guests on a trail ride, leaving the foal and her mother behind. And of something combustible lingering in a storage shed adjacent to the barn.

"My dad was visiting his family. Working at a table saw in

their driveway. He must have smelled smoke or heard the explosion. Anyway, he abandoned his project." Again I imagine my dad, always Johnny-on-the-spot at the first sign of need, dropping whatever he'd been doing and racing to respond. Like Chris Hemsworth as Thor, except not nearly as impervious. Like the gladiator of goodness.

The reporter writes at full tilt. I go silent and wait for her to catch up. Still, I need to press on while my courage holds.

"The mare escaped. She was crazed, trying to find a way back into the barn. But already it was engulfed. The roof, collapsing. A housekeeper called 911. Saw the foal run out. When the fire department showed up, all the horses were accounted for. It wasn't until after they'd doused the fire that they realized . . ."

Lucy's furious scribbling comes to a halt. She looks at me, stricken. "Wait. Are you telling me that your dad . . . ?"

Another deep breath and I'll get through. "Investigators figure my dad helped the horses escape. But he must have still been working to free the foal when the roof . . . all the flaming debris . . ."

For a long moment I stare at the untouched mug of tea I'm holding on to for dear life. "The main beam fell on him." Just saying it makes me catch my breath. "Maybe he'd already been overcome by smoke. We don't know. They transported him by Life Flight. He never regained consciousness."

This time, when my soft-focus remembrances dissolve into dark and haunting imagery, I let my mind go there. Scenes flash, sharp-edged. The phone call. My mother's scream. Wild eyes. Shattered glass. Weeks of hysteria, followed by months of hopelessness, followed by years of ash gray. My world, blanched.

"Oh." Lucy's eyelids flutter. "I see." She taps her pen on the page. "And you say this happened"—she flips back a page—"thirteen years ago? Have I got that right?"

"Thirteen summers next month," I say quietly, more to myself.

"So you were . . . how old?"

"Three weeks away from my sixteenth birthday."

It takes the woman a moment to regroup. At last, she looks back over her notes. Then shakes her head. "I don't even know what to say, Audrey. It's a nightmare. I'm so, so sorry."

"Thank you. I like to think he didn't suffer." I have to believe this.

"And this is why you're hoping to resurrect the inn." Her voice is gentle. "Because of what happened to your dad."

Is it? I nibble at a cuticle. "I only know that the property was a place of joy for a lot of people, for a lot of years. There are so many stories. I only know mine. And now it sits broken. I get the feeling it matters to others, not just to me. Perhaps many, many others. If not, then that's fine. I'll move on."

Somehow.

"But if it matters to Charity Falls, then I'd like to see it restored to Charity Falls," I say.

Thirty-Four

Nearly every square inch of the Trading Post Café's dark-paneled walls is covered with relics—antique rifles, rusted saws, faded black-and-white photos of Charity Falls' early days as a logging town. There's even one of old barrel-chested RJ Buck, the town's first mayor, sporting his signature ten-gallon hat. He had a personality to match, I'm told. RJ built a blue-roofed farmhouse on his cattle ranch just outside town—the farmhouse that years later would become the Sugar Pine Inn.

At some point he also built a humble house across the road for his ranch foreman. For the last fifty years or so, that small, white clapboard house has belonged to my family.

Paige is at her Saturday art class with Cara Murray, but I needed a chance to talk to her mother privately. Nina delivers my slice of chocolate silk pie and a glass of milk. This is a textbook case of stress eating. Although prayer might be a better remedy for the pickle I find myself in today.

Minutes later, Nina slides into the booth across from me.

"Did you make this pie crust?" I ask.

"I make all the pies." Her sable eyes shine with pride.

I moan in gratitude. "It's dreamy."

"So what's up?" Nina keeps her purse over her shoulder. I need to make this short and sweet. She deserves to go home and put her feet up.

I set down my fork. "Actually, it's something I've been meaning to bring up for a while." At my serious tone, Nina's relaxed expression turns to concern, and it dissects me. I never wanted to add to this woman's burdens. "I . . ." My throat's dry. I take a sip of my milk. I can't meet her eyes. Cannot do this.

What slips out is, "I've noticed Paige has trouble seeing clearly at certain distances." Because I am a big-time coward. And I'm stalling. "I mean, her up-close vision seems fine. But—"

Nina's relief is evident. "Yes, I know. Poor girl. We made an appointment at the health center, but they're always so backed up."

"Oh. Oh, good. That's great." I force myself to meet her eyes. The flavors in my mouth turn sour. *Just rip off the Band-Aid.* "There is something else, Nina. My last day at Homer's is coming up. This Tuesday, actually. I need to be home—you know, back to the Bay Area—by that weekend. I only ever meant to stay in Charity Falls long enough to—"

Nina interrupts. "Wait, does Paige know? She never told me any of this."

"Not . . . exactly."

"Not exactly?"

Heat creeps up my neck and pools in my face. I hang my head. "She doesn't know. And I have no idea how I'm going to tell her. I've been trying to—"

Nina's mouth hangs open. "She's gonna freak!"

"You think?" Could it be I've been willfully living in denial of how important my friendship has become to Paige? "It's not like I won't be back to visit. She can call me whenever she wants. We can stay in touch over FaceTime." My words pour out in a flood, each one more inadequate.

Nina sits frozen. The intensity of her glare communicates anger—no, hurt. Hurt tinged with fear. Fear for her daughter's heart. Nina's looking at me now like I'm no longer her daughter's savior.

I'm her enemy.

"You want *me* to tell her? Is that it?" She spits out the words.

"No, no. I can do it. I just wanted you to know."

Nina's out of the booth in one smooth movement. She hikes her purse strap higher on her shoulder and hardens her chin. "*I'll tell her.*"

———⌒———

As if this day could sink any lower, I return to find a glossy Coldwell Banker sign posted smack at the end of Daisy's driveway. Which should thrill me. Isn't this exactly what we've been working toward for the past two months? The house looks like a million bucks with its pristine white siding and picket fence, tidy lawn, and that Benjamin Moore Heritage Red front door. Not to mention mounds and mounds of lavender and a profusion of blooming daisies.

Mission accomplished.

But instead, the sign feels like a headstone. Mine.

I pause inside and let my purse slide to the floor. With fresh eyes, I take in the interior. Gone is the cozy clutter of my childhood memories. Gone is the dust-collecting décor scattered everywhere so that your eye didn't know where to land. The space has been professionally edited—by yours truly. Today it evokes simplicity and charm. Today the room is light and bright, with its creamy-white walls, woodwork, and fireplace surround.

My eye is naturally drawn to the green velvet chairs flanking the fireplace and the mantel vignette. For this I shopped other rooms of the house, choosing a framed landscape, a pair of tall iron candlesticks with white tapers, and Daisy's antique brass clock.

The low bookshelves that wing out to the corners of the room now house tidy rows of books arranged by spine color. I've grouped a few of Daisy's favorite owl figurines on a tray.

This space is inspired. This space is elevated. This home is dripping with hygge.

And soon this place will belong to a stranger.

"Hello?" My voice echoes in the sparse living room. "Anyone home?" Oh, that's right, Dean had a doctor appointment in Bend. They must have decided to grab dinner before heading back.

I meander toward the bookshelf and run my fingers over Daisy's Austen collection. Heck, I'd live in a place like this in a heartbeat. But chapters end. So do whole books. Someone else gets to fall in love with this house now.

I sink into Daisy's well-loved damask loveseat. Throwing good posture out the window, I roll forward, bury my face in my hands, and let the sobs come.

Thirty-Five

Daisy

Myrtle Rose mews. She stares through the sliding glass door into the inky night. "What's up, bossy pants?" I say. "That old tomcat come back around? Ohhh, *I* see what's got you all in a snit." Out on the patio, Audrey reclines in the moonlight. And she seems to be enjoying a glass of wine. Well, good for her.

"You've taken a liking to her after all, haven't you, Miss Myrtle? Me too, old girl. Me too."

I step outside, surprised when the motion-sensitive light doesn't come on. Audrey must have turned it off. "Daisy, look," she says over her shoulder. Her voice is hushed, infused with awe. "I can't believe how clear it is."

I'll take this as an invitation.

Settled into the other Adirondack, I peer heavenward. Starshine glimmers against a pitch-black canvas. The Milky Way stretches like a river of light. "It's indescribable," she says. "I'm going to miss this. Also, *shh*," She holds up a finger. "Listen." We wait. Then, a soft, melancholy *hoo* over in the pines. Then another.

When Audrey turns to me, I read weariness in her eyes. "Oh, Daisy. It's been a day." She sips her wine and falls back.

"You know, you don't get any bonus points for solving your problems by yourself. Have you not heard anything from Paige?"

"She won't take my calls."

"I'm so sorry, honey. She'll come around. These things have a way of sorting themselves out."

"Ha. You sound like Dad. He used to say, 'Everything is sortoutable.'"

"He got that from Dean."

"But it seems like ever since I arrived *nothing* has gone to plan."

"It rarely does."

"But . . . well, two more shifts at Homer's and I'm done."

"I have a feeling you've left your mark on Charity Falls."

Audrey sighs. "Why do I feel more like I've painted the town black? I'll feel better when I have a plan."

"I think you're awfully hard on yourself."

"I've heard that before."

"Considering the setbacks you've run into here, I'd say you don't give yourself nearly enough credit. But then again it isn't your first rodeo."

Audrey tips her head. "What do you mean?"

"You've had practice facing disappointments. If there's a secret sauce, Audrey, that's probably it—practice. Some people never, ever learn that we can't measure our life based on whether or not our expectations are met. It's not a question of *if* life will disappoint us. It's only a matter of when. How often. How deeply. The unexpected life *is* our actual life."

Audrey turns to me. "How can you say that? After all you've been through, all you've lost. Your sister. My dad. Camille. And now, in a way, your husband? How do you move past the heartbreak?"

"Oh, Audrey. Grief isn't something you move past, ever. It's something you learn to carry. That ache, the one that won't ever quit, that's how you know for sure it meant something in the first place. It mattered then, and it still matters. So we pick it up and carry it every day. And honey, we have got to allow our disappointments to draw us closer to God, not give us an excuse to drift further away."

Okay, I've said my piece. Maybe I should just let the stars do the talking. "But what do I know?" I add. "I'm just an old fuddy-duddy."

Audrey lays her hand over my arm and gently squeezes. "You know plenty. And I don't take it for granted."

A patch of gray clouds drifts across the moon. The owl calls. Audrey whispers into the vastness, "I think I understand now why I stayed away."

"From God?"

"From here. From you and Dean. I've been steering around a black hole of sadness for years, afraid of what might happen if I got too close. What if I fell in, you know?" She wipes a tear. "Seeing *your* grief up close, on top of mine, well. I think I figured it might sink me."

"Oh, honey. That's understandable. It really is."

"You know, my feelings about this place are complicated. Honestly, I was . . . and this may sound silly . . . sometimes I was jealous of Dad's time up here. I mean, I loved it when we all came together in the summer. But the rest of the year, it seemed like he was gone a lot. It probably wasn't all that often, but when I was young I didn't get it. To Dad, this place was always home. And he loved you guys so much."

I can't begin to recount all the various circumstances that brought Danny home. There was Dean's shoulder surgery. Often he came in the fall to winterize the sprinkler system and check our wood supply. Whatever needed doing, whenever. "Oh, Audrey," I say. "Sometimes holding on to resentments is our way of guarding our hearts. There are myriad ways to run away from our brokenness. I don't need to tell you that it's not healthy."

"Yeah." Audrey's smile is wobbly. "I tried to pretend I didn't lose something so . . ." A single tear trails down her cheek. She doesn't wipe it away. "So precious to me."

"He was more than our nephew, you know. He was our son."

"I know."

We stay like this for a time, without a use for any more words. Finally Audrey rises and gives me a soft peck on the head. "I think I'll go in. Good night, Daisy."

"I won't be long behind you."

"I love you."

I am no sage. But until tonight, I have missed being able to play at the role. What, I can't help wondering, have I ever done to deserve a heaven-sent delivery of hope, in the shape of a young woman with the same eyes as Danny?

I gaze at the limitless expanse overhead. The owl *hoo-hoo*s.

> *God of Our fathers, whose almighty hand*
> *Leads forth in beauty all the starry band*
> *Refresh thy people on their toilsome way*
> *Lead us from night to never-ending day.*

Thirty-Six

Audrey

Tuesday afternoon, Homer and I watch Alauna, a sales rep with the up-and-coming boutique paint company Aberdeen & Moss, exit the store. Somehow her loose-limbed stride, in a flowy dress and knee-high suede boots, communicates both professionalism and that easygoing nature I've come to identify as quintessentially Central Oregonian. The woman doesn't possess an ounce of tightly wound city veneer. Probably spends her weekends on a stand-up paddleboard.

Homer folds his arms over his chest and addresses me. "Well, what do you think? She made quite a presentation."

In truth, my heart is still drumming out a symphony. I'm spellbound. These brochures fanned out across the paint counter flirt with my weakness for pigment-dense colors with evocative names. A foggy green called Mizzle? A moody violet called Stella's Sofa? I'm all about this. I move one of the large samples back and forth under the light, admiring its gentle luster. No wonder Alauna said they're winning awards.

"This is cutting-edge," I say.

Homer scratches his head stubble. "But is it a good fit for us?"

Again I peruse the colors of the small-but-growing manufacturer's Heritage Collection. Immediate inspiration unfolds, a nuanced palette of hues appropriate for the intricate interior details of Whittier Mansion. Which doesn't necessarily mean this product is right for Homer's small-town clientele.

"It's super innovative," I say. "And the fact that they're based right up the road in Bend is crazy. Plus, Alauna's awesome. She'd be easy to work with."

"Agreed."

I consider the pleasing, eco-friendly shades of what they call their PNW Collection. There's something here for every unique corner of the Northwest. Mountains, desert, coast. "The local decorators are loyal to you, Homer. They seem to *want* to shop here, and they represent a discriminating clientele. I'm sure they'd appreciate this option."

Homer appears to weigh my input—as if it's actually valuable to him. When I suggested this meeting after Alauna pitched the product to me last week, he said, "If you think it's worthwhile, schedule it." How blessed I've been to have had men in my life who've affirmed me. Starting with my dad.

"But," I say, "your average paint customer is a DIYer on a budget. When it comes to large projects, upscale products like this will be too pricey. But for smaller projects? I see them in here all the time tackling small, manageable projects they've seen on their favorite home improvement shows or Pinterest. Fixing up a mudroom, or installing a shiplap or board-and-batten wall. Painting an accent wall an interesting color. That one's a major trend right now.

"If they fall in love with one of these colors, it could be an easy sell. Especially if someone explains the value to them. Density of pigment means less coats. Less coats means less work."

Homer hums in agreement. "Could be good for our image. Our brand, as they say. You two sure hit it off. You seem to speak the same language."

I grin. "I can talk about color all day."

"It's good to have a passion."

I've enjoyed my time here at Homer's in ways I could never have anticipated. I get to listen to people describe their projects and offer advice when it's helpful. Sometimes customers will even stop by to share before-and-after pictures.

Out of the blue, Jan's huge, round voice rings across the store. "Well, look who's here. Daisy Needham, *yew* are a sight for sore eyes! Ya know, I recently had a dream about your marionberry scones. The ones with that heavenly sprinkle of coarse sugar and lavender on top? Thought I'd died and gone to heaven."

Daisy bats the air dismissively. "Oh, pshaw. Ancient history. But it's nice to see you, Jan."

Something about the direct way Daisy approaches the paint department gives me the uncomfortable feeling this isn't a warm-'n'-fuzzy social call.

"Am I interrupting?" she asks Homer.

"Not at all," he says good-naturedly. "Just pickin' your niece's brain while I still got the chance. We're going to miss this gal. She is one sharp cookie. And in case I don't see you later," he says, addressing me directly now, "I know I can speak for the whole team when I say that we've sure enjoyed having you." He pats me on the upper arm. "Don't be a stranger now."

Daisy waits until Homer rounds the aisle. "Can we talk?"

"Sure. I was just about to take my break." I stash my blue apron under the counter.

Outside, Daisy's yellow bike leans against a post. "You rode? Good for you." I gesture to a bench. "Would you like to sit down?"

Daisy wrings her hands in a way I've never before seen her do. "I'd rather walk. Would you mind?"

"Is everything okay?" I ask.

We've covered half a block before Daisy stops. Her fingers shake as she unzips her floral fanny pack. "I found this at the post office."

She scans for privacy before unfolding a piece of printer paper—as if it were something indecent.

Only, I recognize it as one of my flyers.

"Are there any more of these?"

You bet there are. How else was I going to call attention to the inn after being turned away from City Hall with no new information about the identity of the property owners or the corporation they hide behind—Elijah-Grace LLC. Fine, I'd thought. I just needed to be more resourceful.

So I created a public notice of sorts. A poster with side-by-side images of my two paintings and a number for concerned citizens to call with any information.

"There are others," I say. Seven, to be exact, if you count the one my aunt's clutching and the one in the newspaper lady's possession. "Why, Daisy? I'm not sure I understand what's wrong. I guess I should have mentioned it to y—"

She fists her hands, crumpling the flyer. I've never seen Daisy so worked up. "Audrey, there's something you need to know. Something I should have disclosed sooner."

"Okay."

"Try to understand, this isn't about you. I've been, well, caught in the middle here. Oh heavens, this is all my fault."

I flinch. "What? What is all your fault?"

"You see, I assumed . . . I *hoped* your concern about the old Sugar Pine would fizzle. That nothing would come of it. But now that you've drawn attention to the situation . . ." She says this like it's a bad thing. Hasn't Daisy always encouraged the crusader in me?

"Honey, listen," she continues. "Do you remember the role Camille played for so many seasons on Broadway? The one she's known for?"

"Sure. Of course." What has this got to do with the price of tea in Charity Falls? "Grace Kelly. Not that I ever got to see—"

"Grace, Audrey. *Grace*." A slow dawning. Is she saying . . . but no, that wouldn't make sense. "Oh, honey, Elijah-Grace LLC is the Carters. It represents Nash and Camille's holdings—properties, movie rights, and so on. Elijah was their younger boy's name. The son who drowned."

"I can't . . . but wait . . . that means . . ."

Daisy's expression is bleak. "Yes. That they own the property across the street from us. And I would give my last tooth not to have to be the one to break it to you."

A couple approaches. We stand silent and wait for them to pass.

"I don't understand," I say finally.

"When Camille moved back six years ago, the place was already in bad shape. The people who bought it from the Milligans planned to restore it and reopen it as the Sugar Pine. Well, you already know that part. They started renovations, tore into the place, removed the old sunroom. I still don't know why they abandoned their plans. Maybe they ran into unforeseen costs. For some reason, they boarded it up and put it back on the market."

Daisy lifts a hand to caress my cheek. "Honey, Nash and Camille felt very much like you do now. They hated to see it go to pot. So they bought it, and they had plans for it. Amazing plans. Cade could tell you more about it. But then, of course, Camille got sick. Life stopped. Dreams died. Plans fell off the table. I think it's safe to assume that Nash no longer has the heart for it."

And I, Audrey Needham, may have singlehandedly brought the community's most beloved citizen—the pride of Charity Falls—a wagonload of unwanted attention. I think I'm going to be sick. "Oh, Daisy! What have I done?"

"Let's just get those posters down. I'll help. Just tell me where they are. It's possible nothing will come from—"

"Oh no!" I clap my hand to my mouth. All the blood vessels in my head constrict at once. "Oh, Daisy, that's not all of it." I have to speak it. Words that I can't wish away. "It's going to be in the newspaper—I mean, it's . . . someone's writing a story about it."

I need to call the reporter, stat. With shaking hands I pull out my phone. Juggle it. Barely rescue it from falling to the concrete sidewalk. "I'll stop the story." Yes, that's it. I've got to stop it.

"Wait. Slow down a second. Audrey, what are you talking about?"

"A reporter from the *Messenger*—oh, Daisy!—she saw my flyer and asked for an interview. I'm calling her. We can stop this. I *never* meant to bring Nash or his family any trouble."

"Alright. Okay. Let's think this through. Yes, you do that. Call the reporter."

I scroll for her number. "What day of the week does the paper come out?"

"Wednesday."

"That's tomorrow!"

"Honey, stay calm. For all we know, they aren't planning to run the story right away. It's not like it's major breaking news."

"I got her voicemail. I'll leave a message." Can I even retract my interview? Is that a thing? "Is there anything else we can do?"

"I'll call Sam Peabody. Better yet, I'll ride over to his office straightaway. Oh, it's probably well after business hours. But I'll try."

~

After leaving messages for both Lucy and her editor, there's nothing to be done except hope the story doesn't run in tomorrow's paper. And pace the guest room. How will I ever sleep?

What's my mantra? Oh yes. *Stop beating yourself up.* And also, *Things will look brighter in the morning.* That one's questionable. *Everything is sort-outable?* Problem is, I don't yet know what I'm going to have to sort out. Where will the pieces fall? How sharp are they?

Ugh. I have got to switch mental tracks. Can someone my age get a brain aneurism? If so, I may be well on my way. And then what? I see it playing out. The paramedics show up, discover I'm the one who threw shade on Nash and Camille, implicating them as small-town slumlords.

"Oh, *she's* the one," they'll say, repacking their gear and leaving me to my quick demise. Am I being overly dramatic? Tell that to my body.

Yoga? Would it even help?

A bubble bath? I'm unworthy.

Thirty-Seven

"There appears to be some confusion," Miss Brittany says on Wednesday afternoon when I arrive at Charity Falls Parks and Rec to pick up Paige. "I told Paige you were here, but she insists you're not her ride. Lemme just check with the office. Her mom may have called in a change."

I try to act casual. But I've got one eye out for any sign of Paige and the other on Brittany's hushed conversation with a lady at the front desk. Over Brittany's shoulder, the receptionist keeps flicking narrow-eyed glances my way. I can't help reading them as sanctimonious. Heat prickles my cheeks.

Brittany approaches, expression apologetic. "Yep. That's what happened. We got a message from Paige's mom saying there's been a change. Actually, she said the change to Wednesdays and Fridays is permanent. So, yeah. It sounds like some wires got crossed somewhere. Sorry about that."

Can Brittany read me? Is it obvious a pair of uncommonly sharp kids' scissors is piercing my heart? Wednesday was one of *my* days. And today is my last.

"But it's nice to see you! Hey, have you given any more thought to the book club? We met last week and I told them *all* about you. We purposely chose a fluff book in case you want to join. You said beach read, right? Sooo . . ." Brittany scrunches her shoulders up around her ears adorably and smiles. "We chose *Sand Between My Tomes*. I already started it, and let me tell you, it is the perfect palate cleanser after a couple of heavier reads. Whoops! I shouldn't tell you my thoughts yet. I—"

I hate to cut off a book enthusiast under any circumstances, but in this case . . . "Brittany, sorry—"

"Call me Britt."

"*Britt*. It's just that I don't have a lot of time." Less than twenty-four hours, to be exact. "Would you mind asking Paige to come out for a minute? I'll just wait right here."

"Oh, sure. No problem! I'm sure she'd love to see you. Be right back."

Brittany reappears several minutes later wearing a considerably tighter expression. "Sorry, Audrey. She said no. I'm sure it's nothing personal. She's been kind of in a funky mood lately. Is everything okay?"

Tears pool. I blink them back. I should probably attempt to disguise my disappointment from bookish Miss Brittany. But today I have nothing left in my emotional dress-up trunk. I'm gutted. At this rate I'll have to leave without saying goodbye.

"Would you like to leave her a note?"

"Yes!" Suddenly I could kiss her. "Thank you, Brittany—I mean Britt. I'd really like that."

"No problem. Need a piece of paper?"

"No, I'm good. I'll just be back in a minute."

I'll have to work fast. Sounds like Nina could show up any minute. Nothing like an imminent deadline to get the creative juices flowing. An image appears in my mind's eye, and I start speed-sketching, all the while darting glances in my side mirror for the first sign of Nina's car. I scroll to a selfie on my phone for reference, from the day we wore ourselves out doing cartwheels in the park. In it, our cheeks touch, and Paige's smile reaches her eyes, lighting her whole face.

I lean back and consider it. This will have to do. After scrawling a few loaded words at the bottom, I race toward the building. The toe of my shoe catches on the curb. I barely manage to stop myself from falling.

The moment I hand over the drawing in exchange for Brittany's promise to give it to Paige, a weight lifts. I can breathe again, knowing I've been able to communicate my feelings to her. A fraction of them, anyway. The sensation of relief dissipates, however, the moment I step toward the glass exit doors.

I'm about to come face-to-face with Cade Carter.

Of course it would be him. Saving the world, one child at a time.

The subtlest flicker of his eyelids tells me that he, too, senses the invisible caution tape suspended in between us. He tips his chin. "Hey, Audrey." A tepid greeting. I'm trying to read his face. Did he see the flyers before I took them down? Did his father? Or worse . . . have they seen the newspaper article?

"Oh, hey," I say. "You must be Paige's ride." No point in trying to disguise my open wound. I haven't the fortitude to paste on a smile.

"And you must be leaving soon."

"Tomorrow." What else is there to say? *I'm sorry I ruined everything? Sorry I so vividly confirmed your original suspicions about me? Not to mention I've subjected your wonderful family to public reproach?* There's a multivehicle pileup of apologies clogging my brain.

The sooner I leave town, the better for all parties involved. Humiliation is eating me up. Failure may not be fatal. But by its very definition, mortification is.

"Well, I'd better get—" He reaches slowly for the door handle. I step aside. "Right. Bye, Cade."

A corner of his mouth quirks ruefully. "Take care, Audrey."

Cade's aqua-sky truck is parked directly next to Harriet. Our vehicles wear a matching film of red road dust. Funny, I've never gone so long without washing my car.

Stupid, stupid tears.

To get in the driver's side, I have to walk sideways in order to clear Cade's large, chrome side mirror. As I do, I can't help noticing what's resting on his dashboard. A disheveled copy of the *Mountain Messenger*.

I feel sick to my stomach. I've definitely overstayed my welcome in Charity Falls.

Thirty-Eight

Lucy wrote a fabulous article in the *Mountain Messenger*. A real heart-wrencher.

Her piece, and the accompanying photo of the deserted inn, will no doubt stir up exactly the kind of collective community outrage I desired.

Trouble is, I no longer desire it.

Trouble is, and I can see this so clearly now, my passion has been misplaced. And it has effectively alienated me from the entire Carter family. By extension, I've caused Aunt Daisy pain and embarrassment, no matter how she tries to placate me.

Somehow I've even found a way to dishonor Camille Bettencourt—may she *please, please, please* rest in peace.

Everyone will be better off when I leave tomorrow morning.

In Bend tonight, I purchase the only edible item Target's Starbucks kiosk has to offer, a packaged gluten-free brownie with seven thousand ingredients listed in print too tiny to read. If I break down and eat it, I know I'll feel even more hopeless. But this isn't merely about to-brownie or not-to-brownie. This is about the warmth that keeps crawling from my torso to my face, the queasiness I can't shake.

Shame clings to me like dragon scales. Because any way you stack it, I've done more harm than good in Charity Falls.

I thumb-type a message across the miles. As much as I hate to be a downer, texting Tawny is my last resort.

> Driving home tomorrow. Made a mess of things here. I'll be shocked if the sheriff doesn't send a squad car to escort me out of C. Falls.

My cell rings. "Say what? What's going on? It can't be that bad."

"Tawny, I'm super salty right now. You might regret this call."

"Out with it."

I provide Tawny with the thumbnail version, up to but not including the part where I ran into Cade, and altogether omitting the part where I zoned out for an hour scrolling through Bob Ross memes. Which was worth it, if only for *Ever make mistakes in life? Let's make them birds. Yeah, they're birds now.*

"Hmm. What does Daisy think about it?"

"She says it's a fine kettle of fish."

"I don't know what that means."

"Yeah, me neither."

"Okay, well, calling yourself 'lower than a wart on a troll' is a little harsh."

"You think? And here I almost said 'a wart on the butt of a troll' but then thought better."

"And what about Cade? What did he say?"

"He only had about three words for me, and two of them were basically *good* and *bye*. The tables have turned and it's my turn to apologize, Tawny. I just haven't been able to come up with the words. I've never, ever been so ashamed."

"Everything will look brighter in the morning. Where are you anyway?"

"Target."

"This late at night? What are you doing?"

"Besides reorganizing a display of onesies?"

"Shocker. Meanwhile, I'm down here eating cake over the sink so I don't get crumbs in my bed."

If Tawny can still make me snort-laugh, there may yet be a flicker of hope. Well, a speck of a flicker. "I figured the only retail therapy I could justify was shopping for Ava's baby shower while I'm still in a state with no sales tax. You should go to bed. I need you to be at your best tomorrow for my next counseling session."

"Ooh, no sales tax! In that case, can you pick up a case of newborn Pampers?"

"Did you say a case?"

"I guess? I have no idea, I just need a bunch for one of the weird shower games. Hey, since the shower's on Saturday, you should just stay here, with me. Why drive to the Bay Area and back? I won't take no for an answer. Text me tomorrow and let me know when you'll get in. Okay, *mwah*. G'night."

"Wait. Tawny, don't hang up! Does it have to be Pampers?"

"No, of course not. Whatever you think. I mean, as long as they're free of toxic, ozone-depleting chemicals. She'd hate that. And as long as they have some kind of cute designs—oh, but not *Sesame Street*. Ava's got that weird complex about Big Bird."

"Right, got it. Good night."

Ten minutes later, I've eliminated Target's generic brand—Ava's too snobby for that—as well as the one that claims it's cruelty-free. Twenty-four percent of online reviewers rated that diaper a one, and as far as diaper blowouts go, they offer no promises. So I've narrowed it down to two brands.

This is too stressful. I have no bandwidth for decision-making. Tawny will have to make the call.

Me
Still up? I can get 76 Pampers with shea
butter for $27.49 or 128 Huggies Little
Snugglers for $43.49. Both say no synthetic

fragrance. Also, I hate to break it to you, but if eco-consciousness were Ava's guiding principal, she wouldn't be using disposables.

Tawny
You don't need me for this.

Ok, I'll go by reviews. Huggies 4.7, Pampers 4.6.

This just in! Pampers has Target's "clean" icon, guaranteed no unwanted chemicals!

Just go with the Pampers. Pamper is practically Ava's middle name. 😂 And buy yourself a new outfit while you're at it.

I don't deserve nice things.

Thirty-Nine

Thursday morning, a bleak haze obscures the Cascades. Smoke from a forest fire many miles west of here. Great, I can't even say goodbye to the mountains.

Harriet is packed way more snugly than when I arrived in Charity Falls. I've inherited so many books from Daisy, I could practically start my own Sweet Reads. Other scores include a super-sexy, vintage, mid-century-modern end table with childhood memories attached. And my grandparents' hand-stitched wedding quilt.

Those old sketches tucked in my blue vintage suitcase now have plenty of company. Daisy surprised me with a stack of cards and letters she and Dean received from my mom and dad over the years. But what I'm especially humbled to now possess is a cache of Dad's artwork. Pieces I've never before laid eyes on.

Oddly, there's something similar in our styles.

Evidently during his time at Cal Poly, Dad completely geeked out on botanical illustration. I've got an old sketchbook filled with his pen-and-ink studies. *Jasminum officinale. Rosa californica. Delphinium grandiflorum.* The ones he colored are absolutely dreamy. I had no idea he ever burnished his own paper, mixed his own pigments. Holding his Royal Horticultural Society Colour Chart—a second-edition, dated 1966—I nearly frothed at the mouth. *Oh, Dad. What treasures.*

Aunt Daisy and Uncle Dean's goodbye routine whisks me back in time. At the end of every summer visit, our partings never varied. It's a dance for which I suddenly remember all the steps. Once I'm in the car with the engine running, Uncle Dean will sweep his feet together and perform an over-the-top military salute. Meanwhile, Daisy will rest her hands on her hips, dressed in a stoic smile that I now realize has always hidden a world of emotion. She'll keep it simple. She won't blow kisses. When I turn out of the driveway onto the road, she'll simply raise her arm and hold it high until I'm out of sight.

And that's exactly how it happens. Only this time, I'm helpless to stop the bubbling up in my chest. The brimming in my eyes. The ache that hurts so good because it means I'm leaving filled with something I've long denied myself. Love. Family.

These are the riches I want to share with Paige. And I'm going to give it one more try, come what may.

If only the Sun Country Apartments, where she and her family live, could be repainted in Aberdeen & Moss colors, it might actually be homey. I approach the ash-gray building. It's Nina's day off, and her car is in its spot in front of unit number nine. After ringing the doorbell, I stare at the front door mat and the pair of yellow flip-flops I bought for Paige.

The smell of sausage cooking drifts through a crack in the kitchen window. Nina answers the door with a smile that's surprisingly encouraging. She wants to bridge the divide, I can tell. "I got your text," she says quietly. "Paige is in her room. She's supposed to be getting ready for her eye appointment. I don't know if she'll see you, but we can try. Come in."

"Is Arlo home?" I'd love a chance to say goodbye to him as well.

"He's still asleep."

Right. It's only half past eight, and the boy is on the precipice of puberty. Nina and Cade have their work cut out for them.

Inside, I gasp. A painting of a horse hangs on Paige's bedroom door, something that smacks of Cara Murray's instruction. I recognize Fancy's coloring. Bold strokes of mahogany and white. Streaks of black in her mane. Nina knocks, then cracks open the door. "Paige, honey, someone's here to see you."

My eyes meet Paige's briefly before she moves out of my line of sight. "I'm busy. Tell her I'm busy."

"Paige, please," I say softly. "I know you have an appointment. Can I talk to you for a quick second? I brought you something."

Nina dips past me. "I'll be in the kitchen," she whispers.

"Paige, may I come in?"

"Whatever."

I enter slowly. Among the clutter of clothes on her floor, I spot the drawing I made for her. I pick it up. "You know, I meant what I wrote here. I'm your forever friend."

She folds her arms and turns to face her closet. "No you're not. You're leaving."

I lower myself gently to the foot of her bed, setting down the Ziploc bag of gumballs from Homer's next to me. "Can we talk?"

Her chin quivers, and she turns another degree to hide it. Damp, dark strands of freshly washed hair cascade down her back. I long to help her comb it out. French braid it. But she's not my doll. She never was. She's a sensitive child with a malleable heart and soul, and what she needs is more people in her life she can count on.

"I'm sorry, Paige. I messed up. I shouldn't have waited so long to tell you I had to leave. I just . . . I didn't want to think about it. I knew it was going to be hard for me, just like it's hard for you."

"It's not hard for me. I don't want to be your friend anymore."

"Are you sure? Because friendship takes work, but I think it's worth it. It's all been worth it to me, even though now I have to miss you while I'm in California. The best things in life take work, Paige. And sometimes they're wonderful and fun. Other times they hurt." We're at a silent stalemate. "Your horse painting is beautiful."

When she wheels around, her face glistens with tears. She stomps to her bedroom door and yanks the horse painting down. A thumbtack whizzes past my face. "No it's not! It's stupid! I'm stupid!"

"*Nooo*, honey . . ."

Paige claws at the drawing on my lap, and it flutters to the floor. "*You're* stupid!" She swipes at the gumballs. The bag smacks against her dresser. Gumballs roll to the carpet. "And I. Don't. Want. To be. Your. Friend. *Anymore!*"

Nina reappears, sending me a doleful look. "Oh, manahuu, sweetheart . . ."

Paige rushes to her mom, buries her face in her chest, and clings. Her shoulders convulse. Her mother is safe.

And I'm a monster.

Forty

DAVIS, CALIFORNIA

Charcuterie boards are ingenious. They satisfy my artist's soul. Color, harmony, taste, texture. And best of all, from one visual masterpiece, everyone has the opportunity to create their own.

Under a banner that reads "Oh Baby It's a Boy!" I attempt to arrange prosciutto, cheese cubes, cornichons, water crackers, two kinds of olives, and a blob of homemade, honey-sweetened stone-ground mustard on a Lilliputian paper plate without throwing off the visual balance. These plates are far too small. I'll have to come back for the mozzarella balls and strawberries and dark chocolate squares.

Ava sidles up next to me with her prominent belly. Can a woman get any more pregnant? She looks amazing in a form-fitting dress in baby blue with large pink roses and an off-the-shoulder ruffle. "Audrey, you weren't kidding," she says, slicing into a block of cream cheese dripping with the marionberry pepper jelly I brought from Oregon, "This jelly is the bomb. I'm obsessed."

"Me too." I'll have to come back for some of that too.

"Oh! Audrey, this is my neighbor Lydia." I greet a woman who's probably close to forty, with gorgeous long, loose curls. Like the style I was going for today, but hers turned out much more picture-perfect. "Lydia, this is the friend I was telling you about. The designer. I bet she can solve your furniture dilemma." Ava disappears, leaving her neighbor and me to chat.

Lydia's pleasant. But she's quite verbal about her distaste for party games, and Tawny is about to get things rolling in that department. She worked hard to put these together, and I'd like to support her.

But Lydia only wants to talk decorating. Ten minutes later, I'm still tethered to the kitchen island with her while Tawny passes out pens and paper to the crowd of guests in the great room, and I'm doing my best to pay attention to both. It sounds like the object of the first game is to name the celebrity based on their baby photo. Fun. But I suppose I should view the woman before me as a potential client.

Still, I look for an opening to break off the conversation with lovely-haired Lydia. We've already covered her living room furnishings and moved on to the new bedroom and bathroom she'd like to add.

"So," she says, "is that the kind of thing you do?"

"Well," I say, eyeing an open chair near Tawny's mom, "with major structural changes, you'll for sure want an architect. But you may also want an interior designer." I explain that larger architecture firms, such as the one I'm interviewing with this week, often have designers on staff.

"Got it," she says. "Then what's the difference between an interior decorator and an interior designer?"

As we've been chatting, I can't help noticing Lydia's unusually plump lips. And her exquisite eyebrows. Microblading? An analogy materializes. "Loosely speaking, you could think of the differences between an architect, an interior designer, and a decorator like the differences between a plastic surgeon, an aesthetician, and a Sephora salesperson. *Very* loosely speaking."

"Oh! That makes perfect sense!" she says.

Did it? Tawny's holding up the first picture. That smile, that button nose . . . so familiar. Sandra Bullock? "You know," I say to my new acquaintance, "this game looks fun. I think I'll go join."

Later, Tawny walks me to my car, carrying two plates of left-over food Ava's mother insisted I take home. *Home.* Now there's a concept as clear as dishwater.

She passes the food through my open window. "Call me Tuesday. I want to know how your interview goes. And hey, I see that look. Cut yourself some slack. You're doing the best you can."

The Saturday traffic ebbs and flows as I plan my week. Monday, I'll clear out my desk and tie up loose ends at DeSoto. Tuesday holds a drive out to San Francisco's Marina District for my interview with Crabtree Interiors. Then it'll be back once again to the city on Friday for the Whittier Mansion walk-through. Next week I'm on tap for a team conference at the Beckenbauer-Vandersteen office. So let the collaboration begin. Time to pull my professional facade out of my metaphorical closet.

I'd sure be more comfortable if I had more than one interview lined up. Unfortunately, I've all but exhausted my Bay Area connections, which yielded no shortage of no-openings-right-now and I'll-keep-my-ear-outs. Should I investigate the LA market or wait and see what shakes here?

Is it even possible to have clarity about the next right thing while still down on yourself for the last wrong thing?

Again I see Paige's face, twisted in rage. Nina's slumped shoulders. The disappointed demeanor Daisy tried to hide. And the sparse response I got from Cade. When I finally texted my apology, I received two words, *thank you.* I only hope he honored my request to convey a heartfelt apology to his father as well. What must they think of me?

Nothing I don't deserve.

The highway lines are hypnotic. I sense a sugar crash in the offing. With a two-hour drive ahead, I may need to pull off for coffee. But it isn't just the three-layer vanilla cake coming back to haunt me. Playing the part of a happy, supportive friend at Ava's shower while privately shouldering this remorse has taken everything out of me. Wearing a mask is exhausting, even for an expert mask-wearer like me.

But if Cade is any example, there's a way to live in peace with failure.

Lord, this is too heavy. I can't bear it alone.

I sense I'm approaching an important aha moment. But the overhead sign says the exit to I-680 is just ahead. I flick on my blinker and merge right, annoyed. Clearly I've spent years allowing external pressures, never-ending motion, to keep me from doing the inner work necessary for a life of freedom and wholeness. I've missed too many off-ramps. Truth is, I've pursued distraction on purpose.

It's hard to make heart connections from a hamster wheel.

There are myriad ways to run from our brokenness. Have I been running? Am I running now? Busyness, success—oh, please, can't I just call it a strong work ethic?—has been my safe harbor. Anything that kept me focused on externals.

The trouble with externals is they fool us into thinking we're in control. Until we're not.

Stay with it. You're getting somewhere.

What is this drivenness I've allowed to fuel me—to *form* me—if not an outward expression of an inward wound?

Name your wound, Audrey. It's time.

251

Forty-One

How strange to find the front door of DeSoto Design locked during business hours on a Monday. At my knock, Joshua appears through the glass, smiling with all his pearly whites showing. He welcomes me with a side hug. "Good timing. Maleficent has left the building."

I hand him a kraft gift bag tied with orange ribbon. "For you. A few provisions from the Beaver State."

Inside, a faint trace of sandalwood still lingers. But the soft instrumental strains are gone. No more high-end clients to bewitch into a spending mood, I suppose. In their place is something shockingly twangy. I narrow my eyes at Joshua. "Is that . . . Carrie Underwood? Really? Country? You?"

"What can I say? Mondays call for my 'Georgia Jukebox' playlist. I'm still reppin' my roots. I trust you'll keep it between us."

"And what's this about?" I drag my hand over my jaw and chin. Joshua's as fly and well-shellacked as ever. Light refracts off his pomaded black hair like a solar flare. But I've never seen him with cheek stubble. And evidently I've missed teasing him.

"Something new I'm trying."

"Huh. I like it. You've always been a hair too perfect. Made me feel shabby."

The phone rings, and Joshua spins toward the reception area.

"Gotta take this. Grab a box," he says, with a nod toward a corner housing a jumble of items—rolled-up area rugs, stacks of boxes, a whiteboard, wall art.

I pass through the wide, empty space that used to be occupied by the conference table. The Asian-influence kitchen island is also missing. Despite Joshua's occasional updates over the past weeks, I can't shake the feeling I've stepped into an alternate reality. One in which our studio is no longer on point.

Not *our* studio. All my contributions, all the hours and effort, have turned this into nothing more than my previous place of employment.

My desk space appears just as I left it, except for two additions. Dust and a plain manila envelope. There's my calendar, still open to May and the word *Oregon*. My parlor palm. The horse figurine little Billy wanted to hold during my last client meeting. I flick the corner of a business card from what feels like another life.

The envelope holds a neatly typed letter with DeSoto's gold-embossed logo. *Dear Hiring Manager, It is my pleasure to strongly recommend Audrey Needham . . .*

Astonishing. I hadn't even thought to ask Pilar for a letter of recommendation. But why not send it digitally? "Why a hard copy?" I say aloud, as much to myself as to Joshua.

Joshua's digging into my gift bag. "Oh, I didn't have your personal email. We just killed most of the individual DeSoto .com email addresses. I don't know, maybe she thought a signed copy was more . . . *personal*." He punctuates that last bit with a wink.

"Right. Maybe," I say.

"So hey, don't leave without jotting down your email address on this here little notepad. Oh, and also, per the boss, I'm to send you *the list*." At my quizzical look, he says, "Potential clients. People who've tried to reach Pilar and been informed by her incredibly charismatic EA that she's—" Here, Joshua pauses to make air quotes. "*On leave . . .* which, as you know, is code for *focused on winning her husband back.*"

I'm still adjusting to a strange new sensation whenever I think of Pilar and her family situation. Empathy.

"They're solid leads, Audrey. You really might want to consider contacting them as a private business entity. I'm supposed to send the same list to Keiko. Pilar said you two could duke it out. Nah, she didn't say duke. That was all me. Dude! What is this?" Joshua tosses a wad of orange tissue paper over his shoulder with a flourish. "Dark chocolate hazelnuts? You shouldn't have. But I'm *so* glad you did. Ooh, coffee!"

"Clean sourced in Guatemala. Micro-roasted in Charity Falls. Also, that marionberry pepper jelly is about to change your life."

"Crazy."

I turn my attention back to the envelope, this time focusing on the attached note written in Pilar's tight, angular script.

Audrey,

Letter of rec enclosed. For future correspondence, please provide J with your personal email. I asked him to print copies of your drawings from significant projects. Make sure it's all there, whatever you need. With such a strong portfolio I don't think you'll have trouble finding work. Did you hear from S. Beckenbauer? I put your name forward to him about a project in Pacific Heights. As I said in my letter of rec, you're extremely talented with color curation. Sales, on the other hand . . . not your strength. Or maybe it's just not your passion.

Best of luck.
PD

So the referral was Pilar's doing. Who knew?

Having emptied my desk, I take one last gander around the place. "So, is everything going?"

"Kinda sorta," Joshua says. "She sold a few things. But the built-ins stay. They become leasehold improvements."

"What happens with the lease?" I haven't thought about that.

His lips twist into a sardonic half smile. "If, for example, we were in default, I wouldn't be at liberty to say."

"Ouch."

"Oh, you have no idea what I've been dealing with. It has been one Herculean disaster. All I know is that I walk out of this office next week for the last time, and the rest is none of my biz."

"Any luck finding a job?"

"Luck? Luck's got nothing to do with it. You are looking at the next PA to none other than *Darika Patel*." He emphasizes the name as if it's supposed to mean something to me. My mind scrambles, but I can't connect it to anyone. Not in the design world anyway.

Joshua harrumphs. "You're killing me right now. Darika Patel. You know, Womentrepreneur of the Year? She launched that AI-enabled platform for leadership training? Still nothing? Does *Fortune* magazine's '40 Under 40' ring any bells?"

My head hurts. "I haven't exactly been keeping up on things."

"Of course not, you poor thing, you've been off grid. Anyway, guess who will be accompanying Ms. Patel to Paris, France, where she will be speaking at an international tech conference?"

"Uh. Taylor Swift? Kidding. Josh, that's incredible! You'll do great. And hey, thanks for keeping my plant alive on top of everything else you've been dealing with." I hoist my box higher. "Well. Guess I'm off. Hope you know I wish you all the best."

"Dude, don't be giving me that pathetic look. Did I not mention I'm going to P-a-r-i-s at the end of the month? Paris, Audrey. This boy's going to be A-OK. And so are y-o-u, b-t-w."

Walking to my car, I'm confounded by my lack of emotion. And me, go independent? Get a business license and all that? Sounds overwhelming, I'm ashamed to admit. After all, there are all those Darika Patels of the world out there winning awards, finding seed money, starting world-changing enterprises.

Dad's words float between my ears. *"You can do anything you put your heart and mind to."*

Yes, Dad, but what? What's the thing I'm meant to give my heart and mind to?

One thing's for sure, I haven't the stomach for duking anything out with anybody.

Forty-Two

The following afternoon, I cinch the hood of my petal-pink sweatshirt and descend a wooden ramp to Marshall's Beach. Never mind that the oversized hoodie clashes with my interview outfit. It's beyond chilly on the San Francisco Bay, and to my current thinking, the Sweet Reads logo takes any ensemble up a notch.

My feet hit the sand. I slip off my heels and carry them by the straps.

Seagulls caw. The Golden Gate gleams. A man helps his little girl fly a kite. Salt air mingles with the faint scent of seafood from Fisherman's Wharf. Over the choppy blue waters, white sails dart in all directions. I sink into a cross-legged position and hug myself for warmth. Other than this mean wind, it isn't an altogether bad place to weigh the offer I just received from Crabtree Interiors.

And to pray.

Crabtree is bigger in size and scope than DeSoto, and they've carved out a solid niche on the peninsula. Despite my nerves, when Gerard Crabtree and his interview panel asked my salary requirements, I surprised myself and reached for the moon. And no one batted an eye. How long have I been underpaid at DeSoto? Still, taking into account the hour-long commute, I'll need every cent of that starting salary. I should've gone for more.

Not that I've accepted the position yet.

If I'm willing to be honest, I've never exactly *desired* to work in the city itself. Renovating historic homes would be stimulating. But those taut, oversmiling faces in Crabtree's office weren't lost on me. I know professional pressure when I see it. And spending every Monday to Friday in this frigid, fog-drenched place? Never will it appeal.

Still, it's a major international city. A respectable offer. A step up. And more pertinent, it's a bird in hand.

After my interview, I cruised the posh hilltop neighborhood of Pacific Heights. Figured I'd scope out the parking situation near Whittier Mansion, mitigate any chance of botching my first impression at Friday's walk-through. Good thing I did. Places to park are almost nonexistent. I'll have to build in extra time to walk a number of blocks.

As one is prone to do in Pacific Heights, I ogled the palatial homes. Sadly, only a drone could get a view into Spreckels Mansion, originally the residence of the sugar tycoon's family, now Danielle Steel's. Not that I blame her, but she keeps her estate well concealed from street-level lookie-loos. Nevertheless, in spite of that substantial hedge wrapped around the place like a great green caterpillar, I managed to glimpse two Rolls-Royces. So that was a win.

Icy wind whips a coil of my hair around. I tuck it into my hood. If only the wind would oblige long enough for the sun to do its job.

Lest I too hastily rule out the idea of running my own design business, I called Mom last night and asked to chat with Jeffrey. Which was a first. As a former business owner—he ran his own optical lab for over thirty years—I hoped he might offer advice. To my own list of concerns, Jeffrey added new ones. Legal considerations, liability insurance, business taxes. The need for a good CPA. And the greatest drawback—self-promotion. As Pilar pointed out so bluntly, I haven't exactly excelled at upselling furnishings. How will I ever sell myself?

Just thinking about it all makes me prickly.

And while the work with Beckenbauer-Vandersteen is lucrative and laced with possibility, it's also short-term. More of a side hustle. Will it lead to other projects? Maybe. I can't pay rent with a maybe. I need to accept the Crabtree offer. Suck it up. Deal with the commute.

I rub my ears for warmth. Must leave before numbness settles in.

At least I'm somewhat relaxed. If my stint in Charity Falls taught me anything, it's that I need to pause like this more often. For processing, yes. But also, to listen.

I stretch my legs out in front of me. Point and flex my feet. Countless fine grains of sand run cool between my toes. For a moment, I'm weightless.

"How precious to me are your thoughts, God! Were I to count them, they would outnumber the grains of sand."

If I've learned anything, it's that I don't need to ruminate on this job question forever. I can choose *not* to overthink all the possible ways my life could go sideways. It's not like the world is made up of people working jobs perfectly tailored to their preferences. Nina Marinovich comes to mind. I picture her wearing her ever-present apron, working her fanny off at the Trading Post Café all week, then spending Sundays on her hands and knees cleaning vacation rentals.

My mouth lifts in a private smile. Yesterday, when I called to check in on Daisy, Nina picked up the phone. For a moment I thought I'd misdialed. But no, Nina had popped by with cinnamon rolls and to sit with Uncle Dean while Daisy ran errands. A friendship has emerged between the two women.

Emotion presses behind my eyes. This sweet, unforeseen scenario, this joyful sense of satisfaction easily eclipses my highest professional accomplishments.

Made possible because you gave of your time to pursue Paige.

I want to accept that voice, the one I often hear affirming rather than tearing me down. I'd like to think my time spent in Charity Falls was more of a blessing to my loved ones than a curse. Although nothing is official yet, Daisy's agent informed her that someone's close to making an offer on their home. Part of me feels ecstatic for them. The other half could use a cup of stomach-soothing ginger tea.

By the time I return to Charity Falls, someone else may occupy the house.

A frisbee lands close by, spraying sand on me. A toddler with a mop of light hair runs toward me, gritting his teeth in a joyful grin. I roll to my knees and flick it back. My throw curves sharply right, well beyond the boy's reach. Yikes. I could use some practice. The child brings to mind Cade's towheaded nephew. And Cade's low, lazy voice. *"My man Griffin."*

Thoughts of Charity Falls inevitably lead to thoughts of Paige. The hollow ache behind my ribs expands. If only I could somehow make her understand how much I care, how much I miss her twinkle of playfulness. Dare I plan a surprise visit once my life falls into shape? Of course, as public enemy number one, I'd have to sneak in and out of town by the back door. Does Charity Falls have a back door? I can't bear the thought of running into Cade.

And yet, we're never meant to carry shame. Hadn't Cade himself said those words? Is it possible I've interposed humiliation where humility is meant to live?

Paige is too young to survive on wishes and promises. But maybe I could help her recognize that with regular nurturing, long-distance friendships *can* be maintained. Can't they?

I'm lucky if I see Tawny twice a year.

I hereby vow to never again presume upon Tawny's friendship.

Loving another is vulnerable. Building your life around love is a risk. I mean, look at Daisy. Her heart is shattering.

Only, that's not true. Because she has entrusted her heart to the author of love itself.

I, on the other hand, have questioned God's goodness. Was sure I'd found weaknesses in the fortress of safety he allegedly provides. If I'm going to love freely and deeply, I'm going to have to rediscover trust. I wouldn't know where to begin to sketch a predictable, pain-free life for myself anyway. It's a myth. I can't know all the things.

Oh God, I give you my muddle. Because I got nothin'.

The wind pauses. Warm rays seep through my sweater.

My creator isn't only in Oregon, among towering ponderosas and fathomless canyons. He's findable everywhere. And I'm hardwired for moments like these. If I hope to contribute anything of true and lasting value anywhere in the world, I need this.

I need him.

Forty-Three

I awake from a deep sleep. My brain chooses not to. Where am I? Muffled voices. A banging door. My nose tickles with the aroma of moisture. Mustiness. My eyes flicker open. An oak-veneer closet with a fist-sized hole in it comes into focus. This is my room. This is where I live, the closet-door hole a gift left behind by a previous tenant.

In the corner, the TV is still stuck on the YouTube channel I fell asleep to last night, Tranquil Mountain Scenery. Words at the bottom of the screen inquire, "Are you still watching?"

Hey, brain, I don't need to solve global poverty quite yet, but I'd be obliged to know what day it is. I tap my phone awake. Wednesday, the ninth of August. Oh my.

At least this year I have a plan.

By the time I've gone for a short run and showered, the house has cleared out. All my roommates are off to their jobs and—woot!—the Ninja blender is available. But when I open the freezer, I find not one empty ice cube tray but four. I shake my head. Looks like I'll be drinking a green *un*-smoothie again today. Which is to say, the furthest thing away from one of Daisy's savory omelets. I throw back a sip, and a tremor passes through me. But hey, it's fuel, and the day is young.

Considering today's date, I think I might be okay. Maybe even a little buoyant. I assess my reflection in the mirror. Periwinkle floral-print ruffled midi skirt. Ivory cardigan. Ballet flats. When I venture to imagine my father's response, his approval washes over me. I don't fight it.

I twirl.

What would Dad think of my life? This room I call home? Despite my best attempts to infuse warmth and style, installing floor-to-ceiling curtains and layers of texture, it's still a damp, cheerless space beyond what another faux-leather toss pillow can remedy. I gather the two plants that are clearly terminal and head for the kitchen trash. At least my succulents have still got a shot.

———

Tucked in the heart of Silicon Valley, the Allied Arts Guild is a historic Spanish-style complex of artist's studios, shops, and gardens. How felicitous that I'm able to locate a frame shop in the same vicinity. The framer on duty is profoundly pierced and tatted and goes by the name of Fabio. To Fabio I entrust two of Dad's best botanical drawings.

From there, I amble through the Guild's lush courtyard, past glossy green citrus trees and soft yellow roses to reach the aptly named Café Wisteria. The perfumed air is heady.

I square my shoulders and request a table for one in the Blue Garden.

"Something to drink while you wait?" the hostess asks, jangling silverware as she sweeps away the extra place setting.

Iced coffee isn't my thing, but it was Dad's. I order their Creamy Iced Coffee.

At the center of the sunshine-dappled patio, birds gossip along the rim of a circular blue-tile pool. A fountain babbles. The profusion of hydrangea blossoms in all directions are the most unfathomable shade of blue.

"Let me adjust that umbrella for you." My waitress smiles

blithely, tucks a strand of caramel-colored hair behind her ear, and takes my order without writing it down. As if we're old friends and I've stopped by today for a long-overdue visit. I splurge on the Crab Avocado Eggs Benedict without a trace of guilt. Well, mostly.

So what if my first visit here was that ill-fated date with Kyle? The memory's as faint and anemic as this day is vivid and blooming. Besides, despite what the number of place settings at my table seems to indicate, I'm in excellent company. Male companionship, if you can believe it.

I miss you, Dad. But I feel you with me in this place you would have loved.

Gratitude pools in my chest for the family I was given, if only for a while. How readily, though, my mind drifts to Paige and Arlo. To Nina, and to all the countless shredded-apart families out there. Families in acute anguish, families enduring long-term crises.

Oddly enough, Paige's dad is incarcerated for effecting the same kind of tragedy that robbed my dad of his mother, and therefore, me of my grandmother. A fatal mistake by a man who by all accounts is otherwise a decent person. What kind of shame must he battle, sitting in prison while his family languishes? Has anyone ever told him he did wrong, but that doesn't mean he *is* wrong?

I sip my drink and watch a swallowtail try to decide which of the blue asters tastes best.

If only I'd known to ask Dad how he dealt with his childhood wounds. *I'm so sorry.* When Dad was faced with the unexpected life, God provided Daisy and Dean. In ways people still remember, my father chose to water the world where he'd been planted.

So maybe his life hadn't come up short after all. Maybe mine hasn't either. Maybe a brief, meaningful life, with the promise of something beyond, is in itself the gift.

Anything more is grace.

I inhale deep, drawing the balm of acceptance into all those inner places where I've too long secreted away grief and bitterness. On a sudden breeze, wind chimes trill angelically. When I tilt my head to listen, I can almost hear my dad's tender whisper. *I'm sorry too.*

But the painful parts of my past aren't anyone's fault. They just are.

He simply did his next right thing. And I'm not meant to bury the ache. Like Daisy said, it's perennial proof of the goodness we shared.

The love that marks me. Dad's love—and his approval—is like the honey-vanilla aroma of this garden. Like the scent of a flower I can neither see nor touch.

I dab the corners of my eyes with my napkin. It's nice to be unhurried like this. To sit with my feelings. To notice. This is new. I like it.

When I return my card to my wallet after signing the check, I find a missed text. Dread clutches my chest. I blink hard. The last thing I ever expected was to hear from Cade Carter again. I can't imagine a single thing in the world that could destroy this day faster and more completely than another rebuke from him.

Instead, when I open the message, I find a gift.

> "To have been loved so deeply, even though the person who loved us is gone, will give us some protection forever." ~AD

I read it again. And then again. This is a *Harry Potter* quote. Gradually its significance pierces me. Albus Dumbledore spoke these words over Harry. He wanted Harry to understand that the love of his long-departed mother was still in his very skin. That evil couldn't touch a person marked by something so pure, so good.

Does Cade know what, for me, today signifies? Was it mentioned in the article? I hardly remember. The kindness of it is nearly unbearable. This feels a lot like an overture of forgiveness I haven't earned.

Still, I straighten my spine and compose a grateful response. Then I lean back, imagining myself suspended on a pillow of God's grace stuffed with fragrant petals from every genus of blue-flowering plant.

"How was everything?" I startle when the waitress appears with my receipt.

More than likely, she notices the wet shimmer in my eyes. This concerns me exactly zero percent.

I swallow hard. "It's been . . . heavenly."

Forty-Four

Daisy

You'd be hard-pressed to find a more charming event than Charity Falls' Founders' Day Parade. So what am I to do on Friday afternoon when good old Rob invites Dean to watch it with the guys? Here's what. I'll say, *so be it*. I've never missed the parade before, and you better believe I'm not going to skip it this year. Besides, the smoke has finally cleared, the mountains are out, and it's a gorgeous, fresh-air day.

Insiders' tip: The only way to get around today's downtown tourist traffic is on two wheels.

With my bike polished and helmet buckled, I'm pretty pleased with myself. And I'll wager God's pleased with me too. I have spent more than my fair share of days feeling tempted to give up. But lately I'm much more curious to see what he'll do next if I *don't*.

Also on the plus side, Dean isn't here to wring his hands over my choice of outfit. No ifs, ands, or buts about it—eighty-five degrees dictates my denim skort. He'd be on me like Velcro if he caught me out riding with even these few square inches of bare leg showing. Not because he's a prude. No, Dean's got it in *his* head that one of these days I'll lose *my* head and end up bloodied and bruised.

To which my typical retort is something along the lines of "Oh, fish sticks, Dean. At my age, if I go down, a little road rash will be the least of my worries."

I draw a red scarf around the brim of my straw hat, tie it with a big bow, and then tuck the hat into my bike's front basket. Might as well attend in style.

Honestly, you'd think this was New York City's Fifth Avenue on Thanksgiving. Parked cars line every side street for a quarter mile in any direction. I stake out a vantage point on the north side of Birch, in front of the donut shop.

But then—"Daisy! Daisy! Over here!" Judy waves wildly at me from across the road, as if she thinks I've completely lost my hearing. There she is, amidst a pod of people I know to be only a sampling of her progeny, and yet she's flagging me over to join their party.

Indeed, Judy has chosen the better. If I cross to her side, the sun won't be directly in my eyes. And yet, the first parade entry noisily advances to my right, Charity Falls High School's raggle-taggle band. Despite the cacophony of trumpets, flutes, and drums closing in, I sneak across the main drag.

On the other side, I say a quick hello to Judy's daughter— the one who makes all those homemade hippie-dippie cleaning products—and her fresh-scented grandchildren. "You remember my Richard," Judy says next. "He's visiting from Arizona."

A distinguished-looking man with thin, receding hair says, "Nice to see you again, Mrs. Needham," and I cannot overstate here how grateful I am for Judy's mental nudge. I haven't laid eyes on her oldest boy since he went by Ricky Poison, wore eyeliner, and fronted one of those eighties hard-metal rock bands with fluffier hair than Charlie's Angels. Insurance salesman now, I believe. He must be pushing sixty!

Turning to me, Judy has to shout in my ear over the oncoming symphonic march. "I'm just here for the corgis," she says.

"I'm hoping to see my friend Nina," I shout back.

A little later, while the rodeo queens clop by on horseback, Judy turns to me. "What do you think? Any chance you can break away for next week's prison ministry gathering?"

I give her a sideways frown. Without Audrey . . . "I don't think—"

"Corgis!" Judy crouches to pivot the shoulders of her tiniest great-granddaughter so she doesn't miss the oncoming cuteness overload.

With a nod to every founding family that endured the Oregon Trail, along come four grinning, short-legged fur balls sporting calico bonnets and harnessed to a miniature covered wagon. The volume of cheering up and down the street escalates. These pups are a perennial crowd-pleaser. Come December, they'll return for the Christmas parade donning Santa hats and pulling a tiny sleigh.

"Why don't we just do it at your house?" Judy says after they pass. "We could set up at your table, use the kitchen counter for packing."

"Oh. Well . . ." Indeed, to her thoughtful suggestion I can produce no rebuttal. "Guess I don't see why not," I say. I'm observing Judy's preteen great-grandson out of the corner of my eye. He's gathering handfuls of candy tossed by a woman dressed a little too provocatively, if you ask me, in a Wild-West saloon-girl costume.

A slow, steady drumming alerts me that Nina's group might be next. Sure enough, under a banner that reads, "The Confederated Tribes of Warm Springs," a group of Indigenous people march, dance, and ride horseback in full powwow regalia. I've always enjoyed this part of the parade. After all, they represent the region's earliest inhabitants. Long before white European settlers, this land was lovingly tended by the Wasco, Walla Walla, and Paiute.

I elbow Judy. "There she is! That's Nina!" Draped in beads that shimmy when she walks and a colorful purple wrap with detailed embroidery, she's absolutely stunning. Her dark hair is swept off her face and tightly braided, then embellished with a single feather—maybe from a hawk? Never before today have I seen Nina wear bright-fuchsia lipstick. What fun.

I do hope Paige and Arlo are somewhere nearby watching. They should be proud.

It seems to me that Nina's been taking baby steps to break out of her isolated, nose-to-the-grindstone existence. Eager as I am to see that family find their way, I take comfort in knowing that God is even more passionate than I am about their healing. Some miracles take time.

Next up is the Corvette club. "Hey, look, it's Luanne!" I say, waving. The fleet of mismatched colors and vintages stops right in front of us, and they rev their engines. "That's her sixty-two," I say, turning to Ricky Poison. Luanne returns our wave from behind the wheel of a convertible the same shade as her lipstick. If I wasn't from around here, I'd presume the full-figured woman in oversized rhinestone sunglasses at the front of the pack was the undisputed queen of Charity Falls and everyone else just the common folk.

Proof to the contrary comes, however, when a high-stepping Appaloosa at the back of the previous group sashays out of position, clip-clopping first to the left, then to the right, drawing everyone's attention. He then pauses, raises his tail, and deposits a mountain of joy directly in the path of Luanne's 'vette. Judy elbows me and snickers. Laughter rumbles through the crowd.

Rather than proceed, Luanne waits like the royalty she may very well be as the car club's president until a volunteer whisks the offending pile into a dustpan.

Following the parade, our party disbands, the street reopens, and I exchange my sun hat for the bike helmet. I take what I hope will be the least-traveled detour around town. Even still, it's slow going.

My emotional tank is brimming after seeing so many familiar faces today. I'm content. A bit daydreamy, even, as I cut right through the post office parking lot and pedal between two rows of parked cars. *Note to self: Research whether corgis make good companions. Asking for a friend. But also not.*

Sudden movement seizes my attention. Something dark. An SUV lurching in reverse. I swerve, but too sharply. Can't regain control. *God help me, I'm going down.*

Forty-Five

Audrey

It is a truth universally acknowledged that an overthinking woman, desperate to make a good impression, must cycle through at least seven wardrobe changes before ultimately circling back to outfit number one. In my case, the very ensemble I pressed and laid out last night for my participation on the Whittier Mansion team.

I scowl at my full-length mirror. "Argh. Good enough!" The gargantuan pile of clothes at the foot of my bed that didn't make the cut repulses me. And now I have the privilege of hanging it all back up. I kick a lone, mutinous black-suede bootie toward the closet.

It's good enough. *I'm* good enough. Pilar DeSoto put me forward for this. Steffen's team extended an invitation. And if any of my new colleagues have a problem with the fact that I don't carry a chichi, six-hundred-dollar Coach briefcase, which seems unlikely now that I articulate it, that's *their* problem. I happen to adore the affordable blush-colored version Mom and Jeffrey gave me last Christmas.

You're not alone. There it is! The only other voice I'll make room for in my head today.

Failure isn't fatal. Okay, you can come along too.

I'm streaming chamomile-mint iced tea into a Hydro Flask when my phone rings. Really, Mom? Isn't this parental behavior a little excessive? Just last night, she assured me I was under a twelve-foot-thick, extra-chunky-knit covering of prayer today. A ping tells me the call has gone to voicemail. I'll wait and listen in the car.

But the call was not from Mom. It's a voicemail from Daisy. Bless her heart. Another layer of prayer covering. I'll take it all.

As soon as I'm safely on the 101, I hit the blue playback arrow. A faint voice. *Not* Daisy's. Straining to hear, I can only pick out the words "Judy Schmidt" . . . "urgent" . . . and "as soon as you can."

Where's that prayer covering, ladies? Already I've lost my peace.

Why would Judy be calling on Daisy's phone? What would she consider urgent, unless . . . *No*. Before I complete the thought, I've already flicked on my right blinker. I need to get off *now*. I angle my car. Listen, people, I *will* force a Kia-sized opening in your demoniac stream of traffic. Ready or not, I'm coming through.

Has something happened to Dean? Or . . . *no*, it can't be Daisy. Grim scenarios flash through my mind, each more horrendous than the last.

"Now stay calm, Audrey," Judy says, when I call her back. "Daisy has taken a spill on her bike." *Please say it's nothing serious.* "I'm here with her at the hospital." *Hospital?!* "Well, not with her now. They took her for some tests. I didn't know who else to call. She asked me to wait before I phoned you, but I just—"

"Thank you, Judy. I'm so glad you called."

"I just felt you would want to know."

"Absolutely. What kind of tests?"

"They need to rule out internal injuries. But Audrey, she's in such terrible pain. Her neck. They think her shoulder may be dislocated, but they can't treat it until they get an X-ray, and the ER's a madhouse."

"Where's Dean?"

"Rob is with him now."

"Is he okay? Does he know what's going on?"

"He's agitated, as you can well imagine. I don't know what we'll do about overnight, but we'll figure something out. I suppose I'll head over there later. I just hate to leave her alone here."

"Anything else? How's her head?"

"She's lucid. That's all I can say about that. I've been trying to distract her from the pain. Scrolling through photos of Mary Puppins—that's my new mini-pinscher. But it's no good. She's really uncomfortable."

I don't realize I'm shaking until I attempt to jot down Judy's phone number. "Okay, I'll call you back, Judy. As soon as . . ." As soon as what? "As soon as I can." What an inadequate thing to say.

How did I end up here in the Panera Bread parking lot anyway? People walk in. People walk out. At the nearby intersection, a woman dressed up as a slice of pepperoni pizza waves a Domino's sign, grinning and gyrating like she's auditioning for The Wiggles.

As if everything is status quo. As if my aunt isn't in the Bend, Oregon, hospital and I'm not five hundred and seventy-seven miles away, parked at a stupid mini-mall.

Think. I bounce my forehead against the steering wheel. Send up a quick prayer for Daisy. *Oh, God, please.* Then one for clarity.

What was Daisy doing riding her bike, anyway? *Says the girl flying through traffic at seventy, wrapped in a thin layer of steel.* But something like this was bound to happen! I should never have left.

Dean's agitated. Judy's strung out. Internal injuries? What if Daisy's in the hospital for days? Dean needs someone familiar. Someone comforting. What can I do from here?

A whole lotta nothing.

Meanwhile, I've signed a contract for a project that launches in an hour and a half. I'm legally committed. Which means it's time to paste on my business persona, Audrey the watch-me-dazzle-you design professional, and blow away Steffen et al. with my astute commentary. Not to mention the mansion's owner. *"Make the client feel they're the most important person on the planet,"* said a certain Bay Area design maven who may in fact be rethinking that business philosophy at this very moment.

A woman who watched her rising empire be leveled overnight by the very thing that built it. Ambition.

But still. I wouldn't want all that research I've done into historical color palettes of Romanesque Revival architecture to come to nothing. Would I?

Except. Except this time, I don't know if I can make it fly. This time I'm pretty sure I haven't got the heart or the stomach for it.

Time seems to halt. There's only this moment, and me.

What power a moment holds. And the choices we make in each of them. I think about the choices I've made.

Then I think of Dad. Of the single moment in which he'd smelled smoke. A choice. One that was not in the least motivated by self-preservation.

Above all, love.

For some reason, I think of Cade and his brother, Eli. In the middle of the flowing river of Cade's life, there had been a single moment. In it, he'd made a choice he'll forever regret.

I think about Daisy's parting words. How she took my face in her hands. About the strength in her eyes, and her benediction. "Now go," she'd said as we stood together on her porch. "Go and make your dad proud."

I turn the key. Harriet purrs. I've never been more certain about my next right thing.

Forty-Six

BEND, OREGON

By the time I arrive at the hospital that night, visiting hours are long over. An eerie hush pervades the building, and the fourth-floor charge nurse goes out of her way to appear unapproachable. "You do realize it's after midnight," she says, as if I'm a complete and total moron.

"Please," I say. "I won't go in. I only need to lay eyes on her. Just a peek."

Upon finding only two names listed under Daisy's family, one of them mine, she gives a curt nod toward room 417. "*Just* a peek," she says. But no sooner does she direct me to the room than she gets called away from her station—in the opposite direction.

Here's how I see it. Already today I'm a contract breaker. A duty shrugger. In the professional world, I'm a regular hoodlum. What are the ramifications of breaking a professional agreement? The long-term consequences to my career? I'll find out soon enough.

Think I'll take my chances with Nurse Cranky Pants.

I enter Daisy's room on tiptoe. The space is oddly tranquil. A single under-cabinet light casts a soft glow. Still, the sounds are all wrong. My aunt belongs among wakeful owls and that whispering

276

sound her aspens make in the breeze. Not this incessant beeping of monitors.

Daisy's pearly hair disappears into the crisp white pillow, and her body seems slighter than ever. Two butterfly bandages mask her right cheekbone. Crimson abrasions, shiny with ointment, mar her sweet face and left arm, testifying to how recently she made contact with the pavement. Her right arm is immobilized in a sling.

I barely alight my tush on the edge of a standard-issue side chair, lest it creak. And I watch my aunt's chest rise and fall. This is enough. To be close at hand.

The 411 on Daisy is, first and foremost, a hallelujah. About the time I crossed the California-Oregon border, Judy's call came in with the results of Daisy's scans. Her upper right side took the brunt of the fall. Two rib fractures. Shoulder dislocation. Fracture to the forearm. Severe bruising to her hip and thigh, but thankfully no fractures there. No obvious internal injuries, although they're keeping a close eye on a couple areas.

I don't deceive myself. Daisy and Dean Needham have a whole community to love on them in tough times, because year upon year they've loved on their community. But I'm family. I'm a Needham. And right now I'm anxious to hold Daisy's hand in mine, to be the one to bring her ice chips or whatever. To tell her I love her. And something else. Something I should've said long ago.

An alert sounds, two bell tones piercing the silence. *Din-don. Din-don.* Over and over. Daisy's eyelids flutter. As I'm flying out the door to fetch a nurse, a husky guy in scrubs nearly body-slams me. I stand back, observing his body language. Once I'm convinced there's a complete lack of concern there, the tension in my shoulders eases and I remember to breathe. The nurse sets to work replacing Daisy's IV bag. He looks her over, scribbles on her chart, then offers a smile on his way out.

Daisy is resting comfortably. Dean, on the other hand, might be a very different story. Last I heard from Judy, he'd finally gone down for the night. Will he sleep through with Daisy gone? What will tomorrow hold? Will he and I pick up where we left off or, after only a week, will I have become a stranger to him again?

I should probably start heading that way. After all, there's nothing for me to do here, and Judy's got Mary Puppins to think about.

Daisy's eyelids quiver, then flicker open slightly. Then close. I move to her bedside. The room smells like bandage adhesive and antiseptic. But leaning closer, I inhale the familiar scent of her hairspray, and an herbaceous smell that is Daisy's alone.

Her eyes fly open with a look of confusion and panic. As if searching through a haze from far away. "I'm here," I whisper, gently stroking her good arm. She works to focus on me. Recognition sets in, and her neck and shoulders visibly relax. Her lids close. "You're still in the hospital."

A single, faint nod. "Dean?" she whispers.

"He's fine," I say. "Everything's going to be just fine." I take her left hand gently in mine. "I love you, Daisy." It isn't enough. Through sheer will of force, I manage to wriggle more words past the wet lump in my throat. "You mean the world to me."

Ever so faintly, she squeezes back. There's so much more I want to say. But already she has slipped away, receding into the fog of sleep.

Forty-Seven

"Don't worry. You'll get it, Uncle Dean." I watch Dean's rusty wheels struggle to turn as he slides letter tiles around the corner of the Scrabble board. He agonizes to assemble even a three- or four-letter word. Today, I feel more affection than sadness. I'm coming to realize there's more to my uncle than the sum of his memories and mannerisms.

He's always been affable. But when he was a strong male physical specimen, he kidded a lot. And I mean, a lot. As much as I miss that, I can't help wondering whether some of it was a show. There's a gentleness about him now that gives me an idea of the kind of child he might have been. The inner child he's carried with him all his life, now unconcealed.

My new working theory is that my uncle was a sensitive child. Born only two weeks after the Japanese bombing of Pearl Harbor, how could he not have been? Like it did for so many Americans, the war created a family dynamic in which he'd had an absentee father and a mother living in uncertainty. Often, he joked about his father's gruffness as a hardened World War II vet. So maybe humor, for him, was part personality, part coping mechanism. A way of dealing with the harshness of life.

Hmm. Maybe to some extent I do this too.

This notion helps me come to terms with the new version of

Uncle Dean. I no longer see him as less than he was. In some ways I figure I'm seeing a side of him he's never shared before.

Still, back in the day, my uncle sure had a sweet, seemingly bottomless repertoire of dad jokes that helped put the fun in summer. I wish I'd written them all down. Once, when we all tent-camped by the Metolius River, several huge crows kept stalking our campsite for food. One got ahold of Troy's sandwich, and he chased it off, waving his arms wildly and shouting, "You black devil! Stay away from my food!" To this day, we still give Troy a hard time about that. But the punch line came later around the campfire. Uncle Dean had scratched at his beard—he wore a short beard back in those days—in a way that foretold we were about to be in for it.

"You know," he said, and immediately we all knew to start warming up our groans. "It's a little-known fact that, before the crowbar was invented, most crows drank at home." I chuckle. It's still a good one.

I only wish I wasn't laughing alone. And then I get to wondering, *what if* . . . "Uncle Dean, do you remember when we camped along the Metolius, and those crows kept attacking our food stash?" Dean smiles, but there's not a hint of recognition. "And you made a joke about the crows. About the crow*bar*. . . ?" I wait for a light to come on. Blank stare.

"The Metolius is a beautiful river," he says. "Have you ever been there?"

"Yes. Yes, I sure have, Uncle Dean. Thanks to you, I've been there."

"My grandfather used to take me fishing . . ."

Little does Dean know, he fished there just last week with Rotary Rob. I listen, fascinated, as he describes in astounding detail a steelhead trout he caught seventy years ago. Remarkable. But not the story I was looking for.

Of course, most of the time, when our family visited in the summer, my uncle was away at work during the day—he held the same job in quality control for a machine shop for over forty years. Or he and my dad would be outside working on some project or another. And in the evenings, old friends stopped by the house to visit Dad and Mom, which often led to a round of adults-only poker. So I can't say I ever experienced one-on-one time with my great-uncle. Until now. The old Dean was warm and loving and funny, but he certainly never once deigned to sit through an hour-and-a-half game of Scrabble with me.

I pat him on the hand before rising from the table. "I think I'll heat up some cinnamon rolls. Would you like some decaf, Uncle Dean?"

He considers this, unhurriedly. "Okay. That would be nice, thank you." Life moves at a slow, simple, deferential pace around Dean now. *I* move more slowly and thoughtfully when I'm in his company, and that's not a bad exercise for me.

"It's the darndest," he says, propping his elbow on the table in frustration and resting his head in his hand. "Sometimes I can't remember things." I move behind him, rest my arm on his shoulder, and lean in, poised to help. What my uncle needs are some vowels.

"Maybe this Y will help." I slide it closer to the letters he's contemplating.

Suddenly he sees it. "Haha! Lookie there! Fly!"

"Yeah, and if you put it there in the corner, with the triple word score, you'll knock me right out of contention. I may as well go get your prize." After placing his cinnamon roll and coffee on the table, I return to the kitchen and load another decaf pod in the Keurig for myself.

"Mmm," he moans, licking his finger, "a *synonym* bun." He chuckles softly, and I see something dance behind his eyes. "Just like the ones *grammar* used to bake."

"Oh no," I faux complain. "You did *not* just do that, Uncle Dean!"

"Grammar," he says again, raising his eyebrows. And I'm left

281

to wonder at the miracle and complexity of the filing system in his poor, addled brain. There is, I notice, a major new development in Uncle Dean's joke delivery. The man can no longer keep a straight face.

I rest my hand on his arm, and together we laugh like there's no tomorrow.

Forty-Eight

Is it possible to quietly sneak in and out of Homer's without causing a scene? Fat chance. Jan's Audrey-detection system goes off the moment I head for the gumball machine. "Oh my, look what the cat dragged in!" she all but shouts. "Goodness, come let Jan give you a hug, sweetheart."

And then Silas appears, popping up out of nowhere like Shaggy in *Scooby-Doo*. "Calm down over there, Jan," he shouts. "It's only Audrey."

"Silas," Jan returns, "telling a country girl to calm down is like trying to lick your elbow. It ain't gonna go well."

"Nah, I'm just messin' with ya, Audrey. How's your aunt doing? We've been wondering."

Jan's out from behind the counter, arms outstretched. In seconds, I'm wrapped in her mama-bear hug. "Yes, how's our sweet Daisy? Poor thing! I've been praying." It no longer surprises me that such news could make its way to Homer's Hardware in under forty-eight hours.

"There's a good chance they'll release her this afternoon," I tell them. "The healing is going to take some time, though."

It's hard to ignore the pile of boxes stamped with the Aberdeen & Moss logo crowding the paint section. "What's all this about?" I ask Silas. Somehow I'm still keenly interested in what's happening at Homer's. Even if I only came in today for a gumball. Or did I? "Did Homer decide to bring in their line?"

"Yeah, take a gander." Silas produces a small box filled with Aberdeen & Moss paint-and-stick samples.

Gah. The colors this company has developed are my absolute catnip. "These are super nice," I say. They feel nice to the touch too. "But it'll take some rearranging."

Silas releases a dramatic exhale. "Yep. That's my problem. Their display is pretty sweet, though. But see, if I put it here, it would stick out into the walkway. Oh! I almost forgot. When the rep came in to take our order, she asked me to give you something. Now where did I stick it?"

While Silas flings drawers open and scratches his head over where he might have left the whatever-it-is, destiny apparently deems it good and right that today I receive not one but two gumballs for my quarter. How about that?

"Hang on, it's in here somewhere," Silas says, still searching.

I stand staring at the rows and rows of paint cans in aisle one for a long moment. Then I study aisle two. Then aisle one again, envisioning various arrangements. "Have you thought of moving the Minwax display to the left?" I ask. Silas pops his head up from beneath the counter and joins me. "If you did that, it would create an overlap, a hidden space behind it—see?—where you could store backstock. Then you could cut down on the number of facings of something . . . maybe the tint base?"

Silas scratches at his angular chin. "I think I see it. So, then we could slide everything down—I mean, *I* could."

Honestly, if I didn't have somewhere to be right now, I wouldn't mind helping at all. "Just an idea," I say.

"I like it." His eyes widen as he removes something from the pocket of his apron. "Oh, here it is." With a flick of the thumb that's meant to look tricky, he snaps a business card into my hand.

"Turn it over. Alauna wrote on the back. She wanted you to have that link. Something about a job opening. Of course, I told her you live in California. She seemed disappointed. But, well, here you are. So, there you go."

On the back of the card, I find a handwritten URL. Something about a job? Okay. Mildly intriguing. Certainly unexpected. "I private-messaged you on Instagram," Silas adds, "but we're not friends on there . . . so, maybe you didn't get it."

Right. Because who needs more friends? Abso-posolutely not me, with my glittering, voluminous social circle of Silicon Valley movers and shakers and my dizzyingly busy personal calendar. No, not Audrey I-Don't-Need-Anybody Needham. You know, come to think of it, here's the real mystery. Why had a sweet kid like Silas I'm-Just-Messin'-With-Ya Rudloe even wanted to befriend a clueless highbrow like me in the first place?

Once I'm back in my car, I place Jan's gift for Daisy in the shade of the back seat and smile. The woman would not, under any circumstances, allow me to be on my way without promising to deliver a full, unopened bag of Dove dark chocolates. Huge earrings, huge heart, that one.

I lift the Aberdeen & Moss business card to the sunlight, admire its understated logo in soft, mossy-green matte ink. Why does holding this tiny slip of cardstock between my fingers feel momentous? I sense possibility. But, oddly, my pulse isn't racing in that wild, adrenaline-rush, better-jump-on-this-professional-opportunity-as-a-catalyst-to-happiness sort of way. In fact, my body's relaxed. I feel grounded. Serene.

This is better. This is a heart-whisper. A huge lump in the throat. A warm hug of reassurance. Proof that I'm seen and adored by the one who matters most. And, perhaps, a prompting.

So, what's to delay me from visiting the website Alauna provided right this second? Only one thing.

I open Instagram and friend Silas.

~~~~~

Once parallel parked along the street near Nina's apartment, I pop the orange gumball in my mouth. I'm saving the pink one for Paige, if she'll accept it. I'm fairly sure I haven't attempted to chew a massive gumball since the days when I drew my inspiration from Franklin the Turtle. Before Tobey Maguire resurrected Spider-Man. Before iPods! Back then, I thought the epitome of courage looked like Blossom, the cape-wearing Powerpuff Girl of the extraordinarily oversized pink eyes and formidable super-powers, defending the world from animated intergalactic bad guys.

Today, courage looks like walking up to apartment 9B.

Not long ago, the bravest thing I'd ever done was take the measurements of a living room while Danny Glover napped on the couch. Today? I can eat alone in a restaurant, and like it. I can walk away from a career-making opportunity. I can open my heart to relationship, knowing full well it promises not only immeasurable gain but inevitable loss.

I can do *this*.

Again today, there's a mound of flip-flops by the doormat. The aroma of bacon. Only a little over a week ago, I stood in this very spot, on what will forever be remembered as one of the worst days of my life.

I straighten my spine and knock. The door opens, no wider than the width of a twelve-year-old boy's face. "Hi, Arlo." I hope he doesn't think my voice sounds too gushy, too grandmotherly. It's just so good to see him.

He gawks at me wide-eyed for a long moment, then flashes a grin starring those two extra-large incisors of his. "It's Audrey!" he shouts, then disappears, leaving me staring at nothing but a corner of a wall in shadow. Was he shouting to his mom? I didn't notice whether her car was parked in its spot. Or could he have been shouting to Paige? I rest a hand on my abdomen in a way that sometimes steadies me.

All at once the door swings wide. Paige is before me, and I barely catch a glimpse of her face before she's on me like a tattoo, flinging herself into my arms. "I'm sorry!" she says into my chest. "I didn't mean it! I didn't mean what I said."

"Oh, girl," I sigh. Stooping to meet those arresting brown eyes, I place my hands on Paige's shoulders. "Listen to me. You had a right to be upset, okay? I'm sorry too." When Paige's chin quivers and her eyes fill, something locks into place in my heart and mind, solid as a bank vault. A promise I suddenly know I can make. "And hey—" I smooth away the tousled hair from her face. "Hey now, look at me, Paige. Hey." I wait till her eyes connect with mine. "This time I'm not going *anywhere*."

The moment the words leave my mouth, I know they've just become true.

Paige wraps her arms around me. Over her shoulder, in the shadows of the apartment, Nina watches from a distance. Hugging herself and swiping at her eyes.

Forty-Nine

Monday evening after dinner, Daisy rests at home on the damask love seat. She drifts in and out of sleep. Herbal tea steeps, and Dean and I work a jigsaw puzzle together. It's a child's puzzle with large pieces, but he seems to enjoy the sense of accomplishment. Despite our donations of boxes full of puzzles to the thrift store, the hutch still contains an assortment. Dean chose the one with baby kittens.

A rapping at the door takes us all by surprise. I flip on the porch light and peek through the glass. Nothing, and I mean nothing, in my nearly three decades of life experience has in any way prepared me for Nash Carter's appearance there, filling my view in the golden glow of porch light, donning a black-felt cowboy hat and carrying flowers. I open the door to reveal not one but two Carter men come to call. *Oh, mama.*

"Apologies for the late hour, Audrey," Nash says. "Hope it's alright. We've only just heard about what happened."

Moths dance in the yellow light near his face. I'm going to go out on a limb here and assume my aunt wouldn't want me to leave this gentleman outside, no matter what I've done in the past to offend him. Not to mention the other, equally dapper gentleman with him. Daisy's had a good day today, her first full day home from the hospital.

"Please come in," I say.

Nash enters first, dipping his head slightly, and removes his hat in that humble, polite way I've seen done in Western movies but never witnessed in actual flesh-and-blood life. "Good evening, Daisy. Well, hello, Dean."

Daisy beams. "What a wonderful surprise, Nash. Oh, you shouldn't have. Those are stunning." The flowers find a home on her TV tray, and she fawns over them. "I adore lilies! Thank you."

"Yup. You and Camille both," Nash says.

Daisy likes lilies? News to me. But then, I'm finding this whole concept—the one where my aunt has vintage-level friends, people who know intimate details about her that I don't—somehow surreal. Also, can this be the same man I accidentally outed in the *Mountain Messenger*? I haven't caught a hint of indignation. Such a class act. Which threatens to resurrect my feelings of disgrace.

After a too-long pause, my brain reengages. "Can I offer you both some mint tea? We were just about to—"

Nash sweeps his hat vertically in the air. "Oh, no thank you, we won't stay. Just wanted to see how the patient's coming along."

When Nash moves to sit opposite Daisy, Cade joins me in the tiny space that barely qualifies as a foyer. "Hey," he says, with an expression I'd like to read as coy. More likely, what I'm seeing is my loss of esteem reflected there.

"Hey."

I've seen city guys try to pull off a Pendleton cardigan, only to ring as pretentious. On Cade, it fits. "I'm sorry about all this," he says, darting a glance at Daisy. "Wish I'd known sooner. I've been gone for work."

"It could have been much worse. We're choosing to be grateful."

"I'll bet."

"By the way, thank you for the text. The timing was really . . ." I sigh. "It was incredible timing. It helps to know someone understands."

"I do." His eyes falter. "December second for me."

"Your mom?"

Cade nods. "Hey, um . . ." He stuffs his hands in his pockets and leans back on his heels slightly. "Actually, there's something I've been wishing I'd get a chance to show you."

"Oh?"

"It's kind of a surprise."

"Good surprise?"

"To be honest, I'm not a hundred percent sure how you'll feel about it. I hope it's good."

"Okay, now you've got me ridiculously curious."

"Got any free time tomorrow? I could pick you up."

I glance at Daisy. "Ooh, that's tricky. I need to help out here. I mean, unless it could be early, before Dean's up and around."

"The earlier the better as far as I'm concerned."

"I'd need to be back by, say, eight thirty."

"Pick you up at seven."

Shall I take this as a move beyond forgiveness, toward friendship? I'd get up at any hour for the chance to add another nail to the coffin of my shame.

~

Earlier, I attempted to FaceTime Tawny. No answer. Finally tonight, my phone hums on the nightstand.

Ugh. Missed your call! What's up?

It's not that I need her stamp of approval. More like, she deserves to be among the first to know.

What would you say if I told you I've decided to stay in Charity Falls?

I steeple my hands and hold my breath. Okay, maybe I *have* been craving her blessing.

Spectacular news. 🤩 🤩 🤩 I have goosebumps.

> Really? I mean, the Bay Area is a beautiful place to live. I just made it into something it's not. Not for me anyway. What if I repeat the same thing here?

Can it really be that easy to remodel a life? Also, I'm tempted to spill about Cade's mysterious invitation. But why torment her?

You won't.

> How do you know?

You're not the same person.

Fifty

The next morning, I'm up at six o'clock and already wide-eyed. Again, I have my mother to thank for etching untold volumes of seventies music onto my young, impressionable mind. And I know from experience there's no point in fighting it when an Eagles tune gets stuck in your head, until it finally decides to move on to the next person.

Which means today I'm takin' it to the limit.

Cade said to dress comfy-casual. So thank you again, Ava—this calls for cropped jeans and my go-to flannel. What did he say about shoes? Ah, yes. Shoes I "won't mind getting dirty." Oh, *those* shoes. I look past two pairs of strappy sandals to my neon-pink runners. How dirty could they get?

Strange. Something about today feels unmistakably different. Like I've just deplaned and I'm suddenly faced with an Uber driver holding a sign that reads "This way to Audrey's new life." Do I trust the sign? The driver? I'm on jelly legs. But—thank you, Eagles—since I'd rather not go to the grave still singing about how the dreams I've seen lately keep on turning out and burning out and turning out the same, different will have to be my new mode of travel.

And today's mode of travel, as it turns out, wins the grand prize in that category. When Cade pulls up in a massive truck-and-horse-trailer setup and leaves it rumbling in the middle of the road while he hops out, it's clear I'm in for different.

Wow, I mouth, approaching the gleaming wall of white and chrome that's blocking the road in one direction. "Are there horses in there?"

"Not at the moment. But it can accommodate up to four."

"That's all?" The cab-over section alone looks more spacious than my Menlo Park bedroom. "Is this your dad's? I don't remember seeing the trailer at the ranch."

"Yep. It's his brand-new baby. And this is its maiden voyage. Figured I needed a maiden."

"Oh great. Like the *Titanic*? I'm not sure I'm dressed elegantly enough for that form of demise."

Cade's eyes take a languid jaunt from my head to toe before returning to meet mine. "You are, uh . . ." He clears his throat. Is Cade Carter nervous? Of little ol' me? "You're just right. I mean, assuming you don't care about those shoes. Hop on in."

Hopping isn't the best way to describe my ascent into the passenger side of the truck. More like, launching.

Cade maneuvers the rig onto Oregon 126, heading west through the pines. There go the Eagles again. *So put me on a highway . . .* Have I waited long enough before prying? "So, is this the surprise?" I'd say it qualifies. "Or is there an actual destination?"

He darts a sly glance at me. "You'll see."

Goodness. With that smirk, that dimple, how is it Cade hasn't found his way onto the big screen like his parents?

"First, a disclaimer. I've never driven a rig like this. I can use the practice. Also, I brought chai. Hope that's alright." He gestures to a pair of insulated mugs in the center console.

That explains the peppery aroma. "Thank you. This is amazing."

"Cab's a little dusty."

It's somehow comforting, the normalcy of Nash Carter's habitat on wheels. A scattering of the usual items—set of keys, phone charger, pack of gum. Because Nash Carter puts his chaps on one leg at a time just like, well, not me.

There's also a novel. "Is this your dad's?"

"Nope. That's mine."

"I've heard of this author. My brother's into him. Isn't he super prolific? Sci-fi, right?"

"Yeah, or epic fantasy, I guess you'd call it. I don't even try to keep up with everything he writes, although I get a lot of reading in at the station between calls. Pretty sure this one's the fourth book in the series. As you can see, it's got a gazillion pages."

"Yeah, that's a fatty." I take my first swig of chai. Still hot. Not too sweet. Nice.

He chuckles. "It's basically a doorstop."

Maybe Cade is willing to act as if the article in the *Mountain Messenger* never happened, but I can't go on pretending like this. My one texted apology was far from adequate. So I say, "Cade, I'm guessing you learned the date of my dad's accident from the article. I'm completely mortified to think you read it. Or that your *dad* did."

He turns to me with eyebrows quirked. "You mean, the article that shall not be named?"

I laugh lightly. "Oh, okay." So he's trying to put me at my ease. But truly, I should not be let off so easily. "I need you to know that if I could undo those things, I would. I never in a million years meant to bring negative attention to your family."

He reaches across the console, rests his hand over mine. "It's okay. Really." Well, this is rather sweet and unexpected. Not to mention a bit electrifying.

"*Really*, really?" I ask.

"*Really*, really." Suddenly his expression morphs from empathetic to wide-eyed, and he wraps his thumb and forefinger around my wrist. "Besides, there's no way *this* can be the hand responsible for all those flyers."

He's right. I have the tiniest wrists known to mankind. "What can I say? I'm delicate."

Cade lifts my hand and performs a mock inspection before returning it to me. "More like a force to be reckoned with."

"Reasoned. I prefer to be reasoned with. But seriously, I'm still embarrassed about all that—the flyers, the article. Facing your dad last night . . . that was excruciating."

"You should really move on. We have."

"Really?"

"Do we have to go another round with this? You're pretty hard on yourself, you know."

"That's basically what my friend tells me once a week. Tawny's the grad-level psych major from whom I have, for some reason, been granted a lifetime supply of unlimited counsel. For free."

"Nice. And what does she say about it?"

"She says I need to act as if my inner critic is a blithering idiot."

"That'll preach." We exchange a smile that feels like an unspoken agreement to circle back to where our friendship left off that time we met over my favorite bistro table in Sweet Reads. "And I mean it, Audrey, if there's any ugly talk about my family going around, we aren't hearing it. My dad's used to keeping a low profile in town. He tends to order online, keep to himself, that sort of thing. A lot of people probably know he's here, but he figures, out of sight, out of mind."

Hmm. Thus the tinted windows on this truck. "I can understand why he'd want to maintain privacy. But it sounds so isolating."

"It is. But we'll see. He's coming around. Things might look different for him very soon."

Curiosity niggles, but I don't ask Cade what he means. I've already overstepped my bounds with his family one time too many. So instead I say, "You know, I hear *different* isn't always a bad thing."

Out my window, the landscape changes abruptly, from pine

green to black char. I noticed this burn area when I drove the girls to the lake and wondered about it. "*Oh man,*" I say. "I knew Oregon got hit with some pretty devastating forest fires over the past few years, but it's so sad to see it for myself."

"For sure. This one's from three summers ago."

For half a mile on either side of the highway, blackened stumps point up sharply from the ground like tines on a hairbrush. On closer inspection, though, itty-bitty pine saplings, vivid and green with new life, have sprung up all across the forest floor.

"You know, fire isn't necessarily a bad thing," Cade says, as if reading my mind. "Ultimately, it cleans up the understory, thins out weaker trees, opens the forest to more sunlight, nourishes the soil."

"So many animals are displaced, though. Or worse."

"Yeah. That's a hard truth. On the other hand, it's also regenerative. When heavy brush gets cleared out in a fire, it actually increases the water supply. Fuller streams. New kinds of plant life. And new plant life means healthier wildlife. Some plants and trees couldn't even continue to exist without fire. Every so many years, they need the extreme heat in order to open and release new seeds."

"Huh." We're back among the lush, green ponderosas now. But I sense a takeaway in this for me. Something to do with divine rhythms. Ashes. Renewal. Hope. "You sure know quite a bit about this stuff," I say.

Cade shrugs. "I can be kind of a nerd about random topics. So, thank you, Audrey, for attending my TED Talk."

You're also funny.

As we share a laugh our eyes connect, and an emotion warm and liquid-like spreads over my ribs. When I'm sure his gaze is on the road, I observe him out of the corner of my eye. Cade doesn't look like any of the guys I've been attracted to in the past. *Hold up.* Did I just admit to being attracted to him? Allow me to squash that right here and now. The only thing I want from this moment is to enjoy the delightful camaraderie happening between us.

If I overthink it, I'll be out of my element in an instant. I'm tempted to say out of my league. But that's not quite it. Cade is just . . . different. There's that word again.

"Alright, here we are." Cade flicks on his left blinker and waits with the patience of a golden retriever for an opening in traffic adequate for a fifty-foot-long vehicle.

"You're doing great, by the way," I say, as we turn onto a narrow gravel road.

"Ha. Thanks. But here's where things might get dicey. I need to find a place to park this beast somewhere along here. Somewhere I can be sure I can turn around." For the briefest of seconds, I contemplate the wisdom of parking in the deep forest with a guy I don't yet know well. But in the same moment I know the vetting is over. He's been weighed, he's been measured, and he has definitely not been found wanting in the trustworthiness department.

Once parked, Cade fishes something off the floor behind my seat, and we jump out.

Now what? I wonder.

"Now we hike," he says, as if reading my mind. "It's not too far. Don't worry, I'll have you back by eight thirty as promised. Unless, of course, we get lost." At that, my head snaps his direction. "Kidding. See the sign?" Tacked to a tree ahead, a piece of weathered plywood states that there's a camp hidden somewhere nearby, Camp KeeToWaNa.

"This way," he says, leading me off the forest road and straight into the woods. I don't see a path. "Shortcut," he calls over his shoulder. "Trust me."

In for a penny, in for a pound.

Fifty-One

"Those clouds are insanely cool," I say. "They look like alien space-ships hovering." I say this mostly to myself, or maybe to the one who dreamed them up. Together Cade and I have been trekking through a fir-scented wood, weaving between manzanita shrubs and some kind of yellow wildflowers.

I hesitate to ask Cade to downshift, but it would be nice to enjoy my surroundings while we hike. Then again, he's the one setting a pace that will get us back before Daisy and Dean need my help. Still, I can't stop tipping my chin to search the blue depths overhead, pondering, like Mary Oliver, "that tall distance."

Take that single cloud off by itself, for example, the one that resembles angel wings.

"Lenticular," he calls out, covering the ground ahead of me with long, confident strides.

"Huh?"

Cade raises his voice. "They're lenticular clouds."

"Oh! Awesome." *Slosh*. I halt in my tracks. Cold wetness permeates my right shoe. So much for keeping them clean *or* dry.

My faithful guide turns back and takes in my one-foot-in, one-foot-out stance. "Oh, sorry. I meant to warn you. This part is marshy."

I pick my way more carefully now and promise myself there *will* be days in my future set aside just for hiking. Days when time isn't an issue. Maybe I'll even break down and get some of those—what had Ava called them? Oh yeah, give me all the ugly river-walking shoes. Sure sounds like a winning idea now. *I've gone over to the dark side, old friend.*

Cade waits for me to catch up. "It's right up ahead," he says, grinning. "I'm counting on this being a good surprise. But first we have to cross this little stream." I skitter down a short, rocky embankment and plot my course across several large, wobbly rocks. Fun. I haven't felt so alive in a long time. Cade reaches a hand to steady me as I land on the other side. As I make my way up the embankment, I feel his hand ever so lightly on the small of my back.

For the next I-don't-know-how-many steps, that brief, light touch makes me forget all about the scenery, and even my soggy foot.

Ahead, a large canvas teepee signals we've arrived at the camp. The property is owned by YoungLife, Cade explains. Weathered cabins are sprinkled around a petite teal lake. We pass a rustic outdoor amphitheater with a half circle of benches that brings to mind some "Kumbaya" moments of my younger days. The whole place appears abandoned.

"Camps are done for the summer," Cade says. "That's why we're here. Follow me."

The air shifts. Something smells sweet and earthy and familiar. Horses? A small corral comes into view. Next to it, a stable of timeworn wood. This explains the halter and lead Cade carried from the truck. Soft whinnies greet us as we near the stable. And out of the shadows steps a blond mare with a fair mane.

The palomino is breathtaking. "Oh my," I say. "Who is this beautiful creature?" She approaches with warm, welcoming eyes and ambles directly toward Cade. More whinnying and tail swishing as he hops the fence. Something about their reunion moves me deeply.

"Audrey, meet Topaz."

"Aww. She's sure a pretty thing! Is she yours?"

A corner of Cade's mouth lifts in a tender smile. "Let me bring her out." I study the horse as he slips the harness over her muzzle and adjusts the fit. She keeps nudging Cade playfully. "We loan her to the camp for a couple months in summer. She's great with the teens. There were other horses, but she's the last to leave."

"Ah. The horse with a ministry. She looks happy to be going home." I can see why Topaz would make a good riding horse for youth. She's a nice size, maybe fifteen hands tall, with an air of serenity. Cade leads the horse to a shady spot and ties her off. When I stroke her velveteen neck, she turns her head toward me. Brown eyes, wise and tender, return my gaze, unblinking. The pale hue of her mane and eyelashes . . . *I got this—Pantone's Almond Buff*. My fingers explore the hair behind her ear, so supple. The elegant contours of her face.

I can't explain it, but for some reason, this horse feels like my spirit sister.

"How old is she?" I ask, turning to Cade.

I find him leaning against the fence, watching us. There's that odd, poignant little half smile again. "Thirteen," he says, with a flicker in his gaze that seems meaningful. But I have no idea why. "Actually now that I think about it, she just had a birthday."

When Cade steps toward Topaz and me, something inside threatens to break open. What's happening here? Why do I feel so fragile? He stuffs his hands in his front pockets and sweeps the ground with his gaze. "Audrey, I brought you here because I wanted to tell you Topaz's story, what I know of it anyway." My eyes dart between the horse and Cade.

"My parents bought her six years ago," he continues. "She'd been raised on a working farm in Terrebonne—that's a little ways northeast of here. She was well cared for. But my mother . . . well, after they built their home in Charity Falls, she decided to track her down."

"Track her down?"

Cade releases a breath. "You see, Audrey, Topaz was born in Charity Falls thirteen years ago." He waits to let the message behind the words sink in. "In a barn—across the street from your aunt and uncle's house . . ."

A shiver travels across my skin. I swallow hard. No, this can't be. I cross my arms. "Cade, stop. What exactly are you trying to tell me?"

But I already know. Somehow I know. I am staring into the eyes of the foal my father rescued. This golden beauty, this winsome creature, has been alive for the past thirteen years—because my dad has not.

I'm still frozen, attempting to process this information, when a woman approaches. She wears hiking boots and a wide smile. "Aww," she says, "I'm going to miss Flawsome. Hey, Cade. Good to see you."

Cade brightens. "Hey, Bridgette. Yep, it's our turn. *Flawsome?*"

The woman laughs. "One of the girls took to calling her that, on account of her grease spot. It's actually become a great inroad to talking with kids about their imperfections—real or perceived."

I search Topaz. "Grease spot?"

Cade circles to her left side, strokes a hand down a dark patch about the size of an oval dinner platter beginning high on her neck, beneath her mane, and cascading down to her shoulder. In a way it does look like someone smeared a handful of grimy engine oil across her neck. I run my hand over the tobacco-colored hair.

Cade smiles. "It's not super unusual. We were told that sometime when she was young, that patch of hair just started growing in like that." He gestures to the woman. "Audrey, this is Bridgette with YoungLife."

"Audrey Needham," I say. Somehow I shake her hand and produce a smile despite this strange all-over numb sensation.

"Well," she says, then kisses Topaz on the muzzle. "It's time to go home, you beautiful thing."

I follow at a distance while Cade leads Topaz back the way we came. I appreciate that he knows not to force conversation. My thoughts are too scrambled, my heart too bloated. The significance of this development laps over me in waves.

"Sure you don't want to ride her?" he asks for the second time.

I shake my head. "But thanks." It's too much. Too much, too fast.

Still, when we arrive back at the forest road, Cade hands me the lead rope. I hesitate, but only for a moment, knowing he needs to prepare the trailer. The ramp comes down with a loud creak followed by a thud. Topaz blinks. But she doesn't startle.

"Well, girl," I whisper, stroking that soft patch behind her ear. She meets my eyes. "Sure seems like you've made peace with your past. Maybe it's time I do too."

Cade is back at my side, smelling of cardamom and Christmas Eve. He touches my upper arm in a gesture of familiarity that feels just that . . . familiar. Natural. I know he feels it too. An accompanying revelation is equally mind-blowing. This could change everything.

"Look," he says, breathy. "I realize I took a calculated risk bringing you here. If I made the wrong decision, I'm sorry. I just thought—"

"No. It's fine," I say, handing him the lead. "This is an amazing surprise. In fact, it just might be one of the most remarkable things that's ever happened to me."

Cade visibly relaxes. His mouth tips into the crooked smile so familiar to me now, and his lake-blue eyes shine as if he's warmed through with pleasure. *Those fathomless eyes.*

"You once told me you had some things to figure out," he says.

I nod.

"If you don't mind me asking, have you?"

I tell myself he's asking because he's a caring sort of person. But I sense a question behind the question. Something like, am I the kind of filly who's likely to bolt again?

Something's happening inside me I can't explain. All the cells in my body tingle. Is that a thing? I swallow hard past the tightness in my throat. How to answer him? I'm not sure I can take credit for figuring things out so much as having them revealed to me. Like scales have been falling from my eyes.

"It's kind of like this," I say. "I like graph paper. I *love* graph paper. All those tidy little boxes for guidance. For a long time, I guess I thought they'd keep me safe." Cade narrows his eyes and studies me.

"But now, I'd say I'm learning to listen to that still, small voice instead. To see what kind of picture takes shape when I follow my heart. So my answer is . . . yes."

Cade runs a hand over Topaz's neck and pats her twice. He presses his lips together, wrestling back a smile. But when he looks at me, his eyes dance. Ever so briefly, his gaze drifts down to my lips. I swallow hard.

He clears his throat. "Well, you know what they say, Audrey. You always come out of the woods better than you went in."

Fifty-Two

Daisy

If there's any perk to all these doctor appointments, it's that I've actually made strides in a new novel. In fact, I'm so engrossed I don't even notice Audrey's white sedan pull up to the curb at the rehab center. Suddenly she's approaching my bench. Sunlight paints her long waves shiny copper.

"Oopsy!" I say, tucking my eReader into my handbag. "Sorry, honey. I should've been watching out for you."

"No worries. Sorry you had to wait. Costco was a zoo. Here, let me carry that." Gratefully I relinquish my purse. "What did they say? Do they think you'll be playing pickleball before the month's out?"

"First, it's only been two weeks. And second, I have about as much interest in playing pickleball as rollerblading in a string bikini." Audrey lets go one of her snort-laughs. Poor girl. It's going to take her a while to recover from that visual. Taking care not to jostle my right arm, the one in the sling, she helps me with my seat belt, closes my door, and circles to the driver's side. "But I'll tell you what," I say once she's in, "if I had a nickel for every time one of these medical experts told me that my accident should have left me in much worse shape, I'd be—"

"You'd be lucky if you could afford Chick-fil-A. Sandwich only. No waffle fries for you."

"Okay," I say, chuckling. "But hear me out. You see, I keep telling the doctors that all summer I've been stretching every day and doing some of those Pilates exercises you showed me. And every time, they say, 'Yep, that probably made all the difference.' Audrey, do you know what the hip-fracture statistics are for septuagenarian bike-accident victims? Not in my favor!"

"You've probably got good bones too."

"They said that as well. My point is, you got me into a routine. Heaven only knows how much worse off I'd be right now if my muscles were still all cinched up like a Christmas goose." I give Audrey's arm a gentle squeeze and wait until her eyes connect with mine. "What I'm trying to say, honey, is *thank you*."

Audrey steers out of the parking lot. But her smile lingers, and I can see that my words have done their work. Why is it we erect such needless fortification around our hearts whenever praise comes our way?

"Actually," I say, "now that you mention it, Chick-fil-A does sound good."

"Great plan. Start counting those nickels."

I point out a sprawling older building. "We used to bring your father there to swim," I say. "There was no public pool in Charity Falls back then, and this one was brand-spanking new."

The half-hour drive here to Bend has always been something Dean and I enjoyed doing together. The reason for going never made a speck of difference. He used to say, *"Daisy girl, I've got to go on up the road and get a part for the lawn mower,"* or what have you. *"Want to come along for the ride?"* And I'd say, *"Bend isn't up the road, you goose, it's south."*

We'd start with nothing but a grocery run or a dermatology

appointment and make a day of it. It's different now. We often take the bus. And our conversation runs in circles, if it runs at all. So this is a delight, coming to "town" with my niece.

"There it is," I say, running my eyes over a beige, three-story structure set back from the road, looking for all the world like a four-star hotel. "Whispering Pines." In many ways, it's fancier than any place I've ever lived. Chandeliers and plush towels and fresh flowers and all that.

Audrey flips on her blinker. "Let's drive around it. You can remind me which one's yours."

"You wouldn't mind? Yes, let's do." More often lately I find I'm looking forward to something altogether new and different. Today's one of those times. "And you'll really help me decorate? But only if you have time."

"Daisy, I'll even bring the Coke floats. All you ever have to do is ask."

I imagine Audrey will have her own ideas about redecorating our little white house as well. Won't that be a kick? What an unforeseen silver lining, watching the old roof over our heads become a new roof over hers.

Some days I have a hard time imagining there's enough to keep my accomplished niece contented in Charity Falls. "Audrey," I say. "I hope you know how proud we are of the woman you've become. But you're still young. There's a world of possibility in front of you. Are you absolutely certain this is what you want? It's not too late to change your mind. A woman's prerogative and all."

Audrey pulls to a stop in the parking lot, kills the engine. "Daisy, everything I want is right here."

"What is, honey? Tell me. What's here for you?"

She pivots in her seat to face me, and I see it now, a sheen of moisture over her eyes. The corners of her mouth tremble. "You."

Fifty-Three

Audrey

"Um. Wow, you sure clean up good," Cade says, greeting me at the front door of the Carter home. "I'm really glad you came."

Cade and I haven't seen each other for nearly a week. Not since the day I sloshed through the woods and met a certain palomino with eyes that penetrated my soul.

Okay, so I may have stepped up my act a tiny bit for this . . . whatever this is today. Cade's invitation was cryptic. At least this time there were no wardrobe guidelines. I may have spent more time than I care to admit trying to make this half-up, half-down hairstyle appear thrown together. But sundresses are always my go-to. And these thrift-store bead earrings? It's been a minute since I've worn them, is all.

Unhurriedly, he leads me through the great room, past the massive rock fireplace. There's such an ease about the way he moves, making me aware of my tendency to hurry even when hurrying isn't called for. We cross a thick Persian rug done in earth tones with a hint of rose. I love this space. Masculine yet openhearted.

As I follow him deeper into the house, I recognize Cade's soft-green long-sleeve as the same one he wore that first time I saw him, in Sweet Reads. I can't even begin to calculate all that's happened since then. I feel I've been shaken hard and aired out like a dusty rug. But I do believe I'm better for it.

"This is my favorite room," Cade says, gesturing for me to enter ahead of him through wide-open French doors. *Oof.* I wouldn't mind moving in here myself, *today*.

Wall-to-wall books line dark wood shelves on two sides of the library. Goodness, there's even a rolling ladder. I'd call that a stairway to heaven. To my left, a wall of glass looks out over the juniper-studded canyon. Add to this a fireplace, overstuffed leather chairs, a moss-green-velvet pin-tuck sofa, and equestrian wall art. If the room could speak, it would say, *Curl up and read awhile*.

And sitting like a portrait in the middle of it all is America's favorite cowboy.

"Hey, Pops." Cade says. I hate that we seem to have interrupted his reading. But Nash closes his newspaper, and his warm welcome puts me right at ease. He slips off his wire readers and rises, as if we're the best interruption in the world.

"Well, hello, Audrey," he says. "Nice to see you again. Tell you what, son. Why don't you two head out back. I'll catch up with you there in just a few."

Outside on the patio, the day's rising heat infuses the air with sage and spice. Cade sits down next to me on a comfortable sectional. There's a gentle concern in his eyes. "How are you? I've been wondering. I'm sure the whole Topaz thing must've come as a shock."

My gaze circles toward the stables. If only I hadn't left my sunglasses in the car. It's another high-luster day, and sunlight is brutal on eyes that have seen days of intermittent tears. *So, Cade, here I am, Flawsome Audrey.*

"Truthfully," I answer, "kind of a mess off and on. But in a cathartic way. I think meeting Topaz is helping me process some things I'd been putting off for too long." Here I have to stop and breathe. I'm still tender, prone to being overpowered by sensations both piercing and poignant. "To look at my life in a different light."

His smile is disarming. "I've really taken you through the mud, haven't I? What about your shoes, have they recovered?"

"Temporary setback." I regain my breezy tone.

He fixes his eyes on mine. And there's that half smirk I can't always read. "Maybe together we could, uh, search for a better trail . . ."

Exactly what are we talking about here? Shoes, or something else?

I'm so in my head that I don't hear Nash until he's upon us. He carries a roll of papers I recognize as a set of blueprints. "Now, Audrey," Nash drawls, taking a seat across from us. "I've a feeling you might be interested in seeing these. It's why I asked Cade to bring you here today." He sets the roll between us on the glass table, and the pages unfurl slightly. "In fact, I could actually use your help—if you're interested, that is."

Is he thinking of remodeling? I try but fail to make out the project name printed in blue ink along the edge.

I feel Cade's eyes on me. "You see," Nash says, "my wife loved Charity Falls. Not just Charity Falls but this whole region." He stretches an arm to indicate the expansive high-desert vista. "She traveled to many places, but this was always home. In fact, she would say, and I'd have to agree, that it made her who she was."

Aunt Daisy once told me Camille was raised somewhere near here. On an alpaca ranch, I believe.

"Course, like most young people, she was bustin' to get out and conquer the world. But as the years went by, she kept feeling a stronger and stronger pull for home. By the time we made the move, Camille had long been ready to get out of the industry. Out of the limelight. I figured I'd still take on a film here and there, if it seemed worth my while. But for the most part, we both got to the place where we were ready for a quieter life. Ready to dream new dreams."

Nash rubs his chin. "See, years ago we visited a youth ranch in Idaho. Beautiful spread. A place where they took in horses who had experienced some sort of trauma—abuse, neglect, that sort of thing. And then, what they'd do was, they'd invite kids out. Kids who'd also run into one kind of trouble or another. Kids in the foster system. Kids who'd experienced things kids should never have to experience. Well, Camille and I were so moved by what we saw. The stories. Man, they just got to ya." Nash pats his heart with a fist. "Something about pairing a child who needs emotional healing with a horse who needs the same . . . the impact is . . . well, you'd just have to see it to believe it."

I picture Paige when she was first introduced to Fancy Nancie. How Cade managed to gentle her fears. How the horse helped her access greater confidence.

Nash continues. "There's a bonding that can happen between the horse and the child. And, well, sometimes it can wedge open a hardened heart when nothing else will. The way we saw it, these folks had a ministry of hope. For many years, we supported that ranch and others like it across the country. Still do, matter of fact."

Cade stands. "Excuse me a minute. It's getting warm, and I should have offered something to drink."

"Thank you, son. That'd be good. I'm a bit parched."

Nash laces his hands together in his lap. "So anyway, Camille and I showed up here—oh, a little over six years ago now, guess it was. Kind of skulked around, searching for a piece of land. Of course, we couldn't help noticing the condition of the Sugar Pine. Such a shame, you know. And Audrey, let me tell you, I thought Camille might blow a fuse. She was downright agitated. Wouldn't let it go. So we began to think on it—well now, is there maybe something we can do about it? Maybe we could open a youth ranch right here in Charity Falls."

Cade returns with a pitcher of ice water and three glasses. He fills the glasses, then leans back with his hands behind his head. I like seeing him relaxed. In fact, I'm becoming quite a fan of the general tempo here at the Carter ranch.

Nash nearly drains his water glass before continuing. "And this, what you see here . . ." He unfurls the blueprints across the glass table. Cade jumps up to grab two pieces of kindling from a stack by the outdoor fireplace. He positions them to hold the pages open.

"This is that dream," Nash says. "We got the ball rolling, and then . . . well, as you know . . ." Nash's voice trails off, and he gazes out toward the canyon.

"I understand," I say, nodding. I can't imagine how devastating it must have been for everyone when Camille became sick.

"Never saw it coming."

"So the project got sidelined," I say, leaning over the plans. It doesn't take but a moment to identify the subject of these renderings. This is the old inn property. A piece of wood hides the project name. I slide it an inch.

Sugar Pine Youth Ranch, it says. The date establishes these plans as five years old.

Nash nods. "Well, yes and no. You see, an integral part of the plan had been finding the right horses. And Camille, bless her heart, she was still hell-bent on seeing that through. At first, it provided a good distraction." He chuckles softly and shakes his head, remembering. "First thing she does is get it in her head to search for Topaz, see what became of her. And I'll be doggone if she doesn't find her. That was some kind of miracle."

Nash's eyes go hazy. His gaze drops. "But, well, you probably know the rest. The cancer advanced quickly. Took every ounce of the fight she had in her. And then—I'll just be real transparent with you here, Audrey—and then, it used up all my fight too. The grief was too thick to see over. Still is, some days."

I nod. I know a bit about grief. Seems like no amount of personal accomplishment can insulate us. Not even fame. Not if we're willing to truly love someone.

"Truthfully, I couldn't even look at the place after Camille passed. It seemed to represent not only her death but the death of our hopes. And so, as you've witnessed, the property continued to suffer from neglect. At my hands." He lifts his palms. The regret in his eyes pains me. "Now, I gotta say it. I'm not proud of that. And I'm especially sorry for you, Audrey. For Daisy. For Dean. It couldn't be easy to see it like that, day after day, considering everything it represents to your family."

I sip my water. Something has been shifting while Cade's father shared so openly. I can no longer find Nash Carter the movie star in the person sitting across from me. All I see now is Nash Carter the man. "Thank you," I say. "But it's really okay. I understand. *We* understand. Anyone would understand, Mr. Carter."

"Please, call me Nash."

I take my lead from Cade, who seems to want to give his dad a moment. The three of us sit together in comfortable silence, watching a chipmunk skitter in and out of a nearby pile of rocks.

Nash clears his throat. "So, uh . . ." He looks at me and waggles his famous salt-and-pepper eyebrows. "What do you think? Go ahead, take a closer look. I've decided—well, with a little push from Cade here—I've decided it's time. I'm ready to see Camille's dream come to pass. Ready to help some kids who need just a little bit of understanding . . . and hope." He nods toward Cade. "*We* are ready now, isn't that right, son?"

I don't need to look at the plans. I've only got four words for these men, and if I hold them in a moment longer I'll burst. "How can I help?"

Cade and his father break into broad grins that, juxtaposed like this, are shockingly similar. In fact, if Cade wore a mustache . . .

"Obviously, this is going to take a team," Nash says. "And, well, I've heard such good things about you." He shoots a meaningful look at Cade. In turn, Cade snags my gaze for a beat. And then another. Something about his quick, coy smile sends a flush of delight all the way to my toes. "We've got our work cut out for us. But for starters, *since you asked* . . ." Nash winks. "We could use some design help."

What's there to think about? "I'd love to," I say.

"You'll be paid, of course."

"Oh, I don't think I could take—"

He holds up his hand. "Now, now. We can tangle about that later. Just give it some thought, and let us know if—"

"I'm in." The laughter that erupts between the three of us feels somehow holy. Like a new beginning becoming sanctified. I feel light and fizzy. Carbonated. "Are you kidding? I am *all* in."

"Well, alright!" Nash slaps his thigh. "Here's where it's at. I've already got a builder in mind, so I'll let him get to work on permits and such. Sadly, I'll be out of town for a bit, shooting in Wyoming. It's a little project Camille encouraged me to take. She loved the script. The producer's been willing to wait, but I can't very well put it off any longer. Time to get back on the proverbial horse. Might even do me some good. Well, that, and *this*." He gives a nod to the blueprints. "I'm hoping while I'm gone, you two might run with it."

Nash shifts in his chair. His tone turns wistful. "You know, Audrey, Camille would have loved to be involved. Matter of fact, she filled a notebook with ideas, even some rough interior sketches. I'll have to dig that out. Maybe you'd be willing to take a look at what she had, see if there's anything useful there. I can assure you, though, she'd be thrilled to know you're the one on the job. Who knows, maybe she does . . ."

Nash sits forward, leans over the drawings. "But here, have a look. Here's the site plan. I'd love to get your thoughts."

I run my eyes along the property lines of the roughly ten-acre plot, which I now see for the first time is shaped like a trapezoid, widest at the back where it borders the national forest. Here's the creek meandering through. Here's the shape of a tree, depicting the location of the landmark sugar pine that stands at least one hundred feet tall. And here's the footprint of the farmhouse. The only change to that structure the architect has plotted appears to be a proposed addition, fairly large and labeled *Banquet Room*. "What's this?" I ask.

Cade sits up straight. "We figure we'll use that space for community gatherings. Provide music and dinner—something casual like a barbecue or a buffet. Give an open invitation. Let locals tour the ranch and learn about the ministry. Seems like a good way to get people involved—recruit volunteers, raise funds, that sort of thing . . ."

But I'm no longer listening. My mouth has fallen open and I'm staring uncomprehendingly at something else on the plans. "What? I don't . . . what is . . . ?"

I lift my eyes. Search the expressions of these two men who appear more similar every second. And the tenderness and anticipation I see there might be my complete undoing. Tears press. Because there's another proposed structure drawn here, this one to the north of the farmhouse. In tiny, neat-as-a-pin architectural lettering on Nash Carter's blueprints for Sugar Pine Youth Ranch is a name that will forever occupy prime real estate in my heart.

My father's.

Daniel Needham Memorial Equestrian Center.

Fifty-Four

Cade flings open the refrigerator door. "Chunky or creamy?"

Food is the last thing on my mind after the meeting with his dad. My head's still swimming with the news about the youth ranch. Especially the idea that the Carters have chosen to memorialize *my father* with the proposed equestrian center. Not Camille. Not their deceased son, Elijah. My dad.

I'm dying to see Daisy's face when she hears.

"I, uh . . . creamy, I guess?"

Cade tosses items into a small cooler. After I agreed to take a walk with him down to the stables, he got it in his head we should bring along something to eat.

I hop onto a barstool at the island to watch. But already Cade says he's good to go. Which may be the fastest picnic lunch assembly I've ever witnessed. This guy's going to have a hard time relating to my Olympic-level overthinking skills. Well, moving forward, I see no value in attempting to disguise any of my personality quirks. If we're going to start spending time together working on the ranch project, he's about to experience them all firsthand.

"Sure you wouldn't rather take the quads?" he asks, as we head out the side door. What I need is to work off some of this weird energy before I self-combust. It's an all-new sensation—some kind of kinetic tranquility. Like that odd collision of atmospheric weather patterns that somehow alerts you when a rainbow's about to appear. Only, all of that is happening inside of me. "I'd much rather walk, if you wouldn't mind."

Cade turns to me as we head down the path along the canyon's ridge. "So . . . good surprise?"

"The ranch? Amazing surprise. I still can't get over it. Cade, this is a place for kids like Paige and Arlo!"

"Exactly."

"I'm speechless."

"In that case, how about this? Tell me something I don't know about you."

"Woo. Okay. Um. May as well start with the big stuff."

"Absolutely. Bare your soul. I'd really like to know more about a girl who wipes down other people's kitchen counters."

"Yeah, that right there might tell you all you need to know. Alright, here goes. I have a serious case of bibliophobia. It's untreatable, really." Cade scrunches up his face. "The fear of being caught without reading material," I say.

"Ahh. An affliction I can relate to. What else you got?"

I shrug. "Me and broccoli don't play nice. When I was six, my mom found a mushy blob of it in the dryer. And here I thought I'd been so clever to excuse myself from the table saying I needed to use the restroom."

"So basically you have a criminal mind."

"Is it criminal, though? Or strategic?"

Cade chuckles. "Alright," I say. "I'll give you one more. I cannot for the life of me pull off a beret. It's one of life's greatest disappointments." It's true. Berets are the cutest—on other people.

"Hmm." Cade stops walking and faces me. He scans me so thoroughly that I feel a blush creep up. "That's hard for me to accept. I'd actually like to ring in on that."

"Don't hold your breath. Okay, that's it. Your turn."

"Wow. It's a lot to take in. But I appreciate your honesty."

"So?"

"I don't know. What would you like to know?" *So many things, Cade. So many things. The list is growing by the minute. Starting with, how is it you're still unattached?*

"First crush?"

"Ohh, she goes right for the jugular." Cade feigns a bodily death spiral. Then he shrugs. "Fine. Lindsay Lohan." And now his neck has gone crimson. His ears too. I really should have taken it easier on him.

"I respect that," I say. "Did you ever meet her? Seems like you might have traveled in similar circles."

"Yes. And are you kidding? I was fourteen, dotted in Clearasil. She was older. I avoided her like the *plague*."

Now that I have treated Cade to one of my signature snort-laughs, the pressure is off. It's all downhill from here. And for the record, my ridiculous laugh inspires his own, at my expense. The man howls so hard he has to hold his stomach.

We continue down the path, humor still lingering through a twinkle in his eye. "Okay," he says, "here's one. Steel yourself. This may shock you, but I once had a tattoo removed from . . ." Cade indicates his left forearm. "From right here, and I'd rather not say why."

I turn his arm over, inspecting the area closely in the sunlight, searching for remnants. "I'm not sure I buy that."

"Suit yourself. Cost me a fortune in laser treatments. I was determined."

We near the stables. It occurs to me that until recently, I've become accustomed to a certain margin of personal space. Maybe I've even orchestrated it on purpose. But over the course of my friendship with Paige, a major hugger, I've had to get over it. And at this moment I don't miss it at all. Because somehow while we've been walking, Cade and I have inched closer.

As if by some magnetic force, our arms now graze lightly. I'm aware of the warmth of him. The strength of him. And when he slides his hand behind mine and laces our fingers, a chill races through me.

So much for extinguishing that kinetic energy.

"This way," he says, and his mouth curves into a smile so beguiling I'd reconsider my lifelong broccoli boycott just to experience it one more time.

Already, Topaz and Fancy Nancie are at the pasture fence vying for our attention. Copper strolls out as well. We feed them each a handful of oats. Next Cade leads the way around the far end of the stables. Out here beyond the bevy of equestrian buildings, a stand of mature ponderosas offers precious shade. He motions to a rocky promontory overhanging the canyon. I choose a spot to recline. The rock is surprisingly cool.

"*This view*," I say, adjusting the folds of my dress. I feel his gaze on my profile. How is it that my hand already misses the feel of his? "Do you come out here often?"

"Sometimes. Great spot, right?"

"Mm. Yes. Is this like the Oregon version of your Haleakala getaway?"

"Kinda. What about you? Do you have a secret place?"

I consider this. "Not really. Guess I'm still looking for mine." A long-buried memory gets tickled. "Actually, when I was a kid I used to imagine God could only hear me from the top of our plum tree. Also, by the way, your spot is no longer secret. But I might be persuaded not to share the coordinates."

And there's that sideways smile I've taken to daydreaming about. "What's it going to cost me?"

I put on my hard-bargaining face, which is a joke. I couldn't haggle to save my life. Instead I laugh. "Got anything to drink in there?"

Cade grins wider and holds up two sparkling waters. "Passionfruit or grapefruit."

I'm not about to attempt the word *passion* right now. "Grape-fruit, thanks." He places it in my hand, and I welcome the chill. His gaze lingers, and I'm aware we're having a moment. Something has shifted between us. Something unspoken but growing louder.

Nervously, I tuck overgrown bangs behind my ear. Oh dang, that's never been a good look for me. I flip it free.

Why should I suddenly care so much what he thinks? Because when was the last time I met someone so principled and selfless, with a dimple in his right cheek to boot?

"So, how did that go for you?"

"Hmm? How did what go?" What have I missed? It isn't easy to focus when there's a hummingbird or three pirouetting inside my abdomen.

"The plum-tree technique. Did you find a direct line?"

"Oh. I guess so. Yeah, for a while it seemed very effective. But a time came when I started listening to that oily voice whispering in my ear, making me question whether my prayers were going anywhere."

"Snape, for sure," Cade says, hissing the *S*.

I tip my head ever so slightly and smile. "*Exactly*. Anyway, lately I've been working on finding ways to reconnect with God. Actually, I'm beginning to wonder if the voice of heaven doesn't sound an awful lot like my aunt, or my mother, or Tawny. Hey, what are you making over there?"

Cade has produced a jar of peanut butter, a package of flour tortillas, and a knife. "Allow me to introduce you to the peanut butter burrito. I strongly recommend you don't knock it till you try it."

"Way out here beyond the edge of civilization? A lot of good it would do me to complain." Also, good thing I brought mints.

He shoots me a sly smile and licks peanut butter off his thumb. Geez, he's attractive. Is he used to having this effect on women? Has Cade Carter ever been a player? I don't sense any lingering traces of it. In fact, I've been picking up on an old-school culture of respect among the Carters. It's palpable in the way Nash talks about Camille.

Later we wander into the indoor arena, where Paige rode her first horse. Maybe that's why the sweet, warm air in here sizzles with possibility.

But when Cade tells me I'm beautiful, I deflect the compliment with a jest. I'm not sure I'm ready to let him know that his words, and that way he's looking at me now, hit their target. Also, something's the matter with my knees. I'm wobbly.

Still, I want to be done playing ding-dong ditch with others' feelings. Not to mention my own.

What would happen if I stopped meting out my love so cautiously?

Cade narrows his eyes at me as if to communicate that I've been keeping things too on the surface. He tucks a strand of hair behind my ear. Okay, in this case I'll allow it.

He wants more. He wants deeper. I sense it. Which feels both thrilling and threatening. But hey, it's all good. I'm still in control here. Because I'm the one who gets to choose which way to weight it.

And still. If I have any hope of leaning into different, I'll have to begin with daring.

"Hey," he says huskily, turning his body into mine and circling an arm behind me. "Have I mentioned how happy I am you decided to stay?" His voice resonates through me.

I make fleeting eye contact but shy away from the intensity I find there.

Instead I rest my head against his chest.

"Audrey, you . . ."

He's petting my head with a tenderness I've never experienced, and I'm hanging on his next words. *I what?* What am I in Cade Carter's eyes? Eyes I've grown to trust.

"You inspire me. The way you care about others. Daisy. Paige. You're genuine."

Muting every inner argument, I *choose* to receive this.

"I think I'm right where I'm supposed to be," I whisper. His heartbeat hammers against my ear.

The next thing I know, he's brushing the hair from my face. And suddenly what my mind is still scrambling to process, my body welcomes like a homecoming. When he buries his fingers in my hair and presses gently on the small of my back, I take the risk.

I tip my chin, knowing what I'll find. His lips, waiting for mine.

Hmm. Very nice. Very, *very* nice.

Fifty-Five

Daisy

Myrtle Rose winds her too-skinny body through my legs. I prop my slippered feet on the coffee table and bend to scratch her head. She's not exactly a pretty thing anymore, what with her rheumy eyes and crooked tail, bless her. Probably has some special sixth sense about the fact that her cat days are numbered. Off to the bay window she slinks, as is her routine, pulling off a surprisingly graceful leap to her cushion. Or should I say, her throne?

Audrey will be up soon. More than likely she'll join us out here in the quiet, before the starlings twitter and this periwinkle twilight melts to blue.

Although, come to think of it, I've reason to believe she had a late night. I feel my eyes soften and smile to myself, remembering how she fluttered around here last night in that breezy floral wrap skirt I like so much. How she circled in and out of the kitchen chattering on about this and that and nothing at all, pretending not to be a ball of nerves while waiting for her dinner date to pick her up.

I suppose I didn't help matters. Why, against all the better judgment I possess, did I ask if she was developing feelings for the man? What a goose.

Audrey responded with some rambling threads about the value of friendship, about not overthinking things, and also something I couldn't quite follow about Pendleton sweaters—which were all interesting tidbits but, of course, not the answer to my question. Well. What young lady wouldn't be fluttery, testing the waters with a man like Cade Carter?

Oh yes, I remember fluttery. Fluttery is how it all began with Dean, of course, and look at us now. And that is *not* a look at us now, we're so old and pitiable. No. It's a look at us now! Look what we've weathered. Look how we've loved. Look how we've *been* loved.

Look what happens when you don't know what else to do, so you just keep showing up.

After Audrey left with Cade, I sat side by side in the Adirondack chairs with *my* date. We drank lemonade while the golding sky set aglow all those Shasta daisies Danny planted once upon a time. We watched a pair of violet-green swallows swoop and dive while a warm breeze rustled through the aspens. This is new for Dean—the poor man used to find it impossible to sit still. It's an astonishing gift to me.

I'm not always a fan of this new, subdued version of my husband, but I sure don't miss the agitation that seized him in the earlier phases of the disease. Dare I say he's often peaceful? If you'd tried to tell me years ago that one day my Dean would be a willing birdwatching accomplice, even chuckling contentedly now and then, I'd have said you're nuttier than a PayDay bar.

I know, Lord. Time to close my eyes and join you in our secret place, where even silence is praise.

I sip my coffee. Then I shift in my chair by the fireplace, trying to find a more comfortable position for my arm in its godforsaken sling. What a nuisance. This recovery has not been a cakewalk. Then again, easy is overrated. Discomfort just means I'm still alive on God's green earth, thank you, Jesus.

For I consider that the sufferings of this present time are not worth comparing with the glory that is to be revealed to us.

Yes, I receive that, Lord.

Besides, had I stuck the landing during my pathetic stunt show in the post office parking lot, who's to say whether Audrey would have chosen to stay?

"God never denies our heart's desire except to give us something better."

Thank you for that truism, Elisabeth Elliot. Yes. What could be better than knowing Danny's child will continue to make her home here after we move? As Dean's sunny personality dims, what could be better than to be gifted with Audrey's?

Draw her heart to yours, Lord. Make this house, for Audrey, a place of comfort and peace. As you have for us.

A while back, I asked God for courage. I believe I also dared ask that he reveal himself.

Can't say I'm even a stitch more brave. I keep thinking, *I can't do this again today.* Over and over. But then I look back, and it's been done. So it seems that weakness works just as well.

As for the sign I hoped for, well. Instead he gave me a mirror. To know him, to relate honestly to him, I have to present my truest self. To acknowledge those dark clouds that were globbing up my soul. Fears. Hidden resentments. Woe-is-me-ism. Not because he wants to shame me. Because he delights in helping me.

I'm here, Lord. See? My eyes are closed and I'm listening. Starting . . . now.

But *yuck.* There's the no-longer-appetizing aroma of last night's meal, the feast of chicken tacos and cookies Luanne dropped off. And my goodness if we haven't *still* got a freezer overflowing with meals from caring friends. So. That lingering meat-and-onion smell? Let's call it a *good* smell. It means I'm loved. Provided for.

And now there's Dean, clearing throat phlegm in his sleep. Mm. What can be said for this? It too isn't an altogether bad sound. It means we've been granted intimate companionship for five decades. Long enough to earn the blessed privilege of sharing our old-people noises with each other.

Thank you.

A car purrs past. And another. And yet another. I still remember when early morning traffic was a rarity here. But. Road noise represents community. And there's no reason to believe this ongoing influx of new people moving to Charity Falls will end anytime soon. Can I blame them?

They show up, wound tight as bobbins, talking too fast, driving even faster. *And here's what I wonder, Lord. Are they truly moving to a place, or are they running from another?* I suppose it's both. Comes a time we all need a do-over. In a world that applauds pretense and eschews the small and simple and servile, we're all yearning for peace. Peace, and a true homecoming. That place where our heart is finally at rest.

I know this because I long too. And I'll continue to long.

Because that place is not this place.

But now, there I go again. I've stopped listening and started yacking. My, how I can pontificate. Not to mention wish and whine. *Forgive me, Father, for allowing my less-than-glorious ruminations to crowd out your glory.* And yet there's grace enough for that! Which, in the end, is all I need.

I may not hear your voice today, Lord. But I hear you loud and clear. You are the giver of better things.

Kiss me again this morning with your love. Strengthen and refresh me, so I can refresh others. Show me where to find the holy in the hard. And in this land that's idyllic but still somehow inadequate, turn my eyes.

Keep me facing homeward.

Fifty-Six

Audrey

Painted robin's-egg blue and tucked like a hidden Easter egg between Charity Falls Coffee Roasting and Haute Diggity Clog Shoe Shop is a small gift shop called All the Feels. Out front, a chalkboard sign suggests, "Have a great day on purpose." You'd be hard-pressed to find a better selection of candles or bath bombs anywhere else north of Silicon Valley. This afternoon, it's where Paige and I browse for her mother's birthday gift. More accurately, Paige browses. I sniff.

"What about this one, Paige?" I unscrew the lid of a lovely brown candle sprinkled with rose petals. "Mm. I like this. It's called Cocoa Rose." Paige dutifully trudges over from the display of stuffed toys. She inhales a whiff, or at least flares her nose, and pulls a face. "Really? You don't like it?"

"I don't know."

"How about this one, Lemongrass? Ooh. Snickerdoodle!"

"I don't know, I don't know, I don't know."

"You don't know what you like? Or you don't know what your mom likes?"

Paige shakes her head. "I don't like smelling things. And I don't know what my mom likes. She doesn't like perfume."

"Oh, Paige, just try this. Orange Blossom." I can't get enough of this one myself, and I keep circling back to it. They must've snuck some kind of intoxicant into the wax. No. It's reminiscent of my childhood. Of the citrus trees that grew in our backyard in Davis, the ones my father lovingly tended.

"Mom likes penguins. I'm going to get her this." The baby penguin she holds up isn't exactly realistic with its exaggerated proportions.

I smother my disappointment. Just because I don't buy myself candles doesn't mean I need to force them on others, like some kind of clean-burning-candle pusher. "You're right. I'm sure she'll love it."

"If you like that candle so much," Paige says, "then why don't you buy it for yourself?" She offers this resolution like the future United Nations delegate I believe she's destined to be. It's an honest question, not a jab.

Yes, Audrey, why don't you just buy it? Because I believe that all these years this ridiculous symbolism of mine has somehow kept me safe? Or due to a self-imposed but oblique sense of loyalty to my dad? Or maybe I won't buy it because self-denial equates to holiness and purchasing a seventeen-dollar candle will demean me in the eyes of my digital budgeting app, which by the way *has no soul.*

Is this the kind of woman I hope Paige becomes?

I join her by the stuffed-animal tower. "Okay, that thing is adorable. May I?" Her face brightens, and she places it in the crook of my arm like an infant. I have to say, these huge button eyes and extraordinarily long and fuzzy gray arms do offer readily accessible emotional support.

Paige watches me replace the Orange Blossom candle on the shelf, taking care to position it evenly with the one next to it. Her mouth hangs open. She looks crestfallen. "Aren't you going to get it? I thought you liked it. It's super pretty."

Am I really going to deny myself this little thing because long ago I set the absolute cap on the number of candles in my home at zero? No, that's not why.

It's because buying it would signal that I'm finally ready to let go.

Scorching heat isn't inherently evil, of course. It's one of God's brilliant ideas. *Literally* brilliant. Who wants to live in a world where there are no stars to outshine the darkness? At its core, the sun is something like twenty bazillion degrees. So you could say my father's good heart simply led him too close to the sun.

Also, fire wields no power over things of lasting worth. Just look at my dad's legacy. Seeds of goodness planted. Kindnesses remembered. Soil regenerated.

"You know," I tell Paige, "I think I *will* get the candle. Thank you for helping me decide." When Paige full-on beams, I know there are few things I wouldn't do to see that smile again. And again, and again. I exit All the Feels with, well, all the feels.

In fact, today's win is deserving of a fist bump if I do say so myself. Where's that Silas when I need him?

"Want to stop at Homer's?" I say, as we head down Birch in the direction of her apartment, swinging our robin's-egg-blue shopping bags.

"Sure."

"Hey, can I share a secret with you?" Her eyebrows shoot up. She's sure cute when she's curious. "I miss my dad today." And I do. The orange blossoms have done it to me. I don't actually expect a response from Paige on this topic. But then it comes.

She focuses on the sidewalk. "Me too."

"Hey, Paige, I want you to know, you can talk to me about all that, anytime." She looks away. "No, really. *Anytime*. It doesn't have to be today." I've said this before, but it bears repeating.

Paige tucks an arm around me in a PDA I'm quite good with. "And I've been thinking about something. What do you think about me becoming your *official* mentor? You know, like Arlo and Cade?" She removes her arm from my waist. Have I said the wrong thing? "You don't have to answer right away," I add.

She doesn't.

In fact, it's not until we've finished visiting with our friends at Homer's and we're approaching her apartment that Paige finally responds. "I don't want you to be my mentor," she says.

"No? Oh." Gut punch. "That's okay." Does that mean I stink at this big-sister thing?

"I want you to be my friend."

~

Once Nina and I have our "girls' night in" calendared, I hug Paige goodbye and retrace my steps through town. To usher in this weekend's epic "Whispering Pines or Bust" moving party, Paige and her mom plan to join Daisy and me for *Encanto* and baking. Now that Daisy's out of her sling, she's been experimenting with a little delicacy she's calling Earl Grey biscotti. Who'd have thought?

Between Arlo and Cade, and Silas and his motley bunch, we were able to tell Pastor David at Sunday's service, thank you very much, but we've already got the moving crew covered. David had said he was very *moved* by Daisy's showing of friends. *Ba-dum-bump.* So cringey. He could stand to take a few lessons from my uncle.

What a world, where a girl who's been willing to allow the relationships of her heart to dry up like the high-desert soil can be given a second chance. If you're lucky enough, as I have been, love waits. Because time doesn't.

Passing High Desert Home & Design, I return a wave through the window to Ruby. Or maybe she was scrubbing the glass. Regardless. It's a great day to have a great day on purpose in Charity

Falls. And while it has never been my job to fix the world, it seems this is the place where I may get to do a teeny bit of good.

Who knew that fighting for a cause just because it's right can still be wrong? In retrospect, my crusade on behalf of the inn was disingenuous. Loving on family, investing in Paige, and working with kids at the youth ranch once it moves into high gear next summer—these things are right. At least, right for *me*.

I step inside The Box Office and locate my new mailbox. I turn the shiny gold key. And there it is, my first piece of mail. Payment for services rendered. My first paid commission, for a plein air painting of that adorable bed-and-breakfast over near Salem. It's no great fortune. My Clurk app isn't going to pop out a hallelujah notification. But maybe it's a seed, the humble beginnings of something fruitful. And when my job at Aberdeen & Moss begins next week, I'll be honored to start paying rent to my favorite pixie-cut landlady for the privilege of occupying a certain little white house trimmed like a cake in Shasta daisies.

The Aberdeen & Moss position is bound to stretch me. But the team seems fairly chill and like-valued. As their color curator, I'll have a voice into product development and selecting new color ranges. Plus I get to style rooms for photo shoots. The hours won't be full-time, at least not at first. But this worries me exactly zero percent. I'll have margin for what's become meaningful.

Most of all, I see these things as generous provision rather than my identity. Point is, they keep me here with the people I've come to care about, in a common land painted uncommon hues. Among cinnamon-barked trees and steel-blue mountains and skies like liquid gold. Met with such extravagant vistas, the questions don't so much fall away as fall into perspective.

Because while answers sometimes bring me peace, they can never bring me home.

A yellow slip of paper in the box tells me I've also got a parcel to claim. A gentleman behind the counter hands me a package that's large and flat, stamped with a Menlo Park return address, and perhaps the most considerate gift I've ever given myself—two of my father's botanical prints, newly framed.

Juggling my robin's-egg-blue shopping bag and this package, I continue down Birch Avenue feeling anything but displaced.

Of late, a morning chill seems to hint at fall's approach. And when the fields of sage turn school-bus yellow and the geese depart, this is where you'll still find me. In winter I'll be here as well, wearing anything that'll keep my head warm other than a beret. I've come to prefer a place where the people jaywalk and deer use a crosswalk.

So here is where I'll stay. Watering the ground where I'm planted, like my father before me.

Fifty-Seven

Tawny
I'm jealous, picturing you in Oregon.

Me
How exactly do you picture me? In what setting?

White-lace Regency gown like Emma's—you know, in the 2020 film—your paintbrush is poised over an easel in a field of sunflower and pine.

Not my favorite adaptation.

Just humor me . . . with the other hand you sip tea, that amazing head of hair blowing in the breeze, deer prancing, robins singing over you. Oh, there's an eagle too.

Not quite my present reality.

Where are you?

"Run like you have to get to the _____"
~Hermione Granger

Ah, library.

Studying up on color science.

Oh yes, tomorrow's the day. You'll crush it.

And if I don't . . .

And if you don't . . . ?

And if I don't I'll still have you.

Aww. Hey, do yourself a favor. All those
books you're perusing? Just leave them.

gasp As in, don't shelve them?????

Think of it as an emotional exercise. From
your therapist.

You can't just leave books lying all around
like some sort of literary miscreant.

Fine. But leave one. Librarians love their
jobs. You can do this. I believe in you.

Audrey???

crickets

Myrtle Rose's
5 Rules for Life

1. Stay close to your people.
2. Be still and notice the birds.
3. Don't judge the mouse-catching prowess
   of other cats . . . or dis on your own.
4. Sometimes it's preferable to let the mouse
   get away.
5. See rule number 1.

THE END

Author's Note

Inspiration for this story came not only from my imagination but also from meaningful personal experiences that quietly steeped in my heart for years.

It's no secret in my neck of the woods that equine therapy offers remarkable healing potential for wounded young people, as well as for the differently abled. I've witnessed it firsthand, both at Crystal Peaks Youth Ranch and at Healing Reins Equine Assisted Therapy. I'm grateful to these inspiring Bend, Oregon, nonprofits for stirring my heart and informing this story.

Years ago, while working for The 1687 Foundation—a nonprofit publisher that distributes free Christian resources to the incarcerated, first responders, military members, and the at-risk—I must have read hundreds of letters from inmates reaching out for hope, for Jesus. I was also made painfully aware of the impact incarceration has on family members. During a prison ministry conference, an articulate young woman spoke about how, as a young girl, she liked to imagine the concrete guard tower of the prison where her father was incarcerated as a castle. The same brave woman shared that whenever she heard well-meaning people refer to her as "at risk," she yearned for them to infer that she was "at risk of accomplishing great things."

Another story seed arose when a writing assignment introduced me to the Central Oregon Partnerships for Youth (COPY) program, facilitated through the Deschutes County Sheriff's Office. Through this wonderful program, volunteer mentors are trained and then matched with a youth who has an incarcerated parent.

Thank you, readers, for taking this journey and opening your hearts to characters who taught me and touched me. I pray my story nurtures honor and understanding for the many for whom this kind of family crisis is, sadly, a lived experience.

Acknowledgments

Special thanks are due my agent, Cynthia Ruchti, a woman in a category of excellence all her own. For the way you brim with creativity, wisdom, and joy, lavish it on me without reservation, and for never wavering in the quest for our "yes."

To the exceptional publishing team at Revell. What an honor to be part of your distinguished family. Rachel McRae, I could not be more grateful to you for taking a wild chance on me and seeing to it that my beloved fictional friends in Charity Falls are now friends to so many others. Kristin Adkinson, your insightful suggestions and the care you took with your editorial polishing cloth show on every page. To Brianne, Erin, Hannah, Laura, Karen, and Katelyn, as well as those I didn't work with directly but who played a role in bringing this book into the world, thank you.

Garth, how is it you never doubted this day would arrive, made countless sacrifices without ever complaining, and shared this dream every step of the way? You are my person.

Marissa, Sean, and Chelsea, you'll never know how much you inspire me. You hold my heart.

My longtime critique group, the Daring Sisters—Melody, Nancie, Marlys, Nancy, Dani, Brenda, Kim, and Allison. What can I say, ladies? You make me a better writer and a better human. I treasure our kinship. And your baked goods.

My ride-or-die prayer team—Diane, Todd, Robin, Jeff, Madisynne, Judah, Kim, and Michael. There's *gnome* place like home church.

Sharon, Lee Ann, Mari, and Chuck. For loving and believing.

Renee, who decorated my world with laughter even as she journeyed home.

Above all, my Savior and friend, Jesus. Nothing rivals a life of following you. Even a publishing dream-come-true. You are indeed the giver of better things.

Kit Tosello is an award-winning writer of big-hearted small-town contemporary fiction, as well as inspirational essays and devotionals. She arranges words with tenderness, humor, and, ultimately, hope. If she's not writing, Kit is probably out exploring the great Pacific Northwest, spoiling her grandkids, or sipping tea while reading several books at the same time.

Kit operates a tea shoppe with her husband in a small, Western-themed Oregon tourist town full of big-hearted folks, not unlike the setting of *The Color of Home*. She freelances as a journalist and an editor, writing personal-interest stories for the local paper and editing nonfiction for a major Christian publisher, among other clients.

A member of Cascade Christian Writers since 2010 and a multi-award winner (Cascade Awards in 2016 and 2019), as well as a member of ACFW, Kit has hundreds of articles published. She's a contributor to anthologies including *The Kitchen Devotional* (Revell, 2024), *So God Made a Mother* by Leslie Means (Tyndale, 2023), *Miracles Do Happen* (Guideposts, 2019), and *Fifty Shades of Loved* (Little Dozen Press, 2012).

During her earlier career as a kitchen designer, Kit launched a lifestyle blog, *The High Desert Home Companion*, featuring design news, home décor inspiration, and recipes. Today you can find her at KitTosello.com, inspiring readers to live fully into their God-given stories.

Meet Kit

Visit Kit's website to sign up for her newsletter, stay up-to-date on the latest news, and more.

KitTosello.com

 Kit.Tosello.Writes    Kit.Tosello.Writes   KitTosello